BLOOD AND BISCUITS

BOOK ONE OF THE SUPERNATURAL SUPPORT GROUP

Blood and Biscuits

https://www.amazon.co.uk/dp/B094NYRQ77

ISBN: 9798503169805

Copyright © C. M. Allen

Front cover – George Ander

All rights reserved

For Isaac, Etta, and Margot.

For Esme,

And for all my family.

Dedicated

To all those that suffer in silence.

You are none of you alone.

An aside…

I support the Oxford comma. It is irrefutable, it makes sense, and it appears frequently throughout this story. To not use this powerful piece of punctuation would be a travesty in my mind. If you disagree, then I disagree with you.

If you disagree again then take a step back, make a cup of tea, and have a word with yourself.

I make no apologies.

For Those Belonging to No World...

Do you feel worthless? Or lonely?
Struggling with the trials and tribulations of everyday existence?

Is your death getting in the way of your life?

You are not alone.

I will be holding weekly support sessions, Monday from 19:00,
St Ellin's Church, Ellin's Island.
No admission fee. Coffee and biscuits available.
If you want to chat or just get anything off your chest then come
along and talk to me.

**I will not judge. I will only listen. Too many centuries have
taught me not to base perceptions on surface detail.**

I look forward to meeting you and, hopefully,
helping you come to terms with who and what you are.
Communication is the best medicine for the mind.

You will see.

- V. Eliade

Week One

The Vampire that Cared

BASEMENT VAULTS,
RUINS OF ST ELLIN'S CHURCH,
ELLIN'S INDUSTRIAL ISLAND,
NORTHERN ENGLAND.
THE START OF THE SUPPORT GROUP.

"So, how has everyone's week been?"

There was a murmur around the dimly lit room. Coats shifted, decaying wooden chairs creaked and echoed. Nobody wanted to say anything, or had nothing to say. Yet they were all there for some reason or another, their stories would give the empty night sustenance.

The man who spoke did not look like much: tall, thin, in his middling years, a bent and broken nose beneath a few inches of dark hair. He was not especially handsome or unique in any way save his shining brown eyes. However, the group would come to realise he was far more than he seemed. He was a force beyond understanding, a will of sheer power buried within somebody who should not be underestimated, granted command through his presence alone.

'*They are on the touchy side,*' he thought. '*Hardly surprising. Tact and approachability will be needed.*'

"Please, I am only here to help. What is said within these four walls *stays* in these walls. I do not share information, not unless somebody's life is in danger." He paused and monitored their faces. One shuffled uneasily, another folded their arms defensively, feigning ignorance. The man sighed internally; outwardly he smiled pleasantly and spread his hands openly. "Look, I know it is difficult.

Blood and Biscuits

I know you are all here because somebody else told you to, or perhaps threatened to bind you in silver if you did not, but forget all that. You are here because you have found courage. Focus on the moment, on the here and now - perhaps I should start?"

He could *feel* their eyes glance at him. There was a palpable sense of acceptance, as if broaching the subject of pain was enough to break whatever hurt locked their mouths. He retracted his smile to a slight curve, wondering what shut-away aspect of his self he should prise open to a gathering of absolute strangers.

This was the first week of the Support Group and the sorts of issues known as 'teething problems' had not yet begun. And in this particular group, teething problems was more than simple idiom: it was reality.

"My name is Vladislav Eliade and I am a vampire. You will probably think me of Russian descent, though I am Romanian. Yes, I know, how stereotypical for a Romanian to be a servant of darkness. Well, that is something you will have to learn to deal with, I know I certainly have over the years." Nobody reacted. Vlad chewed his lip, keen to help others, not so keen to reveal much about himself. "When I had friends, they would call me Vlad, or even V, which now makes me sound like an annoying energy drink or a disease one might catch on a late-night train. You can use whatever name you feel comfortable with, I honestly care not."

Another rumpling of clothing as the gathering eased. It was a fraction of a motion, though Vlad discerned it anyway. He possessed staggeringly powerful senses meaning he never missed anything. He had made sure the first meeting would be held on sanctified ground beneath a full moon – it always felt right to be out and about then, and the skies were especially clear that night. The stars twinkled above as the gleaming moon hung high, like a boastful white coin, all visible through the narrow windows near the basement ceiling.

In the moment's hesitation somebody finally spoke, catching Vlad off-guard.

"That's not a story."

"I beg your pardon?" Vlad asked politely, picking up his cup and sipping. He knew it was supposed to be a strong brand of freeze-dried coffee but it was tasteless. He had made it jet-black yet his taste buds had long since died, with only the few remaining relegated to the tang of iron and a little salt. "I am not sure I follow."

The speaker was a young woman, stark pale in complexion, waist-length, sleek-black hair draped over one shoulder. A thick coat covered her long dark dress, ending in scuffed and dirty trainers. Vlad smiled at her; the look went unreturned as she spoke again.

"You only told us your name, not your story. Why've you set this ridiculous group up? What's gone so wrong in your half-life that you seek redemption in listening to others moan? Masochism? I don't think you are who you say you are."

Vlad blinked. The light flickered and the accusation wiped from her face.

"Just what the hell was that?" another asked, worry in his voice. "Buggered electrics in a place like this. Too old to keep going much longer."

Sipping his coffee again – for the pleasure of warmth over anything else – Vlad placed the cup upon the hard floor. The pottery rang perfectly across the cold concrete. He laced his slender fingers together and fought the urge of his inherent rage building and unleashing hell itself. Though that monster lurked inside it would never become him.

"First of all, thank you for being here. Secondly, I honestly do want to help. Look at me, you know what I am, you know I am incapable of lying when on holy ground – that is partly why I chose this church, so you could all trust me. But since you – I am sorry, what was your name?"

"Lucille," the young woman offered. Her misted voice broke as she struggled the name out. "Lucy, for short."

"Lucy it is," Vlad responded in kind. There was another shuffling from the group and Vlad regarded them all. "But since

Blood and Biscuits

Lucy here has taken the first step in helping herself by just attending I can say I am glad I came tonight. We appear few in number but I count four in total, and that makes four of us seeking some kind of betterment rather than sinking to our base urges and becoming less than our desires. Now, my story. Yes, of course."

Vlad cleared his throat and unlaced his fingers, wondering where exactly to begin. When at last the answer arrived, he was surprised with how easily it came, having expected to gloss over his history, as he always did.

"I am...well, I am a vampire. There is no simpler way of saying that, and I certainly never mince my words. I have been a vampire for a long, *long* time." Vlad uttered the last part with such gravity every *scent* of disturbance in the room focussed on him, every eye captivated despite their anxieties. "That, really, was the realisation that turned me to thinking about my time here, on this good green earth. Hundreds of years in servitude to a curse and I cannot recall ever being *happy*. Have any of you ever been happy as you are? Satisfied with what you have become?"

The others shook their heads and Vlad nodded.

"No, but then I could have guessed that. Still, so many years and I have yet to find one good reason why I should carry on instead of plunging a stake through my heart or finding an astonishingly efficient tanning bed." The group chuckled and Vlad felt them relax further, a change in air pressure softening on his icy skin. "Those thoughts are strong in me all the time. Did any of you know that vampires are born with every trait their human counterparts died with and are incapable of change? Some vampires are permanently overweight, others irreversibly addicted to alcohol, modern variants unable to rid themselves of embarrassing haircuts, et cetera."

Vlad hesitated, waiting for the inevitable question. It came quickly from a slightly older man wearing dark jeans and boots, a worn leather jacket and balaclava covering his face entirely. Vlad tried to see his eyes but there were only minute slits revealing nothing.

"So, what did *you* get stuck with?" he asked quietly, an Edinburgh voice hissing strangely.

Vlad cleared his throat once more, preparing for the inevitable laughter.

"When I was human, I suffered greatly from depression."

Vlad braced for the smirks and the sniggers yet nothing came. The group stared blankly at him, or Lucy and the Scottish man did – the third person's face remained concealed. Vlad's eyebrows shifted in surprise and he loosened the tension in his body, feeling comfortable in the situation.

A sudden sliver of hunger sliced through his stomach and Vlad paused, allowing the blood urge to pass and clear his mind once more. When he spoke, he was determined to explain his position to these strangers, to convince them of his intentions. If that meant exposing the raw sides of him then so be it.

"I was turned a long time ago, bear in mind, and there were no networks of support nor systems of mental health services. Many corners of our society *still* struggle with a simple discussion, let alone attend a place where people go to clear their heads and get things off their chests, as it were, so you can imagine what it was like living through times when simply declaring your love for somebody of the same sex was illegal." The Scottish man shifted as Vlad continued. "There *was* no recognition of mental health and people simply…got on with it. If you bled you were sewn up, if you caught a fever you could die from it, that was it. Did you know these days it is neither sword nor disease but suicide that is the single biggest killer of young men?"

Lucy shook her head. The masked man remained motionless. Vlad sensed a splinter of pain jab from him. Vlad nodded gravely.

"Indeed it is, and many young women suffer through things I could not hope to imagine, and could not possibly empathise with, though my sympathy is great. And then there are people like us: the strangers, the outcasts…"

Blood and Biscuits

"The invisible freaks," the third and final member of the group whispered, a woman by the sound of her voice, her body transparent, clothes fluttering upon a non-existent breeze. Her face was veiled, her voice shadowed by time, creaking and groaning with dust.

"No, never the freaks," Vlad replied sternly. "We are the extraordinary, the supernatural. You might not be proud of what you are – I have certainly despised what I am over the years – but that does not mean you cannot be proud of *who* you are, proud of your choices to overcome whatever ailment has befallen you. We are not governed by our curses, we govern *them*. Do you understand?"

The group was silent. It did not matter now, the important thing was they were *there*. He continued through memories of fire and blood to deliver all he could to heal their pining souls.

"You know, I used to self-harm as a human." The admission caught everyone off-guard. Vlad sucked his teeth. "Hm. A lash was my choice, cutting stripes down my back, or a flame to my legs. Anywhere I could get that feeling of control again. Nobody would have understood but *I* did, *I* knew why I did it."

"Takes a lot to stop doing that," the hissed-voiced man said darkly. "Everyone struggles stopping. So I've heard…" he trailed off.

"I did not stop."

Vlad sensed the feeling of the room plunge and he sat straighter in his chair.

"I never discovered the trick to stopping and now I am permanently lumbered with my depression, I find the curative of my claws brings balance back when all else fails. Scoring my flesh returns that control to me when I am overwhelmed by my despair, yet as if to mock me I no longer scar. My power heals me again, leaving no trace, as if I am not worthy enough to see the results of my battles. No stories of the flesh to remind me, only the sensation of my despair retreating.

Blood and Biscuits

"There is no cure for depression in humans, this much is known, there is only help for the suffering. Help comes in many forms but evidence shows that staying silent, trying to drag your way out of it by yourself, can actually worsen it. Conversation improves the mood, relegates darker thoughts to the back of the mind, and by discussing our problems we can work through them, *accept* them. This acceptance is the key. As a vampire with depression, I cannot banish the dark creature that follows me, waiting to suffocate me, but I can forget it for a time. I accept this and it does help.

"I did not know what was wrong with me, when I was human, only that I suffered from a mind that would focus on nothing other than sheer and utter misery. I had good things in my life, a wife, a daughter, and the comforts of money, yet there I was, tortured daily by the ravages of despondency and sorrow. I was a failure of a man, or so I believed."

Vlad breathed deeply. The move was a long-ago habit from when he had been alive. He needed no breath anymore, his lungs long since shrivelled and blackened, but Vlad sometimes still enjoyed the practice of drawing in cold, sweet air. Besides, the motion helped bring all wandering attention back to him, a real-life pause for dramatic effect.

"So, one day I found myself perched upon a cliff edge and facing the Black Sea, ready to jump to ease my exhausted brain of its horrors. Ready to end my world and remove the burden of myself from my family. And that was when she saw me."

"She?" the balaclava'd man asked. "You didn't mention her. Oh, you mean your wife."

"No, my goodness no. My wife never knew of my illness, nor of my intent that day at the cliffs. Hiding one's internal damage is something one becomes acutely practiced in, and it is always the closest to us that see it last. No, *she* was my maker, the creature that turned me into the *thing* I remain today." Vlad practically spat the word, feeling its glass shard slice his tongue. "The vampire Izanami, ancient and hungry was she. Izanami spied me from the treeline and intercepted before I could complete what I was most indecisive about, and took me up into the skies with the aura of her *mastery*, a power I abhor above all our kind possess."

"If it's what I know of vampires then I don't see the problem with it," the man-in-the-balaclava said smoothly, a note of desire staining his tired voice. "The ability to convince people of anything you want. Sounds like a dream come true. Could make them stop staring at me, accept me, or just leave me alone."

"Indeed," Vlad replied sharply, his tone whetted to a keen edge. "Or you could simply walk into a bank and take what you want, rob people blind, tell people to stroll right off a bridge, convince them to stop breathing, tell them to go on a rampage, to remove their free will and take their choice from them. Sound good to you?"

The room fell quiet again and Vlad regained his composure. They did not deserve condescension.

"My apologies, I do not mean to sound angry. It is another facet of mine, to view everything through a lens of pessimism, and on occasion I fail to repress it."

"Is that a vampire thing? Or the depression you were turned with?" the hiss-voiced man asked. Vlad tried to focus on any flesh he might have exposed but there was nothing. He suspected the man was a shade or a ghoul.

The vampire laughed quietly, the first he had had in quite a while.

"It is, unfortunately, not a vampiric trait but mine. I wish I could blame it on something, or some*one*, else but alas it cannot be so. I have always had a rather bleak outlook on life, and now I have a bleak outlook on death."

"So that's it?" Lucy asked suddenly, a venom edge to her voice. "You were sad and now you're permanently sad? And now we're just going to sit here and have, what, a lovely time? A big laugh? Your problems are nothing like what I'm going through, I knew this was a waste!"

Lucy stood haughtily and grabbed her bag to leave but as she stepped towards the door a figure appeared in the frame, and she halted motionless. Vlad stood quickly, marching before Lucy as she backed away. The vampire folded his arms and took measure of the stranger.

Long, dark, ragged hair hung in sweated locks to his shoulders, clothes draped in tattered ribbons from arms and waist, a long and heavy musculature beneath. Olive-toned flesh rented by old scars, decorated in new blood. A body of raw strength and history, the man's face grizzled by horrid experience, his hollow eyes steeped in pain and rage. His feet were bare, hands freshly scratched and torn.

The stranger set Vlad's spine immediately in an electric storm of warning signals. He knew exactly what he was by the feeling in the pit of his stomach, though the *smell* of the wild and of the iron grip of fury was a strong indication, too. Vlad tamped down the innate sensations of hatred and instead spread his arms and smiled at the man, blocking Lucy completely. If he attacked, Vlad would have to do what he could to protect the group.

"Welcome, my friend," Vlad said, exercising more caution than intended. "Are you here seeking help? Or have you stumbled in by accident?"

Vlad held the man's deeply penetrating gaze, centuries of practice bolstering his determination. There flecks of yellow in his irises, pupils dilated despite the basement light. The newcomer glanced behind then backed fearfully into the basement, making certain the door was clear of whatever threat pursued him.

He stared around the room and then at himself, looking at his hands and body in confusion as he slowly replied.

"I…I…didn't mean to disturb…I only wanted…shelter for a moment, I think," the man hesitated. He stared at the group. Vlad stepped between them once more, making sure there was no challenge to his movement.

Blood and Biscuits

Vlad glanced at the man's back as he spun, assessing the table in the corner with the coffee and packets of untouched biscuits. A series of injuries bled down the lower right of his back, several gashes lined his shoulders, and heavy bruises coloured the muscles. It might have been a full moon outside but holy ground and electric lighting sheltered the man, their combination reversing the transformation, their reach extending across the wastelands beyond.

There was something about the stranger, a feeling, a sensation growing in Vlad's mind.

"Then come in, get warm and safe," Vlad said pleasantly, ignoring his worries. "You will be fine down here, stay as long as you want. Help yourself to coffee or tea – sorry, only the dried stuff. Biscuits as well, though they seem to be unpopular."

The grizzled man looked at Vlad properly, clearly measuring his lithe, confident form. Vlad wondered if he was marking him as the biggest potential threat.

"*Vampire.*"

The single word escaped the man in a low growl, his eyes unreadable.

"Werewolf."

Vlad met the man's tone respectfully and held his ground, showing equality determinedly.

That strange something about him *scented* again, something beyond the werewolf. Vlad could not put his finger on it, it was…confusing.

The vampire thought there would be a problem, and when the man stepped forward he felt every dead nerve of his body react. Yet there came no assault and the man stopped before Vlad and nodded once, a slight curve to his eyes. The newcomer pointed back at the doorway and shivered with cold.

"Nasty out there. Real chilly up these parts, surprised it ain't snowin'. Glad I stumbled down here, good for a bit of light and a chance to catch me breath."

Blood and Biscuits

"You have stepped into a place of good fortune, friend," Vlad noted casually, indicating the basement. "Come, if it is not because of this group then tell me why you are on this island, if you can remember."

"Huh, alright. Before the moon came out, I crossed that bridge over the river, thinkin' I'd not be discovered. Most times, the transformations ain't so bad, I can sorta' get myself into some fields or surround myself with water or lock myself up somewhere before it gets real terrible, but there's another powerful moon comin', I can feel it, and if I've another episode as bad as last time…" he trailed off worriedly.

"Ahh yes, the blue moon," Vlad acknowledged as the group stared, transfixed by the werewolf. "Worst of its kind for your folk. Can turn any normal werewolf into an absolute force of nature, not that they need the help."

"The very worst. *Don't* ask me about it."

"I had no intention," Vlad said. "But what brings you down here?"

"Men. Young men, actually. Drinkers, by the smell and noise of 'em. They'd've passed on without findin' me but I sneezed, of all things, and they found me out, hidden under one of them abandoned factories. They were just there to graffiti but when they discovered me they…they…"

"They attacked," Vlad finished for him, and as he looked, he realised the man was not particularly old, perhaps early forties. His advanced appearance was a facet of exhaustion, rage, fear, and the ravages transformations had upon the body. "I assume you were human-form at that point? Yes, I thought so, or else they would be dead. That must have been very confusing for you – this island is…strange, to say the least. There are many things about it that are not as they seem, a haven for old magics and ways of life lost to the histories. Odd happenstances like the ability to keep you from transforming in certain places will occur from time to time on this island, like a waypoint of randomness in reality. You are safe down here, I swear it. Nor will you find hindrance should you decide to move on."

"I can't guarantee your safety in return," the man said, almost mournfully. "I'm incapable of safety."

"Fear not, I am more than adept at handling myself and my associates."

There was a pause of understanding between the strangers, two creatures of immense power and even stronger natural hatred, finding a sort of distant acceptance binding them. Then the newcomer sighed and shook off his shivers, that odd scent coming from him again.

"Coffee, you said?"

"Indeed, I did," Vlad smiled. "It should still be hot, given the expensive container. Please help yourself. Join us if and when you are ready. We shall resume our session to save time, if you do not mind?"

"Knock yourselves out, I'm leavin' soon as I'm clean and recovered."

Vlad nodded once again and returned to his seat. When he sat, he realised Lucy was back in her chair, staring wildly at the werewolf as he crossed the basement and poured himself a thick black stream of coffee. He sliced open a biscuit packet with a single nail and tipped six onto a palm. Vlad was satisfied they would not be disturbed and turned to continue the session, noticing Lucy's chair was a fraction of an inch closer to his.

"So, where was I? Ahh yes, we had become badly sidetracked from my initial question, the one I intended to be the planter from which we would grow the great vines of our meetings. Who does not enjoy a good metaphor, eh?"

"*Meetings* plural?" the balaclava'd man asked.

"If you find this evening helpful then I see no reason not to continue," Vlad admitted evenly, already imagining in-depth sessions and how he would provide more than just biscuits if need be. "I am sorry, I have yet to ask you your name…"

"Jacob," he replied easily. "But Jay's fine. In fact, maybe just go with Jacob."

"Wonderful. I knew a Jacob once, a fine fellow he was. I do like the older names; it makes me feel as if I am back from when I came. A pleasure to meet you, Jacob. And yours?" Vlad asked of the veiled woman.

The person shifted and glided in their seat, and Vlad realised she was not touching the chair. A true ghost, a spectral form withheld from death through an emotion so strong it had imprinted on reality itself, stopping the deceased's mind moving on to the underworld. She was fascinating, her ghostly voice rippling like through water.

"I was…am…called Sarah, I believe. That sounds odd, like it doesn't quite feel right on the air, maybe it's not my real name, maybe this place isn't real and I'm the only thing in it that exists, a waypoint of randomness in reality." Vlad raised his eyebrows: Sarah had copied his own phrasing. That was a surprise. "I'm tied to this place, the hallowed halls of this church, and in my half-existence I haunt the matter and boundaries of my reluctant home, flowers and all."

"Oh!" Vlad said without thinking. In that moment, the wolf-man slurped from his coffee and devoured all six biscuits noisily, his hunger echoing around the entire basement, ricocheting off old piles of musical instruments and mouldering wooden pews lifted from the halls above. Lucy leaned round to stare at the man with wide eyes, her sleek black hair brushing her lap in a dark river, but Vlad was keen to press on. "Oh goodness, I am sorry, Sarah, are we trespassing? We can leave, if you would like, and find some other place? I did not see you enter, you were already here, so I-"

"No! No, please don't go," Sarah groaned in a hollow way. "Please, I would be alone once more. Your company is greatly pacifying for me, in ways I haven't felt in decades. I can already feel my…mind…finding some stability, like an empty page filling in properly, the words rushing together. I would have you stay a while longer, else I'll return to my empty corridors to exist only as a forgotten memory again, to sing forgotten songs and talk to forgotten people like I've done for years."

"It would be my honour," Vlad said. He became quickly aware of the werewolf approaching. He allowed his senses to surge a little and take in the man's scent, the wilds and winds of his life, the cursed blood solidifying on his back, the minute sounds of pain he made: all quiet to human senses yet a powerful symphony to a vampire's.

With finality, Vlad turned and gazed up at the man. The stranger's eyes were locked onto Sarah's veil.

"You're a ghost?" he asked slowly. She nodded mournfully and her form drifted a little lower. The man continued hurriedly. "Sorry, I don't mean to be rude, was only a question. But…that's amazing! I'd heard of vampires, 'course, and ghosts, too, but now I've met them both, I…I recognised vampire from his smell, 'cause he don't have one, but ghosts? That's a different kinda' nothin' altogether."

"I am only a shadow of my living self," Sarah said quietly, her translucent dress clouding upon the air, the edges billowing. "Less than that, for shadows must have material form to create them. I have no presence upon the world and leave no mark, only what you can see. I don't even know what I am, only what I feel and how little I can think."

"Right, I see," the man said measuredly. Then, in a quieter voice: "God, I never thought I'd meet a real ghost. You're fascinatin'."

Sarah did not reply but there was a definite change in how she held herself, if there was such a notion. Vlad addressed the werewolf whilst indicating one of the many spare chairs.

"Pull up a seat if you want to join…please, what is your name?

"Cain," the man almost growled.

"Cain. This is just a little gathering of sorts. You are more than welcome-"

"No, just the coffee, thanks," he interrupted hastily. "It's keeping me warm. I'll move on soon, can never afford to stay in one place. Though this little room seems to be stoppin' me from transformin' again…why *is* that?" he wondered aloud, staring round then at himself.

"Holy ground," Vlad explained, pointing round the church basement. "And the electric light. Neither is enough by themselves, but together they are a mighty force against your natural curse. Obviously, that has only become apparent since the turning point of electricity."

"Huh," Cain muttered thoughtfully. "Wish I'd known that twenty years ago."

"If you did not know it is hardly surprising. Information on werewolves is scarce at best."

Vlad longed to help him, despite his natural instincts to tear his head off, but refrained from saying anything. It was not his place to force anyone's choices. He had relegated himself to a position of observation and listening only, hundreds of years of ill-mannered disrespect on life having taught him quite enough.

"Well I am proud you are all here, through one way or another," Vlad stated at large. "It is good you have chosen to remain, Lucy, for I feel I may help you more than you want. Despite our obvious differences, I am not the man you think I am, a beast of depression and blood. I am centuries old, plus forty-one atop in human years, so I have seen many things, *experienced* many things you could not believe. Wars and cataclysms so destructive, so vast, parts of worlds ripped asunder forevermore. Emotional pain unspoken, festering so long it destroyed whole lives and sent waves through friends and families."

Vlad looked to Cain but saw he was tending the wounds striping his back, too preoccupied by his wellbeing to care for anything said nearby. Older scars lined his shoulder blades, many curved in wicked slashes. That odd scent shook off the man again and Vlad finally realised where it was coming from. The stranger's blood reeked of it, too fine a matter for human detection, a sensory overload for Vlad. He tried not to lose focus on the others, though as he spoke he could not ignore the man's blood.

He did not smell like any werewolf Vlad had ever met before.

"Yes," Vlad muttered, turning his head away, "I have made many mistakes, and most I cannot ever hope to redeem myself from, but this group is one way in which I might bring some good back to the world."

"Even if it's for a bunch of freaks like us," Jacob hissed.

"*Again* with that word," Vlad strained. "We are nothing but products of nature – or God, if you so believe." Jacob rolled his eyes at the notion but Vlad pressed on. "It is only what we choose to do, how we choose to act, that separates ourselves from others like us. Can we not say the same for the humans from whence we derived? Many murder, rape, steal endlessly, many that could be described as irredeemable monsters by their own kin. Are they not simply acting on their urges, too? No, they stand governed by choice and choice alone, condemned by them. What makes us so different? Fangs, immortality, physical presence…mere vestiges of perception, nothing more. If you think and act like an animal then you *are* an animal, regardless of species. *That* is my point, *choice* is my point. I am a vampire but I choose not to act with the sick and violent connotations that precede me. This helps calm the sadness I carried over from my humanity, if not heal."

Lucy shifted again in her seat. Vlad hoped she drew something positive from what he shared.

There was an explosive sneeze from behind and when everybody looked, they saw Cain holding himself steady, hand clasping his nose. He looked ready to fall over from the stress on his face. After a short moment, he exploded again, the noise like an angry bark, limbs shuddering violently.

"Bloody *hell*," he muttered angrily. "Always when it's proper embarrassin', too."

"Are you alright?" Vlad asked cautiously, wondering if this was Cain's form of transformation forcing its way through. "Do you require assistance in any way?"

Cain seemed sheepish and stood slowly, evidently finding control of himself.

"I, err…I get allergies."

"Allergies," Lucy repeated slowly.

"Yeah. As a human I'm, ugh, allergic to…I'm allergic to dogs, alright?"

"You are joking!" Vlad exclaimed before he could stop himself. Cain shook his head miserably. Lucy stifled a laugh.

"No, and it's worse than it sounds. Every full moon I turn into a monster, and then that last human part of me decides I'm allergic to myself! You any idea what that's like? It drives me insane."

"And so you hide on abandoned industrial islands so you do not harm others in your way," Vlad acknowledged.

"It's mostly the shame," Cain muttered.

Vlad hesitated, his unbidden despair conjuring jokes at the poor man's expense, but he shut his mouth before he spoke without thought. Instead, he tried a different approach.

"I would not have thought dogs and wolves similar enough for that sort of thing to cross over."

"What can I tell you?" Cain said, bare arms spread dejectedly, nose bright red and sniffing. "It's always been this way, just gets worse come the full moon."

"It must've something to do with your curse," Jacob offered quietly. "From the little I know, blessings eradicate ailments and protect someone in certain ways but curses make matters worse, so your dog allergy – sorry to trivialise it – must be made worse, enveloping wolves as well. Do you suffer around poodles now?"

"Well this has gone off-topic," Vlad murmured as Cain responded.

"Now you mention it, yeah I do."

Blood and Biscuits

"Curse is the reason then," Jacob finished.

"Because poodles?" Lucy said disbelievingly. "You realise you've diagnosed a man based on poodles."

"They are hypoallergenic, so reactions are quite rare, if at all. You learn many things living as long as I do, and apparently that is a piece of information I have unwittingly retained," Vlad offered.

Jacob made a motion with his gloved hand that said he agreed.

Suddenly, there came a noise from beyond the entrance, a sound of jeering revelry. *Humans.* Vlad's skin crawled and leapt with the fires of agitation and desire, and suddenly he was exercising every ounce of strength he possessed to repress the urges telling him to kill, tear, shred, feed, to drink and drink and drink until all essence, all life force, all blood was his.

Immediately, Cain was at the entrance and poised, side pressed to the cold stone, every fibre alert. His breathing quickened, eyes becoming carvings of fear, long fingers tensing and twisting, toes gripping the floor as if to pounce.

Vlad raised his hands, palms facing Cain, and spoke softly.

"All is well, my friend, they should not find us here. The light is too dim to be seen far away unless you are a werewolf. Be still and they will pass."

Cain said nothing, nor did he look at Vlad. Every muscle in the room tensed until the laughing calls drifted on, the clinks of bottles and scuff of drunken footsteps disappearing. Then, when silence returned, the room breathed again and Cain went back to tending his wounds.

Lucy made a hiss.

"Well we make for a fine show," she spat, her tone almost a quiet shriek, an undercurrent of fury breaking through. Vlad did not think anyone else noticed but whenever Lucy showed heightened emotion her shining hair seemed to come alive. Lucy pointed at each of them. "We have a lonely ghost who can barely remember her own name, a werewolf who's allergic to himself, for goodness' sake, a clinically depressed vampire, and – wait, Jacob, what's your story?"

Vlad *smelled* something stir from the man, his balaclava a visor only for his face, not for his emanations. Jacob shuffled uncomfortably in his seat but made no motion to remove his headwear.

"Well I..." he hesitated, being put on the spot evidently causing him great discomfort. "I heard of this group and thought it might be able to help me, that Vlad here could offer support. That's all, that's my story."

"So you were bored," Lucy said spitefully. "Very nice, I'm sure you really struggled with that. What're you hiding under that thing? Why are you wearing a mask?"

"I wear it so people don't do what you're doing and start asking too many questions. And I'm here because I get phobias, too, alright?"

"Phobias...

"Yeah, like going outside and getting accosted by annoyingly curious people."

"Are you insane!"

"No, I'm not, I'm vegan."

Lucy frowned.

"You're here because you're vegan? That's why you've hidden your face, because of the social shame? It's more acceptable nowadays,' she added bitingly.

"That's *not* what I meant!" Jacob spat. "It came out wrong. Being vegan and being me now, it's...it's hard, alright? But that's not the point, I didn't mean any of that – *God* this is difficult!"

"Then how *did* you mean it to come out?"

Jacob visibly balked and rose in anger. He reacted.

"I tried to kill myself, alright? You happy? I tried to kill myself and now I'm here because I'm scared of what I'll do next. I saw the advert for this place and thought it was my last shot, *jeez*."

Blood and Biscuits

Lucy sat back and folded her arms defiantly, a strange look on her face. She seemed to Vlad like a mix of shock, pity, self-revulsion, and indignity. Jacob, of course, discerned none of this.

"I tried to end it all before I became this freak because of my damned life, and then again when I realised what I was. But it's pretty bloody difficult to die when you're already dead, and that drop wasn't big enough that I couldn't just…piece myself back together again."

"Christ," Cain muttered from the other side of the room. Only Vlad heard: the werewolf was taking interest. However, his focus needed to be on the immediate group, Vlad felt the heat rising to a critical level. He decided to dissipate the sparks before they took flame.

"Why are *you* here, Lucille?"

Using somebody's fullest name gets their fullest attention. Lucy snapped round and focussed on his depthless eyes entirely, mouth caught open.

"Why *are* you here?" he said again, changing the emphasis. "You have spent a great deal of time complaining and finding excuses for others, and you have even attempted a classic storm out at my expense, but we have yet to pierce the heart of why you are here, if you will pardon the vampiric jest."

"That's none-" Lucy began but Vlad interrupted.

"None of my business? I understand that, yet here you are anyway, at a group you must have known was designed to unearth problems of anxiety, to talk them through openly. That was what my advertisement plainly stated. Can you honestly blame me for trying to reach you now you have come?"

"You don't know anything about what I've been through, and what I'm still going through."

"And I would not pretend to, yet you might help yourself by letting us understand and empathise in some small way. I put no pressure on people that do not wish to talk and only want to listen and be around others but I draw the line at accosting others. From your anger, I see you are desperate to talk. That is how any of us can recover, by shifting tiny problems to cause an avalanche of better things to pass. To have discussions and conversations, to debate and socialise, to lessen the weight of our emotional burdens. To *share*."

"You make it sound so easy for monsters," Lucy said, hardly above a whisper. "Like the right word said in the right way's all it's going to take."

"Only because I have lived through many centuries of suffering. Constantly, I stave off the clawing negativities invited by the demon of my despair. Yet a lifespan such as mine, without fear of frailty, does provide certain…clarifications, shall we say?"

Lucy stood indignantly.

"And from my looks you assume I'm young, is that it? You don't know what I am, you couldn't possibly know." Lucy folded her arms defensively and Vlad saw in that moment she was exactly as old as he had assumed. Perhaps pushing thirty years, no more, with a slight Irish accent.

"Then tell me. Tell *us*, if you can, what you are and why you are here, surely that is why you came. I am intent on helping anyone – yes, to make up for many atrocities that I would undo if I could, but also because there is good in all of us and I will expose it if I can."

Vlad kept his posture calm, face neutral. Lucy stood for a moment as Sarah's veiled gaze drifted between them; Vlad wondered what her ghostly mind conjured, what she could possibly be thinking. Jacob, face still hidden and unreadable, said nothing, body language impassive and stoic, whilst Cain prowled the basement's perimeter, coffee in-hand, checking all narrow windows were sealed. His paranoia leached into the room, putting Vlad's heavily fortified mind into a state of unrest, seeking to undo the mighty iron walls he had spent years building to imprison his power.

Finally, Lucy sat again and tucked her wild black hair behind her ears, high spots of rare colour at her cheeks, fingers clasping and flexing oddly as she held back powerful feelings. A flicker of black power danced along the edge of her hand and was gone again as she took a calming breath.

Vlad leant forward and looked at every member of the group, taking all three of them in at once, none noticing the strength Lucy had just shown.

"I may not look it, I may not seem it, but I promise you that I have seen more in my time than you can dream of. I am the epitome of horror and if I were to let my urges surface, I would be a force of absolute evil upon the world. That is *not* an exaggeration. Yet under all of that lurks the warmth of a man that honestly wishes to do *good*, to make this the start of something bigger, to let people like us rectify the mistakes of our forebears, to alter opinions of us now. To open us all to a brighter world that could one day, possibly, accept us for who and what we are. Yet that has to begin somewhere, and I truly believe that *we* are that beginning. Us. Now."

Even Cain was poised, his stalking paused as he evidently eavesdropped. Vlad thought he would return to his wound cleaning but a moment later the werewolf spun and marched up to the vampire angrily. Vlad stood quickly to protect the group.

"There is nothing you can do, you walking bat," he snarled, "*nothing*! Not with what's out there, not with what I've heard of. You imply you're so bloody powerful but all I see is an arrogant, empty man talkin' to a bunch of terrified kids as if he can really cure them. She's right," he added, jabbing a finger at Lucy who shrank into her chair. "You don't know what anyone's been through, you don't know a damn thing. Just because you're old, just because you've been around and seen a lot, it doesn't mean anything!"

Vlad stood his ground like an island battered by the sea, parting the man's boiling lupine rage and directing it away from the others. He kept himself relaxed as the man snarled.

"This ain't natural. This group, whatever you're trying to build: you're going to fail. It's in our natures to burn and kill whatever gets in our way when we lose control. Vampires are all the

God damned same, just entitled monstrosities playin' at noblemen, lording it over everyone else."

"You said you have never met a vampire before yet you talk as if you have known our kind your whole life," Vlad pointed out easily.

Cain's eyes sliced narrow.

"You callin' me a liar? 'Cause I don't lie, *friend*. I might not have met your kind but I've heard of 'em, I've seen the results of their hunger. And if I say you lord over us then I mean it."

"You are wrong," Vlad muttered in a hushed voice, willing the utmost placidity into his dead veins.

"What did you say?" Cain thundered. "What did you just say?"

He gave no time to respond. His long-fingered hand shot through the air and made to grab at Vlad's throat. It was the move of a desperate man, yet one filled with the fires of a thousand suns as the wolf buried within the blood howled and flooded him with strength. Vlad did not move. He did not need to, for when the hand came to his neck the vampire simply stood and let him grasp and squeeze as hard as he could.

Vlad lowered the smallest measure of his control, the mental walls encasing his power, and pushed an ounce of darkness into his flesh, allowing his power to fend off the attack. The light of the basement flickered and the air grew icy. Vlad's eyes became as twilight.

Jacob and Lucy stumbled back off their chairs as they moved to get away from the fight; Sarah hovered where she was, hardly aware of what was happening.

Within the man, the wolf roared and gnashed its furious jaws but the supernatural figure it attacked refused to cave. Cain could not crush Vlad's throat, he could not even disturb the skin as the vampire took a simple step forwards, forcing the wolf-man backwards, bare feet grinding against the floor, tearing gouges from the stone.

The basement light flickered again.

"Remove. Your. Hand."

Vlad felt revulsion for himself as he spoke the words, Cain evidently fighting the mastery the vampire layered over him. The barest trickle of power threaded through as Cain's exhausted shoulder muscles tightened and struggled against the poisonous darkness seeping into his mind. Vlad knew what the man felt was a voice on a deathly cold day persuading him to leap into the ocean where it was warm, the most convincing sound somehow enticing him to make the entirely illogical decision against his better judgment. The mastery was a force of influence, the smallest amount of laced language inflicting the largest amount of dominance in a person's mind simply by challenging the foundations of their choice.

Vlad hated the mastery, it was truly vile.

"I…can't…" Cain groaned, his hand clenching and unclenching, sweat beading his forehead. "It's…impossible…"

"I said remove. Your. Hand."

However, the mastery could not quite break through the vicious thoughts of the lurking beast, the man's curse too foreign even for Vlad's extensive knowledge, and there suddenly came a sound from the other side of the room, a haunting call of suffering.

Vlad broke his concentration and looked aside. Lucy crouched against the wall, head clasped in her hands, her body huddled as if warding off an invisible assault. Her once-mirrored hair hung dulled, thick strands floating freely upon the air. Her mouth was cracked unnaturally wide and unleashing a scream so long, so piercing, and so filled with the utter sorrow of the dead that Vlad realised in that moment what she was.

"Banshee," he whispered.

Then the focus of his dark power was lost and Cain's hand gripped harder, finding weakness in the throat. The fingers crushed Vlad's flesh and he cried out in pain, his imprisoned beast tearing free in retaliation. His fangs ripped out, eyes becoming the very night itself, and Cain lifted him bodily, slamming him to the ground with a formidable force, the holy ground burying the wolf just beneath the surface. Vlad shouted in shallow shock as the banshee's scream grew and grew and Jacob howled in distress.

With a short shriek, Sarah rose and flew through the ceiling, lost to the church above as she finally recognised the fight breaking out in her basement.

In the confusion, there sounded a clamour of metal striking stone from the entranceway and Vlad smelled blood, fresh, slick blood. Tainted with alcohol but good enough to kill, to consume. Seven young men poured into the basement, hands clutching sharpened wooden sticks and lengths of rusting chain, faces twisted in ugly sneers. Many jammed fingers in their ears to block the sound burning from Lucy's mouth.

Jacob backed away quickly. Cain retreated from Vlad and headed into the nearest corner, eyes flittering fearfully. Lucy's scream rose to a fever pitch until, at last, the front man of the invading force lunged and grabbed her by the hair, his fist closing in a violent handful, lifting her as if she was only paper.

Lucy's voice strangled and black tears cascaded down her face like ink as the man clutching her grinned wickedly in the low flickering light, face scarred and flushed with the pleasure of the hunt. His heart a void, Vlad ghosted elegantly to his feet, hands hardly brushing the ground. His mind instantly became frigid as a mountain stream, every sound the clearest ring of crystal upon his thoughts, rage forged into a beautiful, shining pinpoint of razor-thin focus. All of him was aimed at the trespassers that would dare intrude on the people he had promised to help.

Lucy's captor smiled ever wider at the sight of this narrow, middle-aged man practically gliding across the floor to meet him. Vlad kept himself purposefully unthreatening, his features dispassionate as he eyed the leader, allowing nothing to penetrate his mask, simply standing and reading him. Just reading.

"Please, put her down."

No mastery in his words. Throughout his years, Vlad knew that the best approach to many a situation was finding mutual respect and exploiting it.

The smiling leader's breath was so powerfully alcoholic Vlad nearly stepped back. The odour was astonishing to his enhanced senses but it did not override the strength of blood beating through the human's living veins. Vlad wanted to rip the man apart and drink every drop of him but that would undermine everything he sought to achieve with the group *and* undo the last two centuries of good behaviour.

The leader spoke and his friends laughed, nudging each other jovially, their weapons dangerous even in clumsy hands. However, that was only if they could come close or move fast enough to get the opportunity. "This some kinda' horror book club out in the middla' nowhere? We came for the freak at the back," he pointed to Cain, "but I feel'ike takin' screamy here out for'a tour of th'island," he slurred, "show her a real man. What'd you all think?"

"Sounds good to me," one replied.

"Some great heights round these parts," another snickered, his hands spinning a length of chain. Vlad watched them all, his gaze passing unnoticed, even though the drunkard before him was staring directly into his eyes.

"That is not going to happen," Vlad said calmly. "I have asked nicely, now I will tell you: let my friend go or there will be consequences."

"An' how's that?" the leader asked viciously, moving closer still, breath like acid on Vlad's face. "You'll go *vampire* on us? Is that it?"

Clearly, the barb was meant to shock Vlad but he was too focussed to pay any heed. Another of the men drew a short knife, a switchblade, and brandished it wickedly, the weapon *smelling* of cheap iron. Vlad raised a single eyebrow in challenge.

The leader raised his stick above his head and brought it down slowly as a warning, expecting Vlad to flinch. The stick bumped harmlessly off his face and the man grinned again.

"Who's a tough bloke, eh?" he churned sluggishly. "He's a tough, tough bloke, boys. Well let's see how tough he really is."

With a long swing, the leader raised the stick again and whipped it down through the chilly air with a huge effort, this time to kill. Vlad did not move and the pole crashed against his skull.

Terrified, Lucy and Jacob shouted but when the stick connected it blew apart as if striking rock, shards of wood blasting everywhere. The leader staggered, staring stupidly at the remaining splinter in his hand, too drunk to realise what had happened. In a panic, the man with the blade lunged wildly and stabbed Vlad in the abdomen – Vlad *allowed* him to. The knife plunged into his flesh and blood blossomed across his shirt but Vlad only smiled grimly and pushed a step forward, shoving the man backwards with a stumbling cry.

The intruders gasped as Vlad permitted a measure of power to seep into his eyes, turning them into two soulless pits of the night sky.

"*I warned you*," he muttered, power layering his voice.

Vlad would accept the darkness once more.

Like ten thousand slivers of jagged ice floating upon a silent river, Vlad released his control, released the blockades he had built, and unleashed the twilight shading his black heart. Growing power pumped through his dead veins and the monster inside roared as the vampire's strength flooded his body, turning the air a choking cold, lining the basement's every edge and corner with evil.

The invaders stumbled backward, the leader's grip on Lucy faltering. She struggled, her hair still caught, and her resultant cry of pain and fear only tipped fuel onto the fires of Vlad's anger.

The vampire's shadows grew and burst from his form, wrapping him in the stillest cloak that stole the light. Darkness spread from him and became wings of a terrible presence, gigantic and ragged in the flashing basement light. Every human face struck with utmost horror, becoming deathly pale as Vlad opened his jaws and four huge canines tore free, glinting wickedly, his cheekbones shifting into snakelike angles. The vampire threw his arms wide as his heart's darkness became horns upon his head, curling and sticking in points of black mist, fingernails sharpening into blades of dark metal.

The men raised their weapons, each pathetic stake and chain held like bastions of salvation, and Vlad smiled grimly, his depthless eyes humourless. Moving faster than sight, the vampire vanished then reappeared an eighth-second later, one hand clasping four stakes – they looked like twigs in his powerful grasp –the other holding three lengths of rusting iron chain. The humans glanced fearfully at their hands and the leader finally relinquished his grip upon Lucy's hair. She darted away to Jacob across the room, eyes streaming rivulets of black-streaked tears. Her stare, however, was defiant.

"You…you…" one man struggled.
"This is evil," another man whispered. "Evil, evil, evil!"
"Don't kill me! Please!" the leader cried.

Vlad spread his vast wings and left the ground, towering over the quivering scraps of men like a demon sent to cast judgment and fire. The knife fell from his stomach and clattered to the floor. Vlad crushed the sticks easily in his fingers then pushed power into his other hand until the chains embraced their decay, their rusted lengths degrading so quickly they became brown ash floating to the floor, joining the knife.

"*Run away*," Vlad whispered, his voice like two speaking at once, words written in mastery. Even through the ocean of darkness pounding through his veins, the act disgusted him. "*Never return. You will fear this island until the day you die and your bodies return to the nothing from whence you came. Tell all you see of the evil of this place.*"

Blood and Biscuits

Every eye trained on Vlad and he threw his head back and roared a dark scream so horrid, so pure, that the walls of the undercroft shivered and the church's foundations shook loose rock and dirt. The electric light snapped on and off and the humans screamed and fled, their feet pounding the shaking stone as they stumbled up the stairs and disappeared.

The light winked out completely and all about the room was darkness and shouting. A moment later, light returned and Lucy, Jacob, and Cain looked around desperately until they found Vlad back in the centre of the room, sitting calmly upon his chair, legs crossed. His hands clasped firmly in his lap and he looked normal once again, though he was somehow even paler. Sarah reappeared through the ceiling – she was humming tunelessly.

"Bloody *hell*!" Cain hissed, his face a picture of dread and awe, the strange scent mixed with the iron in his blood pulsing a little stronger. "What on this good earth was that! That's like nothing I've ever heard of from a vampire, that was demonic."

"Not demonic, my lupine friend, only the powers of an ancient vampire."

"But *still*," Jacob said, pushing round the upturned chairs to stare at Vlad in awe. "I'd never have imagined something like that!"

"The older we are the stronger we become, and the more we learn," Vlad explained, folding his arms. "I have been by myself for a long time and have spent many years in quiet places wondering what I am capable of."

"It was like something from hell; I thought you wished to live only a passive life?" Cain asked disbelievingly, eyes still glancing to the entrance for signs of movement. However, the humans would not come back.

Jacob came to Lucy's side to see if she was alright. Sarah simply hovered and continued humming.

"I did, and still do," Vlad replied carefully, "but I can exercise interest in the dark side of me, can I not? I am, after all, still human on some level and curiosity is their greatest asset, *and* their greatest downfall, as you have just witnessed. I can tell you this: I have spent thousands of nights alone, out across endless plains, practicing what I am capable of and exploring my power as I have grown older. On a smaller level, that sort of self-appreciation, that intimacy, is important to truly understand who one is, let alone *what*."

Lucy edged forward, her sleeve wiping away tears. She laid a hand on Vlad's wrist and shivered at his deathly cold. Her body shook a strange thrum of dying power and loosening command. She crouched and met his eye, a quivering smile on her lips.

"Th-thank you," she managed. "No one has ever done that for me before."

Vlad swallowed dryly and returned her weak smile.

"I doubt you have met many vampires like me."

"No, that's not what I meant," she continued as Jacob and Cain, their eyes flicking nervously, put the chairs to rights, ordering them back into a circle. Vlad noticed there was now one more seat. "No one has protected me before. So thank you, Vlad, I was wrong to doubt you. Maybe I'll give this group another chance."

Lucy stepped away, the slight warmth to her fingers leaving impressions of heat on Vlad's skin – he could even detect the pattern of her fingerprints. Lucy sat in her chair and folded her arms, eyes downcast with a strange look playing upon her face. Vlad looked to the others.

"Will you all stay alongside Lucy?" he asked solemnly, hopefully.

"After that display?" Jacob said amusedly. "You can have more than that. S'only fair, considering you've shown us *your* true self."

Stepping forward, Jacob drew his fingers under his balaclava and pulled it off slowly. When he was free, Vlad felt a sliver of surprise catch in his throat.

"A wraith," he whispered, trying not to stare rudely at the decayed flesh and partially exposed teeth of the man's face.

His sunken eyes were bare of irises, only pupils staring from yellowed sclerae. Scars made from skin devoid of muscle and water drawn tight over bone, a lopsided grin finding his face, one showing more than a little jawbone. He was black but now any patches of skin unfettered by curse had paled dark-brown, revealing the evidently handsome man he once was.

"A wraith?" Lucy asked quietly, any shock at Jacob's reveal hidden. "I've never heard of your kind before."

"You might know me better as a 'zombie'," Jacob said lightly, skipping over the term disgustedly. "But I hate the word, makes me sound like a beast, a *thing*. I'm not a thing but a man infected with an incurable curse."

"You and me both, mate," Cain muttered, clapping Jacob on the back. He, too, showed no reaction to the wraith's face. Jacob smiled warmly, evidently touched by the morbid connection. Then Cain pulled a face. "Hang on, didn't you say you were vegan? How in the hell does *that* work! What kinda' group is this again?"

"I was vegan my whole life," Jacob said defiantly. "And turning this way hasn't changed that, though I do have to make concessions somehow, considering I can only survive on brains now."

"A most unfortunate turn of events," Vlad said. "So, let me guess: you keep the ethos of veganism whilst surviving by obtaining brains via…donations?"

"Grave robbing," Jacob muttered.

"Ahh," Vlad finished as Lucy stifled something unreadable and Cain's face grew alarmed. "A most understandable option. Fresh and unneeded, lives already lived and not taken by your hand. Free range, if you will."

"Exactly, though I think 'organic' might be closer," Jacob said brightly. "It's the best I could think of, given the circumstances."

"It's quite brilliant," Lucy said reassuringly though her eyes looked sick. Jacob smiled again, his cracked and yellowed teeth bare.

"You see?" Vlad said, indicating between them. "None of you are alone, and if you give to this group then I will do all I can to help improve your lives. It will greatly improve mine; I can already feel the benefits of simple conversation and companionship."

Vlad looked at each in turn and saw their hesitant faces glow, though whatever Sarah thought was lost, her veiled face a mystery. He was not sure she was even capable of true independent thought.

Lucy nodded.

"You've done more for me than most already, so why not give this a try?"

Vlad nodded back to her and looked at Jacob. The wraith shrugged.

"I'm in just to see more of what you can do."

Vlad grimaced but accepted anyway. He looked to Sarah, prompting her with her name.

"I wish only for company in this awful place," she echoed, her words riding the walls as disturbed waves across a deep lake.

"And company you shall have."

At last, Vlad looked over at Cain as he took the fifth and final chair opposite the vampire, a new coffee in his hand. He positioned what remained of his clothes over the necessary parts of his body and gave a sly look.

"Why not, eh? Gives me something to do in a place I can't hurt people. Probably move on after this, though, so I won't get too comfy. I can talk a while, ain't like I'll see you again. Sorry about the, uh, strangling – Vlad, is it? Don't know what came over me."

"It is quite alright, I have suffered a lot worse than an angry werewolf squeezing the life out of me. Or the death out of me – that has a nice ring to it. I am just happy you were not transformed, else I fear the balance would very much have been tipped in *your* favour. And considering the light went out for a second I was convinced we would see your wolf form tonight."

Vlad said nothing of the scent in his blood but he knew he could not allow this man to run off into the night after the session finished, never to be seen again. He needed to convince him to stay, to show him this church meant safety.

"To be honest, I did feel it risin' in me when the electrics tripped. Glad it didn't last long. S'pose I can blame the full moon for my behaviour earlier."

Cain tried to smile but failed, and Vlad saw shame behind his gaze.

Then Vlad spread his hands and looked at them all.

"Well as an opening for my first ever attempt at a support group, I think it has been a rather interesting evening so far. A vegan wraith searching for some sort of personal redemption, a ghost suffering from the worst in loneliness and isolation, a werewolf allergic to himself, a banshee with deep-set anxieties, and a depressed vampire. It sounds like the plot of a bad film or an odd comic from the eighties." Despite the ragged tensions still lurking in the shadows, the group let out the barest shudder of a laugh. That sound told Vlad a thousand things. "Let us return to admissions of what makes us most vulnerable and sharing them with complete strangers for the hope of clemency, shall we?"

In awkward unison, the group agreed and Vlad placed his hands gently upon his knees. He considered them all, tried to get thoughts of the werewolf's blasted blood scent from his mind, and then he asked a question he still had not found the answer to, the one that would form the basis of every week's session should the Support Group continue.

"So, how *has* everyone's week been?"

Fig. 1. The rusted chains.

I am always fascinated by the wonders of my powers; such horror and yet such strength in darkness. I turned their chains to rust like the wind blows away the leaves of autumn.

Fig. 2. A simple switchblade.

I remember every blade that has ever stabbed me yet this tiny thing is one of the most offensive. I mean look at it! I know the human was not to know with whom he was trifling but a cheap switchblade is, frankly, rude. My stomach recovered within seconds.

On Flowers and Silence

Rain glossed the island in sheets as a foul wind bellowed. Vlad grasped his hands together then unknotted his fingers, facing the ghost.

"Thank you for sparing the time to talk with me, Sarah, I was hoping we might be properly introduced. Get to know each other a little better."

"Oh, it's no bother, it's not as if I'm going anywhere. I had a few duties to attend to - realigning the atmosphere in the eaves, singing sweet poems to the gravestones, regaling the bats with foul sailor songs..."

Vlad snorted but Sarah did not laugh. In fact, the vampire realised she was being completely serious. This was the side of her he needed to expect the most, he thought.

"Well thank you anyway," he ventured, hoping to glean anything he could from her. "It is nice to speak to somebody out here when all others have left, it reminds me this island was once a place of life, just as all dead places once must have been. I am sorry about that business with the humans and the werewolf, it was disrespectful to bring such blasphemy to these grounds."

The memory of that foreign scent in Cain's blood snaked into Vlad's mind again, teased the demon of his depression, casting a pale gloom across him, and then it danced away. Cain had only stayed a short while after the group had left, then he, too, disappeared into the night.

"Think nothing of it," Sarah echoed. "Matters of humans and wolf-men cannot be helped. You may have more luck taming wolves than the terror of wild men. Ask away with your question."

"I actually have two questions, my first is this: what is it like to reside here, in this church?"

Sarah drifted away, floating to one of the thin, barred window slits along the ceiling and peering out into the night. Slowly, she trailed her spectral fingers through the iron bars, the spattered glow of rain-soaked moonlight illuminating her in white. It was an eerily beautiful moment.

"You know, a lot can be said about silence," she muttered. "The living don't seem to appreciate it. All humans ever do is fill their lives with as much noise as possible, be as *loud* as possible, and they miss all the subtleties of the world around them. Have you ever emptied your head of all things, just for a moment, and simply...listened?"

"Many times," Vlad admitted, running a thin, pale finger along the back of a chair and staring at nothing in particular. "Vampires sometimes meditate, usually when they form a new residence; it is a way of tuning themselves to the surrounding area, feeling for the land, the types of ground there, the animals living above and below it, the humans residing nearby to feed on. I think, in those times, I know precisely what you mean."

"In my moments of silence, I like to free my head of all its burdens. I don't know why I'm telling you this; though we've known one another a handful of moments, I feel like I've always known you. Is this what friendship feels like?"

"I have always had that effect with people," Vlad admitted, hoping he did not sound arrogant or conceited. "I do not know why but after only a short time knowing someone, they seem to start telling me things they would not dream of saying to their closest friends. Perhaps it is the stranger phenomenon, the idea we might reveal a side of ourselves to somebody unknown because we assume we will never meet them again."

"As if strangers are journals with a face," Sarah mused. "Journals we voice our entries to that offer comfort in return, becoming pages we never look back on but always know exist somewhere, holding our information tightly and not judging us."

Vlad smiled.

Blood and Biscuits

"A wonderful sentiment. So what you are saying is you enjoy the silence here?"

"In a sense, though too much can become louder than any human might offer."

Vlad chose to leave the matter there.

"Alright. My second question, if you might permit it, follows thusly: do you think of this church as your home?"

Sarah's spirit bobbed for a long moment, evidently considering the question with a gale of thoughts. Vlad was not entirely certain she truly understood what he had asked but it mattered not; what mattered was right then, she was not alone.

"This church is no friend," Sarah finally replied smoothly. "It is a broken hive, a once-place of forgotten things. So much love has buzzed through these walls, walked and danced the halls above, I can feel it soaked into the stone. Every face this church has seen it has shown back to me over the years, as if to mock me, binding me to its consecrated grounds with dry, cruel humour. The only moments of happiness afforded me are the yellows and pinks of daffodil springs, the hope that life still grows, of daffodils and bees, of sunlight and trees..."

"Poetry, it would seem, has followed you into death. Were you fond of the artistry of words in life, Sarah?"

"I was...I was a...a writer, I think. Was I an author? No, not an author, not of novels and epics. But the presumed simplicity yet subtle complexity of words were my love and my vice...yes, that's right, they were my everything. Until he came and showed me more than just ink and paper, showed me what love could truly mean beyond the confines of scripted bounds."

"Words are our best means of developing relationships, even with ourselves," Vlad added, not pushing on the matter of love; he did not know how Sarah would react if he pried. "We think on what we wish to address of our inner psyches and seek to rectify anything we do not like, conversations with our own minds. Yet silence can be our own enemy, too; we avoid our most brutal parts with silence, which is why I do not wholly agree that absolute quiet is best for every situation. Sometimes we crave the words of others to fill the vacuum within us."

"Words set us free, set our minds beyond the trappings of our physical and spiritual forms with the limitless expanse of our imaginations. Why do you think I love foul sailor songs? They're freeing in the ultimate sense. They're brash and rude but they offer dialect and profanity in unshackled droves. We present strict sides of ourselves to others, sides we want them to see so we can't be judged for who we really are, but that's not freedom, that's self-repression. Instead, I choose *imagination*. With creative language, we give ourselves many options and then choose one, and set words to that choice to create immortality with our mouths, our fingers, our minds. Stone, paper, wood...we drive home our thoughts and make them real; that's pure beauty. Beauty I can only share with myself, no-one to hear my words."

"You are not alone, not anymore. My problem is I always treat myself harshly with my words, I feel I am bound to pre-conceived notions of perfection. I long for the ability to simply let go and communicate on a more open level. I envy your sense of linguistic liberty."

"Nobody has ever envied me before," Sarah muttered, her hand falling from the window's bars.

"Well it is true. I wish I had known you in life."

"Perhaps you did. Perhaps we were great friends but forgot one another. Perhaps we were both flowers dancing together in the wind, petals blooming and colouring the fields then drifting with one another upon the breeze, forgotten and renewed in dazzling forms to find each other again. Perhaps silence is the thing that brought us back together, the desperate longing and utter, devastating beauty found only in the quiet that we both crave driving us toward one another over and over through time. Or perhaps we both think too much and can't seem to let our needs drive us when we should really let them."

Blood and Biscuits

"Which of those would you like to believe?" Vlad asked, almost sadly.

"It doesn't matter what I believe. Ghosts don't get choices, we get only permanence and the absolution found in that hard truth."

"No. You are a person before anything else, before any title or existence. You are a person and people are granted choice, no matter how easy or hard it comes to them."

Sarah floated for a moment, her silvery fingers back to passing through the bars of the window gently, as if she wanted to feel the cold iron in her grasp, rain on skin she no longer owned. Then she gave a small laugh, almost imperceptible, even to Vlad's powerful senses, and turned from the vision of the night.

"Then I choose the breeze and the flowers. Two acts of life caught in one act of randomness, the ability to peer at the event in two ways: the wind stealing the flowers for its own gain, and thereby stealing beauty itself, or the flowers harnessing the wind and taking their own freedom. Both are short lived but for a moment there is such joy to be had."

Pacing the room and moving his hand through the air as if conducting some invisible orchestra, Vlad thought a moment.

"Do you know *why* the daffodils around this church grow strange pink flowers from their stems, Sarah? I have never seen their likeness before, it is most strange."

"They are beautiful, aren't they? So beautiful. I call them my spirit roses. Sometimes, I feel their beauty's made just for me. So small an act of kindness from the graves and the world. I will pay them your respects."

Vlad said nothing else. He suspected, despite Sarah's phantom form and inherent inability to change emotionally, she had revealed more of herself than she would ever know. A minute later, she was flying back through the church basement and humming aimlessly to herself, pirouetting occasionally and bowing to nothing in particular. Vlad watched her drift away and disappear through the ceiling, feeling the last two flurries of hope and joy escape with her, the ghost that felt too much. As he considered her words, Vlad doubted she would remember anything of the conversation they had just had.

Week Two
Do You Believe in the Soul?

**BASEMENT VAULTS,
RUINS OF ST ELLIN'S CHURCH,
ELLIN'S INDUSTRIAL ISLAND,
NORTHERN ENGLAND.**

"Once again, please do not feel pressured to say or share anything. It is good enough you came back; I was not sure after the first trial session you would return."

There was a murmur of assent and a watery smile from Lucy - Vlad was especially glad to see her again. He did not think she would return, not after the humans.

The vampire sat relaxed, thoughts calm, and looked to them all openly.

Jacob moved as if to speak but stopped, hands falling heavily into his lap. He had a dark-cloth, empty-seeming bag tucked under his chair. Vlad smelled a flicker of once-living tissue from it and a scent of pain from the wraith. Jacob glanced to the doorway and checked his watch.

Vlad turned to Cain – he looked tired, more so than someone his age should have been – and extended a hand in his direction, exuding calm. It was a move representing solidarity and respect, glossing over the strangling incident the week before.

"Things got a little…emotional last week and I believe the importance of proper British formalities became lost in the turmoil. Let me extend my apologies for my behaviour."

Blood and Biscuits

"Oh, err...that's alright. Me too. The full moon's gone now and I've lost some of that natural anger that comes with my curse. Same thing every month, same excuse, it just builds in me 'til the moon's out, and–"

"–and you become something you are not, something you consider a sickness that cannot be cured. A punishment for a crime you never committed."

"Yeah," the man replied, his unsure face gaining a modicum of strength. "It's not been said like that before. I'd ask how you'd know what to say but what's the point, right?"

"Correct," Vlad said with a smile. "Though I would never dream to suppose I know your past and your pain, I can at least offer a great deal of empathy from person-to-person. I will always hold to the opinion that my own servitude to darkness is a punishment for my own attempted suicide, it brings me surprising peace, though it does nothing to help my dour turns of depression. Regardless," Vlad sighed, "I notice your allergies have departed. That must be a relief, however temporary."

"For now," Cain said. "They'll come back as well, always do."

The men shook hands as Vlad reminded, "Do remember to grab a coffee and some biscuits, I believe you were a fan last week."

"They weren't half bad," Cain admitted as he stood and walked to the table against the wall, his form lit strangely by the low electric light. "Appreciate it. Anyone else want anythin'?"

"I'm good," Jacob muttered. "I can't have too much coffee, it won't sit well in my stomach. And you wouldn't want to be around for the result."

Lucy, however, raised her hand.

"Chuck me a chocolate biscuit?"

Cain obliged and fished one out of a new packet. He aimed the biscuit and threw it deftly across the circle, and Lucy caught it easily and smiled. Vlad took a measure of gladness at the act of familiarity, as if for the briefest moment they were all friends

Blood and Biscuits

enjoying one another's company.

"Thanks," Lucy said and bit into the biscuit gratefully. A flicker of relief passed over her face as she chewed.

"No problem," Cain muttered as he returned, coffee in-hand.

"I feel heavier today," Sarah suddenly said and everyone glanced at her. Vlad cocked his head; her spirit floated lower than the previous week but that could mean anything. Emotional weight was her burden, unfettered by earthly laws as she was, so her altitude might well reflect her mood.

When Sarah said no more the matter was dropped.

Vlad flexed his fingers and breathed deeply into his stomach, his long dead and blackened lungs fluttering uselessly as his diaphragm did all the work. He felt air move over his vocal cords, sensed his voice created by the vibrations: that was the sole physical purpose of breathing now. The thought gave him a strange, distant comfort. He took a sip of coffee made fresh a quarter hour before, but as always he could taste none of the bitter flavours described on the supermarket branded packet. He could smell them, right down to the type of soil they were grown in, but his taste was dead save for blood, salt, and capsaicin molecules in spicy foods. The coffee was quite simply a lukewarm drink in place of blood, a poor substitute to keep his hands busy, rather like a smoker replacing cigarettes with carrot sticks.

Those not addicted to blood or nicotine would not understand.

"Any more, err, self-harming?" Jacob asked quietly, slowly, feeling for Vlad's mood.

Vlad shook his head.

"It is quite strange but no. This would be the first time in a long while I have gone a full week without slicing my skin. Hmm, I had not even considered it…"

Vlad made to speak but something stirred in his body. The sensation grew from his stomach but was not isolated there, and he hesitated a moment as he waited for the feeling to subside. It had nothing to do with coffee: this was starvation. Thoughts of his own blood only intensified the situation, so he set aside methods of retaining mental control, paid them no heed.

The starvation sensation took a minute too long, dragging at his insides like a thousand clawed, desperate hands, but then it was gone again and the vampire shook off the urges of blood and death. It was stronger than last week's and had been growing the past few days; he knew how to heal this pain but he could not acknowledge it, not yet.

Vlad knew he needed to be strong enough to last a little longer.

"Anyway, I shall start again," Vlad continued, "with the quietest yet most profoundly deep of my questions: how was everyone's week?"

Nobody answered, as predicted, so Vlad nodded acceptingly.

"Then I will begin," he announced, counting off the days since he had last fed without missing a beat. "It seems that is only fair, considering this was my idea."

Vlad breathed again.

"My week was...an interesting one. Yes, that about sums it up. There were highs and lows, all things considered. I suppose it began well enough after last week's meeting. I went home and occupied myself with a film or two - silly things about guns and car chases and poorly written women incapable of looking after themselves."

Vlad opened his mouth to continue but Jacob chimed in.

"Typical male fantasies,' he muttered. "Always play out the same. Not exactly Éric Rohmer."

"Ahh, a film lover?" Vlad asked, welcoming the brief distraction.

"Not really; used to be – used to love them, especially French cinema – but I don't own a TV anymore, and can't exactly walk into a theatre without causing widespread panic."

"That is a shame, I find them to be terrific escapes," Vlad

noted. "And considering I spent much time in France in the thirties and early forties I am well-versed in French cinema of that era." Jacob shrugged resignedly and Vlad continued. "Anyway, that is beside the point. I watched these ridiculous action films and decided to take a walk. This is not something I normally do; being around living, breathing life causes me great difficulties, but I was feeling buoyed by the previous meeting's success."

"It had its moments," Lucy said with a knowing grin, part-hidden by shining midnight hair.

"I admit there was a shaky aspect to the proceedings," Vlad agreed half-heartedly.

"Shaky! We got annexed by humans and you went full-vampire on them! Probably landed the guys in some division somewhere; they're definitely gonna' need psychiatric help." Though Cain's tone sounded dry Vlad caught respect there.

"Indeed," the vampire muttered, ashamed. "Though I assure you, that was not 'full vampire', as you call it."

The group shuffled in their seats. Vlad could not tell if they had suddenly leant away from him subconsciously or were setting their attentions firmer. He was glad to see Lucy no longer looked at him with frustration.

"I do not really sleep, not in the same sense as many of you. There is a part of my brain that finds rest useful but I am always at least partially aware during those short periods. Sometimes I meditate to attune myself with my surroundings but other than that I am awake constantly."

"I think that'd drive me nuts," Cain marked, tapping his head for emphasis, long fingers moving with surprising grace. "Can't imagine a world without sleep, I kinda' remember being a big fan of it before I…became what I am, I s'pose. But then, you *like* sleep when you're young."

"Quite," Vlad responded. "And supposedly many new vampires do struggle with the change. It would not seem it but the sudden lack of sleep and adjacent introduction to being eternally alone with one's mind is one of the biggest difficulties after the transition of joining the blood-hood. I certainly-"

"Blood-hood?"

Vlad stopped. It was Sarah that had interrupted. When they all stepped down into the church basement she had simply been there, floating half an inch above the same chair as before, humming away. If Vlad had not spoken to her alone earlier in the week, he would have been convinced she had not moved since the last session.

"Yeees," he said slowly, trying to work out her truncated question. "That is what it is sometimes called."

"Only amongst an inner circle of vampires, as far as I know," Sarah commented, her words ricocheting off the ceiling, back to Vlad's highly sensitive hearing in a dozen separate voices. An ethereal choir. "That would mean you've not been alone for so long, as you suggest. I remember this though I don't know why…"

Suspicion leached into every eye.

"Well, I have not been alone my entire life – or death. I mentioned last week my creator, the vampiress Izanami, did I not? She was ancient even when she came to recreate me in her form, from the Japanese old world moving across what was Europe back then. She forced me to love her and in return I was her unwitting slave, the man to do her bidding. After I was reborn of her blood, Izanami took me into her circle – that is the collective noun for a group of vampires."

"Isn't it coven?" Lucy asked genuinely, sincerity plain on her face. Her innocence made Vlad smile rather than grimace.

"No, that is a common mistake. A coven refers to witches, and trust me there is a vast difference between the two beings."

"Hang about, witches are real?" Cain asked suddenly, light-brown hands turning pale against his steaming cup. "Why've I never heard this? I feel it's somethin' I should've been told about, given my situation."

"I would imagine information on many of us, if not all, is scarce at best," Vlad noted. "Consigned to legacy and myth only, with the merest of sightings from those escaping the evil clutches of our forebears the only real details penetrating society. And those victims are always scoffed at, mocked, derided as lunatics, attention seekers. It cannot be easy suffering as they have only to be dismissed as deranged."

"But…witches," Cain said again and Vlad shook his head slightly, grinning lopsidedly.

"Apologies, I become awfully side-tracked sometimes. Perhaps I am a stickler for the sound of my own voice." The group chuckled and fell into a detectable ease, as it had last week, only this time it came a few minutes earlier. "I do not wish to get into it but witches do indeed exist, as do many other beings outside the realms of 'normality'. Look, this is completely aside from what I was saying before – what *was* I saying?"

"You were talking about films," Jacob stated.

"Ahh yes, well I was actually divulging my week. Let us fast-forward a bit; I went out for a walk. This was a little before dawn so I felt fine doing so, physically anyway. Not that the sun bothers me anymore, I overcame *that* little setback centuries ago. So, there I was, strolling down the high street, when I heard something ahead. It sounded like a cry, a muffled scream, so I sped up, wondering if somebody was hurt."

"What was it?" Sarah asked. She sounded roused, as if the notion of someone's anguish ignited her spirit. Vlad supposed it was the particular amalgamation of her remnants, her unique emotional combination wreathing the only impression she made on the world, the imprint of pure feeling giving her a visible presence. Her interest in the morbid gave clues on how she died.

"It was a young woman, possibly no older than thirty. Her dress was ripped, she was crawling away across the wet ground. There was a man bearing down, older by a few years and built a lot larger, intent burning in his eyes."

"Oh God," Lucy muttered, putting her hands to her mouth, eyes shining over her fingers. "That's terrible."

"Indeed," Vlad spat. "A most heinous crime, detestable and entirely human in its quality."

"What did you do?" Jacob asked as Cain sipped his coffee, avoiding looking at anyone. When Vlad hesitated, Jacob misread his wordlessness. "You did nothing?"

"Of course I did something," Vlad responded, quicker and harsher than intended. He measured calm into himself. "Apologies again, I did not mean to snap. Look, after what happened during last week's evening session, I tried very hard to maintain control on my darker self; that was what the walk was for, and the films. However, this man advancing on a defenceless person – and I admit, in a rather old-fashioned way, I was riled further by her being a woman, and I make *no* apologies for this – it stirred the worst side of me again, still fresh from the human assault last week."

"Jesus, what did you *do* to him?" Cain asked, the slightest satisfaction curling his eyes. "Whatever it was he deserved it."

"I did not attack him, if that is what you are referring to," Vlad qualified, running his hand through his dark hair and finishing his coffee. At the memory, he could feel his curse gripping his blackened heart again. "Not in the physical sense, anyway. But I did engage him with hypnosis, my vampiric mastery."

"Oh nice!" Cain exclaimed, grinning at Jacob jovially. Vlad could not see his face but he assumed he smiled.

"No, it is not nice," the vampire said sadly. "It is the foulest gift, and not so morally different from some techniques used by predators to *get* vulnerable people like that woman into the situation she found herself in. Coercion at its most intimate, whereby I speak magic, if you can call it that, and invade another's soul. Take away freedom of thought and commit them to little more than slavery at your own discretion."

"You used mastery to lead him away from the woman," Lucy confirmed thoughtfully.

"I did, and I am not proud of it."

Lucy's face changed then, like she was feeling two warring

emotions.

"But…but you stopped him! What does it matter how you did it? You stopped a woman from what sounds like sexual assault and you didn't kill anyone, that's a win!"

"I know what I did was right, I *know* that," Vlad said, running his hand through his hair again, "but that does not stop the hatred I have for myself for taking somebody's free will away. Do not look at me like that, Lucy, I could not bear the thought of you thinking me foolish; I have a conscience the same as anyone else, and it guides me in everything I do. Remember that I had already used mastery on those men that attacked us earlier in the same evening?"

Vlad did not mention the hypnosis he had used on Cain before the humans had attacked, he did not think it wise to speak of.

"And you saved *me* from that," Lucy said exasperatedly. "You did what you had to and stopped a crime from happening. Do you regret *that*?"

"No! My good gracious no, not for one second. What I did was necessary, it had purpose, it was needed."

"Exactly! So how is this with the woman in the street any different?"

"I – I do not know, I…struggled greatly with my choice, became devoured by it. It weighed on me so heavily I flew home and did not leave until two days ago."

The vampire felt the air of the room change; it was only a fraction yet the alteration was palpable to him. He glanced round and saw every member of the group staring at him with an unknown feeling. The first to speak was Jacob.

"Vlad, you did *nothing* wrong, absolutely nothing. Mate, you stopped a girl from suffering something horrific, and earlier you saved Lucy from getting dragged off. In my eyes, you're a bloody fine bloke. If you ask me, the wee turmoil you're struggling with is 'cause you used mastery so much in one night, not because you used it at all. Must be a side effect of your depression."

Cain nodded and the distrust and violence from the previous

week between vampire and werewolf was lost to the abyss. When Cain spoke, he was evidently quietening his usual growl.

"Don't listen to that voice in your head, Vlad, it ain't worth it. What you've got is an illness but it can be beaten. I'd heard of vampires before, sure, but I'd never seen what they're capable of until last week."

"I am not the same as most vampires. You must have been sickened by my actions," Vlad muttered, shame rankling his insides like mud and poison.

"Far from it," Cain said wolfishly.

Lucy reached across the small space separating herself and Vlad and lay her hand on the edge of his arm. He peered through her shining hair, the fibres flowing independently according to her mood, and saw she was looking at him differently.

"What you did was right, Vlad, it was *right*. I know you feel like crap but that'll pass, I'm sure of it."

When she let go it seemed to take some of Vlad's burden with her, physicality and emotionality combining and departing his small world.

Vlad felt he could say nothing and he was glad when Jacob filled the void with his quiet intonation.

"Huh,' he chuckled half-heartedly. "Realise what's just happened?"

"What?" Vlad managed.

"Role reversal."

"Excuse me?" Lucy asked pointedly.

Jacob shuffled awkwardly.

"Well, you know…Vlad started this – us – the group, obviously intending on helping people that need help. But *he* was the one in need, and *you* just gave that to him. Seems it's easier opening up to a bunch of randoms rather than people you know, so maybe Vlad's just gotten a dose of that, too. I'm only saying – I probably shouldn't have, maybe I've ruined it."

"No…no you haven't," Vlad started just as Sarah spoke.

Blood and Biscuits

"I feel lighter," she whispered and her body rose a little higher from her seat. "Like there was pressure before but now it's gone. Ooh, I feel the church getting brighter, that's nice. Thank you for being here with me and brightening my church."

That was all she uttered and Vlad smiled at her.

"You are welcome," he replied, a warm sensation filling the void surrounding his motionless heart. He enjoyed Sarah's company yet her very presence always filled Vlad with a heavy sense of sadness, too.

"You see?" Jacob said, satisfied, indicating Sarah and Cain. "Seems we're here for a reason, Vlad."

And in that instant, Vlad realised for the first time since they had met, he was the vulnerable one. Lucy had momentarily set aside the banshee curse consuming her every thought to expose her caring side, the beautiful mind beneath. Jacob revealed a deeper wisdom than his age perhaps suggested. Their help as a group, however brief, was enough to bring the vampire back from the precipice of sorrow from which his personal demon so sorely wished him to jump.

And then the moment lost its edge.

"To be fair, she probably shouldn't have been out alone. The girl you saved, I mean."

Vlad and Lucy looked quickly to Cain and the werewolf sat straighter in his chair.

"What's that supposed to mean?" Lucy asked, ice cracking across her words, lacing her voice with cold meaning.

"Easy, she shouldn't have been out alone. This is nasty, yeah, and she didn't deserve it at all, don't get me wrong, but if she'd been with someone this wouldn't have happened in the first place."

"That is not the right thing to think, Cain," Vlad said. "You do not know her circumstances, you do not know why she was in the position she was in. The fault lies squarely with the man, you need to understand that."

Lucy sat forward, arms crossed dangerously, fingers biting into her flesh.

"Alright, *mate*," she spat, "what do you do when you go out for a drink, then?"

"Eh?" Cain said thickly.

"It's easy," Lucy said, repeating the werewolf's breezy tone. "When you go out for a night on the town – or at any time, for that matter – what do you do to prepare yourself against assault or abuse?"

Cain chewed his lip for a moment, a scent of agitation grating off him jaggedly.

"Nothin'," he finally muttered darkly. "Never really thought about it before."

"And that's your right, to live your life as you see fit without worrying something's going to happen to you. But it's also your privilege, Cain, do you understand? It's a privilege for you because you're a big man, because girls and women don't get to feel so safe, because while emotional vulnerability might be an issue for you, with your transformations, *sexual* vulnerability isn't. Maybe I'm different from human women but I remember feeling like that once, a long time ago, and I still do when I walk into town. However, I can read articles and I see the news. Every day, girls and women go out and suffer serious threats and real abuse at the hands of disgusting, vile men, just for wanting to live their lives."

Cain tried interjecting but Vlad shook his head, teeth gritted. This was Lucy's turn. Cain needed to listen. Jacob's eyes darted between them as Vlad kept his senses alert, tempering the room should moods flare.

"Keys in their hands as weapons; planning their routes home before they've even left to go out; never leaving their drinks alone and making sure *they're* never alone, even for a moment; never relaxing. When you walk home after you've had a few, do you panic at every shadow? Keep your ears pricked at every sound? Have to worry about every single person you think's following you? Ring somebody so it looks like you're not alone?"

"No. No, I don't," Cain muttered, guilt now mixing with

agitation.

"No, and you shouldn't have to. And neither should girls but they do it all the time. You've never had to think about it before. So whatever that poor woman was going through isn't for you to judge. She's just lucky Vlad was there, most don't get that salvation."

Cain took a deep breath then exhaled heavily.

"You're right, I'm sorry. I didn't mean to…to say what I did. It was the man's fault entirely, you're dead right. I'm sorry."

Cain sat back and clenched his jaw but Vlad saw Lucy soften, just slightly. She loosened her arms, back muscles losing their tension.

"It's alright. What you need is education, just like most, but for now you've heard me, and that's what's important."

Cain nodded and thumbed his nose, a sliver of shame peeling off him.

"Well," Vlad said after a few seconds' pause. He did not want people to focus on Cain any longer, he had taken enough for the moment. "What has been said has been said and I cannot think of anything else for *me* to mention. I suffered through that haunting week as my depression hit its lowest point in months and then dragged myself back up once more. Nothing further to say on the matter."

Sitting back in his chair, his body radiated waves of shallow contentment, a rare feeling for the vampire as he considered its worth.

"So, who's next?" Cain asked, long fingers intertwined passively, clearly desperate to move things on. "Wouldn't be fair if we all go silent, seen as Vlad here spilled his deepest."

"Off you go, then," Lucy said, a dangerous twinkle in her eye.

"Me?"

"Why not?"

"I got you that chocolate biscuit and you verbally spanked me in front of everyone, seems on balance you go next as payment,"

Blood and Biscuits

Cain grunted.

"Add it to my tab," Lucy countered. Jacob blinked at Vlad. The vampire raised a single, solitary eyebrow but said nothing.

Cain chuckled.

"Fair enough. So where to begin, eh? Where to begin after that dressing down from Lucy…oh, may as well start like Vlad did: after last week's impromptu session." Cain cleared his throat. "I didn't mean to come down here, you know that, I was scared and confused. The full moon and this island were causin' havoc with my transformation – I only remember flashes of the wolf, like I'm drugged or it's someone else's story conjuring false memories."

"You've got to remember *something*," Jacob said curiously.

"Mainly fury and blood; I thought it was a dream at first but I know I was human inside them factories along the riverbanks. I can remember thrashin' about but I was definitely human-form then, must've been one of them spots of old magic you talked about, Vlad, and then them human gits must've found me while I was delirious with the moon fightin' that magic, I guess. And then there was runnin' and…light."

"Light?"

"Not just light, *a* light."

"St Ellin's Church. The light from the basement," Vlad said.

"And that's where I ended up, so maybe that's right."

"I didn't hear you approaching," Vlad noted. "There are not many that might deceive my senses. In the future, I shall increase my power to keep a better watch over the island as we talk."

"Well, I think the one saving grace my wolf has is his ability to stay quiet when he wants. I know vampires are s'posed to have clever hearing but werewolves are notorious stalkers, and mine's no exception from what I understand. Plus, soon as I stepped near, I transformed back."

"We didn't hear you," Lucy said, looking at Cain curiously. "Doesn't it hurt?"

"It's excruciating," Cain hissed. "But I internalised the pain

Blood and Biscuits

outside and waited a bit on the stairs to listen to you guys and see what was what."

"The holy ground and electric light power do stretch a bit beyond the church. It must have been distressing," Vlad acknowledged. "From what I have witnessed, the change is torture."

"You have no idea," Cain admitted, a flash of something shuddering through his shoulders. Absently, the man rubbed his back and clicked his spine. Then he glanced at Vlad and Lucy. "I misspoke. I guess you do. I meant more on the physical pain."

"I know what you meant, Cain, and I took no offence. Nor, would I assume, did anyone else here."

Cain looked round at the others and obviously recalled where he was and who surrounded him. Nobody raised it as an issue and Cain continued, relief defining his face.

"After the session I didn't want to go back outside. Those guys might've still been here but more to the point I was safe from transforming, you know? It was good of you to stay behind, Vlad, and thanks for the extra coffee and biscuits, Christ knows I needed the energy. After you'd gone I slept for a bit on the floor then left at dawn, safe again for another day," Cain finished.

Vlad remembered Cain shivering and eyeing the doorway nervously after everyone had left, aside from Sarah. She had watched the two men absently and hovered for a little while, then coughed politely and promptly disappeared through the ceiling.

"Yet it was only the second night of the full moon," Sarah resonated, a force of quiet observation and calm intelligence. "Though I already know the answer, I ask for the rest of our friends here: whatever would a man such as yourself do next?"

"Would you believe I bought a sleepin' bag and came back?" Cain asked, almost suggesting he was admitting something embarrassing.

"If you felt you needed to return then you were free to do so," Vlad began. "I quite understand the notion, I cannot imagine it can be easy finding safe places to inhabit during the full moon's nights.

One must take advantage of anything one finds."

"I'm always on the move," Cain sighed, rubbing his hand over his arm more vigorously than a simple itch would have required. "I can't remember the last time I just...*stopped*. Just stopped in one place and found I could stretch out and...I dunno'. I just want to stop," he groaned, "get this constant moving-from-place-to-place thing done."

Vlad had something else to say but he stopped himself. Sometimes he had the unfortunate habit of speaking too often, of offering yet another piece of information he hoped would convey wisdom, but this time he fought that side of him. He assumed his urgency to speak was another side effect of his ever-wavering mood, as if his words buoyed him against sinking further into depression.

Vlad sat back and listened as Cain continued undisturbed. This was, after all, a collective designed to encourage the strength of its individual parts.

"I guess it was nice to come back to somewhere, even if I barely knew the place." Cain gazed round the basement blankly. "I got some food from a bank, some old clothes from a charity shop. Camped out here a few days – I didn't see you, Sarah," he noted suddenly. "I've only just realised!"

"Perhaps, but I knew you were here, warding off my loneliness. It's always nice having the living around, I like to hear them breathe," she replied mistily, veil unmoving as she turned her head to peer at him. Vlad noted a minute translucency change, light shimmering through her spirit as Sarah said, "This is my church, I am tied to it, and I know her walls and her secrets. I am always aware here."

"Oh," Cain said slowly, unease tightening his facial muscles. "Well...super, good to know."

"Thank you for letting me watch you sleep," Sarah whispered.

Jacob looked between the ghost and the werewolf. Instead of letting go of the nervous laugh he clearly held back, he decided to

Blood and Biscuits

break the silence with a question.

"So, did you stay here all week?" he asked.

Cain shook his head.

"No, once I started recoverin' from the transformation aches and the wounds them humans gave me, I went and stayed in a hostel – I'm still there now, actually."

"Do you find that helps with getting some kind of stability?" Lucy asked and Cain dipped his head.

"Yeah, lets me set a base of sorts and see about gettin' money together from odd jobs. Not got any friends. Got a couple careers advisors that don't ask questions. They sometimes find me casual work, no strings attached. Labour, warehouse stock, and the like. Been shiftin' boxes the last two days for extra weekend pay, it's been good."

"That is terrific to hear," Vlad said finally, leaning forward with a slanted smile, fingers steepled elegantly. His stomach twisted in starvation again. "Simple matters are the foundations of better lives, I have found. And it *is* terrific, Cain, I am honestly glad you found something to construct with."

Vlad felt a measure of warmth from Cain and knew that was enough.

"So, I suppose if our friend here feels he has said his piece then it is somebody else's turn," the vampire remarked. "Any volunteers from...?"

"Could I say something?"

All heads turned to Sarah. She hovered ever higher above her chair.

"Of course, please go right ahead!"

"Thank you. Two days ago, I went to the graveyard beyond the north wall – I like to see the names; it gives me comfort knowing there are those that came to rest here while I remain imprisoned against my will. I walked between the tombstones, reading the dead and wondering on their lives...I think I remember a few of their funerals. And then I felt you all returning to my church. So that was nice."

Vlad raised his eyebrows and waited but Sarah had finished, simply floating pleasantly. Eventually, she started humming.

"Thank you, Sarah," Vlad finally said, not really knowing how else to respond. Her casual use of the word 'walking' carved into his thoughts. "That was good of you to share with us. Any…anyone else?"

Jacob's red-rimmed eyes watched Sarah strangely. Vlad could feel a disturbance in his mood as he hesitated warily, clearly not grasping the hollowness of the ghost's presence.

"Yeah…" the wraith began slowly. "Cheers, Sarah. You all, err, mind if I go next? I feel good enough to speak and time's ticking on."

"Please, the floor is yours. I am still listening," Vlad assured, standing gracefully as if lifted by the air itself. "I am just going to make myself another coffee. Anybody want a beverage or a biscuit?"

"I'll go for the orangey ones this time," Cain called over his shoulder and Vlad smiled as he moved to the coffee stand, stopping his famished body from trying to glide. He picked up two orange-flavoured chocolate biscuits and sent them soaring to Cain's outstretched hand. He caught them nimbly. "Much appreciated. Must admit, I'm a sucker for synthetic fruit flavours."

"Good to know," Vlad responded, pouring himself another stream of steaming coffee. Jacob spoke on in relative comfort.

"I didn't do much after last week's session, just went home…sat for a while. Wraiths don't really sleep, same as you, Vlad. Drives me a bit wild, got to keep myself occupied. I'd love to go out and see some art but I can't, obviously, and I've no TV, like I said; can't afford a set or a license, what with me being unemployed and-"

"Ahh, you should've said," Cain interrupted. "I'll see if there's anything goin' down at the warehouse, could be somethin' for you."

"No that's alright," Jacob shrugged. "No point. Can't take

this off," he indicated his balaclava, "or they'd cack their pants, and people'd get funny if I wear it at work. Damned if I do and damned if I don't, so it's better to keep alone and scrimp on what I've got."

"Jacob," Vlad said seriously, striding back to his seat and taking it delicately. "If you are in need of anything you will let us know, will you not? To have a potential friend suffering through no fault of his own is deplorable to me."

Jacob raised his hand passively.

"Honest, it's fine. I was homeless before I got like this and you learn a few tricks of the trade. As for my week, that was kind of it, really. I sat and read a few books, did some puzzles, went online when the free Wi-Fi from the bank opposite my bedsit booted up. That was until Friday, when I started getting hungry again."

"Ahh, that's not great," Lucy said.

Jacob nodded.

"You're telling me. Usually I keep an eye on the obituaries in the papers and online but somehow I'd forgotten this time so I'd no idea where to go for fresh food. God, that sounds odd."

"Yeah, and I thought *I* was weird," Cain muttered, eyes wide. Jacob snorted.

"How long buried can a body be before you can no longer consume their brains?" Vlad asked as casually as if he was enquiring about the weather.

"A few days past death? Maybe ten at a push, if I'm desperate. And I was, the anger was overtaking me. That wraith surge coming to drag my consciousness away. I didn't have a choice, I needed to feed or be lost from my mind. So, I grabbed a shovel, a bag, and some food containers then headed out. Speaking of, I brought some with me."

Jacob reached down and unzipped the dark bag by his feet. He withdrew a plastic container and Lucy recoiled slightly. She attempted to cover the move by sweeping her hair back. The container was filled with a light-grey substance with the occasional pink spot. Nobody needed an explanation.

"Anyone mind?" Jacob asked coyly. "I'm really sorry, this is breakfast, lunch, and dinner in one."

"I certainly do not, and I would not think I have any right to, given my own culinary delights," Vlad said matter-of-factly. "Anyone else?"

"Nope, go right ahead," Cain offered.

Lucy simply nodded and averted her eyes as Jacob cracked the container and brought out a mouthful of food as delicately as if he was handling an imperial Fabergé egg. He spoke as he ate.

"I've got a few popular cemeteries I keep on my radar but I didn't know which to use. Ellinsgate's got a big enough population to keep the holes filling. God, this is good, I think I like the hypothalamus best..."

"So, what did you do on Friday?" Lucy asked in sickened wonder. "I can't believe I'm asking this but how does one know where to start when searching for, um, fresh brains?"

"Christ, it *does* sound funny when you put it like that. Properly morbid. And I don't know, I just sort of guessed. Lucky guess, it was, 'cause I came to Verrin the Passive's graveyard and saw a few spots with new flowers on them. I feel awful saying this but I dug both graves up and got into the coffins – you have any idea what it's like knowing I'm disrespecting the dead because of my own selfish needs? And I was a bloody *vegan* before all of this, I hated mindless sacrifice!"

"Well, they *were* already dead," Cain began. "Not exactly usin' their soft 'n' squishies no more. As Vlad said: gotta' take advantage when you can."

"That's not the point," Jacob retorted sharply, repacking his food into his bag. Cain sat back in his chair, arms folded across his chest. Jacob sighed. "Sorry, but it just doesn't compute like that in my head. What I do is monstrous, it's disgusting, and the only reason I haven't caved in and tried to kill myself again is because I'm a coward. Since the first time failed after I became a wraith, I've thought about it twice more, but both times I gave up."

Blood and Biscuits

"That is no cowardly thing, Jacob," Vlad cut in. "To pluck up the courage to take your own life requires remarkable strength, especially when it is to save the lives of others. You should never do it, there will always be help, but you are not a coward for trying and never believe yourself as such. What I say will probably not help but I cannot let you continue thinking yourself weak. Everyone has these thoughts, and I mean *everyone*. Most are not in your situation: some are like me and sick for unknown reasons; others feel they just cannot go on with their lives; most people have bad days, weeks, months. Your worries and your feelings are important, especially to you, and you cannot mark yourself a failure simply because you no longer wanted to exist with your pain. Look at me! I became a vampire when *I* was trying to kill myself! And I would have done it, too, had I not been stopped."

"It's brave is what you are, mate," Cain growled. "Yeah that's right, brave. Not many'd have the guts to survive like you do, and not many'd bring themselves to spare the lives of others by ending their own. Bloody hell, I've contemplated it a few times. I think if there's one thing we've all got in common here it's death, in whatever form it comes. Don't let your mind rule your soul, it'll consume you."

Jacob slumped in his chair, hands flat on his thighs, listening to everything said. Vlad longed to see his face, to connect on that basic level, but he would never ask Jacob to throw aside his dignity because of what someone else wanted. After thirty seconds or so, Jacob sniffed and turned away, his heart clearly growing heavy. Vlad sincerely hoped it was relief that crushed him, not musings on his own worth.

"I just..." Jacob said as he choked. "I never talk about this stuff. I had people, once, but now I'm on my own. I didn't think I'd ever share again." He sniffed again. "Thanks for listening."

"That is all we can do," Vlad said. "Listen and hope to occasionally offer a piece of advice or a comforting thought. The more you share the fragments of your broken selves the more you piece yourselves back together. We are not counsellors, simply a means to offload."

"It's good," Jacob said quietly. "This is a good place to be, I can feel it."

For the second time that evening, a definite note of pleasantness stretched between them all. Even Sarah seemed contented hovering six inches above her seat, her humming echoing round the basement in an eerily beautiful yet sombre reflection.

"Do you believe in that kind of thing?"

Lucy shattered the quiet, addressing Cain directly. Vlad had not thought she would, considering the avoidance she had thus far shown the werewolf, yet there she was defying his misplaced expectations.

"In what?" Cain asked suspiciously.

"A soul."

"Oh, it was just a figure of speech, but since you asked…no, I guess I don't."

"Huh," was all she said, something processing behind her dark eyes.

"What is it?" Vlad asked, curiosity getting the better of him.

"It's just…no, it's stupid. Never mind."

"Please, nothing you could tell us would be stupid. The point of this is not to judge. If it drags you down in some way then release its weight so you might surface and take a breath. Metaphorically, considering only one of us here actually *needs* breath."

Cain rubbed his arm as Lucy glanced up at the ceiling and at Sarah. She shuffled awkwardly before opening her mouth.

"I was brought up in a closed community in a tiny town in south-west Ireland," she began.

"Yes, I thought I noticed a hint of an accent," Vlad admitted and Cain nodded.

"I try and hide it but clearly I'm not as good as I'd hoped."

"I spent a good amount of time in your home country after observing quite the invasion of Henry's forces in County Wexford,"

Blood and Biscuits

Vlad explained. "Some very dark times."

Vlad realised his mistake quickly. He did not intend to talk about his history, that was not the point of the group. He chided himself a fool for letting his tongue wander as it did.

"That's interesting," Lucy said absentmindedly. "My community was deeply religious, *deeply*, and with a heavy core of superstition from your typical Irish mythology, too." Lucy sat back and pointed to herself. "Ironically, they weren't actually wrong. Not about the superstitious stuff, anyway. And I was a big part of that belief, I was fully ready to accept God and the creatures of the night to keep me true and pure until I passed from this world, that was everyone's purpose. One of the big things we believed in was the sanctity of the soul."

"I get that," Jacob said quietly, almost to himself.

"But what do you mean by that?" Cain asked loudly, drowning Jacob out. "Sorry for interrupting, but I'm always confused by this. People say the same thing but always mean something different."

"I don't follow," Lucy said, clearly irked by the cut in conversation.

"What I mean is, can you explain to me what a soul means to *you*?"

Lucy began forming a word then stopped, the sound strangled in her throat. Vlad thought she did not know what to say but a half-second later, he realised something else altogether different.

There was someone stood directly behind him.

The vampire left his seat and spun in a blur of shadow, survival overtaking his consciousness, darkness powering his muscles. As quickly as the power had risen, however, it was gone again, replaced by a moment of immediate calculation.

Vlad took in the figure's well-cut clothes of dark-blue and their long, elegant limbs. They had an androgynous face, the nose sharp and delicate all at once, black pupils gazing from startlingly

Blood and Biscuits

white-green irises, all framed by cut-glass cheekbones and a slim jawline. Their skin shone gold in the low light. The person standing before Vlad was devastatingly beautiful to him.

The newcomer's body was tense, hands held before them passively, or perhaps defensively. Yet it was the *nature* of their hands that held Vlad's attention the longest. Where their arms glistened, their hands were blackened and crude, flesh pulled tight and shining over the knuckles, fingerprints burnt away, nails long-since melted. Vlad saw a sweet aroma of life and vigour about the person but their hands spoke of old infections and burning.

In that instant, Vlad knew whom he was stood before and a shard of ice ran through his already cold heart.

"I would know your kind anywhere," he said cautiously. He wished to extend a hand, to bridge the gap and erase the tactlessness of his words, but halted the blunder. Those charred hands looked to be extremely painful and they spoke volumes of dangerous magic. Instead, he gave a bow and smiled warmly. "Please, join us and forgive me, you simply caught me by surprise."

The newcomer returned the bow as Jacob spoke.

"I didn't think that was possible," the wraith noted, no hint of amusement in his voice as he stood. "Seriously, I thought you were aware of everything."

"One does not care for boasting but I usually am," Vlad responded, willing serenity into his posture, replacing the huge emotional walls about his escaped control. They had yet to speak though their face held no fret or panic. "However, there is only one being to my knowledge that can circumnavigate the senses of a vampire, especially one as old as I."

"I thought I did pretty well last week," Cain commented and Vlad tilted his head.

"That you did, though it was my *hearing* you overcame, Cain, nothing more. I was distracted by the new group but that will not happen again. I know your scent now, and the beat of your heart. There will be no escaping me on this island."

"Creepy," Cain grunted.

"Wait, what are you saying about senses?" Lucy asked quietly. She was stood behind her chair worriedly. "I don't – who *is* this person?"

The newcomer looked between them all, concern colouring the deeps of their significant gaze, but before Vlad could reassure them Jacob stepped forward and removed his balaclava grandly. The visibly open muscles of his disintegrated face shifted as his yellowed teeth, some clear through a hole in his cheek, parted and he broke into a smile of warm recognition.

"They're a faerie and I invited them here. I hope that's alright."

The newcomer sighed, relieved, and Vlad stepped back to let the two embrace.

"You need not ask permission, Jacob, this is an open group designed for anyone to come and take what they need. I did not realise you knew a member of the fae, that is all. However, the more the merrier."

The wraith and the faerie stepped away, the latter's astonishing face finding the twitch of a watery smile. Their ruined hands shivered and the lightning smell of magic burned a little before fizzling away. From all his experience throughout his years, Vlad knew surprisingly little of faeries, most of his knowledge delivered by those he had met banished from their homelands.

One thing he knew for certain, however, was that faeries were biologically sexless.

Though Vlad had never seen a faerie without clothes, nor had the opportunity to ask, he was sure the fae reproduced via methods outside of the earthen ways. This newcomer's face and body spoke of no specific physicality, only a humanoid of utter grace.

Vlad could not tell but this faerie had either faced exile or had overindulged in their magic, given the burns on their hands.

"A faerie?" Cain asked as the new member moved into the room. "First witches, now faeries – you never mentioned them before."

"Indeed," Vlad responded calmly, eyes flicking between everyone's faces. "There are far too many hidden peoples and creatures to recount. The situation never really called for a bullet-pointed list."

"Sometimes I feel the world's much bigger than I thought."

"Oh, it is a *vast* world out there, my friend, but take heart: you are just as important a piece of it as the rest of us."

"Huh," Cain sniffed, crossing his arms again and eyeing the faerie cautiously.

"My deepest apologies for the quietness of my arrival," the newcomer said, their voice echoing in a manner rather like Sarah's. The sound was a symphony of divinity, sweeping Vlad up in its illustrious beauty. "And for the lateness of the hour; I tried to arrive for seven o'clock but my train was delayed and I became lost finding this church."

"Weren't my instructions good enough?" Jacob asked worriedly.

"They were but I could not see the old ruin lines of houses," the faerie said plainly.

"Ahh, that would be because it has rained quite hard these past few days and the muds have shifted again," Vlad explained. "Sometimes the island masks itself and hides its history."

Vlad mused on the notion of a faerie of the Eight Realms, a member of one of the highest orders of magical creatures, riding a poorly maintained train in northern England. He took great pleasure in fantasising what it would have been like buying a ticket or operating the lock on the toilet door.

"It matters not," Vlad said pleasantly, ignoring his traitorous thoughts, "it is good you arrived. Please, let me get you a chair – I assume you would sit next to Jacob?" The faerie nodded and the vampire returned a moment later with the offered seat. Lucy pulled hers out to accommodate. "We were just discussing how our respective weeks were, anything good or bad to unload, anything new, anything old plaguing the mind."

Vlad's stomach clenched again, striping agony down his nerves. The hunger was worsening. He thought he might stop the session short but he did not wish to disappoint anyone or jeopardise their already stained view of him.

"Hang on," Cain added as the faerie sat. "I asked Lucy a question, and it's gonna' eat me up inside all night if I don't get no answer." Vlad heard a note of urgency. The vampire wondered what drove Cain's need for closure. "No offence, mate," Cain added to the faerie, "I promise this'll be quick."

The newcomer raised their blackened hands again.

"Speak as you will, I am the one who interrupted. Besides, I do not think I am ready to contribute anything of worth."

"Presence alone is worth enough," Vlad uttered as he crossed to the coffee table again. "Can I get you a drink of any kind? Biscuit?"

"No, no animal products, thank you," the faerie said.

Jacob grinned lopsidedly and commented with amusement layering his voice.

"You'd think we'd know each other 'cause of our supernatural tendencies, but it was actually an online vegan forum. Worked out the connections later with some coded language."

"And very informative it has been meeting you, Jacob," the faerie commented. "Humans, it would seem, can have acts of kindness when they so desire, and you are a kind-hearted man. It is good that side has pursued you into your wraith form." The faerie looked to Vlad, who was finishing tamping down the last of his rising urge for blood. "If you must know, my vampire acquaintance, it is a belief of the fae that the consumption of any animal, our equals, in any form is an unclean and deplorable act."

Cain chuckled in bemusement but Lucy looked forlorn.

"Oh, now I feel bad, I just ate a chocolate hobnob."

Cain barked a laugh and Sarah descended an inch or so, Vlad watching her carefully out the corner of his eye. His studious observations allowed him to feel closer to understanding the ghost a little more.

The faerie looked mortified and bowed their head to the banshee.

"My sincerest apologies, madam, I spoke out of turn without acknowledging others' views. They are simply the beliefs I was born into; they are not answers to the wider questions of morality. I would offer you satisfaction in my suffering as recompense?"

"Jesus, no!" Lucy cried, leaning away from the faerie, horror scrawled across her face. "No, it's fine, it's fine. You say whatever you want, whatever your name is..."

"Fable," the faerie said quietly.

"Fable, it's nice to meet you," Lucy said quickly, evidently realising things were off to a bad start. "Avoid me, seems it's best for everyone."

Fable cast their eyes down and let their slender, broken hands tumble miserably.

"I have been here but a moment and have already caused upset. I knew this to be a mistake before I arrived, it would be best if I departed before I dampen the evening."

"No, that'd make me feel terrible!" Lucy said hurriedly. "You haven't caused any upset, you haven't done anything wrong. You just spoke your mind and that's alright. Just...don't tell me to punish you, that's all. No suffering."

Fable nodded as Vlad witnessed it all, silent and watchful. When he spoke, it was from a place of contemplation, a crossroads to direct them away from misery and guilt. Life is but a series of paths, of choices, and to walk one rather than any other would always come with risk. Some paths yielded greater or more permanent consequences.

This was a juncture better served for distraction. Vlad engaged Cain.

"So, you wish to know of the soul, yes?"

The werewolf nodded.

Blood and Biscuits

"Kinda'. Already got my own views, was thinking Lucy could share hers. I'm always interested in history and mythology; how different people think of 'em, and so on."

"You really want to know what *I* believe?" Lucy asked strangely.

"Yeah, why not? Got a pretty good idea on everyone else."

"Have you?" Vlad asked as Fable glanced between them in wonder, a withdrawn look to them. "Would you presume to know Jacob's thoughts on the soul? Or Sarah's? Or my own?"

At the introduction of the vampire, Cain grew guarded and leaned back in his chair, a closed look shuttering his face.

"No, I wouldn't," he finally said. "'Course not."

"Indeed, but that does not stop one from questioning. I would hesitate and suggest Lucy does not wish to offer her sense of what a soul is, correct?" The banshee nodded, the matter of her Irish heritage evidently gratefully dropped. "But if you would like I am more than happy to provide you with my own views. You need only ask."

Cain waited a moment then sighed.

"Vlad?"

"Cain."

"What are your views on the soul?"

"Oh, thank you for asking!" Vlad exclaimed dryly. Despite herself, Lucy sniggered and Jacob snorted. Even Fable cracked a grin as Vlad continued. "Go and grab yourself a coffee, this is a heavy subject."

Sarah ascended a half-inch and Vlad noted it down in his memory, storing the movement away with the other minute things the ghost did when some element of the room or the group changed. She was a creature of purest emotion and Vlad was beginning to see how this guided her visual impression.

"Anyone else want one?" Cain asked as he rose to pour some more coffee. "Not a problem if so."

"You know what, I think I will," Lucy said with a half-smile.

"Not that I've gotten used to the hellish screaming but my throat's not sore from last week. One of the few benefits to being what I am, I suppose."

Vlad nodded thoughtfully, his hand rubbing his chin as he thought through everything he knew of banshees.

"Righto," Cain muttered. "You want milk?"

Lucy glanced at Fable then shook her head, her mirrored hair shining, sending loose strands curling round her face.

"No thanks, black's fine."

As the drinks were made, Vlad leant towards Lucy and spoke quietly.

"On that matter, I was wondering: have you ever considered training yourself to see if you can unleash your scream outside of the predictions of death?"

Lucy looked at him out the corner of her eye.

"No, should I have done?"

"Well, it is our nature as human sub-divisions to be curious, I was only wondering if you had ever seen what you are capable of. Just food for thought, you never know what might happen if you pit yourself against yourself. Look at me and what *I* learned to do."

"I never really thought I was allowed," Lucy muttered back.

Vlad snorted.

"Who the bloody hell is going to stop you?" he countered. "It is not as if there are laws on the matter. Anyway, let me not disturb you, just bear it in mind and give it a think later on this week, maybe."

Lucy nodded silently and sat straight in her chair, though where before she had held herself steady now her eyes flickered, the tendrils of her free-floating hair lying flat upon her shoulders in consideration.

The group settled into a strangely comfortable form, Fable's quiet arrival changing hardly anything of the dynamic as Vlad eased his iron grip on the walls of his control, casting senses further and further out until he was certain the island was deserted. Despite his assurances, Vlad was still vigilant after what happened during last week's session, the secret arrival of the faerie no balm to soothe his worries.

However, all was abandoned save for that basement.

Vlad calmed his nerves and rebuilt the walls of control about his senses, sealing them off tightly and ignoring the pounding, roaring tirade of hunger yawning wide in his stomach. Soon, there would be no stopping the craving, that deepening, ravishing starvation awakening the monster within. The vampire did not dwell on the matter and forced his body's urges under his dominion, ignoring the freezing cords knotting inside his veins.

Those walls of strength would not last forever.

"So, where was I?" Vlad said quietly.

"You were going to tell us about the soul," Fable replied.

"What *is* a soul?" Cain asked exasperatedly. "I've got no idea!"

"What do you *think* it is?" Vlad asked quickly, catching Cain off-guard.

"Oh, I dunno'. Some sorta' internal wibbly thing that flies into space when we die."

"An unbelievably strange answer," Vlad mused.

"Well go on, then, what do you believe it is?" Cain asked irritably.

"I believe in a great many things, far more than you perhaps could imagine," Vlad said, "and therefore I have a way of looking at subjects through the *eyes* of many. These differing perspectives provide a sort of clarity that can only be afforded someone that has travelled much and seen considerably more."

"We've gathered that you're old, Vlad," Cain said sarcastically.

"Not old, *ancient*."

Cain's smile faded and ten thousand memories flashed before Vlad.

"And with this length and breadth of life I have accumulated so many viewpoints it would haunt you to witness what I have gained, and what I have lost. It has not been an existence based on satisfying my urges and gorging on the feasts of humanity, rather a struggle for survival, a constant, unwavering need to remain cloaked from the world whilst somehow keeping one foot in its reality to maintain who I am, who I *was* as a man. Like many of our ilk, if I choose not to feed I will eventually become an animal, a creature of such violent and reckless disregard for the beauty of the mind's sophistications that it would tear apart the hearts of those I love, for they would see a form most revolting. It has happened before and it may very well happen again."

  Vlad twisted the empty coffee cup in his grasp then set it gently upon the floor, the quiet clink of its pottery on the cold, unyielding stone a spindle of focus to pull every string of attention back to him, wrapping them about his words. Vlad needed no mastery to captivate an audience.

  "I tell you this because every time I have succumbed to the evilness of my nature, the vileness of the dark tides, I have unwittingly ripped apart something inside those I care for, the thing that holds their love and admiration. The soul. To use a macabre example, think of the parents of a murderer, how they grieve: ultimately, it is not for the violence their child has shown but for the loss of who they raised, an unexplainable connection broken by an act so despicable it cleaves them asunder. You see a part of those parents die, never to be remade, never to be reborn. They move on, as all things do, but their foundations are shattered, building new people out of fractured hurt."

  Vlad paused briefly, letting his words truly sink in. When he continued, he spoke from a place of more than depth. He spoke from *time*. "Then think on how the eyes of the dead appear: they are empty, beyond simple motionlessness. They contain no sight or feeling anymore, shells that once held perspective and passions. The person behind them is gone, leaving only the matter they inhabited. There is a reason the eyes are considered the *window* to the soul."

Blood and Biscuits

Vlad stood and began circling the group, explaining as he journeyed, hands clasped firmly behind his back. He hoped the act would mask the slowly weakening grip he had on the hunger clenching his stomach.

"These are but two foundations upon which I view the soul."

"And in parents that watch their child slip away," Lucy muttered, perhaps quiet enough that none but Vlad heard. The smallest sliver chipped from the vampire's iron walls of control and the low electric light of the church basement flickered. "Was that – was that you?" Lucy asked. Vlad nodded.

"Apologies, let it not distract you."

Vlad regained his self, committing his energies into conveying everything he felt.

"Through all I have learned, if the soul *does* exist, and I highly believe it does, it is no *physical* manifestation residing within us, waiting like a spring to uncoil upon our deaths. It is a reservoir of memory, a gathering of who we are and what we choose to be as we live. Every emotion we have ever felt, every pleasure, every pain, everything that helps us grow, *defines* us, collated together in a force guiding our every movement and action. When we die our souls do not depart lightly, they wish to stay, to continue learning. The gravity of emotion."

As Vlad circled, his feet hardly struck the ground, darkness leaking through cracks forming in the walls of his control.

"If you need further examples, what happens when you sense fear? As an inexperienced child you might simply run and hide or cling to a guardian, but as you grow you learn to deal with such feelings, to compartmentalise and rationalise, to replace terror with knowledge and understanding or to avoid the situation entirely so you never encounter what you know might harm you."

"But that's just education," Cain said. "Your brain adaptin' to pressures and learnin' to cope with negative situations better."

"Indeed, it is, but the thing that drives that education is a *want* to learn, a *need* to learn. You can feel it inside you right now, hence why you asked this question to begin with. This thirst of curiosity is not a quest for knowledge, rather an urge to satisfy a craving, a desire to fill a void you cannot perceive nor explain in any way. Yet that void exists. The vacuum of space is nothingness yet it exists. Anger and hunger are but electrical and chemical impulses processed by the brain, *yet they exist*. Matters of perception, yes, but born from this very force that guides us, driving us to fill it with the knowledge of life, information based on our responses to internal and external stimuli. The soul is the culmination of our emotional intelligence, the result of our choices, the mind behind the mind. Our identity absolute."

Vlad found himself looking at the faerie. Arms loosely folded, Fable sat with deep interest written upon their features. Vlad longed to know what Fable's thoughts on the matter were yet he could not stop, not on as dour a pair of subjects as death and education. Nobody likes to end a conversation on the topic of schooling.

Vlad altered his pace to match his steps with the rhythm of his words.

"Through the countless countries and cultures I have been amongst, I can honestly say the single thing connecting them all is the trust and faith in an afterlife, god or no. There must be some reason to this – you might think *hope* but I think different. Since the dawn of human evolution, and we as sub-divisions accordingly, people have come to realise they are more than walking sacks of blood and memories hurtling through randomness, more than just anger or hunger: they are thought, love, rage, joy, sorrow, trust, care – stories of true and powerful feeling, conduits of choice. All that raw energy must be housed somewhere, a store of emotional memories so powerful it can form an imprint of themselves on the world once they are gone. For sometimes, the soul remains when the body has gone, the matter it inhabited returned to the dusts of the world."

At last, Vlad came to the place he had always intended to be, standing behind the person he had driven the conversation towards.

Floating peacefully seven inches above her seat was Sarah, humming a tune so old it perhaps predated the church she called home.

"Your proof, my friends."

"Wait, Sarah's evidence of a soul?" Cain blurted haphazardly.

"It's that easy?" Jacob echoed disbelievingly. "To speak such powerful words then have the answer floating right here. Faith teaches us more than that."

Vlad smiled and glanced at Fable again.

"Your friend here will confirm for me. I see it in their eyes even if I cannot sense it in the golden beat of their heart. If you would, Fable."

The faerie sat forward and spread the charred remains of their hands, the very act visibly sending stress up their shivering arms. Then Fable's stunning countenance became set in stone as they shook off their pain.

"It is not becoming of me to speak on behalf of one I have just met," they began, "yet the vampire is right. A ghost is the purest form, the remains of our emotional selves when not all of us has moved on, a select group of memories tied to a hugely potent sensation; they are the entire soul but have access to only a little of their memories. That is why spirits find it difficult to recall anything, for there are vast gaps in what they are granted once the body is gone. Imagine trying to remember something from decades before whilst enraged or perform complicated mathematics while upset: near-impossible tasks."

Fable hesitated a second as Sarah began lowering back toward her seat, the volume of her humming rising, her transparency increasing. When the faerie spoke again, they were soft, cautious.

"Your Sarah here *is* a soul. Materially, that is all she is. No body, no mind, purely the collection of who she was. Ghosts can still learn, like you or I, but where we gain experience and knowledge through hundreds of means, spirits can only learn through emotions closest to their own, rather like the development of fondness or hatred for another. If you learn anything about somebody you feel strongly about it is always through a visor of that powerful feeling, colouring your knowledge. When a soul is so torn by a single emotion, so filled by one above all else, then it becomes unbalanced and remains behind in the world, unable to move on, a spirit form to walk the earth until it finds stability once more."

"So ghosts are *souls*," Jacob repeated slowly. All cynicism was evaporated from his tone, Vlad noticed. "That means we all have ghosts inside us, right?"

"Well…" and here Fable hesitated again, returning the conversational baton to Vlad.

"Why stall?" Lucy queried hastily. "That's what you meant."

"The answer, generally, is yes, though what Fable *meant* is some who live in the guise of death no longer possess a soul."

All heads turned back to Vlad as he opened his arms and welcomed them to the realisation of what he truly was: a vacuum, just like space.

"So you're saying…"

"I am the same as any other vampire: I exist without a soul."

Jacob shook his head and Lucy cast her eyes away, but Cain surprised Vlad by nodding. Sarah was now motionless in her seat, sat touching the plastic covering completely, her form heavily transparent. Vlad had not wanted this subject to get out of hand; he could see Sarah was suffering because of it.

"But if that's true," Jacob said with an unsure smile, "Vlad wouldn't learn anything emotionally based. That's what you said, *souls are the emotions gathering within us*. If that's true then how does Vlad empathise with us? Why does he laugh or get angry? He can't have started this group without emotions, that's impossible."

"It is because I am vastly old, Jacob," the vampire stated coldly. "Ancient, I said. And over the first few centuries of my recreation, I discovered some vestige of soul retention inside me, like an ember hungering for more, to burn brighter. A memory of a memory. It is the same force that craves blood, for it is never sated. I helped other vampires understand this inside them, too, and we have since come to train ourselves to re-learn our emotional sides, on some level. We do not build a soul with it but we become emotionally intelligent once more.

"I am a being of cold logic and often singular drives but I have lived for so long I have regained much of my human reasoning and emotions simply by relearning, re-patterning, and reinforcing my behaviour. Young vampires cannot think or act on any sensations other than hunger or pleasure; they lack the subtle nuances of their former selves. It is considered about fifty years, as a rule of thumb, before a vampire can even *hope* to begin regaining their emotional core with sufficient guidance. And as I have gathered up the connections I had lost for so long, so too have I gathered the strength of the vampire, as if the fragments that make up the light of the soul can be reconfigured into the darkness of the twilight beast. The duality of good and evil."

"Therefore, young vampires without emotional cores are evil," Jacob muttered, shrinking into his chair a little.

Vlad shook his head a fraction.

"Not quite, not unless they succumb to their drives and kill relentlessly by choice. They are unbalanced. It is a very difficult road to walk, as with all supernatural beings, but that is the harmony of the soul and its counterpart. Evil is a choice and a very difficult thing to define."

"But there *is* no soul in you," Lucy said, almost frustratedly. "That's what you just told us! So what's there instead? What's this counterpart inside you?"

"Power."

Vlad uttered the word as a whisper yet it blew through the room with the force of a gathering storm. The basement light flickered and creaked in its bracket, sending shadows dancing and skittering from the places they lurked. The breaths of the warm-bodied condensed and froze before them in silver-hung clouds, the smallest amount of Vlad's devilry creeping out into the world, the walls of his control falling mercilessly to his hunger's rising strength.

When he spoke, his voice was infused with darkness. His words did not travel on the air, instead they whirled along the twisting shadows.

"You cannot truly find the soul until you fall into the absence of it. You cannot truly understand the soul until you know the breaking of it."

As quickly as the coldness and the disturbance of the air had come, it was gone again but this time, when Vlad released his power and replaced his control, he found he was weak. He suddenly fell to his knees, heavier than he had felt in a long time, his stomach a pit of screaming nails and broken glass. Immediately, Lucy and Cain were at his sides. Cain lifted him to his feet easily, the wolf strong beneath the skin.

"Thank you, both of you…" Vlad muttered, unable to look at either of them, mind recoiling and shrinking as his mood darkened and sank. It was coming again, the desolation that fuelled his nature. He did not have much time. "I – cannot stay."

"God, don't let a moment like that get to you," Cain said gruffly as he helped Vlad back into his seat. "We certainly don't think any less of you."

"That was not my meaning," the vampire responded. When he looked up, he realised that Sarah had vanished. Vlad was not surprised, not after what was discussed so openly in front of her. "I must go. I cannot be around you all. I swear this will not affect next week's session, as long as I can find blood soon."

"Wait!" Lucy cried, her voice reaching a crescendo of heat, but Vlad had already been enveloped by darkness and was gone.

The creaking light of the basement flickered once more and then its bulb burst, showering the room with the last of its light before it, too, disappeared entirely.

Blood and Biscuits

THE SKIES OF NORTHERN ENGLAND.

'I must find sustenance. Blood. Fight it, do not become the monster. You are a vampire, not a slave. Blood. Make contact with them, they will help. They always help. Blood. She will smile, he will despair, but I am too far gone. Blood. If they cannot help I must risk another raid. But I don't know if there's enough time. I can feel it rising in me again!'

'Blood...'

Fig. 3. The Eye Spiral.

It is not my finest work - I am in a rush for an evening's flight and I shall not apologise - but the meaning is clear. The everlasting soul is created by eye and mind and the Eye Spiral, a classic image in vampiric iconography for reasons of emptiness and immortal longing, displays its creation with beautiful simplicity. I am forever drawn to its notion, as if such ease of art mocks what I am forever denied.

The lashes denote life's experiences coming from all directions; the gaze to the left signifies far sight.

A Crisis of Faith

At the rear of the hall, hands placed upon the font, eyes cast into the motionless holy waters, Jacob stood with his head bowed and back arched. Unbeknown to him, high up on the balcony rails crouched a hooded man, face pale in the darkness, eyes gleaming. He balanced with such precision on the thin stone that he seemed a statue save for the gentle flap of his cloak. The pristine church interior shone with recent refurbishments.

The man eyed Jacob's back then knocked politely on a pillar beside him.

Jacob gasped and looked up, face covered by his balaclava, his shaded, sunken eyes finding the crouched man immediately.

"Who are you? What do you want?"

"Two very classic questions when posed with an unknown intruder," came the curt reply. Effortlessly, the figure dropped thirty feet smoothly, as if gliding on an invisible cushion of silk.

Jacob breathed a deep, ragged sigh of relief.

"Oh Vlad, thank God it's you. You scared the crap - sorry, Hell - no, *life* - out of me."

"It is unlike you to fret over blasphemous language within sacred walls," Vlad noted with amusement. "You have uttered several such occurrences at St Ellin's over the past two weeks."

Jacob shrugged.

"That ain't a church anymore, it's just a broken place."

Vlad made a noise in his throat and clasped his hands behind his back.

"You know, Sarah described St Ellin's that very same way, but her meaning was so different from yours as to nearly change the very words themselves. No church is broken, Jacob, not really. Certain places remember specific things, it is what elevates them beyond mere *buildings*. You might be able to recognise the history and faith embedded in the stone, into the ground itself, the memories of footsteps and song, of people, even after time has left it and ghosts and bats have moved in."

"Is that a reference to yourself?" Jacob asked shallowly as he turned back to the moonlit font. The huge stained-glass window high above the altar sent shafts of coloured silver down to the floor and Vlad stepped into its light, tipping back his hood and folding his arms stoically. Jacob lifted his balaclava in imitation.

"No, it was not. I honestly have not the slightest idea where that belief came from, the association of vampires with bats."

"I'd imagine it's the fangs, the black wings, the nocturnal stuff, the term *vampire bat*, to point out the obvious, and the fact you're both kind of mammals but not really."

"Alright, fair point and well made. So why are you here, Jacob? What has brought you to this church at two in the morning on a Wednesday?"

Jacob did not look up but his shoulders hunched a little more, as if Vlad's question had loosened the rope of a large weight above him. Though he did not know him particularly well, Vlad sensed Jacob was a man of principles, and of considerable emotional burden.

"Huh, the other day when you were talking about the soul, it got me thinking. Thinking about eternal life and all that, you know. This might come as a shock to you, Vlad, but I'm actually a Christian."

"Oh. Actually, that was a surprise."

"Does it bother you?"

"Why on earth would that bother me? We all have our own faiths, Jacob, and I am glad I got you doubting yours. It is important to continuously question ourselves but it is not for anyone else to tell us who to worship or what to practice, just as it is not for anyone to tell us how to live our lives or who to love so long as nobody is hurt."

"That's good to hear, that's something full of hope. Couple generations ago, my family was protestant, being from Ghana, but after one set of grandparents passed away mum and dad moved from

Blood and Biscuits

London to Edinburgh and found more community with the Church of Scotland. Had my brother and me born right in the city. But then when we were teenagers, Mum passed, too, and my brother and I moved down to Newcastle with Dad, and we found solace in Church of England."

Vlad leant against the font beside Jacob.

"I am sorry, I did not know your mother died. To lose a parent is heart breaking but it is especially so when it is too early. Though most believe we only need our parents for our formative years, truly we need them throughout adulthood, too. They shape us as children and then guide us through the infinitely harder later years. I am sorry you lost one half of that influence."

"It's alright, that's at least fifteen years ago now," Jacob sniffed but he could not hide the still-raw hurt in his voice. Then he smiled lopsidedly, his dilapidated face stretching in an almost handsome manner, revealing the man desperate to break free beneath. "You know, she was a really funny woman, that one, had a great sense of humour. We had this old seven-seater, really ancient thing, the rear seats facing out the back. Used to wave at people behind us at traffic lights, make them go all awkward – loved doing that as a kid. Dad used to keep all these supermarket carrier bags in the boot, stuffed down the sides of the seats, in case we needed a sudden mad dash to the shops; he hated waste, he was strange like that."

"Most could stand to be more like your father," Vlad commented and Jacob nodded.

"Aye, he's happy now. An odd one but happy all the same. My nephew keeps him busy, keeps his mind off bad thoughts of Mum."

"You were saying about your car," Vlad prompted, also wanting to keep Jacob's mind off bad thoughts of his mum.

"Oh yeah. Well, this one time, when my brother had a couple friends and we were coming back from the cinema or the park or something, Mum asked how we were going to sit in the car. My brother gets car sick so he has to sit in the front. So I suggested Mum sit in the boot with all the other old bags and she clipped me round the ear."

Without meaning to, Vlad suddenly burst out laughing, his hands on his thighs and gripping the cold flesh, voice booming round the dark church. He laughed for a long while as Jacob chuckled to himself until, at last, Vlad straightened and regained his composure.

"You know, that caught me completely off-guard," he said, wiping his eyes then realising there were no tears of joy there. There had not been for a very long time. "You have a mind for a turn of phrase, you should show it more, it would help you communicate at the group."

"I'm glad you think so, she'd have said something similar. I miss her, I really do. I miss evenings with friends round eating fish and chips, and then Dad'd say he'd want us to eat something from Ghana, get my brother and me thinking about our ancestry. He'd try and make a Kontomire stew or Red Red and bugger them up completely, leaving Mum to show us how to do them properly. She'd do Kelewele fries and Bofrot as a treat – Christ, I eat brains now but thinking about it still makes me hungry. Been vegan the past ten years, too, and still it makes me hungry. I miss the way the kitchen smelled, all those spices and that family connection."

"Did you ever go to Ghana?" Vlad asked.

"Once. Just once. Our living Gran paid, took us to Accra, where she was from. She came to England through the whole colony thing, the uh…"

"The British Gold Coast," Vlad filled in.

"Ahh that's the one, I knew it was something like that. Anyway, we went to Accra. Had a nice time."

"How did you feel when you went there?"

Jacob leant back and stared up at the ceiling, breathing deep into his ragged lungs.

"Like I was back in that kitchen," he finally said. "Home's where the heart is and I missed Scotland, in a weird way. I got to

Blood and Biscuits

Africa and I couldn't stop thinking about my mates back up north, in that stupidly cold, rainy place. Football in the streets, climbing trees on weekends, school and arcades, my first kiss. Strange."

"In the end, home is where you take root, where you draw sustenance from. It is important to know one's ancestry but it does not mean we must stay in one place. Scotland became your home, for better or for worse."

"Aye, ain't that the silly truth of it."

"Ghana, how fascinating. I admit most of my African knowledge lies in Egypt. I take it you have found kinship within *these* walls, correct?"

"At the end of the day, Jesus is the same for all sects: the stuff he stood for, the stuff he died for, the people he loves...took me long enough to come to terms with who I was as a man - as a human - and try to rectify and align that with my faith that I struggled with the days. It's why I ended up getting anxieties, from all the social pressures and judgements I felt I was under, which manifested as...other things."

"You know you will have none of that with the Support Group, right?"

"No, I know, it's going to take some time with Cain and Lucy, I think, but at least Fable's shown me kindness these past few weeks."

"Ahh yes, the faerie I could not sense. However did you isolate your unique sensibilities online, of all places?"

"We sort of got speaking about our lives on a public forum for fantasy tabletop games and vegan forums and then took it private when they saw I was struggling."

Jacob sighed and turned round, leaning back against the font and folding his hands on his lap. "Point is, out of all of this over the years, the one constant I've had is my faith. Sometimes it wasn't enough," he added quietly, rubbing absently at his wrists, "but it's let me know whatever happens I'll always have somebody, somewhere above, watching over me, caring for me when others and myself can't, taking care of me when I'm unable. It's really helped me through a lot."

"That is beautiful, Jacob, I wish I felt the same as you, I really do."

"Well, there must be a reason you're here, you can't have sensed me across town."

"That I did not. To tell you the truth, I was not feeling particularly great after what happened with Sarah on Monday."

Jacob cocked his head a fraction of an inch.

"Why, what happened? You guys argue?"

"No, nothing like that. I am certain she took our discussion of the soul as a direct insult. She left the session before I did, I had no chance to explain myself. I was flying overhead ten minutes ago, trying to clear the guilt, when I detected your presence. I felt it only proper to see if you were alright."

"Ahh, understood. Well, I'm fine but I appreciate the concern, and if it helps, I think Sarah'll be alright, too. She doesn't strike me as someone that holds a grudge."

"She is a ghost. All ghosts hold grudges. It is pretty much the one thing they all have in common, aside from death."

"Oh dear. Good luck, is all I can say. Do something nice for her, something that means a lot, I think she'd love a gesture like that. Incidentally, did you find blood after you left the session?"

"Yes, I did," Vlad said, thinking on the man he had drunk from, the one that had willingly given him a survivable amount. "More than enough for now."

There was an oddly pleasant silence between them, two men standing across a chasm of faith, discussions of the supernatural setting stones to their emotional bridge. Finally, Jacob twitched and looked round the church with a small smile on his rotten face.

"You know, my brother had a baby not too long back. Kid was christened right here, at this font. 'Course, the place was a bit more rundown then, it's had a nice renovation."

Blood and Biscuits

"I do appreciate care and attention put into places of worship," Vlad said, gazing at the church in fascination.

"Your turn to surprise me, science man," Jacob prodded.

"Please, I can appreciate churches even if I do not believe in their divinity. They are monuments to the human condition, waypoints for life's milestones, expressions of artistic merit, fulcrums for conversation, and so much more. Churches, Mosques, Vihāras, Temples, Synagogues, Mandirs…all are of such value to billions, they deserve to be treated with respect, to reflect the care and attention put into them."

Jacob eyed Vlad curiously.

"But you're not the religious type."

"I am not. Though I describe myself as a man of science, it irks me that many believe the two matters cannot be shared equally by one mind. I simply put my faith in things other than gods above. As my confidence in myself and the world has grown my belief in higher orders has diminished, that is all. I am a man of science and a believer in the faiths others have. Whatever sees you happy on your deathbed."

"You're a mystery to me, Vlad. You know one day, I hope we can hang out together, get to know one another outside of churches and support groups. For one thing, you can tell me what it's like living as a vampire in deeply religious societies in the old times."

"Alternatively, you could tell me how you feel being a wraith, a member of the undead, whilst still trying to live as a son of God," Vlad countered. "I made my peace with science and the supernatural hundreds of years ago but you, my friend, are still standing in a church at two in the morning, staring into a font."

Jacob tried to answer but the words strangled in his throat, his normally hissing voice screeching quietly to a halt. When he finally spoke, he did not sound happy about it.

"I'm still struggling with squaring those two together. Curses aren't natural, they're forces against God; I cannot be both, not like

Blood and Biscuits

people of science and faith. I'm an unnatural man trying to live in the eyes of the creator of all nature. Honest, it keeps me from happiness."

Vlad placed his hand on Jacob's arm firmly. He looked deep into the wraith's sunken eyes, pushing everything he had into giving him strength.

"You are not unnatural," he told him but when the man did not look convinced Vlad tried harder. "Curses are natural phenomena, Jacob. Most originate as mind-made constructs, true, but if we denied everything fabricated by intelligent thought and accepted only natural-formed creations then none of what we eat or use or entertain ourselves with is acceptable by God. Do you understand me?"

"Vlad...how can I rectify this? Can you tell me? Please. Please tell me."

"I am truly sorry, Jacob, but I cannot. However, I did not come here to solve riddles of faith, I came here to make sure you were alright. But if it helps, you should know that you are as natural and important to this world as I, or humans, or trees, or flowers, or Fable, or Sarah, or any of the others of the group."

"I guess that helps a little. Can you not mention this particular bit to the group, though? I kinda' want it to myself for a bit more, don't want them judging me."

"Say no more, it is done."

Jacob sniffed and wiped something from his cheek. Then he peered at Vlad oddly.

"Out of interest, how *did* you get in here? I snuck in through a window but I shut it behind me..."

"Oh, I have this," Vlad said brightly, holding up a thin length of leather with a shining brass key on the end of it.

"Just how in the hell do you have a key to a random church in the middle of Ellinsgate?" Jacob demanded.

Vlad grinned.

Blood and Biscuits

"Who do you think paid for the recent renovations? I do hope you like the stained-glass window."

Week Three
Death Finds its Rhythm

**ARCHWAYS AND PRAYER HALL,
RUINS OF ST ELLIN'S CHURCH.
TWO DAYS BEFORE THE WEEKLY SUPPORT GROUP.**

The waning crescent in the sky was nearly spent, payment for the emergence of the new moon. In the grounds of an abandoned church, a figure of sorrow was poised in solitude.

Vlad balanced unswaying with utmost dignity and grace upon the bare, broken arches as if they were a simple floor, arms folded lightly across his chest. He stared through the shade of the lost church, the last of the moon's light shining eerily through the hanging vines and flowers that had long-since reclaimed the stone, casting strange forms swaying across the floor.

In the deeps of the ruins, all was still.

Vlad leapt to the next arch easily and came to the edge of the part-collapsed roof, some tiles still attached - more out of stubbornness than construction – and his senses reached out for anything disturbing the ice-cold threads of the air. Nothing. Vlad mocked himself for the attempt; that which he pursued would leave no lasting trace upon this world.

He sighed and turned away but something caught his eye. A glint of silver, a flash of white light. It darted, back amongst the crooked walls, but Vlad was already moving, gliding and leaping across the arches, his motion effortless, delicate as black smoke.

The vampire stopped and hung upside-down, considering every angle. He wished only to speak with her, not agitate.

Blood and Biscuits

'Where are you?' Vlad thought calmly. *'I know you want to see me or you would not have shown yourself.'*

Silver flashed again and Vlad pursued immediately, shadow chasing light from arch to arch, through vines and stone. In the flurry of flight, Vlad saw her veiled face. They rose and twirled in a dance of the macabre, two affections of death swirling through frigid night air, spiralling the crooked spire until, at last, circling the pinnacle, pitch-black and silver facing one another beneath the gaze of that gaunt, lonely moon.

The ghost's veil remained impassive, yet her demeanour was strangely absorbing. Vlad wished he could have known what she thought.

"Why are you here?"

The ghost's voice came thin and strong, her spirit utterly transparent. Vlad considered a smile but the meeting was perhaps too sombre to deem it appropriate. Instead, as they glided upon vapours of darkness and light, he bared his heart to her.

"Sarah, though I know you care not for what and how I might feel, I am deeply affected by your perception of me after the way I spoke about you days ago." The apparition of Sarah's veil rose and fell upon a non-existent wind, her form ever more apathetic. "I meant no offence by it, nor did I intend for such discussions to grow too far. It was wrong of me to treat you as if you were not in the room, and for that I am sorry."

Still, Sarah said and did nothing, her spirit gleaming in the moon's gaze as Vlad spoke.

"I have spent days in the outright misery of my own emotional reflection. Though it is no excuse, I was starving when last we met. My mind was nearly gone by the time I found blood. However, my actions haunt me still and thinking on how I upset you only drove my sadness deeper. Know that where you have suffered I, too, have suffered."

Slowly, Sarah's opacity began to return. Though the transition was slight, Vlad knew it was of the utmost importance for what he was trying to achieve. They hung in their own mysterious translations of death, balanced like clouds beside the ancient steeple slanted in time.

"You were never a subject of mockery, I would not have you believe that for one moment. Come back to us and let me set our paths anew."

"You think me no part of your collective," Sarah whispered, her words riding streams of the air, filling every corner of the broken church beneath them. *"I wasn't invited, I only arrived. I listened to the tortures of your friends but I never felt a part of you, none of you."*

"That does not matter!" Vlad boomed, his own power-infused tone shaking the church; six tiles dislodged and slipped to the ground, puncturing the moment with their cold snaps. Sarah gasped and clutched her chest as Vlad said: "You are one of us, an important member of our dysfunctional group, and I would see you stay for however long you wish, in whatever manner you choose, heeded by nothing but your own choice. You need not attend if you so desire, but know there will always be a chair for you to hover above."

Sarah's veil ceased its fluttering and she ungripped her chest. Vlad thought for one wild moment he had further upset her. Then, through some miracle, there escaped from her the smallest of laughs, a strange and uncanny noise sounding as if muffled by water, and Vlad knew he had amused her. He believed then it was safe to make his true offering.

"I have for you a gift, Sarah, if you would allow me?"

"A gift?" the ghost replied. A hint of innocent curiosity. *"I've not received a gift for many years."*

"I had imagined so, but this is no material offering, rather something to bring some levity into your home, this beautiful church you have welcomed us all into the heart of. There still resides some electricity in the protected basement so I have procured something that will utilise this. Come, follow me to the ground."

Blood and Biscuits

Tentatively, Sarah lowered as she grew opaquer still, becoming deceptively real, and Vlad gently led the way, allowing the smoke of his darkness to absorb back into his body as he glided down towards the smashed and rotten pews of the church's prayer hall. Something glinted through the twilight, a small box resting upon the font at the rear of the old hall. Vlad led Sarah to it.

The box was black, shining handsomely in the night, its power supply feeding into a back room.

"What is it? I've never before seen its like," Sarah said wondrously, flying around the box, examining from every angle. Vlad noticed her voice had reverted to an almost human quality, her spirit almost solid in appearance, legs visible rather than drifts of mist.

"It is a type of music box," Vlad explained. "You simply activate it and it will play whatever song you wish. I took the liberty of obtaining a storm-proof one and fixing it to the font, so you shall never lose it, nor break it."

Sarah remarked with a sound of joy and astonishment then suddenly grew solemn and gazed down at her hands.

"But I cannot touch it. How might I bring about this fascinating miracle without my hands?"

Vlad smiled deeply.

"It is voice activated."

"Astonishing," Sarah whispered. She leant forward, veil passing through the box harmlessly as it fluttered once more. Then she hesitated. "What would I tell an object like this?"

"Tell it to turn on and then instruct it to play whatever song you want. It has something called 'internet', which means it is connected to, um, something else called '4G'. That is a sort of voice that talks to a big dish in the sky that gives it all songs ever made. You understand what this means, correct?"

Sarah did not respond verbally. Instead, she laughed aloud, this time the noise coming clear and beautiful. Then she spoke a command of reverence, surprise, and anticipation, complex feelings Vlad never thought possible from a ghost.

"Box? Turn on." The little black box *dinged* softly and a blue ring of light emanated from the front. Sarah giggled delightedly. "Box? Play *Quasi una fantasia* by Ludwig van Beethoven."

"The Moonlight Sonata, a fine choice, if a little on the nose," Vlad commented and Sarah laughed again. It was good to hear her joy; Vlad thought it was the first time he had experienced it since knowing her as a ghost.

The music box whirred into life and found a good copy of the old song, and soon the soft, melodic tones of those famous piano notes resonated throughout the abandoned arches. Vlad closed his eyes and listened, letting the tones take him up. He felt for once as if his burdens were lifting from his heavy, heavy shoulders, the despair of his mind retreating for a moment.

The air before his face grew as icy as his own blood and he opened his eyes. Sarah's face was a hand's span from his own, her veil stiller than the night.

"Come. Dance with me."

The vampire gazed at the phantom, a deep thrum rising within, warm and inviting. He gave a tight nod.

"It would be my honour," he whispered.

Delicately, he raised his arms into position, one about Sarah's waist, the other held out for her to lay her hand above. Her touch was hollow but that did not mean it was not real, and Vlad looked at the silver whiteness of her fingers and could have sworn he nearly felt something there, as if their two forms of death could connect. Sarah held herself with such dignity, such composure, that she took Vlad's breath away, so to speak.

Then they danced.

Vampire and ghost swayed and moved beneath the shattered structures of the church to the Moonlight Sonata. Despite their only theoretical contact, Sarah kept perfect time with Vlad's highly trained and experienced steps, the memories of countless lavish festivities and social occasions amongst royalty coming back to him easily in that frozen moment in time. Before he could think, Sarah laid her head upon his shoulder and sighed quietly; reactively, a single breath caught in Vlad's throat and he perceived his very heart trying to beat alive.

Sorrow, joy, longing, guilt, and relief all flooded him in one almighty storm of sensation and shining tears of fresh blood fell from his eyes. He felt as if he held the form of his daughter once more, a hand reaching through centuries to lift from him the sadness bearing him down. This was his purpose, the reason he remained a part of this world.

Yet as soon as the moment began it ended again, and the ghost fell away from Vlad's grasp, her body gliding backwards to float beside the quietening music box. The long song had reached its conclusion, the dance had been danced, and the vampire stood alone once more, cheeks stained with the blood of his ancient memories.

Sarah did not recognise the tears. She simply leaned towards the music player again.

"Magic box? It's me, Sarah. Please play *Let's Dance* by David Bowie."

"Goodness!" Vlad exclaimed as he stood away. "I would not think you to know that one, Sarah."

"It was the final song ever played here," she said happily. "The couple ended their wedding on it, decades ago. It means many things to me, haunting me like I haunt this place."

Vlad nodded acceptingly and moved away as the music player whirred into life again, the first beats of the next song bringing new life and vigour to the church. Sarah whooped and spun off across the floor, and Vlad watched from the entrance for a time, cold fingers upon the doorframe. He mused on the many people that had crossed that threshold to be married, christened, and moved on from life, and he asked himself what it was all worth as he gazed upon the ghost of Sarah dancing amongst the broken beams and vines.

Then the vampire was gone, the last shadow of the night, his purpose quickly rediscovering the threads of her old life.

RUINS OF ST ELLIN'S CHURCH.
THE NIGHT OF THE SUPPORT GROUP.

Vlad sat before the gathering and smiled broadly at them all. Everyone had returned, including Sarah, and there was a different feeling to the air, a sense of understanding. Candles lit the basement in a low fluttering light, the electric bulb above still blown from the previous week. Vlad eyed it with a sigh, a flush of shame filling his veins. He glanced over at a small package on the coffee table he had brought alongside a new wave of biscuits.

Lucy seemed more relaxed. Jacob no longer wore his balaclava. Cain had shaved and cut his ragged hair, and he wore well-fitted clothes clearly bought recently. Fable rubbed their blackened hands together, the same look of unease still written across their face from last week.

'Try and involve Fable more,' Vlad noted internally. *'They probably feel rather awkward.'*

"Thank you all for coming back this week. After last week's…session…I did not think you would return."

"That's what you said at the *beginning* of last week," Lucy mentioned with a slight smile. "And you couldn't stop us then. What's so different this time?"

"I do not know, truth be told. I am just overwhelmed to see you all again. It has been a difficult few weeks for us all; I have done my bit for trying to keep the, um, scarier side of myself under control and you should hopefully see it no more."

"Think nothing of it," Fable said easily, waving the matter aside with a ruined hand. "These things happen quite often and we should not be blamed when there requires no blame."

"Aye, but you did go a bit freaky again," Cain remarked slyly, a toothy grin flashing from behind his steepled fingers. "But since you did such a good job of going full vampire once more – yeah, I said full vampire again – and breaking the light in here we thought we'd see what else you'd break."

"Tell me you are joking," Vlad said crestfallen.

"Of course he's joking," Lucy hissed. "Silly sod's always being sarcastic. Stop it, Cain, you're being a pain."

The werewolf threw his hands up and smiled wider.

"You're right, I'm an arse. Still, I've gotta' say, Vlad, that was quite an exit you made. Care to share? How's your week been, mate?"

Despite himself, Vlad chuckled, the lunacy of the moment and everything that had happened colliding with his own question aimed back at him.

"Yes…yes, it has been quite the week. I am unsure where to start."

"Why not give us a quick rundown after you swept outta' here like some bat out of hell?"

"Nice reference," Jacob cut in.

"Been sittin' on that for days," Cain nodded.

"I can tell. You look all constipated and everything."

Cain barked a laugh and Lucy grinned wide. Sarah rose several inches from her chair and Vlad looked between them all. Then he sighed.

"Last week, I was far hungrier than I gave my body credit for. I have an astonishing grip upon my vampiric side – I call it my 'control', the walls I built around my power long ago through years of practice so I do not unwittingly unleash that which might destroy. You could think of it like a human's inhibitions, only far more frightening and with bigger teeth."

"How often do you have to feed?" Lucy asked lightly, delicacy ruling her words.

"Every month or so," Vlad explained easily. "The less I have to lower my control and release my power the less frequently I must feed, which in many ways makes sense. The older a vampire gets the more they learn to withhold their power, and the less blood they need to fuel their strength, so I need only the smallest amount. However, I think those humans during our first session drew on my reserves a great deal more than I thought they would. Last week just about tipped the balance and I had to leave. I flew through the skies until I decided on how best to feed without hurting anyone."

"I don't really understand how you get…sustenance…without causin' harm," Cain hesitated over the word, avoiding the real term. "You use animals instead?"

"Do wolves eat tofu if they feel sympathy for sheep?" Vlad retorted and Cain pulled a face. "No, vampires cannot replace human blood with that of another animal; I have tried, despite being warned many times, and in each instance, I regurgitated in the most spectacular fashion. Coffee? Oh, that is fine! And the odd bit of whisky? Not a problem, and I can still achieve drunkenness if I set my mind to it. But a bit of deer blood or rabbit gore and I am redecorating Swedish fields with a devastating liberalness to make Jackson Pollock jealous. I had to move away from Scandinavia in the end, you know, it was quite embarrassing. Lovely log cabin, that was."

"Not a pleasant image," Jacob said. He glanced between his legs at the dark bag under his chair. "Then again, we've all got our vices and I can hardly talk: I've still got some of Mrs. Hinchley's left hemisphere and parietal lobe blended in a box. Died of natural causes, bless her."

"Indeed," Vlad said quietly. "My point is, only human blood will do. However, options are limited when it comes to someone like me, who does not ever wish to commit torture on another. Blood banks are one way, though this country's donations seem to be dwindling further every year. The other option, and the one I use most frequently, is having ten rather understanding friends I can trust without end."

"Hang on, you have human friends that know about you? *And* they let you feed from them?" Lucy asked incredulously. "How does that even work?"

"I compensate them for every instance, and I only drink a pint, the same one would donate to the NHS in one of those mobile clinics. I do not *need* any more than that to survive. The problem, however, is the inherent greed of the vampire: once that first fresh taste passes the lips it becomes almost impossible to stop drinking, hence why humans tend to die once caught. I mentioned my control, and that certainly helps withhold the urges, though I arm every one of my friends with an amulet of silver to place upon my brow if I start drawing too much. I have ten donators so I can rotate, as it takes about sixteen weeks for a human to recover the lost red blood cells. I like to account for their holidays and sickness, too."

"That is both genius and disturbing," Lucy said.

Vlad inclined his head.

"Many thanks, my sickened friend. It has taken me a long time to cultivate so many donors that are not only trustworthy with my information – without the use of mastery, I might add – but are also willing to be fed upon. It shames me but I cannot live without it."

Vlad sat back, keen to move on from his self-revulsion. There were a few exchanged looks and Vlad half expected the basement air to grow thinner, but instead it grew warmer, thicker, and he sensed a sort of knowing between them, like they were sharing a private joke or a memory.

"Have I missed something?" he asked cautiously. "There is definitely a weight lifted from you all. Do not try to lie, vampires are built for detecting that sort of thing."

Cain scratched his shoulder awkwardly, not quite meeting Vlad's eyes with his wolfish ones.

"We, err…last week, after you left us in the manner you did, we cleared up best we could, what with the pitch blackness and stuff, and then, err…"

"We went for a drink."

All heads turned to Lucy. She seemed defiant, oft-shining

and moving hair now matte and lifeless again. Her eyes grew wide.

"Yeah, that's right. And it was me that suggested it, too."

"You went for…a drink…" Vlad repeated slowly.

"We did, is that alright?"

Vlad gesticulated in surprise.

"Of course that is alright! I am overjoyed you all decided to do such a wondrous thing! A shared drink has always been a direct course to the deepening of the hearts. How did this come about, might I ask?"

"We all catch the same train,' Lucy explained. "It seemed silly not to waste the evening, as it got cut short – no offence, I know you didn't mean it," she said hurriedly but Vlad waved it away. "There are a few decent bars in town and so we went to one Cain suggested."

"The Parrot and Cracker, they've got a smashin' snooker table," the werewolf said with an almost longing look on his face. "It's a hipster bar as well so the table's there *ironically*, whatever that means. Haven't been since I was last up this way, thought it'd be nice to suggest it and maybe see a face or two I knew. Got my favourite drink, too, unlike the other bars round here. It ain't difficult to do. God, it tasted good. Felt like I'd really earned it, y'know?"

"Let me guess," Vlad said mischievously, pointing at Cain, "some sort of porter or dark ale."

"Close," Cain said with a wry grin. "Very close."

"Close my decomposing foot, *he* ordered a dry martini," Jacob sniggered and Cain visibly shrank into his chair, a rare show of humility for the werewolf. "With a wee olive *and* a slice of lemon on the side, which he *insisted* on."

Cain gestured at Jacob irritably.

"Listen, toothy, that's a really sophisticated drink and I won't sit here and be mocked, d'you hear?"

Jacob laughed again but Vlad nodded thoughtfully.

"That *is* a very nice drink; a fine choice, Cain."

"You see, Jacob? Vlad says it was a fine choice."

"Oh of course he would, the guy's *built* on sophistication."

Vlad's composure lowered and he snorted despite his bearing, and the room felt lighter because of it. Sarah started humming to herself and even Fable cracked a smile, their black and shrivelled hands still rubbing together awkwardly. The vampire turned to the banshee.

"And your drink?"

"Old Scrump Cider, nine percent."

"Good God, you must have been merry after that!"

"I can hold my drink," Lucy said knowingly.

"Hmm…' Cain muttered. "That was until you vomited outside and disappeared quickly after."

"That wasn't the drink," Lucy muttered.

Vlad realised what the problem was and raised his hand to Cain, and shook his head before the werewolf could retort. The vampire continued as if nothing happened.

"Then that brings us to Jacob and Fable. I would hazard a guess for you both but I am afraid drinking is where my powers of deduction crumble, apparently."

"Me?" Jacob asked. "I *am* an ale man, always have been, always will be. Thankfully that's one taste my being a wraith still allows. Brains and ale: could almost be a flavour of pie."

"Ugh," Cain muttered. "And 'cause it's you it'd be vegan pastry, too, gross."

The whole group chuckled and Jacob threw a ball of paper at Cain when he wasn't looking. His long-fingered hand snaked out so fast only Vlad saw. His grip closed around the paper and Cain smiled slyly.

"Nice try," he grunted.

'Wolf reflexes even in human form. Interesting…'

Vlad did not allow his thoughts to show on his face.

"Fable?" Vlad asked and the faerie looked up. "Your beverage?" Fable shook their head.

"I did not drink. It is forbidden for alcohol to pass my lips."

"Yeah, didn't stop you droppin' a couple funny mushrooms in that tea you ordered," Cain remarked and Vlad's eyebrows rose in surprise. Fable allowed a rare, knowing drop in their placidity.

"I said alcohol. I did not say the naturally grown fruits of nature."

Vlad clapped his hands together and rocked forwards with a throaty laugh, his mood sweetened and deepened by the group's travels into fellowship.

"This is wonderful! Oh, I am so happy you all found a moment together, that is more than I could have wished for at this stage. Well done, all of you. Perhaps if I am not bound by my inner demons one evening, I might join you all as well, so long as you would have me?"

"*Have* you? You started all this, Vlad," Lucy almost admonished, and the vampire saw how she had progressed in just a few short weeks, her confidence blossoming. "We'd love to have you with us."

"Exactly," Jacob agreed.

Fable nodded.

"I began only last week but I can see how much your friends regard you, Vladislav – they told me your full name, also. It is wonderfully olden Romanian, by my knowledge of Latin languages. The word conjures rolling hills and houses of colourful woodwork."

"Thank you, Fable, that is very kind of you to say," Vlad replied, sincerity pouring from him. "I often think back to Romania and long to visit once more, it has been too long. I would not think you would have known much of our world."

Fable made a gesture.

"We have watched yours grow alongside ours, displaced as we are in reality. It is always good to maintain connections to the other side, especially if they feel so distant."

"I could not agree more. The links between worlds are vastly important for many reasons. I would very much like to see *yours* one day," Vlad said. Fable nodded tightly.

Blood and Biscuits

"I used to enjoy mead," Sarah said lightly, her hands miming the act of drinking as she spoke. "All honeyed and lovely. It tastes warm even though it's not, and it reminds me of tulips."

"Ooooh, now whenever I'm feelin' flush I do like a mead, too," Cain said with a pleasant expression. "S'nice you can remember it, Sarah."

"I remember many things, fang-man, like the words *you* mutter when you dream," she finished cheekily.

Cain cleared his throat, eyebrows knitting together.

"So, what's *your* drink, mate?" he asked Vlad hurriedly. "It's gotta' be posh, somethin' elegant and refined. Or maybe it ain't, maybe you knock back the cheap ciders like Lucy."

"Hey!" the banshee cried, her umbra voice slipping in a note of screech.

"No, no," Vlad said, "I do enjoy many alcohols, but my personal favourite would be a single malt from Japan or Scotland, wood-charred and peaty – wonderful odours."

"Surprising," Jacob noted genuinely. "From my neck of the woods, too."

"I thought you would appreciate that, Jacob. It is an ancient drink for an ancient man," Vlad spoke, his voice carrying as fine as spider's silk. "Anyway, we came not to discuss the benefits of inebriation in all its many colours and potential projectiles but to share what we can of ourselves. Are we ready?"

The entire group nodded, the tone of the high-vaulted room shifting into a darker space, the shared moment lost but not quite forgotten. The subtle looks each member gave another spoke of the gentlest threads of purpose. Without saying a word, Vlad knew the Support Group was losing its inherent individualism and growing in unity. They truly were just people.

"Come, how was everyone's week?"

"Much better, thanks," Cain began, hesitating no longer. "Got myself upgraded to a single room in the hostel – costs a bit more but the privacy's fantastic. Nobody askin' about my scars, no one wondering why I'm stayin' there long-term. Brilliant."

"A price for freedom," Vlad noted and Cain smiled.

"Pennies, mate."

"Fantastic, Cain, I am glad you are finding a firmer foot. Anything else?"

"No that's about it. Work's good, a few loose ends I need to tie up, but other than that I can't complain."

Vlad accepted the information then looked round the group. Sarah spoke next, her usual dream-like tone echoing as it always did.

"I have had the greatest week," she said delightedly and Vlad smiled to himself.

"That's nice," Lucy enthused. "Anything new happen in particular?"

"Do try not to be jealous, Lucille, but I got a magic box that plays music and speaks to me," Sarah replied mistily. Lucy looked bewildered, as did Jacob and Cain. Fable nodded thoughtfully as if it was the most obvious thing to say. "It waits for me to give it my voice again," Sarah finished, rising another inch or two above her chair until she was a clear three feet higher than everyone else.

"And what have you been listening to?" Vlad asked, determined to steer the conversation from who had given Sarah the box. He was not one for boasting, nor did he wish people view him as someone that held favouritism.

"At first I got excited about many songs from what's known as 'the eighties', so that was good. Then, quite by chance, I discovered something called 'podcasts'." Jacob sniggered and Lucy paused as she stood to grab a coffee, listening to what Sarah said interestedly. "I've heard dozens now, my small world has opened endlessly. Politics has changed a lot since my time. Oh, and people *swear* on podcasts, it's delightful!"

Cain gasped in surprise then let out a loud laugh as the others gave similar responses. Sarah was more involved than usual, Vlad noted, her sentences structured strongly, her visibility less transparent. He thought the music box might serve to return some semblance of reality to her, a connection to which she could tether her emotions and anchor her sense of self. It was Jacob that had sparked the idea in his head for he had been the one to suggest giving Sarah something. Vlad had thought her constant humming might be a sign that she missed music in her life.

Vlad smiled and turned to Jacob, his hands fidgeting a little.

"How was your week?"

"Better than I thought it'd be, I guess," the wraith replied, shifting his focus round the room. "Had a moment of religious doubt – spent a few hours at the church near my flat dealing with being a Christian and, you know, being a member of the undead. Turns out it's a wee bit of a struggle to square the two."

"You're not alone," Lucy said in a small voice.

"You're Christian, too?" Jacob asked, a glimmer of something in his eye.

Lucy gave a half-hearted shrug.

"I think I was – some kind of Catholic in County Kerry. But that was a long time ago, I made my peace with myself and I'm actually comfortable with it."

"You are?" Jacob asked quietly. "How the hell'd you manage that?"

"Well, frankly this curse is already ruining my life enough. I don't need religious guilt as well, over something I don't think is my fault. I didn't ask for this, I didn't choose this, and I think God would be happy with the person I was and still am. Your religion's about how you live your life and treat others; it's not about constantly adding punishment onto punishment."

Silent relief blazed off Jacob and Vlad observed the interaction.

"You really found peace with that? That's amazing, Lucy. You've actually made me feel a little better, thanks."

"You're welcome," Lucy said offhandedly, the smallest fragment of pride fragmenting from her. This was important.

Jacob sat back in his chair, arms crossed, head bowed in

thought, Vlad's own speculations coldly measuring.

'She gave what I could not. What Jacob needs is a peer.'

Lucy crossed to the table of biscuits and coffee.

"What's on offer today, Luce? Any Jaffa cakes?" Cain called over his shoulder as Sarah took up her humming again. Vlad's thoughts cut short.

"Don't call me 'Luce', makes me sound trampy," Lucy grumbled and Cain apologised. "And there are none. Besides, those aren't technically biscuits," the banshee stated matter-of-factly. Cain muttered something about 'bloody pedants' as Vlad watched silently, observing everything, commenting on nothing. The dynamic had most certainly changed; it filled the void of his body with something akin to calmness, a quelling of the rage that was his lurking monster. With the recent blood he had consumed, Vlad was safe from another attack from the vampiric beast, for now. "What's the package, Vlad?" Lucy called over, picking up the small, brown box from the table and looking it over.

"Oh, never mind about that," he answered. "I'll deal with it later. You get back to letting Cain down gently over his biscuit choices."

Cain grunted and folded his arms tightly.

"If there ain't no Jaffas then I'll settle for a custard cream and a black coffee."

"Got any bourbons?" Jacob called over.

"There should be a fresh packet," Vlad mentioned.

"Got it," Lucy said, lifting the unopened pack high. "But I thought you can't eat biscuits, Jay."

"I just wanted to smell one," Jacob admitted heavily. "And they're vegan, too, so that eases my conscience."

Fable looked up, interest crinkling the faerie's gaze.

"You shut your mouth!" Cain exclaimed as he took a proffered custard cream then stood to help Lucy with the drinks. "That's an outrageous claim and a disgusting lie! You tell me there's at least butter in 'em right now or I throw a tantrum."

"No, seriously!" Jacob insisted as he took a bourbon. He sniffed it and smiled appreciatively, a distant look growing in his eye. "Completely vegan."

Fable glanced from Jacob to the dark-brown biscuits. Quickly, two badly damaged hands shot forwards and took up three biscuits, and when Fable bit into the first, their face burst into a look of deep satisfaction. Though he could *sense* nothing from them, Vlad saw pleasure in the faerie for the first time.

Fable said nothing, they just sat and ate their biscuits happily as Lucy and Cain returned with the drinks and handed them out. Vlad took his gratefully and waited for all to sit again.

"This is nice," he said quietly. Only Lucy heard and she patted him on the shoulder.

"I guess it's my turn, then," the banshee said after a short draught of her drink. "Didn't get a chance last time, thought I'd make an effort today. So, my week. Where to start? It was…alright, as far as weeks go. Not the worst, certainly not the best. Still invisible to everyone, that's not changed."

"Eh?" Cain asked. "You're not invisible – oh, you mean emotionally, sorry."

"No, I mean literally," Lucy qualified. "Really, properly invisible."

"It is true," Vlad explained. "Banshees cannot be seen by the living human eye unless they have heard the scream. Remember that none of us here are human; some are not even living."

"Oh," Cain muttered. "That's a big bugger. But what about them folks at the bar last week? You ordered your drink alright, drank it in plain sight."

"No, Fable ordered my drink with their tea and then we sat in that side room, remember? No-one saw me, I promise you."

"Christ, I never knew. I'm sorry, Lucy," Cain said slowly but she waved it away.

"Don't be stupid, nothing you can do about it. Just the nature of my curse, that's all. I go unnoticed, which would have been fine when I was human, except it's made me awfully lonely over the years. Hard to miss something you take for granted until it's too late. Now I have to wait for these weekly sessions to get some sort of interaction again."

"Wait, wait, wait, hang on a sec'," Cain said, fingers tightening into fists as he thought. "Humans *can* see you; those guys did two weeks ago, the sods that came in looking for me. Sorry for bringin' it up again."

"No, I get it, it's confusing," Lucy explained. "Like Vlad said: they'd heard me scream. Remember I was already yelling when those gits walked in and grabbed me? Well, that scream's the link to the real world for banshees, how we become perceptible to humans. You must remember what banshees are…what I am is cursed. A reanimated corpse, not to put too fine a point on it. That curse isn't just for us but humans as well, and when they hear us that's when one of them's due to die, though *when* is a matter for debate. Humans can't perceive banshees until it's too late, and then one'll drop dead, sooner or later."

There was a momentary pause as Lucy leant back in her chair, clearly wishing to be swallowed by the ground. Vlad smiled kindly.

"I am glad you still come," he said softly. "It would most certainly be a duller basement without you, and I realise that sounded sarcastic but it was not meant as such."

"It's fine," Lucy sighed, looking more drained than her deathly paleness seemed. "I know what you mean, Vlad. You forget: banshees see through lies, same as vampires. Although you can't lie on sanctified ground, so that was a pointless thing to say."

"That ability's really a thing, too?" Jacob asked and Lucy nodded.

"A lesser-known skill, but yeah, it's true. And sometimes the invisibility's great, I can go out and not be bothered by anyone, but I always get pulled back home. Always. And when I went home last week I just…haunted the place, I guess you'd call it. I don't really have much to do except wander dark hallways and think on dark things. That kind of isolation makes you very insular."

"It can be quite enlightening for some," Vlad said, "but most view it as a type of torture, trapped by your own mind – not *in* it, that's a different situation entirely. Doomed to exist in complete introverted desolation. Just because you are a banshee that does not mean you would not suffer the same as anyone else. I am sorry this is your fate."

"It would take a miracle to release me from it," Lucy said, her hands shaking in her lap, eyes misting over.

"In what sort of abode do you reside, might I venture?" Vlad began.

"What difference does *that* make?" Cain asked incredulously.

"Would you mind if I explained?" Vlad posed and Lucy shook her head. He had not thought she would agree.

"I will be delicate," he promised, turning to the werewolf. "The difference it makes, Cain, is subtle but to Lucy it will be astronomical. The smaller a residence is the weaker a banshee's binding, that is the way of it. *Physically* smaller. If it is a small house the binding of her soul to the residence is lessened; as abodes grow you start to find the banshee's binding gets stronger and stronger until they can no longer escape, bound to stalk the corridors and rooms, hoping one day to be released from their curse. This strength is measured in time, so a small house might provide several days away before the curse demands the banshee's return."

"That about sums it up," Lucy groaned. "Not only that but banshees are harbingers of the end of life, messengers of the very real death of another. That's why we scream, and the louder the scream the sooner the death is or the stronger our bond to the person. Family members are the bloody worst."

"That's horrid," Cain muttered, arms crossed tightly over his chest, coffee balanced precariously on the edge of his arm, held by a single finger. Vlad watched it as he listened, wondering how long it would take before the cup went one of two ways. He held it in his mind as Cain spoke. "I can't imagine what that means to you. You screamed when that human got hold of you, and it wasn't no normal scream."

"Though I was screaming before he came in, I'm still capable of fear for myself," Lucy said miserably. "And that manifests like it would, like a scream, however it's bolstered by curse."

"I take it you live somewhere quite large," Jacob said, concerned.

"A mansion on a hill."

"Bloody hell," Cain muttered.

"Is that Galloway's Mansion?" Jacob asked curiously.

"It is," Lucy said. "You know it?"

"Only in passing. Creepy place, *really* creepy. Nearly went there on a school trip; very glad I didn't."

"Yours is a most unfortunate circumstance," Fable said to Lucy, their face sympathetic. Sarah had finally ceased her humming and was perched only five inches above her chair. "Is there nothing we might do to alleviate your situation?"

"Not unless you know how to reverse the banshee curse and undo everything I've seen," Lucy said miserably. "And trust me, I've searched a long time. I don't think anything could help."

"How long does your particular binding allow you to leave your mansion?' Vlad asked gently.

"Six hours, no more."

"God, at least it's not a castle, though," Cain added unhelpfully. "Or a skyscraper."

"What happens if you try and stay away?" Jacob asked, a sick sound to his voice.

"I get very ill very quickly."

"Ahhhh," Cain breathed in realisation. "Hence the puking outside the bar."

"Yep. Had one too many and forgot the time. Alcohol disguises the binding's warnings and I waited too long. I think that's the only time I can teleport, when I need to get back. Is teleport the right word?"

Vlad shrugged. He honestly did not know.

"And so you literally disappeared," Jacob confirmed.

"Correct. I'm only forty-five minutes out of town but it takes long enough to get here as it is, so I'm limited even now."

"If it helps, I, too, am bound to my abode. At least you can leave, if but for the barest of hours."

All eyes turned to Sarah, her veiled face revealing nothing of her mood. Yet there was hurt in her tone, the echo of her voice lost, her words landing like the thunder thuds of cannonballs.

"I know, Sarah, I know," Lucy expressed solemnly. "You understand better than anyone else, I think, and I wish there was something I could do for you, too."

"Whatever do you mean?" Sarah asked brightly. "I have my magic box!"

Lucy chuckled quietly and the mood lifted somewhat by a hand of levity. Vlad recognised the moment had passed and Lucy settled back into herself, and so he looked to Fable at last and engaged them.

"How was your week, my friend?"

"It was fine, thank you." The answer was curt and hollow.

Vlad blinked several times and Jacob stared at the faerie confusedly. Cain looked anywhere except at Vlad or Fable.

"Ok...good, then," Vlad said. "I am glad for you. Out of interest, before we continue: would you mind if I asked if we should be addressing you with a particular set of personal pronouns? I am unsure, given the nature of faeries. Many humans do not wish to be identified as one specific gender or another and I would not wish to coerce you if you wish to remain neutral."

Fable tilted their head and gazed curiously at Vlad.

"I do not quite understand, Vladislav."

"Well, it is simply a matter of how we present what we say *to* you and how we might talk *about* you to another. I mean no disrespect but faeries are mostly beyond my knowledge, and I know you as a species largely comprise no specific sex."

"That is correct," Fable confirmed, their blackened hands twitching painfully as they spoke. "Is this…would this be regarding gender words?"

"Indeed it would!" Vlad said happily. "Are you happy with a non-gender-specific 'they-them' set as we have been using or do you identify closer to how we might? Male and female pronouns, I mean, such as 'his' and 'he', 'hers' and 'she', et cetera."

Fable looked around the group with an almost cheerful expression, taking in every face with intrigue.

"Amongst the fae we need no such methods of address – most communication is made through hand gestures and the magic we perform. Yet faeries study Earth and your languages, and I have enjoyed learning to use my prior knowledge of English here. I see more what you might describe as male faces here, so to tip the balance I favour perhaps the female gender identification. I'm no woman but I've heard of their care and strength, and to associate myself with those of the maternal bond would bring me the greatest joy. This I would be proud to identify as in your world."

Vlad heard far more in what Fable hid than in what they said.

"Then you shall be treated as such, Fable," Vlad said. "For as long as you wish."

Fable nodded in satisfaction and sat back again, folding her arms loosely and clearly mulling over the previous discussions with deep interest.

"Very nice," Jacob said, smiling and patting Fable on the shoulder. "I hope you're happy with your choice."

Vlad looked round and suddenly realised that within three weeks, and the addition of two new members during that time, they had finally managed to come to the end of the first question he had set himself the challenge of asking. He stumbled for a second or two, never believing he would make it this far. In all honesty, he had not believed anybody would respond to his online advert at all.

"I suppose we might take a moment here and congratulate ourselves on our supreme victory: we have made it to the second question."

There was a palpable sense of realisation amongst the group, evident in the way they rearranged themselves in their seats – Sarah hovered another inch higher, her humming returning merrily.

"And what *is* this mythical question?" Cain asked dryly, though there was a definite note of genuine anxiety in his voice.

"Do you have anything to unburden yourselves with? To get off your chest? Or is there anything positive you want to tell us?"

"Oh, that was unexpected," Jacob said.

"I thought it would be a good continuation from the first question, to round it off and allow the chance to complete a thought or explanation."

"How many questions do you *have*?" Lucy asked, looking nervous.

"Currently? Sixteen."

"Jesus, Vlad, are you serious! It's taken three weeks to get through the first one, and that's only because Fable abstained. And we start all over each week. Is this some manic vampire habit of getting as much information as possible?"

"No, actually I think it is a feature of my depression," Vlad admitted. "It manifests in very strange ways, one of which is to focus on infinitesimally small details. You should see me when something does not go to plan, I become quite unreasonable. Very well, I will review the questions later and perhaps pare them down. I shall then work on my obsessions a little more. Anyway, who would like to begin?"

"Actually, I *would* like to share," said Fable to the surprise of everyone. She stirred uneasily, the astonishing angles of her face like beaten gold, capturing Vlad's thoughts even as she prepared to lay bare her soul. Lucy reached out and rested a pale palm gently on Fable's shoulder, and the faerie smiled appreciatively. "It's about my hands, as you might have guessed."

"I didn't think you wanted to talk about them," Jacob said.

"It's not my most pressing matter to divulge but it's the heaviest thing on my mind at this moment. Vlad most likely knows what these mean," Fable suggested, showing her hands to the group, "yet there's little doubt he only suspects *why* they happened."

"All I know of the fae's magic is it links to their – sorry, *your* – natural world in its purest sense," the vampire explained. "I have heard tell of hierarchies and Sects of magic, but these were rumours from foreign lands. How far am I from the truth?"

"Surprisingly close to it, you were right to trust your sources," Fable confirmed. "There are indeed hierarchies amongst my people, governed by status in magic and types of birth. Each country of the Eight Realms contains within their factions their own tiered hierarchy, and in-turn these Sects are collectively known as the Choir of the Fae. I was one of the lowest amongst the tiers, a member of the Sect of Light."

"That sounds so beautiful," Lucy said almost soothingly as Sarah's humming became more tuneful and atmospheric in the background. Jacob eyed the ghost curiously – or it could have been in fondness, Vlad considered.

The vampire watched Cain's cup still, the werewolf's attention slipping at a gradual, glacial pace.

"It is," Fable confirmed, "and I wish you had more time to hear about the true purity of my world, but your binding sees you limited more than most of us right now and I cannot be so greedy with time. We have been here too long as it is." Two spots of colour appeared high on Lucy's cheeks and Vlad smelled a slight flash of guilt from her as Fable continued. "All you need know for now is that the Sect of the Light was not enough for me; I was a proud faerie, with many ideas of success and power far above my capabilities, but I was also wracked with sadness and I was blinded by this. To regale you all with the details would most certainly take longer than Lucy can afford."

"Why not simply tell us what ails you the most at this point?"

Blood and Biscuits

Vlad suggested, sipping his coffee thoughtfully. "Then we might unravel the rest of your story as the sessions go on. Excuse me a moment."

The cup fell from Cain's hand.

Vlad removed the slightest measure of his control holding back the strength within him and disappeared from his seat. Moving as fast as shadow, sheathed in the power of his darkness, Vlad appeared beside Cain immediately in the mists of twilight, the werewolf's cup clasped firmly in his cold hand. All of this happened during Cain's reaction to the falling drink, and he practically leapt from his chair when he looked up and saw Vlad towering over him.

"Jesus *arse*, Vlad! What the hell!"

Vlad held his hand out to Cain, the cup balanced upon a single finger with the grace of a feather. The vampire smiled sweetly.

"You might wish to hold this a little more firmly, my friend. Refill?"

"Refill? Refill!" Cain thundered as he placed a hand on his chest and doubled over, panting. "Bugger your refill, I'm having a heart attack. I'm havin' a very real heart attack. Oh Jesus Christ…"

Lucy and Jacob burst out laughing and Fable cracked a wide smile as Vlad crossed the room with a purposeful stride and Cain began feeling his left arm.

"Do not be so dramatic, my friend, I can hear your heart clearly. It is slowing already, currently at one hundred and eleven beats per minute and falling. Your breathing is elevated, your blood has increased by a quarter degree Celsius only. Your vessels are dilated. But these will all return to normal, especially with a new coffee, which you will be more…?"

Vlad let the question dangle as Cain sat heavily and stopped the theatrics.

"Which I'll be more careful with. Patronisin' git."

Vlad returned with the coffee and placed it into Cain's outstretched, shaking, hand. Jacob and Lucy stifled their smirks and wiped their faces clean as Sarah's humming grew louder. The vampire seated himself elegantly and indicated towards Fable.

"Please, continue."

"Like I said," Fable muttered after she had stopped glancing awkwardly between Vlad and Cain. "I was proud and I thought I deserved more power than that which I had been bestowed. It is a dangerous pursuit, the knowledge of magic, and yet it is wildly addictive, rather like one of your earthly drugs."

"Or your fungal ones," Cain muttered bitterly, so quietly only Vlad heard. The man's heart had slowed to resting pace, finding quiescence far faster than most werewolves Vlad had encountered, he noted oddly.

"All you need know today is that I tried too hard to cast my magic beyond my abilities and this happened." Fable presented her hands, front and back, the black flesh cracked and worn. "I can still perform a little basic magic but it is nothing compared to the feats of old. If I try and do too much, I will damage myself further, I am sure of it. Just little things now."

"I would love to see that some time," Lucy said to Fable and the faerie smiled.

"For you? I would grant this instantly."

Lucy's eyes grew wide in astonishment as Fable spread her hand, palm facing upward, and withheld a grimace of pain. Her shoulder twitched involuntarily and Vlad *felt* the strong electrical disturbance signalling magic long before the waves of power arrived. The basement's candles fluttered and every member of the group was transfixed at the point above Fable's palm – even Sarah ceased humming. Vlad leant forwards as the space over the faerie's hand distorted like air above a flame. Fable grunted and several beads of sweat danced down her brow, then suddenly a ball of Light appeared above her hand, shining and gleaming in a dazzling burst of splendour. Sparks spat and fizzled into the air as the orb spun, filling the room with glory, banishing every shadow.

"Whoa!" Cain remarked, leaning back in awe, face illuminated, the smells of intrigue and fear plain to Vlad's senses.

Blood and Biscuits

"Oh wow," Jacob whispered.

The sphere of power was broken and flawed but beautiful in every sense, a spinning form drawing in the candles' glow as if the magic was too perfect to permit any other light to survive before its majesty.

Vlad felt his skin beginning to heat and singe, and he realised what the Light truly was. Though the control containing his power had long since banished the hatred of the sun, Vlad suddenly felt a glitter of danger. This was purest magic delivering true light and it assaulted his flesh like daylight once had.

Fable cried in agony and the Light winked from existence.

All about the basement fell utterly silent and the candles flickered hauntingly in their jars, throwing shadows back into every corner. When next Vlad spoke, he was reverent and tranquil.

"You are a remarkable person, Fable. Truly remarkable. To conjure what you just did with your injuries is nothing short of a revelation. Thank you."

"You are…most…welcome…" Fable breathed, shaking her hands, favouring her palms specifically. "The gift was for all, though the meaning…I hope…will be instilled in Lucy."

"I think I'll remember that forever," Lucy began before she looked at the vampire. "Vlad, your skin! Look at your skin!" she cried.

Vlad waved her away as he felt his flesh already healing.

"Fret not about it, I will be fine in a moment. Truly, it is only a first-degree burn, it will be gone soon."

Vlad glanced at the banshee and saw, with no small amount of surprise, minute black tears pricking her eyes; one had already cascaded down her deathly white cheeks to stain her dark dress. Her mouth hung open in shock, body rigid as rock. Her eyes, however, were the most startling of all: they glowed crimson with the fires of the earth's heart, struck with a vivid heat.

Vlad took in all of her image and felt countless years of understanding fall away when he realised a banshee could lament. It was true that Lucy had shed tears during the first session when a human had imprisoned her by the throat. However, that had been fear, the threat to her own safety; what Vlad saw now was the banshee mourning for herself, for her entrapment in a seemingly endless spiral of the premonitions of death.

Fable, her hands broken by greed, was now a shade of her former self, recoiling back into the form that had slunk to the group for emotional sustenance. Cain, the werewolf that had never felt true kinship, sat with heavy shoulders and looked at no one. Jacob, the man that despised who he was and what he had done to try to end his life, only to linger on unwillingly, twitched in his chair, his face seemingly forgetting the mask of its usual toothy smile. And Sarah, the lonely woman who only wished to feel the love of people around her once more.

'I see myself in all of them,' Vlad thought, and right then a blade of pure feeling pierced his dead heart and gave it meaning again. He grunted and clutched his chest as, for one single second, his heart gave a solitary *beat*. Just once, but the act was enough to send a tidal wave of emotion crashing over him.

Vlad stood and walked towards the centre of the circle, burdens of pride and shame flickering from his shoulders like drifting tongues of flame as he understood the hurt and pain in everyone's eyes. Despair filled his mind, as strong as it always had, yet for once he would not run or hide: he would face his demon and use it to his advantage to help those still seeking his company in that supernatural gathering.

He strode into the middle and turned. He peered into their faces deeply, measuring their trust and their anguish – with Sarah, Vlad could only estimate from the manner in which she sat firmly upon her seat, her body utterly translucent.

Then Vlad spoke with absolute authority, his command over the threads of life and death gripping them, signs of a vampire's protection derived from the curse holding him in immortal darkness.

"You are none of you alone."

Blood and Biscuits

No mastery, no power lacing his words.

Vlad's thin hands fell to his sides. He felt as when he had stood upon that clifftop in ancient Romania, the iron-grey sea falling away far beneath his feet; the day he had died and been reborn. He was laid open as a man then, the true heart of the once-human shining through in his most vulnerable moment, the cloak of the vampire forever lurking beyond, waiting to enshroud him once more.

For that is what makes the monster, the inability to supress the devils of our innermost selves.

Without his meaning, Vlad's power started seeping out and the shadows formed. They grew from his body, starving the basement's candles, turning the air as icy as the frozen wastes of the south, and...

Sudden heat burst in two points across Vlad's ribs and his dead breath shuddered to a halt in his throat, catching audibly as a gasp. It was the most intense fever, dual marks of fire pouring through his body, spreading across his chest until all frigid coldness was gone, and the darkness was absorbed back into him, every trace of shadow retaken into the void of that soulless entity until Vlad was himself again.

The vampire looked down and saw two hands, pale as pearls, upon his sides. He turned and looked into the eyes of Lucy, her black tears dried upon her skin, the spots of colour back at her cheeks. She was a clear foot shorter than Vlad yet she seemed taller then, the mirage of courage. Lucy's eyes cast down and her head fell, and in the next moment she threw her arms around his lithe form and wrapped him in an almost crushing embrace. The weight of who she was and how she felt enfolded Vlad until he had no choice but to stretch his own arms around her and lean a side of his face against the top of her head.

She smelled of the wildness of night and Vlad's eyes squeezed shut as red tears of blood threatened to spill, something he had *no* command over. A deluge of sentiment fell and Vlad struggled with maintaining his dignity, but Lucy only hugged him tighter until he finally let go, unable to prevent it any longer.

When Vlad thought it could get no worse, Jacob joined them and placed an arm round his shoulders, the other about Lucy's waist. A second later, Fable had joined, her long, graceful limbs finding a position in which to comfort Vlad, and the vampire felt himself leaning on them all more than he ever thought possible. Then in a moment of astonishing sincerity, Sarah descended from above, drifting down until her spirit was *inside* Vlad, and for the first time ever the vampire felt the true presence of the phantom, an empty vessel and a foreign soul, two to make one. Sarah resonated within his body and sang such a beautiful melody of old that Vlad had no doubt of how important she was, about what she meant to him.

Sarah sang from behind his eyes and he felt as if he watched the world through her song.

When at last it came time to fit into place the missing link, Vlad knew it was right. The vampire felt a strong hand rest upon his free shoulder and grasp it firmly, and he turned with scarlet eyes to see Cain staring impassively at him, jaw carved from stone. Werewolf and vampire held together, completed by banshee, ghost, wraith, and faerie.

For a single second there came a stillness to the air, a sort of silence through the basement like a giant hand pressing all sound down into the floor. It was a moment of something else, speaking of forgotten powers that had found no joining for many centuries. Only Vlad felt the pressure connect them all as one, and the vampire smiled a knowing smile.

'We are missing only one,' he thought through the sorrows of his mind and Sarah's melody.

Cain's hand left his shoulder and the pressure was gone.

Within himself, Vlad finally found an ember of levity and he cradled it until it burst into life. He released a short laugh and the group's embrace fell away. They did not return to their seats, however, for they knew how much time Lucy had remaining. The session had taken longer than they had thought – there would be no drinks tonight. Lucy's binding would draw her back again, one way or another.

When all was done, Vlad looked to them with fury and joy lighting his eyes in equal measure, fanning flames of determination.

"I will find a cure for you all, this I swear," he said through gritted teeth. "You may think it impossible but I think different, and I *will* one day bring peace to your lives."

Vlad wiped the blood from his cheeks and looked round the basement.

"This church…it will serve as the place where you all begin new lives. One day, though I do not know when, you will walk free from here and from your curses, and I will stand a proud man, alleviated of all his woes."

"You shouldn't make promises you cannot keep," Sarah muttered as she drifted away towards the ceiling.

"I am a man of my word, Sarah."

He wished he could have seen her face but the veil remained ever impassive.

"Thank you for my nice magic box, Vlad, you have made one dream come true."

"You are most welcome, my love."

Vlad took what clemency he could from the beauty of the ghost's last song as she started to echo a different melody, this one a lilting tune, layering in folds of haunting words as she rose into the ceiling and was gone.

Lucy stood beside Vlad as everyone replaced chairs against the basement wall. The banshee grinned lopsidedly.

"You know, she's definitely an odd one. But I really like her."

"Oh, I am fond of her, too," Vlad responded quietly. "I feel it deep in my bones. She is a curious child, one that I long to free from her chains."

Vlad glanced round and saw Cain staring at the blown electric light, a look of consternation plain across his face.

"What ails you, my friend?" Vlad called over. Cain pointed up at the light.

"It's the full moon in a couple weeks. Holy ground's all well and good but it ain't nothin' without an electric light to help keep my curse at bay. *You* taught me that, Vlad. What the hell'm I s'posed to do when the moon's back?"

"Ahh, you have reminded me of the one small errand I needed to complete this evening," Vlad said. He crossed the basement and picked up the small package he had placed on the coffee table earlier. He slipped a steel-hard nail into the taped wrapping and slit it with ease. He opened the flap and took out the single item inside, presenting it to the group. "Penance on my part, and an offering to the church as a mark of respect."

"It's a light bulb," Jacob said. "An energy saver, too."

"Of course," Vlad announced happily. "We all must do our bit for the planet."

"You're joking!" Cain exclaimed as Vlad pulled a chair under the light fixture. The ceiling was high but the light's pendant cable was long. "You have any idea how long energy savers take to light up? You want me to transform as slowly and as painfully as possible, I get it. That's sick."

"No, Cain, I do not. And this is an LED bulb, very rapid. I want to use as little energy as possible because I am unsure in what state the electrics of the church remain. Also, the bulb was on special offer."

"Oh for God's sake," Cain snarled. Jacob laughed as Lucy checked her watch.

"Does anyone mind if I leave?" she asked.

"No, you go right ahead, I will see you next week," Vlad said as he made to fly up to the ceiling. Jacob grabbed a chair.

"I'll do it; I was an electrician before I was turned. I still know a thing or two about dodgy connections. Might as well take a look at the wiring and see if I can trace it back to a fuse box somewhere as well, could do something to improve things around here. Oh sorry, Lucy, bye. See you next week."

"I'll accompany you to the train," Fable said to the banshee as they gathered their coats and walked to the entrance stairs. "I wouldn't be comfortable with you walking alone across a place like this."

"Trust me, if I see any drunk humans again the first thing I'm doing is screaming so loud it tears their flesh off," Lucy responded as they climbed the stairs and disappeared out of sight.

'Now I wonder if she could choose to do that,' Vlad thought.

"Oh, now *here's* a joke for you fellas," Jacob said as he took the LED from Vlad and reached up to the socket dangling from the ceiling.

"Don't do it, please don't do it," Cain practically growled.

"How many monsters does it take to change a light bulb?" Jacob asked with a grin. Cain groaned and Vlad rolled his eyes. "What? What!" Jacob cried indignantly. "That was begging to be said, you know it! Oh don't look at me like that, Cain, you're just jealous 'cause you didn't think of it first. Envy's unbecoming of you."

Vlad sipped the dregs of his coffee and smiled, thinking on many things as he watched Jacob work and Cain make sarcastic comments, the werewolf clearly holding a growing regard for the wraith. Vlad thought on the session and the progress they had made, how he had managed to keep his power protected behind his control despite his depression, and give Lucy the opportunity to speak and Fable to integrate into the gathering more. Vlad realised he had not done much this week but that was largely the point.

As they finished, the vampire thought on the moment of their shared physical connection and the reaction from the air and the earth, and his smile deepened.

'Just one more needed,' he told himself again.

THE INDUSTRIAL COMPLEX,

ELLIN'S ISLAND.
THE NIGHT FOLLOWING THE SUPPORT GROUP.

Vlad balanced upon the very edge of stone and peered out across the island as he had done many times before, eyes touched by the grey knowledge of centuries. He watched with silent interest as the white and translucent form of the phantom spun and whirled in the ruins of St Ellin's church, two miles from the towering factories. Vlad was bathed in a night drenched by heavy rains and mists curling up from the dark and dangerous river far below, and he stood and watched the ghost as she twirled into the sky and fell to the church again, always wondering on the answers he so sorely desired.

Anger tinged his mood and he turned from Sarah, determination biting at him as he stormed down into the factories, an answer yet to be given to a question he had been asking for too long.

Yet. Such pain in these hands. Such unimaginable pain, and yet such love also. To suffer through agony just to bring about a smile of wonder is a harrowingly beautiful notion. It is at this point I would make some witty comment for amusement but I cannot; this gift of light was too exquisite.

The Contemplation of Hidden Things

Torches hung cold in brackets. Tapestries dangled lifeless from high stone walls. Doorways stood seemingly empty and windows glinted dully, a glimmer of magic just beyond them the only hint that some things were not as they first appeared. Looming, carven faces leering out of oddly placed alcoves and strange little recesses, and peering between columns and through windows, spoke of the demonic and angelic figures moulded from the walls, their long bodies trailing behind them with terrifying beauty. Deiform beasts of heaven and hell occupying that silent place, never moving, always watching, opposites together.

Footsteps paced silently and Vlad marched down the long hallways, intent and alert. He had many things on his mind, all vying for any scrap of attention they could find and devour hungrily so that they might grow, but one stood out amongst them. It was a thought of ghosts, of the notion of spirits and their imprint on the world.

'We should not be alone when we die,' he thought angrily, denial obvious even to him. *'To die alone is a tragedy but to live alone in death is far worse. There must be a reversal, some ancient spell or a ritual to counteract the spiritual connection and bring back the mortal body.'*

It had been Sarah's descent into Vlad that had done it. To see the world how she saw, to feel almost as she felt; it was too much to bear, that loneliness, and Vlad now entertained the fires of resolution.

Turning down another corridor, Vlad peered into room after room, deciding on where the best information might be kept; the second floor was good for battlefield lore and the spirits that could haunt such evil places but nothing on their reversal came to him. Not even the Lookout Rook, an observational balcony hanging two hundred feet from the ground, could yield anything. The fourth floor, when its resident suit of enchanted armour was not prowling the halls, revealed only a few tomes on the subjects of ectoplasm and its potential uses in para-medicine, which Vlad found in Education Room XVI, a place full of models of animal anatomy and brain dissections alongside abandoned detailed notes on rotting paper.

Vlad soared back down into the bowels of that hidden place and explored some of the dark chambers of the dungeons, their endless miles glowing blue beneath the gaze of magic scripture as he searched through chamber after chamber, arena after hall, behind ancient statues and through old tunnels on his quest for information that he knew, deep down, did not exist. Even the greenhouses in the high reaches were scoured as Vlad became desperate, moonlight striking the huge planters of soil and twisting columns of painted wrought iron. Statues stood throughout in odd poses, some looking seriously at all the plants no longer growing, while others took on merrier images, as if the light they lived in was enough to satisfy their petrification.

'*Damn. Damn it all.*" Vlad sat on a bench of twisted metal with embellishments of strange foreign flowers and put his head in his cold hands. '*Why did I try in here? I know I am losing my mind if I think there will be matters of ghosts residing in* greenhouses.' Vlad peered through the huge structures of glass to the very end and looked at the shut double doors there, and he felt a sliver of irritation flash for them. '*If I could open you, Irons, I know there would be secrets untold beyond your doors, but you have never shown any inclination of allowing me through.*'

Vlad sighed and pushed himself away. It was time to check the library. Channelling a single shadow of darkness, Vlad disappeared from the long greenhouses and reappeared upstairs in an impossibly large hall, a vast, complex warren of such a wealth of knowledge he had not seen even half of it. The shelves and cabinets of books and volumes stacked so high some touched the ceiling two hundred feet above, the deeps of the library winding through that hidden place in devilish ways, forming pathways of books, roadways of knowledge that demanded exploratory adventures in literature. Many stone levels sat high above, built upon columns so strewn with books they seemed to *stand* on piles of them, staircases spiralling down to the main floor. Vlad blew his cheeks out as he started considering just how much work was ahead of him and he began at the most obvious place, on the subject of phantoms.

An hour in, a shuffling came to his shoulder, near a shelf concerning the matters of medicinal trees, but Vlad did not look round. He had stood too long in one place and one of the library's helpful denizens had come to see if he needed assistance.

"No thank you," he muttered without looking round and the shuffling thing shifted away again, back into the tunnels of the shelves. "No bookworms today," the vampire muttered.

A fluttering high above made him stop, his finger paused on a book entitled '**Ethereal Nature**'. Vlad looked up and saw a flash of something brown and red pass over.

"Now *you* I might use," Vlad said with a smile. He whistled and the fluttering returned. The flying something dropped from the library sky and landed heavily next to him; it twitched its head with an almost mechanical non-fluidity and flapped its chipped-paint wings. "Dearest wordpecker, might I have a moment? Do you have any books on phantom resurrection you might find for me, please?"

The wood-carved bird twitched and flapped its wings again, the magic of animation old but stable enough in its joints and *brain*, its matrix of thought-giving spells. The bird clearly heard Vlad's words and leapt into the air, and then dived into a gap in the shelves and was lost in the ocean of books and scrolls. Vlad waited a moment and the bird returned, much higher in the sea of tomes, a haul of books pushing out and thudding down into Vlad's hands. If he had not been looking, the books would have struck his head.

"Thank you very much," the vampire said when the wordpecker landed before him again.

It started worrying at his hand, its clever magic instructing it to pretend as if it was a real bird; however, the spell matrix enchanting the limbs and head were four hundred years old and that length of time without maintenance from a competent mage meant the magic holding the thing together had gone a bit funny. After a moment, the wordpecker wobbled into the air, forgot how to fly, *thudded* down again, woofed, then scuttled irritably into the shelves, lost amongst the books for the last time.

"As I said: thank you," Vlad repeated dryly, thumbing through the books the wordpecker had collected for him in its waning sanity.

Vlad flicked through their pages but found only unhelpful answers. *'Death is permanent'*, the **Book of Violet Hauntings** said; *'Once the body is gone the spirit cannot be rehoused'* said **A Guide to British Ghostal Regions**; *'Though the mind is almost altogether present in the observed phantom, the awareness is entirely gone, the willingness to live rather than exist dissipated,'* said **A Master Meets the Ghost of Runnerbog Well**. That last one was completely wrong, Sarah was evidence for that.

Nevertheless, the themes of every book remained the same: Vlad could not play God. He was no bringer of life, only the courtier of death.

As wordpeckers fought and squabbled noisily over food that did not exist, Vlad tried a different approach.

Planting his hands on his hips and stooping inside the Fifteenth Century Ghosts section of the library, found by sliding aside the Paranormal Philosophies shelving bars, squeezing down a small tunnel of gigantic dark-tomes, and pushing open a tiny door into a room lit by an everlasting candle, Vlad stopped engaging wild thoughts and let his mind go blank. Considerations of Sarah reminded him of the silence she said people so rarely appreciated. As soon as he released all of his tension, Vlad began focussing on more important details, siphoning out the meaningless peripheral matters and finding even the demon of his depression quietened for once. And as he narrowed his mental gaze, Vlad asked himself one question:

'How do I find what I am looking for?'

The answer came to him quickly. *She* would know. She knew many things about this place.

Vlad squeezed back out and walked with measured steps, savouring the moment as he so rarely frequented this path. He found the winding roads through the library enchanting, as if they were strange ley lines trodden through a forest. Trails led off down shadowed ways, books and scrolls written by European and African scientists and magic casters lining the crooked, leaning shelves in alcoves and shaded ways, and sometimes towering cabinets hid secret shelves behind them, creating newer ways to follow.

And all of it was indestructible, protected by spells that did not allow units to be removed or shelves to be destroyed. One must walk the paths of the library, there would be no cheating.

Between long sections of science and round many high stacks, Vlad wended under a stone archway with a message of literature and education inscribed in Ancient Greek. He stopped before a narrow stretch of thin bookshelves.

With a small smile, he walked to the fourth-from-the-right, of books regarding 'Hillocks and Trollocks', according to the plaque on the shelving unit, and he sought '**Eccentric Stories of Moss-Bottom Warlocks**' on the sixteenth shelf from the floor. He pulled the spine down. Within the bookcase there came a series of *clunks* and a moment later the whole unit slid aside. Vlad grinned: he did so love a hidden passage behind a bookcase.

He marched through the newly made doorway. Torches of emerald light illuminated a small chamber filled with heavy, iron-bound books, these far older than any in the main library, some in languages even Vlad could not read. They were grimoires, filled with strange scraps of spells and illustrations of odd designs depicting horrific enchantments, designs the illustrators had clearly taken great pleasure in detailing. Vlad had poured over the books for days out of pure, sick fascination, but he was not here for them.

Blood and Biscuits

In the centre of the small chamber was a pool of blue-tinted water. A thin stream trickled from the mouth of a marble griffin carved into the back wall. Vlad reached over the pool and tickled the griffin's left ear. Somewhere behind the stone, a small spell roused, and the carving actually *giggled* and the water stopped pouring. Vlad stood back as the pool walls shivered and slid apart, water splashing and rushing down the opening chasm, and *she* rose from underneath. Drips of blue water slid down the head of a beautiful statue, a stone woman wearing a toga. Vlad stood and watched with the same appreciation he always had whenever he sought her counsel.

As the last of the statue came into the room, Vlad admired the hem of her robe where there flashed the hint of a fish's tail, green tinged scales glinting in the emerald light. The statue revolved to a stop and faced the chamber, hands held out as if she weighed two things against one another.

"Good evening, Mistress of the Waves. I hope you have fared well in your underwater lair. I am sorry to only ever need something of you rather than spend any personal time but once again I have a question."

As always, the Mistress' face remained impassive yet Vlad found comfort in that. So many of the lingering spells in that hidden place were so extraordinarily reactive with no mage to tend them that it was refreshing to find one piece still in full control of itself.

"Great repository of information, has it ever been known for a ghost to find new life again, even in the body of another outside of possession?"

There was never a direct answer, usually just a feeling or some sort of sign, but right then nothing came. Vlad nodded and turned away, knowing the Mistress of the Waves would sink into her pool again, when the slightest disturbance announced itself. There were no windows but a small wind blew through the green-lit chamber. Vlad sensed something move and a grimoire lifted from its shelf; the book was entitled '*Haunted Majiks of ye Olde Worldes, of Faithes Aligned, of Matters Darke*'.

Blood and Biscuits

It dropped onto the table with an irritable *thud*.

"I promise next time I shall come here only to talk with you, my beauty," Vlad said gently.

The grimoire's front cover burst open and the delicate leaves fluttered over and over until they came to rest on one page. Vlad knew he was at least partially forgiven.

Approaching cautiously, he read the title of the page: 'IMPRESSIONS OF THE DECEASED, MATTER AND TANGIBLE.' Down the lines of Middle English he read, his eyes drinking the words as he tried to find whatever it was the Mistress of the Waves wished for him to see. Finally, as he grew wary of the statue's magic, thinking she might finally have gone the way of some of the older spells around the place, his eyes caught it. Two short lines. Irrefutable.

'*Ghosts, or souls everlasting, beyond temporary possession of the corpus cannot find solace in resurrection, only the limitless solitudes of haunting ad infinitum. Attempts to the contrary produce only crucifixion for both party's souls.*'

'*The Mistress serves only to confirm,*' Vlad told himself, misery framing his resolution.

Fig.5. The Spirit's Daffodils.

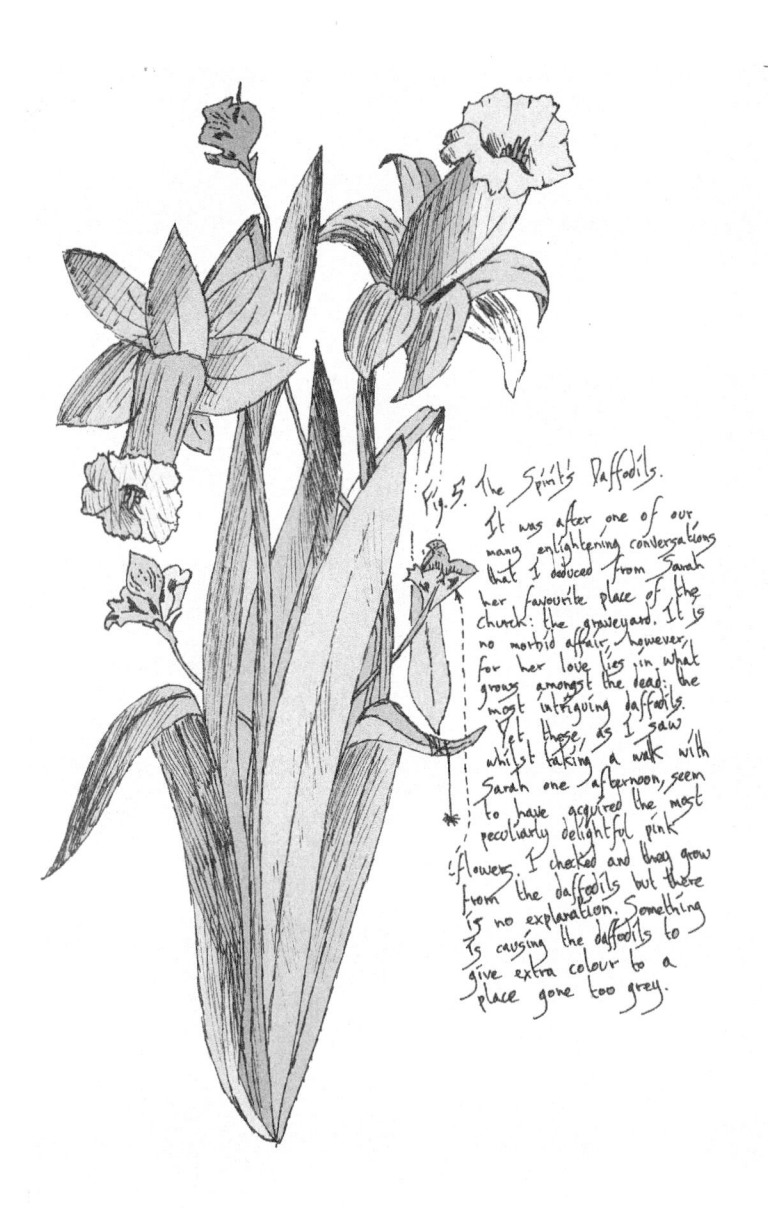

It was after one of our many enlightening conversations that I deduced from Sarah her favourite place of the church: the graveyard. It is no morbid affair, however, for her love lies in what grows amongst the dead: the most intriguing daffodils. Yet those, as I saw whilst taking a walk with Sarah one afternoon, seem to have acquired the most peculiarly delightful pink flowers. I checked and they grow from the daffodils but there is no explanation. Something is causing the daffodils to give extra colour to a place gone too grey.

Week Four
Restraints for the Wolf

OESCHINENSEE LAKE,
BERNER OBERLAND,
BERNESE ALPS,
SWITZERLAND.
SEVEN HOURS BEFORE THE SUPPORT GROUP.

    Vlad stood upon a rise of ice and stone, a claw bared for the flesh at his arm.

    Poised, Vlad shook with rage and near-frozen hatred for himself. He could not think clearly, the burn to slice his skin too hot. He brought his claw down and pressed its razor tip against his arm, ready to plunge and slice, spatter the stone with his blood, but something stopped him. A vision of faces, bright as if before his eyes, danced across his mind and he paused.

    He thought of his friends of the group, how they would seem if they could see him about to fall back on old practices, and Vlad pulled the claw away. He could not do this, could not disappoint them. The demon of his despair roared and slashed at him, trying to throttle his emotions, but Vlad stepped away from it and sheathed his claws again.

    "I am my own master," he breathed. "Even if it as the behest of others' feelings."

    Vlad smiled at his tiny victory and overlooked the snow-white stretch of the Alpine Lake, stillness twinkling and glittering like his long fangs gleaming in the moonlight. Vlad withdrew the canines and tightened the grip of his control, containing his darkness as he strode to the lake's edge, the eerie silence stirring thousands of thoughts. Trees lined the shores, their long silhouettes dripping with shadows.

Dropping a bag upon the ice, Vlad stood a moment and mused on his place in time.

'I am here at this beautiful place once more, come to take back that which I knew I would need one day.'

The lake waters had long frozen over in the mountain frost yet Vlad felt nothing on his bare forearms. *'I trace the first of many steps over the paths of my past. Now there is a flowery thought, even for me.'*

He walked out across the paper-thin ice, not caring for how the water shifted beneath, nor for the spider's web of cracks that followed even his light stride. He stopped above the right place and lowered a small section of his control, allowing a sliver of power to seep out. His senses penetrated the ice and sank into the frigid depths below, diving further and further until Vlad felt the presence of something wrong to his kind. It was ruinously heavy, a vicious poison to the *touch* of his power.

He could have gone anywhere for the material in question but these items were of the purest quality, the strongest of their kind. Vlad had made sure of that when he had buried them three centuries ago.

He sighed then stamped, hard. The ice burst apart like an explosion of glass, water crashing over him in sparkling waves, and Vlad fell into the lake. Immediately he swam, the depths closing in as he relied on his senses for guidance. Needing no breath, his heart remained still as his power grew throughout his body, giving his muscles strength, accelerating his descent.

Vlad reached the lakebed, over a hundred feet down, and sought the anchor-rock, the sensations of arctic char and rainbow trout all about him as fish curiously approached his ghostly form.

Finally, Vlad found the massive rock and reached down. His fingers found its base. He recalled the boulder was over three tonnes but he hauled it up and threw it aside as if it was twenty pounds.

Blood and Biscuits

There, in an airtight box of stone and tree amber sealing, was what he had come for. Vlad unbound the chest from its rusted chains and it buoyed up immediately. He held on tightly as the box shot through the water and broke the surface with a deafening crash.

Dragging the chest up onto the thin ice, Vlad carried the whole thing back towards the shoreline, his clothes freezing to his skin. Upon the darkling shore, he set the box down and broke it open – the lid cracked apart with a satisfying *hiss* and musty air from three centuries ago exhaled into a new world. The influence immediately leached into his darkness; Vlad would not have long, perhaps a matter of hours at most.

Drawing on gloves from his canvas bag, Vlad removed the contents. He placed them carefully in the bag, joining four iron pegs and a spare set of clothes he had packed before leaving England. He tied the bag shut and shivered as his power slowly sucked from behind his control. This was not like being hungry, this was an outside force drawing on his darkness like a leech draws blood from a wound.

He eyed the moon through the beautiful evergreens and knew his time ran thin. Enshrouding himself in his waning power, Vlad erupted from the shoreline in a shower of dancing jewels, droplets spraying as he disappeared, wrapped in a cloak of shadow. The items in the bag dragged at his strength, slowly breaking apart the mental walls of his control, devouring his energy reserves.

Vlad sped for over an hour until he came at last to the skies above the north of England. Cloud water dripped from his brow, power faded considerably. He aimed at the ground, near St Ellin's Island, and saw the industrial complex only he knew the true secrets of, the lights of the abandoned church to the north. Despite his weakness, Vlad smiled.

Then his strength failed completely and he fell a thousand feet through the sky towards the muddy ground, the darkness of his power fluttering away entirely.

Blood and Biscuits

THE WASTELANDS,
ELLIN'S INDUSTRIAL ISLAND.
AN HOUR BEFORE THE SUPPORT GROUP

"*It burns, it dissolves! I can hardly* think *under its weight!*"

Vlad staggered across the seemingly endless wastelands, the heavy bag dangling in his faltering grip, the bones in his arm broken, his right hip shattered from the force of the impact. Both vampire and bag were spattered in mud and oil, the contents enhancing the agony coursing his body.

"*I'm not even touching them and they're burning me. Put them down, step away, set your darkness to heal your bones.*"

Vlad saw a light ahead across the wastelands and tried to increase his pace but the bag's weight was too heavy, his body too broken. He could not stop for the burden he dragged was a gift to alleviate a curse that could otherwise doom the lives of many.

Vlad stumbled a fourth time again and dropped the bag. He was not far from his destination though it felt like a hundred miles.

He was exhausted and he stumbled a fifth time.

RUINS OF ST ELLIN'S CHURCH.
THE START OF THE SUPPORT GROUP.

"Where's Cain? He's usually one of the first to arrive."

"He will be here, do not fret, Jacob," Vlad said. "Something is different about the island and I think it is because he is walking upon it. He will be exhausted so go easy on him." Despite the vampire's weakened senses, he felt confident. He had a great purpose this week, hidden in the canvas bag at the basement's far end, a hundred feet away. "Furthermore, I have taken the liberty of bringing Jaffa cakes this time. Cain is a synthetic fruit flavour man, as we all know. I do not think his wolf nose will miss the opportunity."

Blood and Biscuits

Absentmindedly, Vlad stroked sensation back into his forearms. The bag had left its mark on him, he knew he would be recovering over the next hour. His shattered hip had knitted itself neatly back together, now he waited for the last processes of darkness-ossification to heal his radius and ulna.

'It is worth the price,' Vlad told himself. *'At least the black veins have gone, I need not answer those particular questions.'*

"It's good the light's working fine," Jacob noted, pointing up at the ceiling. "Energy savers used to take a lot longer to heat but this is good quality. The wiring's surprisingly fine under the bracket, too, so no repairs needed right now. If we're planning on being here long-term, though, you might want to invest in some tools so I can properly work on the circuit. I'd use my own but I lost 'em ages ago when I turned, and I can't afford rent, let alone new electrical gizmos."

"I will look into it," Vlad said simply, letting his gaze track the ceiling thoughtfully. Sarah had not yet arrived, which was the first time the ghost had not entered before the vampire. "Perhaps there are several things we can do to this place to make it homelier, though we would need Sarah's permission. We cannot very well make changes to somebody else's house without their say-so."

"What do you think she'd do if we did?" Jacob asked hypothetically.

"Oh, I assume her vengeance would be swift and severe," Vlad muttered. "I have never heard of a completely passive spirit before, and though our dear friend emanates a wonderful charm I have seen flashes of anger in her. It is a common trait, part of the emotional imprint of their souls. As I have told you in private, Jacob, all ghosts hold grudges. Be glad she is not a poltergeist."

"I'll bear that in mind," Jacob said and he wandered away to talk to Lucy by the coffee stand. Vlad looked at them both then decided on something.

"Lucy?" he called over and the banshee looked round pleasantly. "Avoid that bag over there, it will do you no good."

Blood and Biscuits

Her face dropped momentarily.

"Is it what I think it is?" she enquired darkly.

"That depends but most probably, yes. Jacob will be fine but you and I had best avoid it as much as we can. We need not weaken ourselves." Vlad rubbed his forearms again. The crash landing without the protection of his darkness had been particularly painful. "You need not worry, it is for none of us," Vlad finished and Lucy nodded tightly.

She turned to speak with Jacob. Despite the fact they were forty feet away and muttering quietly, Vlad heard every word.

"How're you doing?" the wraith asked the banshee. "Last week you sort of ran off because of your, um…"

Lucy spoke as Vlad started gathering chairs and arranging them in a circle.

"Because of my binding. It's alright, Jay, you can say it. I'm more than used to it by now, even if I haven't accepted its power over me, and I told you all because I wanted you to know. And yeah, I guess I'm fine. The place is so damned big I feel like I've not seen it all. I lurked around the rooftops, too, saw lots of stuff. You know, there's an old observatory beyond the massive garden complex; I've never had the courage to see inside but I might break in there one day."

Jacob said something but Vlad dampened his senses, suddenly feeling he was eavesdropping. He felt a flash of shame. He did not want to encroach on peoples' privacy, that was not the point of the Support Group. Yet his treacherous mind still teased thoughts of an old mansion on a hill with undiscovered mysteries.

"I feel something dark here," a voice echoed from behind. Jacob jumped and Vlad saw Sarah descending through the ceiling. She was opaque this evening. Vlad smiled at her as she positioned herself above her seat and nodded to everyone in turn as they greeted her. "It's in that big bag over there. Ahh, I did look forward to this gathering. I can almost remember the feeling of being around people when you're all here."

"And that is precisely why I began this group," Vlad said as he positioned the last chair. "Thank you for returning to us, I always look forward to seeing you."

"You shall see, hear, and experience," Sarah said pleasantly and then she hummed a tune, her feet kicking in time to the quiet rhythm. "Experience, experience, experience," she muttered merrily.

Vlad discerned Jacob approach.

"Seven seats?" the wraith asked confusedly. "There's only six of us. And one's only ceremonial at best," he added quietly, nodding slyly to Sarah. "You expecting someone?"

"I suppose I am," Vlad replied. "Somebody I met the weekend just gone, quite unexpectedly, I might add. She is...rather extraordinary. Just like all of you, I hasten to further add. If she arrives then you shall see what I mean."

Jacob smiled knowingly, the flesh of his face warping and pitching aside, revealing the rotten musculature beneath. Vlad peered at him in that instant and saw just how handsome Jacob was, irrespective of his damage.

"You know me, I like almost anyone I meet. Lucy and me are quite close now and Fable's already a dear friend. I think I'm slightly in love with Sarah, she's so fascinating. I even wore Cain down in the end, though if the full moon's due next week I think we'll find him back to that irritable, grumpy man we first encountered."

"It is a *blue moon*, Jacob, grumpy will be an understatement. Interestingly, it is the first blue moon coinciding with Halloween for seventy-six years," Vlad said. "But never mind that, I have a plan that will hopefully help Cain's suffering soul. Ahh, Lucy, how are you?"

The banshee finally walked over, coffee perched with considered delicacy in her hand as she pretended to survey the vampire sternly. Then, with a grin, she opened her arms and gave Vlad a short hug. There was more than just meaning in that brief embrace, there also lay the foundations of true kinship. It was a

Blood and Biscuits

beautiful moment and when Lucy released him her face seemed to reciprocate. Then the banshee smacked Jacob on the arm playfully and laughed at him.

"Don't look at me like that, you vegan git, I *am* capable of human emotion, you know."

"I didn't say a thing!" Jacob exclaimed, rubbing his arm. "I was reeling from Vlad admitting he met a young lady this weekend at a...actually, you never said how you met her."

"Ooooh, a young lady, eh?" Lucy said suggestively.

"Oh for God's sake, I outstretch her years by several dozen factors at least," Vlad defended, playing down his age. "Besides, I have sworn off matters of the heart, they never last well for me. And to answer your question, Jacob," Vlad continued as they took their seats in the usual positions – there was nothing set in stone, everybody simply reacted as creatures of habit always do – "I met this woman at a gathering, of sorts."

"A gathering..." Jacob repeated oddly, sounding the word out slowly. "Like this one? Or more of a 'leave your keys in the bowl and grab a towel' sort of situation?"

"No, goodness no, nothing like that! So unsanitary. And you are the only Support Group for me," Vlad smiled. "No, this was huge; hundreds of people, very loud live music, copious amounts of alcohol. I am not entirely sure how I ended up there, in truth, I was extended an invitation online and I decided to take a step towards self-help and ignore the inner voice always hounding me."

"I've heard some people visualise a black dog hunting them, is that how your depression manifests for you?" Lucy asked.

Vlad nodded.

"Despair can come in many forms but for me it seems as if I have this spectre, this demonic force, always following me, always waiting to pounce. Then, one day, it will strike without warning and drag me down in its dark embrace and I will be consumed in that roiling sorrow once more, unable to escape until the demon exhausts itself. I gave it a ridiculous name to disarm him but it had no effect."

Blood and Biscuits

"God, that must be awful," Jacob muttered, clasping his hands in his lap. "I can't imagine how you live day by day with that always snapping at your heels."

"How does anyone do it? They survive. As a vampire, I am forever one step from hell, and as a man I am weighed by the gravity of my mind, pulling me down when all I long for is to be free. However, I am no worse off than anyone else, and I do not pretend to be. I simply hope each day sees Cuthbert one step behind me and not hovering above, waiting to drop."

"You called your demon Cuthbert," Jacob said, hardly able to suppress a smirk.

"Indeed, Cuthbert Peters. He insists on dogging my every step and so I insist on normalising him with a ludicrous name."

Lucy snorted as she tried to ask another question.

"I guess you don't feel like…Cuthbert's descended on you today," Lucy said, biting her lip.

Vlad thought on the matter, considered the impact his journey from Switzerland had had on his body, then shook his head.

"He most definitely has not for I feel lighter, strangely. There are things I can do to stave off Cuthbert, such as keeping myself as occupied as possible; I find work and technical distractions of the mind amongst the best remedies, though the greatest method is significant social contact."

"Yeah, certainly sounds it by the way you partied at a festival all weekend."

Every head turned to the entrance. Framed in the doorway, and looking worse than ever before, was Cain. He was unshaven and his hair, where it had recently been styled and washed, now hung in greasy locks. His dark, heavy eyes held evidence of sleeplessness, and when he stepped into the room, he stumbled and pitched forwards. In a flash, Vlad was beside him, catching him by the shoulders and helping him to his seat, ignoring his burning arms. Cain stank of fried chicken, the scent seemed to encompass him entirely.

Cain nodded appreciatively as Vlad moved across to make two cups of coffee, both for the dishevelled arrival.

"Jesus, you look like crap," Lucy hissed, leaning forward with a worried look on her face. "Really properly rough."

Cain grinned.

"Gee, what a wonderful sentiment, Lucille. Sorry, all, I stopped for grub on the way, got caught up with a mean Hen Commandments chicken meal deal with Onion Slather Sauce."

"Oh eurgh," Jacob grimaced. "You're making me feel sick. You should just have some brains like a decent person."

"Cain, you are disgusting," Lucy agreed, yet something else peeled off her. Was it worry?

"Hello, Cain," Sarah said, pausing her singing. "Thank you and your smell for joining us. The room is balanced again."

"Hi Sarah, it's good to be back." Cain suddenly sneezed then shook his head like a wet dog. "God damn it, bloody allergies are back. Where're my pills," he muttered, patting down his pockets. "Ahh for Christ's sake, I've left them at home!"

"Looking for antihistamines, Cain?" Vlad asked casually without looking up from the coffee table. He held up a fresh packet brought along for this exact situation. Cain strode forwards and took the pack quickly, then he added ashamedly:

"Sorry, didn't mean to snatch." He walked away, pressing out two pills. Swallowing them dry, he sighed: "It's good to see you, too, Vlad. Oh, and Vlad?"

"Yes, Cain," the vampire intoned with care as he tipped coffee granules into the mugs and added hot water.

"I can smell orange. Have you got what I think you've got?"

"Good God, the packet is still *sealed*," Vlad said. "Even *I* have to concentrate to smell them through the plastic."

Cain shrugged.

Vlad returned eight seconds later with two mugs of coffee and an entire box of Jaffa cakes. Cain whooped and smiled broadly, his eyes recovering some of their vigour.

Blood and Biscuits

"Thank you, thank you, thank you!" Cain growled enthusiastically as he tore open the pack and stuffed three cakes into his mouth immediately. In a muffled way, he said: "Bin liffin' on cheap beanff and fftale bread ve pafft few dayff." He swallowed noisily. "Barely able to make it to work. Ugh," he added, poking his finger into his mouth, "got some stuck in me teeth. Actually," he added, sucking his molars, "that was chicken. Nice."

"You are extremely welcome," Vlad replied smoothly, retaking his seat. Sarah resettled her hover with an almost daintiness. "A festival, you say."

"Sure sounds it," Cain grumbled, drinking his first coffee like a parched man given water. "Oof, I needed that. This place have tonnes of teenagers covered in fluorescent paint inside a big sweaty tent with some horrid beat poundin', pretendin' it's music?"

"No, but there was a considerable number of middle-aged humans with ribbons in their dreadlocks, and a lot of steady fiddle and guitar music. I recall a band named 'Gary Davis and the Seedlings' and another called 'The Compost Boys.' There *were* tents – one was specifically for washboard and harmonica bands. The whole thing was fascinating."

Jacob burst into a fit of laughter as Lucy nudged him in the ribs and smiled gleefully.

"That's my positive of the week!" she announced happily.

"You and me both, I was already having quite a good one as it was," Jacob chorused, and even Cain managed a chuckle. Vlad simply looked between them all, bewilderment plain on his face.

"What? Would somebody please explain to me what is so funny?"

Jacob looked at him seriously as Lucy tried to stifle her laughter with a custard cream and, when that failed, her coffee. That failed, too, so she simply turned away from Vlad and spluttered.

"Mate," the wraith began, and Lucy snorted into her drink by mistake. "Compost Boys are a Celtic band. And Gary Davis has been dipping in and outta' the festival circuits for years with different lineups. Last I heard, he was with the 'Twig Twins'. You were at a *folk* festival."

"Good heavens! Is that what that was! I was wondering why there was so much cider. And the lack of shoes was disturbing. People at folk festivals have a large preference for discussing the political climate, I found. Most surprising, considering hardly any could stand straight, let alone hold a serious debate on political complexities."

"It is a wonder," Cain muttered happily as Lucy howled in her seat and Jacob struggled to sip his ice water through a curious cough he had developed. Sarah's humming took on a more melodic tone. "So how the hell'd you end up there?" Cain asked.

"My new friend invited me," Vlad admitted thoughtfully, drinking his coffee and feeling the warmth of it heat the length of his cold throat like a furnace. He could have sworn he almost tasted it this time. "And no, it is nothing of a romantic nature, my lupine friend. She thought it would be a nice, neutral place to meet for the first time and she happened to have free tickets. She told me it was a surprise, hence my confusion. She is very nervous and this was a huge step for her; I would not want her to feel in any way overwhelmed at this group."

"I'm sure she was perfectly well treated," Lucy said, two spots of colour back in her pale cheeks. "If nothing else, all you've presented to us is that you're an utter gentleman."

"Aye, and a scholar," Cain said, finishing his first coffee and picking up the second. He pointed at the empty mug on the floor. "And no more tricks, Vlad. You shook me up good and proper last week and I'm determined not to let you get the better of me again."

"Yes, sorry about that. I own few cups and you were about to smash one. Anyway, this is all beside the point. How *are* you all? How have your weeks been?" Vlad glanced to the door and he felt his senses finally return to their full strength. There was a new force upon the island. "She is on the island. Her arrival will be imminent."

"Ok, that's creepy," Jacob said, the smile leaving his face. He paused and assessed something. "I'm happy to start, it's just where to begin. Umm…well I'm more confident now, certainly in front of you all. No judgements, no stupid balaclava, no more hesitating. It's great, you've all been brilliant with me."

"No problem, we're all here for somethin'," Cain said in what Vlad surmised was meant to be a warmly reflective tone but instead came out as a cold growl.

"Yeah, and this week's been good for me 'cause I didn't have to rob any graves."

"How'd you manage that?" Lucy probed and Jacob grinned.

"Turns out Fable's got a contact at a morgue, and they're more than happy to siphon a few bits of cortex and spinal column from the more intact of the deceased for a couple pounds. You know, the ones who've died of stuff not related to the brain and whose families won't go asking questions about why granny's left hemisphere's missing. Oh yeah, it turns out I can eat spinal cord *and* drink the fluid, who knew? Everything central nervous system-related is up for munchies."

"That *is* fascinating," Vlad murmured genuinely as Lucy's face turned somehow paler and Cain made a noise into his coffee.

"Fable let me stay at hers instead of that awful bedsit, so I've had hot water for the first time in months, and I can walk around without being stared at."

"That is fantastic," Vlad said. "And where is our beloved faerie? She is noticeably absent. The one walking across Ellin's Island is not her, though she *does* identify as female."

The room went quiet and Vlad looked round. Fable stood in the doorway. She smiled broadly, a hint of apology in her eyes.

"I am late," she said lightly as she stepped down into the high-vaulted room. "I am sorry, I had every intention of coming several minutes early but there was a disturbance in my magic and I had no choice but to acknowledge it, to balance it in my mind. These imbalances happen sometimes; I think it is because I have found myself a roommate."

Jacob smiled awkwardly as Fable gazed deeply at him.

"I forget you can circumvent my senses, Fable, and lateness is no issue here. Besides, we have not properly started yet," Vlad said as the faerie strode in and headed for the coffee table. "Do please help yourself; I know you are not a coffee drinker but I hoped perhaps to tempt you with some herbal tea? My new friend said that she was rather partial to fennel and rosehip. She said it had something to do with *her* magic…"

"There's another mage on their way?" Fable asked with interest. "That is wonderful to hear – oh!"

"Everything ok?" Jacob called over.

"Vlad, I…don't know what to say," Fable muttered. "Dairy free custard creams and raspberry and nettle tea, how did you know?"

"I overheard you and Lucy discussing them on your way home last week."

"Vlad, we were half a mile away by that point!" Lucy said, shocked. "Walking past the old mill limits, I remember that clearly. There's no way you heard us."

"I did not mean to pry, only you were both enjoying yourselves loudly and I am quite in-tune with this island now…"

"No, I didn't mean you were spying, I'm just impressed with your hearing! God, I wish I had such a blessing."

"It is not quite as you describe," Vlad admitted quietly. "Though it has had its uses, in many different capacities."

Fable came to the circle with her steaming tea and a handful of vegan-friendly biscuits, and everyone in the room settled, the mood brightening to a familiar tone. Sarah deepened her humming and even though he looked rough, Cain managed a smile.

"To answer your earlier question, Fable," Vlad continued, "there is another mage arriving, yes, and from my current deductions she is about three minutes away."

"I look forward to meeting her," Fable said, her blackened hands less nervous than previous weeks.

"Indeed," Vlad said with finality. He clapped gently and smiled at everyone. "Jacob has spoken but how was the week for the rest of you?"

"Shouldn't we wait for your friend?" Lucy asked worriedly, indicating the empty entranceway for emphasis. Vlad shook his head.

"Oh no, she told me to carry on as normal. Judging by her characteristics, I do not think she would enjoy us waiting for her. Best to act as if nothing has changed so she can slip in unnoticed. Cain, would you care to carry this on?"

"I s'pose," the werewolf grunted. He sneezed explosively again and shrugged resignedly. "As I've already mentioned, my allergies are back."

"*Welcome back, allergies,*" Sarah sang. "*We've missed your sneezy shakes!*"

"Yeah, they're a real peach. It's incredible, havin' my immune system attackin' my own body, really top-notch fun. I can't tell you enough about it."

"But the full moon's not for another week," Jacob pointed out. "What's brought this on so early?"

"It's a *blue* moon – October first and now October thirty-first. S'always worse leadin' up to a blue moon." Cain shifted and glanced at Vlad, expecting some sort of response. All the vampire gave was a thin, bloodless pursing of his lips. This was not his time to speak. Cain trudged on, each word coming thick and heavy, dragging through the man's exhaustion. "Blue moons are beyond torturous; not much can stop a werewolf under one of them. I've missed work, I'm barely holdin' onto my job, I've been kicked out my hostel for speaking disrespectful to the staff, and to top it off I ain't slept in days outta' fear. It's better down in here, I'm not so angry, but still."

Blood and Biscuits

Cain put his face in his hands and rested there for a moment. Vlad felt a spark of empathy, the man struggling to keep his head above water. Vlad hoped they as a group could do something before it was too late, before Cain's curse thrust him deeper down the spiral of rage and self-hatred he inched towards.

Vlad glanced to the bag at the far end of the basement again. Hope filled his voice, a longing to help.

"Focus on who you are, Cain. I know it sounds cliché but I swear it will keep your thoughts straight and this tidal wave of self-loathing at bay. I will not sugar-coat it: this will be extremely difficult, but remember also where you are. You have been through this before and you can survive again. This group was started to aid people like you, and in-turn you have already helped us in ways you cannot imagine."

"How can you stop this, Vlad?" Cain rumbled, staring at his long fingers as if he already saw iron-hard claws and thick hair. "The pain that'll come, I can already feel it growin' down my back, like it's baring its teeth at me excitedly." Cain's eyes grew narrow in desperation, tears pricking the corners. He looked down in shame and indignity, pangs of revulsion affecting his pride. "When it comes it'll destroy me again, and no amount of biscuits and therapy sessions can stop it."

"That is where you are wrong, my friend."

Cain peered up under a heavy-lidded gaze, his eyes darkened by misery. Vlad detected the weakest ember of faith in him, aching for flames.

"No?"

"No, not if I have anything to do with it. You might have lost your hostel but as long as Sarah permits it, you are always welcome here. There may not be warmth but there is light, and there is the promise of the holy ground we sit upon to keep your change at bay."

"But it's the *blue moon*, Vlad," Cain emphasised. "It's much worse than any other full moon: blood, harvest, you name it. You said it yourself weeks ago."

"Indeed I did, and to prove it I have a safeguard, to ensure the wolf may never get out. Do you trust me, Cain?" His face passive, Vlad extended his hand across the gulf stretching between both men.

For a moment they stared at one another in an immeasurable display. Vampires and werewolves were notorious enemies, a seething hatred based on the natures of their curses, on blood chemicals and similarities between their uncontrollable urges. Yet here sat a member of each race in a test of supernature, the sheer power of their minds over their matters.

Vlad's hope for Cain's salvation distilled down to that singular moment, when the werewolf would overcome himself or be consumed by his rage and sink into the abyss of his bane, lost forever.

Cain did not know it, and perhaps he never would, but the crossroads he stood at was unique, and all in that basement sat anxiously, awaiting the reckoning that was sure to come. Cain's jaw clenched and unclenched and his fingers twitched but Vlad never dropped his hand until, finally, the werewolf reached out and took his grasp in his own, the living flesh of one curse meeting the dead flesh of another.

There was no magic, no act of the paranormal to signify the gravity of the moment. It was only a handshake yet there was more in it than could exist in the lyric of any spell. Through that connection, Vlad felt something pull loose from the werewolf's heart and untie itself from his soul. The beat of his pulse slowed, the smell of his agitation lessened, and the true man beneath the exhausting anxieties was revealed.

For the first time in many years, Vlad was in some way at peace with the vampire senses he possessed. Without them he would have been unable to witness such an infinitesimally small change in someone else, the slightest alteration enough to turn back a man from the brink of a seemingly inescapable fate and set him on the course for resolution.

Blood and Biscuits

Cain's shoulders slumped and tears finally broke free from the prisons of his eyes. He sniffed loudly, teeth grinding in the shame he felt at his disintegration. Vlad reached forward and gripped his shoulder, willing strength into him as everyone watched a man break down and release all he had walled up within himself. These were the foundations of the person Cain so desperately longed to be.

"I'm terrified," he whispered. "I'm so *scared* and I can't do anything to stop it."

"That is ok. It is *ok* to feel this way."

"Month after month, I wake up with blood on me, more wounds to try explainin' to some doctor. I got no home, got nothin' to call mine, and the last of any family I abandoned years ago 'cause I was terrified of hurting 'em. You say I'm not alone but is that really true?"

"*Yes*, Cain, it *is* true," Vlad hissed. "You would not keep coming back here if it were not."

"Truth be told, mate, I couldn't stand you when we first met," Jacob said and Cain flashed him a hurt look. Jacob grinned slyly. "But it turns out you're a great guy. And I mean that, Cain. Look, we all feel the same way. It's obvious, isn't it? You want to change, you want to stop this, and you're getting help where you can. It sucks what happens to you, it really does. But we're here, Vlad's here, and he says he can help you. So trust him, like we all have."

"He tried helping me with my loneliness," Sarah echoed from across the room quietly. "No-one has ever done that before. People are terrified of *me* but all I want is someone to talk to, if I can't move on. I wouldn't hurt anything, I was never like that in life. Vladislav is our friend, let us treat him as such and he will in-turn."

Lucy and Fable said nothing but the warmth of their faces radiated so much power that Cain sat straighter in his chair. He breathed deeply, hands relaxing in his lap, every word as building blocks for his soul.

"Thanks," he said barely above a mutter, looking away in embarrassment. "I...don't know what to say."

Blood and Biscuits

"Then say nothing," Vlad suggested. "There is nothing *to* say, but there is something to *do*. Cain, would you be so kind as to go and look inside that canvas bag over by the far wall. There are several things inside it you will need if you wish to best this accursed blue moon next week."

"Christ," Cain muttered as he stood and stretched his back; it clicked and clunked into place and Vlad felt through the man's pain the bones of his spine already shifting and growing. "What've you gone and done now, vampire?"

"Just go and see, but please bring it nowhere near Lucy or I. Or even Fable, I am not too sure of the effects on faeries as of yet."

Fable looked confused but Vlad put up a hand.

"Just…be patient. You will see, and hopefully something else will be explained to me."

Every eye followed Cain as he walked. He stopped at the bag and stooped to unfasten the knotted ropes, and Vlad acknowledged the twitch of his senses telling him his new guest had arrived.

'She is waiting outside. Too nervous to come in? Perhaps,' Vlad thought measuredly. *'Or assuming she needs an invitation. Let this moment pass and if she is still not amongst us then go outside and bring her in from the cold. Make sure she knows there is tea.'*

Cain undid the bag and the folds fell back. His eyes grew wide and Vlad *felt* a mixture of surprise, unease, and even relief flood the man. Slowly, Cain reached in and closed his fist around something. He stood slowly, the muscles of his arms and shoulders lifting effortlessly where a normal man would have struggled. He stepped back to show the group.

Jacob gasped and Sarah hovered lower to her seat, her veil fluttering. Fable's mouth dropped and Lucy uttered an audible "Oh my" as Cain drew out the length of a single chain and gazed at it, end-to-end.

"Good God," he said as the thick, heavy links glittered and sparkled in the light of the basement's new energy saver bulb. "Is this…?"

Blood and Biscuits

"Silver," Vlad confirmed. "The very purest, I might add, and that I can prove without a doubt."

"Ahh," Fable breathed slowly, leaning back in her chair, away from the chain. "That is most interesting, Vladislav. Silver does not have the same effect on faeries as it does vampires and banshees, I think, though it does not do us well all the same. We might not be bound by it but the closer we get the more unfocussed we become. Touching that for too long could devastate what little magic I have remaining."

"Then I am glad I put it so far away," Vlad said.

"Strangely, silver does not affect me on my own world, it is natural as we are and all natural things are connected, but on Earth we become untethered to the Eight Realms and so are unbound in other ways, too."

"You know, one day we really must sit and talk about your home, Fable," Vlad said with interest. "Somewhere nice and quiet with a coffee."

"Where did you get that chain, Vlad?" Jacob asked, standing and walking to Cain's side for a better look. "Flawless, absolutely flawless. Look at the way it reflects the light, it's like looking at bright water. It must be worth a fortune."

"*They* are," Vlad emphasised as Cain put down the chain and reached in to pull out three others identical to the first. "And pure silver is astonishingly difficult to work with without alloy impurities, such as with jewellery, and so the work alone did not come cheap, let alone the materials. But I always pay and the smith was very happy with the price. In fact, I believe he retired soon after to a lovely cottage by the sea for the rest of his life with his family and four horses."

Despite silver's influence affecting only some supernatural beings, such as banshees and vampires, Vlad felt a pang of irony every time he was weakened by the metal: they were amongst the only moments he ever felt human again.

Blood and Biscuits

"But...*why* do you have them?" Fable asked as Cain and Jacob stretched the four chains out and began measuring them roughly with their hands. "There must be reasoning behind this, one doesn't simply have a half tonne of silver at their disposal. This would have taken years to collect before processing."

"Also true, but three centuries ago I was a different man, living a life of paranoia that one day I would need these in the event of another vampire's attack. They would be protection. It was the rationality of a madman but, in a sense, I was not altogether wrong. However, it is a werewolf that needs binding and the protection is from himself."

"You can't hide these for three hundred years without somebody eventually stumbling across 'em," Cain said slowly, his attention only half on Vlad as he held the lengths of his salvation, their links clinking almost tunefully across the concrete floor. "Where'd you hide 'em?"

"In a lake in the Swiss Alps," Vlad said easily. "Buried at the bottom in an airtight box to stave off water's oxidative properties."

"Well that answered that succinctly," Jacob said dryly. "When did you have the time to get them since last week? I guess a plane..."

"I took no plane but I did fly back a few hours ago."

"Oh. Oh, right then," the wraith responded in simple surprise. "Maybe when I'm getting the holiday jitters I'll book a flight on Air Vlad instead."

Vlad smiled and allowed the joke to settle before saying,

"Cain, if you look deeper in the bag – ignore the dirty clothes, I crash landed – there should be four iron ring-pegs and a sledgehammer."

Cain sneezed then rummaged and pulled each out.

"Jesus, you carried all of this while flying?" he asked disbelievingly.

"Indeed, and if the silver had not slowly eaten my reserves, I would have arrived a great deal sooner and not required a change of attire. My arm has only just mended itself," Vlad added, shifting a little to set his bones back in order with a series of sickening *clicks*. Lucy dry-heaved quietly. "Before we leave, we will hammer those pegs into the floor and get a mattress for you, presuming Sarah allows you to stay in her home a while."

The ghost bobbed a little on the air. Or *in* the air; she always moved irrespective of the material world, rather like the phantasmic forms of Lucy's hair.

"That is satisfactory with me," Sarah sighed beautifully. "Perhaps the werewolf knows a song or two I do not and my magic music box can lull us to sleep with foreign fancies unheard by these hallowed halls. I could watch you sleep again and play games with your dreams, how fun!"

"Sounds delightful," Cain muttered, a scared look to him.

"I might even float inside you and use your eyes as my own," Sarah giggled.

Cain shivered visibly.

"Then as long as you are happy here for a little while, Cain, we shall be able to help you through the blue moon, agreed?"

"Why not, eh? Sounds like a wild party."

There was a brief silence as the room evidently thought of what to say next. Vlad allowed the members to soak up the information given; he knew it was a lot to absorb and possibly appeared even a little mad to them.

"While you all deliberate, I will go and greet our guest," Vlad said quietly, standing gracefully. "She has been waiting for some time."

He left the group to wonder over the silver chains – Cain and Jacob picked up the iron pegs and sledgehammer and viewed them thoughtfully. The vampire ascended the entrance stairs and looked beyond the open doorway. Peering through the swallowing darkness, he saw the river mists curling and obscuring the waxing moon, casting strange white forms across the eerie island.

She stood to the side, back to the wall, hands fidgeting nervously. Vlad did not want to startle her. He spoke delicately, considerately.

"Hello, Alizon, it is good to see you again."

Despite the gentle tone, the young woman jumped and stood away from the wall. She put her hands up in the darkness and tripped over her own words.

"I...I...I am s-sorry, I didn't m-mean to loiter. I...I..."

"Alizon, Alizon, Alizon," Vlad repeated, the use of her name helping ease her disruption. "It is quite alright, you did nothing wrong. I did say that when you arrived you were perfectly welcome to come down and meet us, but please do not feel as if you have wronged us in any way."

"I am sorry," she said again, hands pressed together as she gave a small bow of her head earnestly.

"Please stop apologising," Vlad said as he stepped out to meet her. He kept his tall body stooped so as to not appear overbearing; he knew Alizon struggled with large men as it was and he would not have her anymore overwhelmed than she undoubtedly already felt. "And before you further apologise for being late, I might inform you that most people here have arrived late one time or another. I was nearly late today, so do not fret and fuss over unnecessary details."

"O-ok," Alizon muttered, her eyes never once meeting Vlad's. "I didn't en-enjoy the festival as m-m-much as I'd hoped, it was too loud. Your f-friends, down there - do you th-think they will like me?" she asked worriedly, her facial expressions not quite matching her fears.

"I hardly see any reason why they should not," Vlad replied and Alizon smiled nervously. The relief *smelled* genuine to Vlad but it did not reach her eyes and her body language remained neutral. "You will find no blame or any sort of judgement here. We are a calm group, one designed only to listen, to help where possible. I will go first, that might help you ease into the room, alright?"

Blood and Biscuits

Alizon nodded tightly, fingers trembling as Vlad turned and led the way. He had only gone two steps before a small hand plucked at his shirt. Vlad looked back and saw Alizon staring beyond him, her mouth open in a small 'o'.

"Is something the matter?" he asked gently.

"There...is an-another magic caster here," she said quickly, fingers twirling through the air as if playing some invisible instrument. "A faerie, their hands...burned by misuse."

"Astonishing," Vlad breathed, awe reaching his voice. "You are quite brilliant, do not ever let anyone tell you any different."

Another small smile played on Alizon's lips. Once more it did not reach her eyes, though Vlad knew she meant it.

"Shall we continue?" he asked.

"Yes," came her short reply. To another person Alizon might have sounded rude but Vlad knew better. What she said and what she meant were two highly different things, and nothing was delivered purposefully curt.

"I promise, you will find only quietness and order down here. There is nothing to be shy of."

Vlad descended back to the basement as a scene unfurled before them. He stopped, eyes wide, and Alizon looked from behind him, hands covering her mouth in shock.

All chairs had been pushed back and Lucy and Fable were watching intently as Jacob and Cain began taking turns smashing four iron pegs into the floor at the far end of the basement, the dull shocks bouncing round the room as everyone laughed and cheered. Cain's allergies made him sneeze in rhythm to the sledgehammer's strikes and Sarah guided their swings, telling them where best to put the pegs to avoid disturbing the *balance* of the church.

"I am gone for three minutes and this is the chaos that ensues?" Vlad asked. He did not bolster his voice, the sheer magnitude of his presence alone halting proceedings as all turned to look at him and the newcomer, her face only partially revealed behind the vampire. Vlad smiled at the group. "I am not your father, you really have nothing to be ashamed of. I am perhaps upset that I missed the fun but aside from that…"

Vlad moved slowly into the basement, not to make a point but to give Alizon the opportunity to decide for herself how she would approach the room. As he suspected, the enchantress followed him closely as he picked up two chairs and moved them back into the circle. Without saying a word, everyone did the same. Cain stood the sledgehammer against a wall and Lucy placed the iron pegs on the floor. They moved back into position as if slow dancing; Vlad watched them curiously, realising quickly that his very reappearance had invited back the shadows of foreboding. Even though all were present due to his invitation, none were there purely to continue the feelings of despondency admissions of grief and sadness caused. Friendships had formed and they were amongst the group's most important results.

"Everyone, may I be the first to introduce a new friend of mine I met last week, I –"

Vlad felt a tap on his arm. He glanced round at Alizon; she muttered something into her hand only he heard.

"Oh, excuse me: *she* met *me*. Yes, the purpose of the meet was so she might get to know somebody like herself, a very brave move on her part. I told her about this group and that I thought it would help her. So, everyone, this is Alizon."

The newcomer didn't meet anyone's gaze but turned her head to each person as Vlad spoke their names. All were pleasant enough though Vlad could sense unease in the air, an imbalance towards this Alizon who had disturbed the group's harmony.

"This was at that festival you mentioned," Cain said, doing his best to keep his face neutral for Alizon so she felt no threat, Vlad guessed. It would not have mattered; Vlad suspected Alizon had no real notion of how to interpret the subtlety of facial expressions.

"Indeed, it was a most joyous occasion," Vlad confirmed. "But please, let us speak on as if we had not stopped. Cain, did you have anything to add about your week?"

Blood and Biscuits

Cain shook his head, closed and walled up once more.

"No, nothin'. Lookin' forward to gettin' a mattress for the corner and gettin' them chains in place for, uh…*next* week, I guess."

"I shall deliver the mattress after the session is over. It is memory foam, if that is any comfort."

"Couldn't tell you what that is if I tried," Cain admitted.

"Top quality," Jacob explained. "Orthopaedic. It'll be good for your back."

"Oh," Cain said in pleasant surprise. "Smashin' then."

The group took turns regaling their weeks. Lucy had ultimately ignored the hidden grounds of her mansion and instead taken a few tentative visits into town by herself. Jacob had moved into Fable's place properly and the two were currently working out how they could make an income without going outside. Sarah had spent most of her time with her 'magic music box'. As they spoke, Vlad quietly suggested to Alizon that she make herself a cup of tea. She seemed relieved and stood up quickly to move to the coffee table. Vlad wondered how long the young woman could cope being in a group before she needed to remove herself. While the festival had been much bigger, she had shared no space or conversational attempts with strangers; now, she was forced into a tight circle and expected to speak. All eyes were on her.

"Thank you for sharing," Vlad said as Sarah finished and hovered high above her chair again. "I suppose the second question, then. Does anyone have anything to get off their chests? Positive or negative, it matters not. Whatever you need to share."

Vlad looked round and naturally peered at Lucy. She smiled thinly.

"My walks into town, they've been nice. Saw a few happy people out and about, not that they saw me. Banshee invisibility's still a thing, so that's a negative, though I didn't feel a scream coming on or anything, so I guess that's positive."

"Good," Vlad said. "Considering any of them could be due a death soon, that was courageous to take that step. And Jacob, anything to say?"

"Oh, this and that," he began. "But no, I don't really have anything, surprisingly. Quite cheerful this week. No more thoughts about, you know…dark things…" Jacob cleared his throat as Vlad observed him. "I haven't done for a couple weeks now. Had a few online discussions about veganism, watched a couple DVDs with a cheap TV Fable and I managed to pick up, ate some tasty brains. New and usual, all at once."

"I am glad you have found some measure of harmony in your life, Jacob," Vlad said. "However turbulent or temporary that might feel. Let us hope it lasts and you can build from it."

As they spoke, Vlad noticed Alizon finish making her tea and move away from the table. However, instead of coming straight back to the circle she edged *round* the room as if spiralling in. Nobody else seemed to notice, their focus entirely on one another. She moved round and round until, at last, she returned to her seat and sat lightly upon it, as if the chair itself might attack her.

"Fable?" Vlad pushed as if nothing had happened. "Anything to add?"

"Not particularly," she said and Vlad knew there was a caginess to the group with the new arrival awkwardly staring between them all without actually meeting their eyes. "There has been less pain in my hands, which is obviously a relief."

"You still have magic, though," Alizon added suddenly, her quiet voice cutting through with a strange power. "I can feel it."

"Indeed," Fable said, crossing her legs. "I struggle sometimes admitting to myself what I did to burn my hands. I think perhaps if I might one day find peace with my past, I could look to the future to see what it holds for me."

"The pledge I made last week to you – to all of you – still stands firm," Vlad said seriously. "This is not the end for us. There are wonders in the world every day; there is no reason why any one of us cannot find salvation of a kind. And so with that in mind...Sarah, do you have anything you might want to get off your chest?"

"Oh perhaps," she replied mistily, her veil always hiding her face. "Though I love my music box I find that void of loneliness still creeping back to me as it always does. As one song dies and another has yet to find voice, I once more remember I am still trapped by my church – it will be nice to have a big strong werewolf about the place for a little while. I'm thinking about serenading him..."

"Oh Jesus," Cain growled worriedly as Jacob howled with mirth and Lucy laughed into the last of her coffee.

"I don't understand," Alizon said nervously. "They're laughing but I didn't hear a joke." Vlad leant to the side and whispered in return.

"They are only mocking Cain out of mutual friendship, nothing more. There is nought here to worry about."

"Ahh, ok," was all she responded with. Vlad glanced at the young woman briefly, taking the measure of her without her knowledge.

The vampire knew Alizon held a deep and thrumming strength beneath her flesh yet the plain-seeming person sitting slumped and awkward looked anything but a pillar of magic. Her round face was constantly confused or worried, lines furrowed her brow deeply, and her thick-lensed glasses kept slipping down her nose on worn arm hinges. Vlad supposed that aesthetically there was nothing remarkable about the young woman, but in her own way, she was astounding to consider.

"Vlad," Lucy said and the vampire returned his full attentions to the room. "Do you have anything to get off your chest? We know you had a good weekend, at least, what with the festival and everything." Cain shot a tired grin at Jacob and the wraith tipped an eyebrow knowingly, the rotten flesh of his face pulling strangely, revealing more of the tendons underneath.

Vlad relaxed his body and sipped the last of his coffee, placing the mug down, letting the pottery's *clink* draw all eyes to him.

"I have kept myself constantly busy but have done nought of any real note this past week other than take a short trip to the Alpines. I feel as if I have nothing new to share with you all. However, if we delve into the smallest details then perhaps I have had less in the way of dour moods lately; I am not sure why but I have felt brighter these past few days than I have in decades. I can remember clearly every moment I have lived as a vampire and yet almost none of my previous lives have allowed me such emotional clarity."

"Not to sound arrogant or self-centred," Jacob began, "but things have changed for you."

"How do you mean?"

"Well…" the wraith hesitated. "You have *us*. You've shared some dark stuff with us and we with you; that kind of honesty comes with a wee price and we're all paying it now. It makes us closer and gives us more of a purpose, y'know? Something to look forward to, seeing one another." Jacob's Edinburgh accent thickened as he spoke more confidently and Vlad suspected that as the man issued words of welcoming warmth so too did the feelings of home grow in him. With his speech came the roots of his past.

"I do, Jacob, I really do," Vlad smiled. "And I suppose that is ultimately what I would like to get off my chest: I am glad we are all here, right now, in this dingy little basement." Everyone chuckled, all except Alizon, who seemed more agitated by the group's acceptance of the mild rebukes of one another and their place of meeting.

Vlad found they had somehow ended the second question and again he hesitated. "We seem to be perching once more before the doors of the next question, I am unsure –"

"Wait," Cain muttered, finishing his second coffee noisily and pointing bluntly at Alizon. Silently, Vlad cursed himself for not acting quicker to move the conversation along. "Why's she not said anything?"

"Nobody has to say anything if they don't want to," Lucy said darkly, admonishing tone levelled at Cain. "That's not the point."

"But why'd she come, then? Seems she might want to get a couple things off her chest, given she came late an' all. Alizon, is it?"

The newcomer looked up, her eyes never meeting the werewolf's.

"Y-yes," she responded nervously.

"How's your week been?" Cain asked roughly. "Done anythin' special?"

"I...I don't want to..." Alizon stammered and Lucy reached across to touch her lightly on the shoulder, comfortingly. However, Alizon moved away so Lucy could not reach, the banshee's hand falling short. "P-please, don't. I don't want..."

"Alizon, it is alright," Vlad said smoothly, looking hard at Cain. He thought the werewolf would back down but the man's eyes were lit by something, like an unquenchable fire. "Cain, please remember that this is an open group and people are free to speak or not speak as they choose. It is common for new members of any gathering to hold back and remain silent for a while so they might establish their comfort. We are to support only."

"All she'd have to say is 'I don't have anythin' to say'. Then she can go back to bein' quiet 'til the next question. S'always best to talk, we all know this now," Cain noted tactlessly. Vlad knew he was trying to be helpful but the stirring rise of the blue moon was grinding down Cain's already often coarse tone, the inherent anger underpinning a werewolf's transformations arriving earlier than normal. Cain was not himself but that did not excuse the fact that Alizon was clearly feeling distressed.

Vlad assessed the growing aggression in Cain's insistence and decided he would not be able to pacify the situation without help.

He slipped a tiny panel of his control aside and pushed a single thread of influence into his words. It was not the same as mastery, not really, but Vlad still felt a trickle of vileness towards himself for resorting to a similar power.

"Cain, that is enough. Please, go and get some more Jaffa cakes and allow five minutes' calm to enter you."

The werewolf stared for a minute longer and then, predictably, he stood, straightened his shirt, and strode over to the coffee table, shoulders tensed as he withheld a thousand things he evidently wished to say.

"I am sorry about that, Alizon," Vlad began but when he looked round the young woman was gone. He *heard* her walking up the stairs of the entrance and the vampire wondered for a moment how she might react if he pursued her. However, the knowledge of how the group could help her overpowered Vlad's need to give Alizon space and so he hurried after her, leaving Lucy to discuss something unknown with Fable and Jacob.

Vlad only made it up three steps when a vast surge of power burst above. The vampire halted for a second, the walls of his control lowering and the emptiness of his once-soul filling immediately with darkness in response. It was a natural defence and he re-contained it immediately.

Magic was being channelled beyond the church grounds yet despite its raw strength it was extremely well commanded. It was water and earth and life all in one, the cleansing calms of unification, the sweetness of creation unified.

Vlad left the church basement and stopped once more, this time in shock.

Alizon stood with her back to him, head bowed, hands held a foot apart, palms facing inwards. Magic swirled and danced in traces of vivid colour before her. River winds stirred and blew to the heights of the distant industrial complex ranging across the landscape in its skeletal form, and from the ground thin streams of dirt poured into the air. They spiralled round Alizon in a delicate vortex of earthen threads.

Vlad watched in amazement as a shape burst from the enchantress, an electric-blue, hexagonal construct filled with a spider's web of etched lines. Vlad had no time to think as the hexagon spun and spun, faster and faster, until it appeared circular and became deep violet, then brightening purple, crimson, burning orange. It slowed and split apart into two triangles that stretched and rotated, becoming like two eyes. Alizon looked up and stared into her magic's gaze and Vlad felt a powerful sensation of belonging emanate from her, intricate weavings of love and reassurance tied together in the subtle simplicity of emotional comfort, and suddenly Vlad knew where Alizon found the relief she needed from the pressures of life.

The eyes of her magic spun again – Alizon knew he was there. Instead of her power dissipating into nothing it flew above them and became thick, dark clouds that emptied in a torrent. Vlad stepped into the deluge and met Alizon, face-to-face.

"You are a weather witch," he said through the minute monsoon created just for them, rain soaking through his shirt. "A highly skilled one, too. This…all of this…is remarkable! Please, come back down to the basement. You will not be asked to speak if you do not wish it. You made no mistake coming here, Alizon. I will always listen if you wish to speak and I will only offer advice if you wish to hear."

Alizon's gaze very nearly met Vlad's and for the briefest of times he beheld an inner turmoil struggling against a breaking desire, a weaving of finer emotions she could not express like most people. He wondered what it would cost her to look into his eyes.

Alizon glanced away.

"No v-vampire I have met b-b-before knew what I was," she began and Vlad shrugged. "They've sim-simply not b-b-been interested in me."

Blood and Biscuits

"I have been around a long time. I know how to recognise that which I have seen before. I am a terrific teacher but an even greater student."

Alizon bit her lip, the rain matching her mood.

"I-I find comfort in my magic," she said softly. "It has always been there f-f-for me, when oth…others have not. Please, I will…go now."

"If that is what you wish," Vlad said sadly. And then suddenly Alizon opened her arms and, while still looking away, hugged Vlad with surprising frankness. It was a short connection, and she held most of her body away, but Vlad took more meaning from it than most embraces. The vampire could only guess at the toll it took on her.

Then the enchantress released him, turned on her heel, and strode off across the edges of the wastelands.

"Will we see you next week?" Vlad called after her.

"Not if the weather's turning sour," Alizon called back, her hands twitching before her again as the rain cloud finally moved away, following the enchantress across the ancient paths of the old industrial grounds, turning the last patches of dry soil into slick mud.

Vlad watched Alizon disappear then sighed and walked back down into the church basement. The others of the group sat in a heavy fog of silence, two of them abjectly refusing to look at one another.

"God, you're drenched!" Jacob said. "What the hell happened?"

"Alizon made it rain," Vlad replied easily, brushing back the strands of dark hair from his eyes. He looked between Lucy and Cain and sighed as he realised what the source of the sudden gloom was. He sat pointedly. "What happened this time? Come now, we are meant to share. Let us not break what little tradition we have with so few minutes left afforded us before we depart for another week."

Blood and Biscuits

"She started it," Cain growled churlishly. His blood rushed hot and rapid through his veins, Vlad could *feel* it, and the sense of Cain's wolf buried in his body became more enigmatic.

"I did not!" Lucy snarled back.

"I hardly think Vlad cares who started anything," Jacob said exasperatedly as Fable stared in utter disbelief. Sarah's humming had ceased, she looked to be considering retreating through the stone ceiling. Vlad shook his head.

"On the contrary, I find it is always best to begin where a problem started so the root of an issue may be *up*rooted. So, *where* did it start?"

As Vlad predicted, neither party wished to admit who had begun the argument, yet a simple look at their faces determined who had thrown the first punch, idiomatically speaking.

"Cain," Vlad said softly, funnelling all intonation from his voice, allowing only a monotone acceptance to underscore. "How do you honestly believe this began?"

It was a cleverly designed question. It allowed Cain to offer his opinion whilst maintaining that core of guilt one finds when one is asked to be truthful amongst friends, especially when they were technically witnesses. Cain muttered wordlessly for a half-second then spoke up.

"It started when I...*mouthed off* at Alizon," he said with heavy, begrudging admission.

"And I assume that phrase was provided by Lucy?" Vlad asked. Jacob nodded enthusiastically behind Lucy's back as the banshee gained a look of indignity. Vlad spread his hands defensively. "I merely asked. Regardless, if we must leave the session here on a negative note then we might at least talk it through and open it out for thorough consideration, bearing in mind one more of our number will be calling this delightful place home for the foreseeable future. Bad moods and tensions build not through disagreements but through failures to communicate. Arguments are inevitable, but many a perspective is changed with proper discussion. We will heal wounded relationships faster by simply talking."

Lucy ground her teeth a moment then launched into a full explanation.

"I told Cain exactly what he needed to hear, impending blue moon or not. He can't just go *mouthing off* at people he doesn't know, people who clearly suffer from anxiety. What he said to Alizon may not have seemed all that problematic but would have felt horrendous for her. When you aren't confident it can be the hardest thing in the world to put yourself out there and try new things, and God damn it if we've lost a new member because of your brashness, Cain!"

"I said I was sorry and I meant it, for Christ's sake!" Cain called back, voice cracking with the stress of restraining a deeper rage. "It came out wrong and I wasn't myself! I'd take it back if I could."

"And that is exactly what cannot be done," Vlad said, beginning his sentence in a strong voice then quickly lowering it to involuntarily bring everybody's collective mood down. It had the desired effect and Cain and Lucy relaxed a little. Fable sat back in her chair and Jacob lost the concern in his gaze. "And what is done is done. However, we know you were not yourself, Cain, and in these moments, I find it best not to think rashly but instead take a deep breath and await whatever may happen. I believe Alizon will return and in that re-acquaintance, you could offer a different side of you."

"It's the blue moon next week," Jacob pointed out and Cain nodded half-heartedly.

"Yeah, and I'm gonna' be even worse."

"I have a feeling you will be fine," Vlad said calmly, allowing none of his doubts to be betrayed, the word 'feeling' altering the lie and circumnavigating the holy ground's effects on his vampirism. "We will all be here and you have the silver; I hold hope none of your fears will come to pass."

Cain nodded resignedly.

Blood and Biscuits

Vlad looked round at them all as Lucy checked her watch and sighed.

"Indeed," he said. "Perhaps this has run longer than anticipated. A great deal has happened in a short space of time. Apologies to those that feel as if they did not get a chance to speak, I will endeavour to see things through a little more smoothly next time."

There was an awkward silence to proceedings as chairs were tidied away. Everyone clearly wished to put the strange night behind them. Cain looked crestfallen beside the silver chains, his stance evidently encumbered by the pain growing down his spine.

As Vlad paid his farewells to everyone, Lucy lingered and stared at Cain's back. She left quietly and Vlad joined Cain's side. Immediately, the silver tried to pollute his body, attacking the mental walls of his control, draining his power from behind their protection, but he gave no outward sign of the influence. For all that Cain saw, Vlad was simply a smiling man, but inside he was a battleground of wasting strength. Simply the presence of silver was enough.

"Cain, you need not feel foolish – do not try and deny it," he added when the werewolf looked at him irritably. "I can *smell* it emanating off you in waves. Please, let us set up this thing together so you feel safer over the coming nights."

Cain looked at the iron peg he had just picked up then sighed and handed it to Vlad.

"You do it; I'm shattered now. Don't think I could lift the sledge if I tried. Jacob and I attempted breakin' the floor but it wasn't happenin'. I guess you'll have better luck with the hammer, s'long as the silver's not gettin' to you."

Vlad looked at the ground and allowed his weakening senses to feel for the strongest parts of the old concrete: they would provide the greatest purchase. He picked up the other three pegs and hefted their weights. Cain wasn't looking as he chose four spots.

The first peg left Vlad's grip faster than a loosed arrow. It struck the ground with a thunder-crack and the basement shook. Dust billowed in a thick plume. Cain could do nothing but throw his hands up to his head and dance away with a cry of shock as Vlad struck the floor three more times, each peg finding its mark perfectly, burying into the concrete as easily as ploughed soil. Vlad stood back to admire his handiwork.

When the dust settled the sight of four iron pegs buried eight inches deep became clear. Cain coughed and shook grit from his hair, and stepped beside Vlad as the vampire rubbed his chin in a show of mock self-appreciation.

"Hmm, not too bad for a man weakened by silver," he remarked quietly.

"Jesus, Vlad, some warnin' would've been nice!" Cain spluttered. "You're never gonna' stop tryin' to scare me outta' my bloody trousers, I'll have a sodding aneurism before you're done. But I'll be damned if that wasn't impressive."

"My apologies, though I can hear your blood and it tells me you probably needed a little scare to liven you up. Here," Vlad continued as he turned smartly on the spot, "you attach the chains to the pegs while I go and get your bed. I shall not be long."

"And where've you kept this famous orthopaedic mattress? Somewhere nearby, I guess," Cain said as he finished coughing and hauled up one end of a gleaming silver chain as if it was a feather – despite his protests to the contrary, he was not weak.

"In my home," Vlad said simply. "Do not worry, I shall be a matter of minutes. The further I get from the silver the faster I go."

"Righto. I'll just clear my brain of dusty snot then crack on attachin' these buggers."

Vlad walked to the end of the basement and felt the last of the silver's influence on his control dissipate completely. Then, in a hurricane of power, his darkness swallowed him up, and he vanished in the blink of an eye upon the shadows of the night.

THE INDUSTRIAL COMPLEX, ELLIN'S INDUSTRIAL ISLAND.

Vlad stooped and hauled up the mattress he had set aside specifically for Cain. He stopped and thought for a moment, his feet upon the stone only he could perceive. As a moment of clarity passed, Vlad glanced out a window overlooking the entire wastelands and breathed automatically, the old human action still a part of his habitual routine. He saw the tiny light of the church basement still beaming out and he wondered how successful his plan was going to be: the blue moon was notorious for werewolves. Its power had easily stripped away the protective nature of electric light and sanctified ground before. The silver chains should be enough but he had repeatedly sensed Cain's unique and foreign strength and it worried him, and he was not a man whose worry boded well for others.

Vlad lowered himself a second time and picked up a carrier bag. Inside was an expensive whisky from the Scottish Highlands – a drink for a vampire – followed by gin, vermouth, and a pack of pitted olives – a fine martini combination for a werewolf with taste.

At least Vlad knew he could finish the current night with a drink between gentlemen under the fine gaze of the mist and stars. As he moved from the low room into the wide stone hallway, banners hanging grey and lifeless, torches cold in their brackets upon the walls, Vlad looked again to the church of St Ellin's through an arrow slit. The glimmer of Sarah flashed and winked in silver light as she swayed through the night, dancing to stone-shaking dubstep from the early two thousands. Vlad smiled.

Tentative as it seemed, everything was moving into place. She would find peace, one way or another.

The vampire looked back at the room he had left and admired its beautiful construction.

'It is a shame only I can see this place,' he thought reflectively. *'Perhaps one day I might show them all.'*

Vlad walked the hallway with the large mattress held aloft,

his thoughts cutting back to the curious, unknown scent in Cain's blood, mixed with the enormously powerful curse coursing his veins. Vlad suddenly realised he had never doubted himself as much as he did right then. If his fears became realised, and Cain was too strong, then Vlad knew he would have to make a choice.

If Cain escaped, he would have to kill him.

Fig. 6.

The Petal Hourglass.

I have found myself of late thinking on the notion of nature and time conjoined as one; I usually have more pressing things to occupy my life - sorry, death - with, yet more often than not I once again dwell on this idea. Petals falling as the passing of time, how curious.

Once again, my sketching prowess fails me - I have no excuse, I shall just do as everyone else does and blame it on the state of the country.

A Hike Through a Garden

Afternoon twinkled across the mansion in shafts of gold as Vlad picked his way carefully along the rooftop. The deepening sun sparkled throughout the vast overgrown gardens, creating strange, angled shadows snickering along the grounds in gothic script. Roof tiles clicked under his light step; without darkness holding him up, many of them would have slipped or dislodged entirely and he found himself wondering how they had survived any sort of weather.

Looking down, Vlad saw the black hair of a young woman as she stepped out onto a worn, chipped veranda, the wooden roof long since fallen in and eroded away. A breeze blew over the hilltop expanse and her hair moved freely, the strands paying little heed to the passage of the air, instead acting out their own theatrics, emulative manifestations of her mood.

"Good evening, Vlad."

He paused. Lucy had spoken hardly above a whisper. That was the proof she knew he was there, for only his keen senses could have discerned her words from so far away.

"Now how did you know I was here?" Vlad asked, binding his voice to a single stream of darkness so it carried upon the thin breeze, an unseen shadow.

Lucy tapped her head and her heart.

"Please. This is my house, I'm trapped here. I learnt long ago to read the signs my mansion gives when an intruder's around; I can feel you walking on me, like the roof is my chest, the tiles my skin, the beams my bones."

"Fascinating," Vlad muttered and he drifted down on a cushion of darkness to stand beside Lucy. "I must dig out a few books on banshee lore and see if I can educate myself."

"Do you have books like that just lying around?"

Blood and Biscuits

"I know a few along those lines, yes. Anyway, shall we walk? In your call you mentioned the paths round the grounds are rather splendid in the evening; I have only ever passed over on my flights elsewhere so I would be greatly interested in seeing things closer."

"Excellent. Off we pop, then, I've got a thermos of black coffee here we can share, so long as you're not worried about catching a virus."

They burst out laughing at the sheer ridiculousness of such a thing and began marching through the mansion grounds. Sunlight dazzled through the overgrowth and the disastrously unkempt hedgerows, twisting trees growing freely amongst the sparse grasses, lending all of it an atmosphere of gnarled mystery. What untold stories hid in these grounds? What deep secrets were forged here and lost in the vines? Vlad wondered these things as they walked miles through the vast hilltop grounds, circling woodland glades and fringing old buildings that had once been long greenhouses or had sheltered instruments for observing the night sky. The history of it all intrigued Vlad. He had often thought of the house atop the hill but had never managed to find much information on it.

Rounding a copse of trees, the wind peeled past a birch and Vlad's senses ignited. The *scent* of a man came to him as a single dark hair fluttered past his eyes, and he followed its path as it twirled and danced through the air and disappeared across the hilltop. The hair gave off a second smell, this one a foreign addition Vlad recognised. Then the hair and the scents were gone but he did not disregard them; correlation does not infer causation but that did not stop his active mind from wandering and wondering, all the same.

After a particularly long and winding conversation covering, but not limited to, the matters of imprisonment, loneliness, joy, heartbreak, and beans on toast, Vlad finally leant his hand against a hawthorn tree and glanced at the banshee. The scents of the drifting hair crossed his mind again.

𝔅lood and 𝔅iscuits

"So how have you been since last we spoke?" he asked gently as Lucy stopped and peered at a chipped and weatherworn statue of a deer, its front leg raised.

"Oh you know, trapped, mostly. Stuff we've just been chatting about."

She was deflecting.

"I see. And how have you been feeling in this time away from the group?"

"Lonely, as usual. It's been like that for years so don't beat yourself up about it, Vlad, a couple weeks at a Support Group isn't likely to change anything in such a short space of time."

"No but I would hope you have things to consider now."

"I've considered plenty, I promise you. You don't need to come checking up on me, making sure I'm doing alright, I know how to entertain myself, keep myself distracted, that kind of thing. I'm fine. I'm fine!" she added when Vlad looked unconvinced.

"Then it is well you have joined the Support Group. Good company will always be the best sort of distraction. Loneliness is a festering affliction."

"So, you're saying I'm lucky you decided to open the Support Group near where I live, eh?" Lucy jabbed, leaning her face down to a wild lavender bush and sniffing. "Good for keeping cats away, this," she muttered to the purple plant.

"Luck is not what I meant and you know that, Lucy. Perhaps instead of turning everything into a fight you should concentrate on monitoring your mood when you have times of solace. Silence, I have heard, is one of the greatest things we do not appreciate; in moments of solitude, you should focus your mind and your emotions, to get them under control."

"You know I don't like spending time in my own head. It's one of the reasons I joined the Support Group, Vlad."

"And it is one of the things I recommend you work on, something only you can achieve for yourself. Let the others of the group help your loneliness then make your loneliness work for you.

Practice moments of silence and listen to your curse, if you can, that is something Sarah taught me. The more you reject yourself the worse you will feel, our curses are a part of us; of all our differences this, at least, is something we have in common."

"Look, I just…it's not so easy as you say but I guess I can…I'll do what I can but I can't promise anything."

"And you should not. There is not much worse than breaking a promise you made to yourself. However, even just *trying* it will make you realise how strong you really are, Lucy. Now, do we venture into that enormous maze or do we cry cowardice and head to the woods?"

"I suggest the woods. The maze is huge and we'd just get lost in there."

"You do know I can fly."

"Of course, but when you enter a maze you make a promise to yourself that you won't cheat, and breaking a promise to yourself would be the worst thing you could do."

"Oh well played, truly superb."

They laughed as they walked past the entrance to the huge hedge maze and instead marched across the grounds to the nearby woods. Vlad saw the tall stone wall marking the perimeter of Galloway's expanse delve somewhere into those trees.

Through the darkness they plunged, between trunks and scrub, the woods punishingly dense, roots trying to trip Lucy with every other step.

"Is there anything in here in particular?" Vlad asked. "I only ask as there are a lot of old ruins about the place, and a few things left standing mostly intact, like your observatory."

"There's not much, just a few towers and a hole in the ground," came the short reply. "Hardly anything to think about."

"And thought is a powerful gift, as powerful a concept as it is a piece of matter. So go the theories, anyway," Vlad added absently.

"Theories on thought," Lucy confirmed. "You're saying some people reckon thought's a real thing."

"Of course it is a real thing, you are thinking right now, are you not?"

"Yeah but that's just impulses in the brain. Electricity and hormones firing round, pulling out memories and organising what you're going to say, letting you work out problems and stuff."

"Those are things that thought *does*, absolutely, but who is to say there is not more? I cannot say for sure, as I have my own doubts, but many people do indeed believe thought is something more than just small patterns in the brain, that it could be constructed of particles or is guided by some sort of force."

"Like a magnetic field," Lucy suggested as she stepped over a moss-covered log and stopped to retie her snagged laces.

"I suppose that is another suggestion, yes, though I meant in the religious sense. Do you really want to talk about this? I only said it because I was wondering aloud, I did not actually mean to go off on another one of my tangential ramblings."

"No, no, this is great! I'd love to hear what you think on this, I enjoyed hearing you talk about the soul before, after I'd thought it through, and it keeps my mind off other things."

"Alright, if you insist. So, if I understand the theories, people posited that thought, if it were to truly give off some sort of…energy, I suppose, would spread from your mind and interact with the thoughts of others, like particulate interactions. Like…the roots of these trees, growing unseen underground yet connected to one another, striving for the same resources. This means that intellect and emotional reasoning could be combined and intertwined, though all of these hypotheses collapsed when repeat experiments to prove mental connections between pairs of people, the most prevalent being identical twins, failed to produce anything."

"That can't be it, though. If theories exist, a lot of the time they can turn out to be true."

Blood and Biscuits

"And a great many more times they turn out to just be theories, nothing more. We are people, not trees," Vlad stated simply, placing his palm to an old trunk for a moment, feeling for the slow thrums of water and life coursing within. Particulate interactions deep at work. "When it comes to something as important as thought, supernatural scientists have done what they can to try to prove these theories. And in a select few cases, they have found results."

"How?" Lucy asked, no measure of disinterest in her voice. She was not like Cain, who would have been immediately bored.

"Well, para-sciences have re-focussed onto other matters now, but over a hundred years ago there were a small number of studies that seemed to produce fascinating outcomes. The most significant of which was the Rosetta-Forestein Oil Shift Experiment. This involved an empath, a particularly talented person that can associate with somebody else's emotions and read them with their own feelings. This is not the same as thought theory, empaths consciously tune into subconscious brain waves. Rosetta and Forestein, two human mages of high academic standing, got an empath subject and sat them in a room full of jars of oil containing air bubbles infused with magic. The empath was then presented with a series of emotionally impactful images designed to illicit a highly emotive response."

"What were the bubbles for?" Lucy asked as Vlad held back a sharp branch for her.

"Well, after an intensive session of emotional resonance, the bubbles in oil actually *moved*. Only a fraction of an inch but they moved all the same. Strangely, they moved downwards but it was enough for Rosetta and Forestein to attempt another experiment, the Thought-in-Magical-Aether Test."

"I take it this didn't involve oil and bubbles this time," Lucy said.

"No, not at all. Forestein and Rosetta decided not to use an empath subject but instead a human of vast academia. They created a magical field using charged sunstones and amethyst crystals, known magical propagators, and set them in a circle. Lining this circle's circumference, eight bowls of water were spaced equally, and floating within each bowl was a piece of cork embedded with an upright brass pin. The experiment room was kept perfectly still, almost like a vacuum, and the human subject was placed in the magic field's centre and given a series of logic puzzles to solve."

"This sounds more complicated than the last one," Lucy commented. "I take it brass has something to do with magic."

"Out of all metals brass is influenced most easily by magic, yes. It also contains magic very well, such as in vessels. See, as the subject accessed their intellect and began solving the puzzles presented them, they were rotated on the spot slowly, and as they spun Forestein and Rosetta observed the brass pins move, as if *pushed*. Only a little, but they moved all the same, as waves of thought seemingly emanated from the subject and passed through the magical field, physically *pushing* the pins round in their bowls in the same rotational direction as the subject. Is that not fascinating?"

"It really is!" Lucy replied enthusiastically. "And what did they do after this? This proves the theories of thought."

"Unfortunately, that is not how science works, para or not. Others tried the same experiments and came to nothing, rendering the results of Forestein and Rosetta's work void. If an experiment is not repeatable then the theory must be rejected. That is how it goes. Forestein and Rosetta lost funding and eventually disappeared, their theories returned to rumour and postulations only. Others have made different attempts, most notably the King Theory on Stone Interactions, but ultimately nothing definitive has come through. Still, it does make one wonder. I have copies of Forestein and Rosetta's original papers, if you would like to read them some time?"

"Oh I would love that! I'm not big on science but anything on supernatural stuff I can find time for. I think it helps me come to terms with my banshee-ism, weirdly." Lucy checked her watch.

Blood and Biscuits

"Huh, you know we've been walking over four hours now. Your company always makes me lose track of the minutes."

"Plenty of time to get you back before your curse summons you," Vlad said. "Let us find this hole-in-the-woods of yours."

"Alright, it's not very impressive, though. Still, the walk'll give me time to pursue that silence you said Sarah recommended, I've heard it's quite the thing," Lucy added dryly. "Gives me a chance to listen to the birds, they don't hang around much here, I think because of the darkness of me and the mansion, so I like to appreciate them when they're back."

After another twenty minutes of pleasant strolling and listening in quiet, the trees opened a little and they walked out into a semi-open glade, the canopy above gradually reclaiming the space. In the clearing's centre was a split in the ground, a jagged cleft like the bite of an axe, overgrown with grass and weeds. Vlad approached and peered down and he emitted a sliver of darkness as a high frequency *screech*. He waited a moment until the sound returned to him, his senses registering the undulations, the peaks and troughs, and building a map of the hole's interior.

"It is deep," he said, crouching by the hole, "and there is the distinct *ring* of moving water at the bottom. Lucy, this is more than a hole, this is a well. Look," and he pointed beyond the lip of the cleft, at several stones lying nearby, "you can even see the remnants of its wall, smashed apart."

Lucy leant down and placed her hands on the edge of the old well, peering down in fascination.

"Huh, I never once thought that's what this could be. I just reckoned it was a bit of sunken ground."

"Yet you felt it to be important enough to mention on our way in," Vlad pointed out. "It would seem your curse is more linked to these grounds than on first consideration."

Lucy was about to say something else but right then, there came the slightest gust of air from the hole and, with only that as warning, a shrill cry burst from the well followed by a messy flurry of panicked wings. Lucy screamed, her voice echoing through the trees, and fell backwards onto her bottom as the creature flew away into the trees, coming to rest on a narrow branch and proceeding to give a series of very irritable chirps.

Vlad gave a long laugh and helped Lucy to her feet.

"So how do you feel about birds now?"

"Oh yes, you're very funny. I can't *believe* you didn't sense that down there," Lucy hissed, brushing twigs and leaves off her dress.

"I determined a shape and sensed a heartbeat but I thought I would leave it alone," Vlad shrugged.

"Bloody pigeon," Lucy grumbled.

"It was a sparrow, my friend, just a sparrow. Poor thing must have gotten itself trapped then worked its way free."

"Well please don't mention that to the group. In fact, don't mention any of this to the group, I don't want them thinking I've been meeting you in secret, I think that'd make me anxious."

"Absolutely, I will say nothing to anyone. I *might* be tempted to mention the bird to Cain, though."

Lucy shot him a quick look and Vlad narrowed his eyes ever-so-slightly.

"I am joking," he said. In truth, he had mentioned the werewolf to see what Lucy's reaction would be. He had deeper suspicions at work. However, he said nothing of the sound she had made, nor the fact that it had not been any normal scream.

After they finished removing leaves from Lucy's clothes, Vlad sat back next to her and looked up into the little night sky afforded by the thin leaves of the glade. In that moment, the scent of man came to him again and Vlad peered round at Lucy; she was stroking her arm and the vampire saw three hairs that were not her own resting there.

"So how *are* you feeling about Cain?" Vlad asked carefully.

Blood and Biscuits

"What about him?" Lucy asked indifferently, though at the second mention of the name the narrowest sliver of surprise peeled off her.

"The blue moon is fast approaching and I thought, perhaps, you might be concerned for him..."

"Should I be?" Lucy snapped, her hair flicking angrily. She answered far more than she realised in those three words. "I barely got to know Alizon at all and the stupid git scared her off; I don't have patience for men like that."

Vlad chose to hold up his hands.

"Of course not. But if you should ever wish to talk then please do not hesitate to send me a message. You know I will do all I can to listen. Let us just hope we can keep it together for the blue moon, Cain will need us all as strong as we can possibly be."

Week Five
Blood of the Seventh

RUINS OF ST ELLIN'S CHURCH.
TWO DAYS BEFORE THE SUPPORT GROUP.

"I'm glad I called you."

Lucy spoke quietly, her body held tight in the high-vaulted basement.

"I wanted to see him before…I guess before it happens, *if* it happens. It might not."

She was in denial. Vlad *tasted* her worry.

"I understand," he replied quietly, not looking at her but instead the man lying upon the mattress. "Though I can hear something else in your voice. There is another reason you contacted me; it could not have waited until after the weekend for the group to share with. You need to tell me now."

"I forget how perceptive you are," Lucy said, glancing away. "Yes, there's something more. It's…ahh, how do I explain this? I saw somebody from the town had died – I read it online, actually, at the library like I always do, which is how I saw your advert a couple months back. I went down the morning after our walk together, just wanted to clear my head again."

"Somebody had died," Vlad repeated casually. "This sort of thing would not normally bother you. Life and death are the bookends of nature's offerings – what makes this ordinary incident so different?"

Blood and Biscuits

"I didn't see the name but I recognised his face in the article: it was the man that grabbed me, during the first week here. He's killed himself."

"Oh," Vlad said flatly.

"Yeah. Jumped in front of a train."

She said it so matter-of-factly Vlad knew she masked her emotions.

"Dear me," Vlad uttered. "A horrible way to go. I hope it was instant. I do not like to presume, Lucy, but I must ask: why are you so affected by this man's untimely death? He showed himself only to be a threat to you."

"Because I screamed that first night, and I thought, stupidly, it was because you and Cain were fighting. But it's like I explained before: banshees scream when someone approaching their death, it's just a matter of who and when. So I realised when you two were beating each other up those men must've been close enough for my clairvoyance to predict the leader's death. Apparently my curse is working as well as always."

"Ahh, I see. Have you screamed before when someone else was not long for this world?"

"A couple years back," Lucy responded darkly, her voice veiled as she hid a thousand and one things. "I'd love to say I barely remember it but I'd be lying." She paused and considered something. "I guess…I don't know, I can't shake this from my thoughts."

"Possibly you feel you played some part in his demise?" Vlad suggested and Lucy nodded. "You could not be farther from the truth. The certainty, my dearest Lucy, is that whoever they are or whatever the circumstances, everyone develops some grade of guilt when another dies. Everyone thinks they could have prevented it somehow, as if one small correction in the paths of fate could have steered the deceased down a different road and saved their life. Do you feel guilty?"

Lucy said nothing but her eyes told Vlad enough. He placed a hand on her shoulder.

"You are anything but, Lucy. Do you hear me? What you have is a *gift*, a real gift. I know it does not seem it but that is the truth, too. You cannot prevent death. Just as vampires cannot prevent their hunger, werewolves cannot stop the full moon rising, and trees cannot deny the axe. These are unavoidable processes of life, just as your gift is an unavoidable facet of yours. That man was going to take his life, one way or another; the chances are it was because he experienced *me* rather than anything you did. Trust me on that."

"Thanks, Vlad," Lucy said after a moment, wiping her nose on her sleeve. "You've made me feel a little better."

"Then we find success after four weeks of trying! Even after a hike through your gardens do we only now have victory!" Vlad exclaimed and Lucy snorted. "Now all we need to do is deal with *him*," the vampire said, pointing to Cain. He was stirring awake, agony painted across his face in fine strokes. Vlad reached into a satchel by his side and drew out a syringe, pushing a little liquid out to force any air from the tube. He approached as Cain snarled.

"Cain, please let us help you. If I could just inject you quickly it will numb the pain."

A growl rumbled through the basement and they stepped back from the man. Four long, heavy silver chains clinked and rang across the stone floor as Cain bucked and curled, hands grasping his hips, his back, his legs, his arms, anywhere bones grew and shifted in place.

The werewolf was returning. The blue moon was rising.

"MAKE IT STOP!" Cain cried out suddenly and the waiting vampire took that as all the invitation he needed.

Vlad gripped the syringe and wrapped himself in darkness. Darting forward faster than any eye could see, he jabbed the needle into Cain's arm. Instantaneously, morphine flooded the werewolf's veins and soon Cain began to relax, his breathing slowing, heart rate calming. Vlad hissed through his teeth as Cain became almost placid. He withdrew the syringe and dropped it into a waste bag for burial later.

Blood and Biscuits

Vlad knew drug sufferers still sometimes made their way out to Ellin's Island and he would not have them finding his used needles.

Lucy sighed.

"Where on earth did you get high-grade morphine...? You know what, never mind. I'm getting used to your connections, Vlad, considering you've mentioned you can get blood donations from the NHS before. Just tell me you think those needles'll keep Cain down a while."

Vlad shook his head sadly.

"I cannot, not really. You have no idea of what the blue moon is capable. Werewolves are already outlandishly powerful creatures, rivalling the more ancient vampires for strength and surpassing them in wild rage by many factors. If he is even half the man I have measured him to be then his transformed self will be monstrously terrifying."

"I don't understand, there are different werewolf types?" Lucy asked curiously, an edge of fear to her voice.

"Oh yes," Vlad intoned as he pulled on a pair of thick leather gloves and began checking the connections of the silver chains to their iron pegs. The leather would only dull the influence of the silver on Vlad's constitution, unable to prevent his already weakening state. "Like any creature of this world, werewolves are sub-divided into groups – I call them 'clans'. The easiest way to think of it is with humans, as we are descended from them."

"You speak as if we are evolved in some way."

Vlad glanced up at her, his gaze filled with hundreds of years of knowledge, philosophy, and experience.

"That is exactly what I believe, Lucy."

The banshee recoiled before she could stop herself: she thought Vlad believed himself higher than humans.

"I do not see humans as subservient to us in any way," he explained. "I do not believe them inferior. I have seen evil's face and shall never forget it, and from this long life of observation I could never treat others as evil has treated them. I am, by all definitions, descended from my human form. I have earned traits help me deal with new and unforeseen environmental pressures. Hence evolution. The only difference with conventional, natural systems is I have not passed on these new attributes to my progeny, I have developed them for myself."

Lucy hesitated, clearly unconvinced. Vlad sighed.

"Look, it is surprisingly simple, really, but all of us remain interwoven in a never-ending cycle. Humans need us and we need them. We are the agents of their death, and they are the key to our life. Figuring out how both can live in balance without undue slaughter is the answer to the real question nobody asks."

"I…think I know what you're saying," Lucy said quietly. "I'm glad I let you explain, otherwise I might have thought you a madman."

"You should see me when I am hungry," Vlad muttered. Lucy snorted.

"You forget, I already have."

Vlad paused as he worked.

"Indeed," he muttered after a moment. "I wish not for that to happen ever again. I have once more fed from another of my…associates, shall we call them, and I feel refreshed. I knew I would need all of my strength for this next support session, when it comes."

Silence for a few seconds, then Lucy stirred.

"You were speaking of wolf clans?"

"Correct, I was," Vlad responded brightly. "They are lonesome creatures, werewolves; do not mistake my wording for the meaning of packs or tribes. A clan, in this instance, is but simple nomenclature to categorise *types* of werewolf, just like with humans and their races. However, humans are based on cultures and countries of origin, werewolf clans are based on something entirely different."

"So what, random genes?" Lucy suggested.

Blood and Biscuits

"In a sense," Vlad said as he finished with the silver and moved away down the basement. The further he drew the less influence the heavy chains had on his power. "Though not on a DNA level. Werewolves are categorised by the curse of their blood."

"That sounds ominous."

"It is particularly ominous, especially as one ascends the list of clans. Like humans, werewolves have blood types. Only, the proteinous substructures building human types are designated by the genetic determination of parental lines – with a little room for random mutations, of course – whereas a werewolf's blood is denoted by the *design* of its curse," Vlad emphasised. "Here is where I feel I must elaborate: there is more to becoming a werewolf than being bitten or scratched, though these still hold an important part in the process. The physical contact, the wounding, is the *key* and the curse is the *door*. Once the wound is open, the werewolf virus passes to the human, infects the red *and* white blood cells, produces the initial curse, and attacks the host's every cell for a single month, changing their biology to respond to the rays of the fullest moon. But this virus will quickly perish if there is not something to bolster it and keep it alive long enough to convert the host's cellular matter.

"A biologist would express great surprise that such a weak virus can cross the blood-brain-barrier, but that is only part of it. I have observational, *not* experimental, results that demonstrate its crossing of the placental barrier, too, though children affected with the curse die in-utero long before they could ever be born."

"That's awful," Lucy whispered, her hands to her mouth. "I can't imagine anything worse. Those poor mothers."

"Indeed, the suffering they endure as a result of the virus is sickening. They lose their child and then they transform into a mindless beast. Yet it is important to remember it is not the fault of Cain or anyone else afflicted with the virus. It is…simply the way of things. Simply the way of things," he repeated quietly, folding his hands together and thinking on the past.

Blood and Biscuits

"You've done an astonishing amount of research into this," Lucy noted as she and Vlad sat upon two chairs and watched Cain.

"I have. It became quite the obsession for a time."

Lucy crossed her arms and indicated Cain's restless form, the silver chains clinking heavily against the stone.

"I guess you know what I'm going to ask next," she said breezily.

"You wonder what curse type Cain is," Vlad replied. "Well, I do not actually know. This is not a good thing. There is a smell about him, a particular *scent* I cannot determine. Every time he breathes or I sense a root of his hair or he loses blood, I smell this foreign agent in him. It is overwhelming and completely uninterpretable. I have tasted fourteen of the seventeen types of werewolf blood – yes, *tasted*, stop pulling faces – and none of them have contained this strange quality Cain possesses.

"Every taste of those fourteen types spoke of rage in the magic binding them. For that is what the virus requires, the magic of fury sealing it to the blood so it may eventually survive on its own. This symbiosis comes from the light of the full moon, which serves as the base of the curse magic and whatever betrayal fills the night sky's air. The emotional hatred found in betrayal binds to the transferred virus and helps it produce the curse. When I say 'betrayal' I mean the numerous ways one person can foul another, from theft right through to murder."

Lucy's head cocked a little. A part of Vlad wished he had not broached the subject.

"Ok, there are two aspects to the curse: the *design* and the *nature*. Design determines in which clan the werewolf belongs, it is created based on betrayal. This is the metaphysical body of the curse itself. For example, if there has been a betrayal of faith between partners nearby then the werewolf's *design* will see the beast joining the ranks of a higher clan. A burglary would see a lower rank."

"And the *nature*?" Lucy asked quietly, her fingers fidgeting.

"*Nature* is subtler; it affects the strength and ferocity of a werewolf further than *design* allows. If the night's physical attributes are violent, such as a storm, then evidence suggests a werewolf will be stronger than another of the same clan born under a calmer night. Ultimately, the *nature* of the wolf can only change so much, even if a high-clan wolf is born on a calm night it will still be devastatingly powerful, just not as much as one, say, bound under a blizzard. It is complicated, I am afraid."

"No, I think I follow," Lucy said slowly as she watched Cain's convulsing form. There was something deep in her eyes, shining in response to the agony. "Are you talking about weather?" she pushed. "For the night air, I mean."

"Weather, mainly, but also smoke in the sky, the type of full moon, dust on the wind…anything that might physically disturb the night."

"So, if someone's bitten during a monsoon thunderstorm when there's been a murder nearby…" Lucy began.

Vlad twitched an eyebrow.

"Is a monsoon thunderstorm the most violent type of weather you could think of?" He could not help but smile.

Lucy snorted.

"It was," she muttered.

"Alright, then with a murder in a monsoon thunderstorm the created werewolf will be of a very high-ranking clan *and* bound by true vengeance. Practically unstoppable. As I said, it is complex but that is what I have observed. The deeper the hatred and betrayal in the night the worse the magic will be on the host human, thereby forging one of fourteen different emotion-led clans."

"You said seventeen before," Lucy corrected.

"I did, I often set the final three apart because what creates *them* is unknown entirely, they are purely speculative; I have attempted to find out, in many different countries, yet the answers have always eluded me. To the point where, up until recently, actually, I refused to believe they ever existed outside of rumour.

You might find this strange but werewolves do not make the most compliant of study subjects, nor are they usually present frequently or long enough to *be* studied."

"Shocker," Lucy said dryly.

"Indeed. As I tasted these fourteen different bloods, from hundreds of unwitting test subjects, I found they had the obvious threads of commonality amongst their sub-species yet subtly different tones in each sample, and as I researched, I began placing these curses into order. For instance, at the bottom of the list there are the Sânge-Unu wolves, the lowest group comprising just one clan."

"Singee?" Lucy mispronounced and Vlad chuckled.

"My apologies, I used my Romanian roots for the classifications to maintain a thread of my history. Though I predate the Vulgar Latin split into the Romanian dialects, I thought it best to use more modern variants such as general Romanian, which in this case is the word for 'blood', 'sânge', followed by a number. Its pronunciation has no English equivalent; that second letter is an 'a' variant you might try pronouncing as the 'i' from 'ski' then rolling your tongue back to the centre of your mouth."

"Or I won't try at all," Lucy laughed.

"Or there is that," Vlad agreed with a grin. "Regardless, there are seven curse groups comprising seven*teen* clans. I can categorise the final group despite having never met a single wolf from any of its three clans because of whispered stories from several terrified humans, their lives separated by thousands of miles and hundreds of years. That is no coincidence. They spoke of creatures capable of destroying city walls, tearing oak trees apart, scaling the outside of huge towers in seconds…though they are powerful, these are not normal werewolf feats. And I always held a fraction of disbelief in the back of my mind because of the sheer impossibility of it. Until four weeks ago, that was."

Blood and Biscuits

"Oh dear," Lucy whispered, looking at Cain fearfully, whose body and mind were already fighting off the morphine. "Cain, what have you been doing with your life?"

"Your worries are well founded," Vlad noted. "I do not recognise the *scent* of Cain's blood and so that can only mean he is a member of the final group, the Sânge-Şapte, comprising the three most powerful werewolves that can exist: Clan Fuller, Clan Mânie, and Clan Răutate. Thunder, Wrath, and Malice. It is because of his power that Cain's allergies include himself, and why he already succumbs to the blue moon. His infection, however that occurred, and transformations must have been truly horrific, I cannot imagine what he has suffered. Also, I cannot accurately determine the source wound from his body for he is covered in scars, almost all of which are most likely from himself."

"This is really hard to hear, Vlad. And now I feel guilty because hearing it's nothing compared to what he's been through, poor man."

"Oh yes, and I pity whoever has gotten in his way. Hence why I am so cautious of this blue moon."

"God, we're in for a wild support session. I can't see how the hell we're going to cope; ironically, this is sort of the situation I'd have hoped Cain would be around to help with."

"It shall be enlightening for all of us, I believe. I honestly wish nobody turns up on Monday but I cannot stop you; Jacob and Fable have already sent me preventative text messages threatening under pain of second death not to cancel the session. I do not order people around, those days are long behind me. I only guide, making suggestions, helping people realise their full potentials. Speaking of which, did you ever take up practicing your banshee scream? Apologies for the subject change."

Lucy looked as if she would immediately say 'no', but then she stopped and considered for a moment. She bent her head inwards then looked up as if she was testing her throat and searching her thoughts.

"I...did, yes, but I'm not sure I got anywhere," she hesitated.

"You are not sure?" Vlad repeated.

"No, not really. I tried a few times out in the mansion gardens over the weeks but nothing seemed to work. I think I made a couple leaves wiggle a bit but that was it. Don't think I've got the time or energy to explore my potential like you've done with your powers over the years. It feels like I'm missing something."

"You will get there, I am confident in you," Vlad said quietly, never taking his gaze from Cain's restless form. "Perhaps all you need is the right motivation, the hidden keystone to your true self."

"If only such a fantastical thing existed," Lucy muttered cynically. She shrugged in acceptance, or exhaustion. "I guess I could keep trying, there's nothing else for me to do anyway." Her eyes were glassy, emotionless, her *smell* like hardened anxiety.

Cain suddenly groaned, a sound almost like an injured hound, and Vlad's face darkened.

"I have such hope for him that I feel it in my heart. He has suffered so much; he must feel such brazen pain in his soul every time he awakens from the wolf to find he is still alive and not in the sweet embrace of death."

"You're talking about suicide. Are those thoughts common for werewolves?"

"They certainly are," Vlad said, a note of anger stinging his voice. "Imagine waking up every month fifty miles from home, covered in blood, not knowing who or what you have harmed. The final three clans are the rarest for a reason: though the curses that create them are unbelievably uncommon, their human forms cannot live with the sheer horror of their crimes. How Cain has survived for so long is utterly beyond me and so I strive to help him. He might well be the last of his kind."

"It's not *fair*, what they must go through," Lucy hissed. "At least in my case I can control it, to a certain degree, and I can keep myself tucked away, safe from everybody."

Blood and Biscuits

Vlad reached across and placed his cold hand on Lucy's pale arm. She stared at Cain with an almost possessive fierceness. Most curious to Vlad.

"Are there different types of vampire?" she asked with interest.

If Vlad had worn glasses, he would have surveyed Lucy over the rim.

"*That* would be telling," he said quietly and the matter was dropped.

They waited a long while as Cain's breathing stabilised and he found a sort of balance with the morphine.

"There is something else…" Lucy began but before she could finish, she closed herself off again. Vlad sensed an ember of yearning within her but it was quickly quenched, the heat choked from her tongue. "Never mind. It's nothing."

He thought back to the man's hairs upon the breath of the wind at her mansion but Vlad did not push the matter. Lucy's business was her own; he was simply a man that would listen when at last she was ready to speak.

"Cain will be alright, Vlad," Lucy said instead. "He has you to guide him through this."

Vlad clasped her fingers tightly in his other hand a moment.

"And I have you all to sustain me," he said softly.

Fig. 7. The Wolf Clans

Sânge - Unu.
↳ Clan Șiret

Sânge - Doi.
↳ Clan Groază
↳ Clan Angajat

Sânge - Trei
↳ Clan Peșteră
↳ Clan Codru
↳ Clan Vizuină

Sânge - Patru
↳ Clan Întristare
↳ Clan Penitență

Sânge - Cinci
↳ Clan Ură
↳ Clan Urâciune
↳ Clan Pângărire

Sânge - Șase
↳ Clan Rușine
↳ Clan Angoasa
↳ Clan Ascensiune

Sânge - Șapte
↳ Clan Puller
↳ Clan Mânie
↳ Clan Răutate

Fig. 8. The Double Stone.

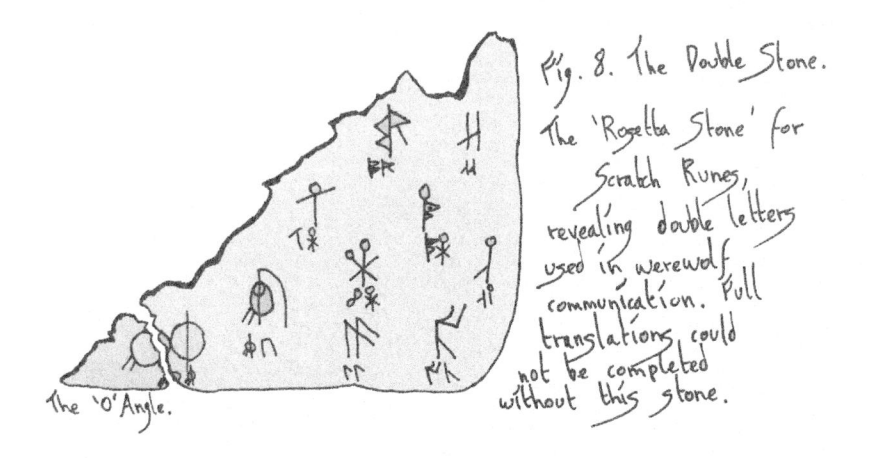

The 'Rosetta Stone' for Scratch Runes, revealing double letters used in werewolf communication. Full translations could not be completed without this stone.

The 'O' Angle.

Fig. 9. The Rune Compass.

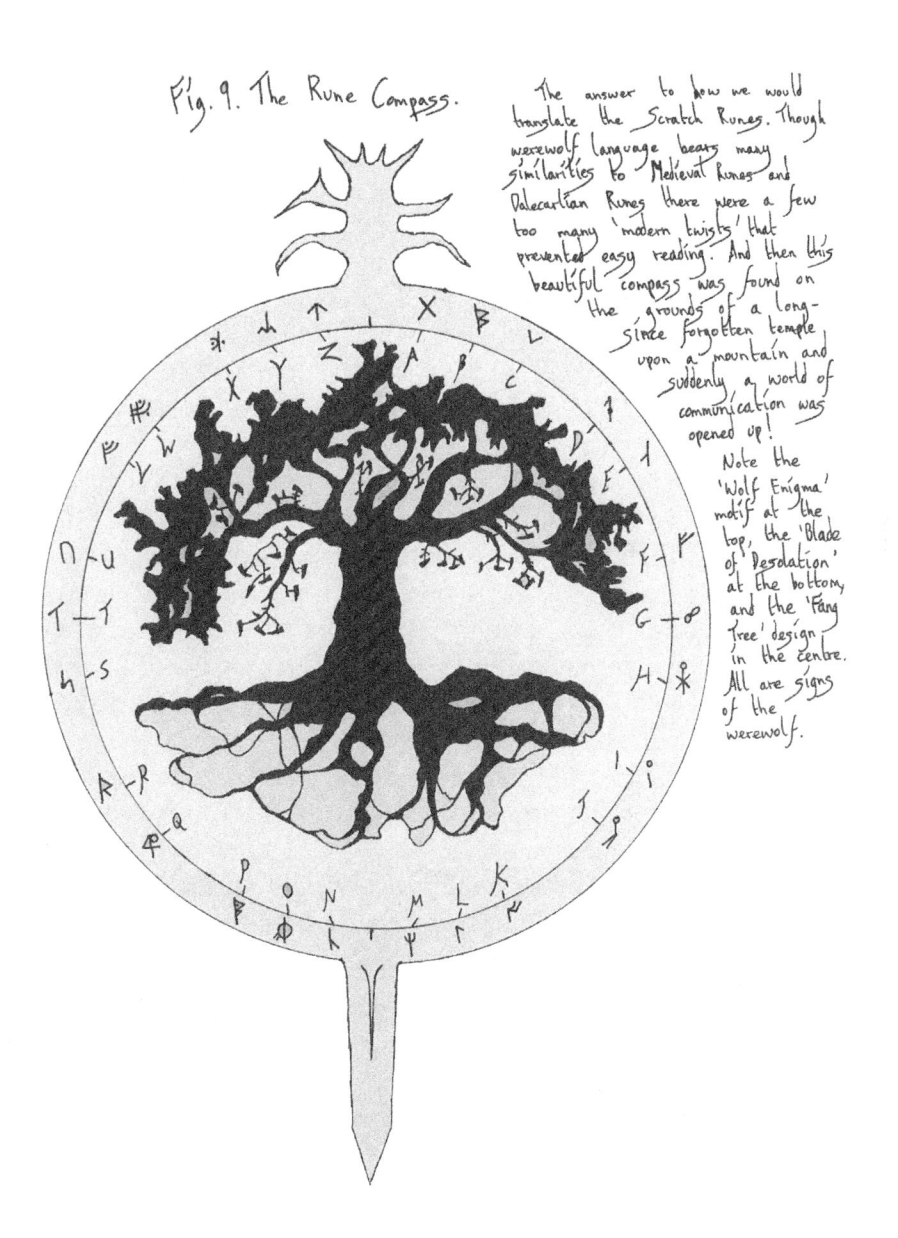

The answer to how we would translate the Scratch Runes. Though werewolf language bears many similarities to Medieval Runes and Dalecarlian Runes there were a few too many 'modern twists' that prevented easy reading. And then this beautiful compass was found on the grounds of a long-since forgotten temple upon a mountain and suddenly a world of communication was opened up!

Note the 'Wolf Enigma' motif at the top, the 'Blade of Desolation' at the bottom, and the 'Fang Tree' design in the centre. All are signs of the werewolf.

RUINS OF ST ELLIN'S CHURCH.
THE START OF THE SUPPORT GROUP.

"He doesn't look good, does he?"

"No, he doesn't. He's in serious pain."

Vlad overheard Jacob and Fable's worry as he put the biscuits and teabags out on the coffee table. Lucy was beside him but her eyes were elsewhere, glancing at Cain's writhing form, his bare wrists and ankles still bound by silver chains. When he twisted to the side, it was evident even through his clothes that his spine had elongated horribly, his hands and feet lengthened and broadened in preparation for housing huge claws and the massive structural anatomy required for the unknown sânge-sapte clan.

Vlad let the Support Group's fear wash over him as he made coffees for himself and Lucy and returned to the chairs. However, this week he did not sit his back to the open entrance like usual, instead he took the seat closest to Cain and had purposefully positioned all others away in an elongated oval. This, of course, came with the detrimental effect of the silver's weakening influence on his strength, but nothing could be done about that. It was only slight, given the distance.

Vlad slid aside a sliver of control and sent his senses across the island, searching for any movement or disturbance. It was a normal misty night in late October, fog curling up from the river, and nothing stirred, no birds, no tiny, scurrying rodents, no Alizon.

The mists would have little impact on the vast blue moon sat heavy in the sky, shining as the silver eye of the Devil.

Jacob fidgeted nervously as Fable laid a hand upon his shoulder to steady him.

"It will be alright, there are more than enough of us here to help our friend in his time of need."

"He's a werewolf, Fable," Jacob pointed out. "Not a drug addict. I think we'll need more than interventions and support groups if we're going to survive his wrath tonight."

"He's bound in pure silver," Lucy offered. "He can't escape that. No werewolf can."

Even so, no face in the room looked entirely convinced as Cain suddenly arched his back and howled a non-human noise, his fingers and legs contorting painfully on the mattress. The chains rattled hauntingly.

Sarah's glowing form appeared through the ceiling and Vlad felt a spark of relief and pride burst within him. He was always glad to see Sarah, though that feeling was tinged by the bittersweet realisation of her cruel, lonely fate, bound to a church she was forced to call home. She could not realise how much she meant to him, not yet.

"Is he awake?" the ghost asked, hovering above Cain, her veiled face gazing down unreadably.

"No, at least I hope not," Vlad said. "If he is then he is doing a very convincing job of feigning a rather painful sleep. He has had multiple morphine injections but I fear the further he travels down his transformational path the less the drug can take effect; his biology simply changes too much to allow such alleviation, his cells no longer responding to the medicine."

"And I doubt there's any real clinical trials on werewolf pain relief," Jacob said dryly. "Then again, there's never a dull moment with Vlad and he's probably got knowledge coming out his ears on gnarly wolf science."

"Unsurprisingly, there is very little on the subject that is of any scientific worth," Vlad admitted. The almighty protection of the unified electric light, the sanctified ground, and the influence of the silver chains was being tested against the dark power still rising within Cain, snarling and clawing to break free and unleash itself upon the island. Vlad felt the silver carve at his own constitution but he divulged nothing of his lessening state to the group. "There is nought beyond the legends and stories we have all doubtlessly heard, mostly in film form. I believe we have Lon Chaney Jr.'s portrayal in 'The Wolf Man' to thank for the popularisation of misinformation we have regarding werewolves, and almost all of what has followed is outrageously incorrect. Rather like with the rest of us, I might add."

Vlad glanced between them all as a vein of quiet contemplation bled its way through the basement, draining what little chance they had left of a pleasant atmosphere.

'Then again,' Vlad thought as Cain's agony bit into his senses, *'there was little chance of pleasantness anyway.'*

"So, let us not dwell on what cannot be changed but instead on what *can*. How was everyone's week?"

There was a murmur and a collective shrug, then Jacob spoke first.

"By and large, it's not been bad, actually. I've managed to get a little money doing internet stuff..."

"Internet stuff?" Vlad asked curiously.

"You know, buying and selling on those auction sites. I didn't want to get technical in case you, err..."

Vlad looked round at them all. Most did not meet his gaze.

"In case I did not understand? Jacob, I am a vampire not a Luddite, I am not *completely* out of touch with today's society! I understand how the internet works and how people use it; in fact, I was most likely using various aspects of it before you were born. Remember that I got you all here *using* the internet, correct?"

"Alright, alright," Jacob said defensively, the tiniest smirk betraying him. "I didn't mean to offend. I wasn't a hundred percent and I made a guess, my apologies."

"Didn't want to get technical," Vlad repeated quietly, crossing his arms indignantly.

"I don't know what an internet is. I first came down to you on a dream," Sarah said mistily, her voice echoing as always. "And a funny feeling of being trespassed on, like you were all walking on my heart. I'm glad I was wrong."

"Thank you for contributing, Sarah," Vlad said cheerfully.

Blood and Biscuits

"You are extremely welcome, Vladislav," Sarah replied with a gentle sigh. "May the springtime of your brain blossom the tulips in your mind."

"*Anyway,*" Jacob said. "That trading stuff seems to be going quite well and I've not run short of brains because of Fable's morgue contact. Big flu outbreak over the county, lots of elderly folk dropping like flies. Not to sound callous – was that callous?"

"It was a tad insensitive," Lucy acknowledged, her eyes darting to Cain.

"Sorry. Put it this way: winter's coming and I'm benefiting. So, err…that's my week, I guess. And my positive things, too."

Lucy waited a moment and then snorted, the black humour clearly hitting its mark. Fable, liquorice-scented tea in-hand, spoke next as Lucy recovered and sipped from her black coffee, several chocolate biscuits clasped in her other hand.

"My week was fine, thank you. I spent a lot of time with Jacob and his new business enterprise – I must say, I'm very impressed that one can make money in this world without ever leaving home. One evening, Jacob introduced me to the wonders of French cinema and his favourite directors, of which there are surprisingly numerous amounts. He attempted to explain some of the history to me but I, being a faerie of the Eight Realms, am magically fluent in most Earth histories. At least I *was*, but since my magic has been almost entirely drawn from my body, I can only use my memory, which saddens me greatly."

"It is a shame you have lost more than your magical abilities but feel assured that we are exactly alike," Vlad said. "A creature of civilisation, that is all. I hardly think we are normal in any *normal* sense of the word. Is that all, Fable?" The faerie nodded, her head almost glistening with gold. "Very good. So moving on, Lucy?" The banshee glanced up and two spots of colour appeared on her cheeks again, the only sign that there was still blood inside her somewhere.

"Yes?" she said in question as Cain gave another long groan.

"Do you want to say anything about your week?" Vlad asked, willing his waning energy into the struggling man upon the mattress.

"I suppose I should. It went quite well, thanks. I spent some time with a friend," she added pointedly and Vlad inclined his head. "And for the rest of it I was mostly alone in the mansion on the hill. You all remember me mentioning that observatory and garden-house complex last week?"

"Not the garden-house but definitely the observatory," Jacob grunted.

"Vaguely," Sarah said absentmindedly. "I wish *I* was lucky enough to have a garden here. All that grows are some beautiful yellow-pink spirit daffodils and some naughty weeds in the graveyard, like the dandelions amongst the Baker and Johnson families between rows five and six. I think the flowers have used the bodies as natural fertiliser. The families aren't happy about the betrayal," she added.

"Morbid," Jacob said in sick fascination as Lucy spoke again.

"If it helps, Sarah, there's little in the way of attraction or shape to the mansion gardens anymore. There's a labyrinth of overgrown plants and broken statues of people and weird creatures, the walls are dilapidated and vandalised, the huge, old greenhouses are smashed and dirty, and the pathways are rotten and disordered by trees."

"That sounds lovely, you must be very satisfied there," Sarah said quietly and Lucy nearly tripped over herself in response.

"Oh, it has a very strange kind of beauty, don't misunderstand me, and the grounds have an eerie quality to them. It's just it seems so desolate now, like all the love and attention once lavished on the place has been taken, blown away on the wind." Lucy quickly turned to the wraith, keen on not comparing herself further to Sarah. "I can't believe you were supposed to go on a school trip there, Jay."

Jacob looked surprised he had been involved, his veined and sagging eyes opening wide, the visible muscles of his jaw slackening a little.

"This was over twenty years ago, mind," he added quickly. "I think there was still an old caretaker there and some sort of National Trust scenario, though I can't imagine why they abandoned the place. I'm glad I didn't go; I think it would have scared the life out of me. Not that I've remained in any way alive," he added, reaching into his bag and pulling out a plastic food container of blended brains.

"I've not been there all that time, just the past few years," Lucy said. All of a sudden, she grew stony and Vlad had a suspicion she did not want to talk about her binding. Her words grew terse and clipped. "That's beside the point, I was just talking about the grounds and how I tried to get into the observatory. Nearly made it in, then I had to go back inside. The end."

"Thank you, Lucy, that sounds positive," Vlad said before anyone else had a chance to remark on her tone and make the situation worse. He turned, wishing to look at Sarah to ask how her week had been, when something suddenly snapped at his senses from behind and a loud, metallic *clunk* resonated through the basement. All about the room fell deathly silent, as if the church itself held a deep breath.

A quarter-second later, Vlad's eyes confirmed precisely what his ears had told him.

Cain's right hand was free of its bond. His wrist had actually *bent* the silver and twisted the links apart.

"Everybody…" Vlad said smoothly, "stay calm. Do not panic."

Cain groaned and a deep sound of something dark and angry rose from within his body. It released as a howl. The group stared in paralysed horror as Cain's clothes strained with a sudden increase in bulk, limbs writhing against his shining bonds as the beast began emerging.

Blood and Biscuits

'The blue moon's power is too much for every protective ward against the curse,' Vlad's mind told him. *'He is phenomenally powerful. The sânge-sapte is real.'*

"Is it happening to him?" Lucy asked fearfully, watching from her seat with a sort of terrified fascination. "How did he break free!"

"Do not hesitate," Vlad commanded. "Just go, get out the church!"

Sarah immediately flew up and through the ceiling; a moment later she poked her head back through the stone to observe from a point of safety, despite the fact she was the only one that could not be harmed. All the rest were petrified, Vlad could smell their terror.

Ripping tore the air and Cain's shirt and trousers burst, every line and seam shredded. The mattress sank under the weight as his skin convulsed and rippled, vast muscles swelling and shivering beneath, his skeleton adding layer upon layer of armoured bone, tendons stretching agonisingly. Long hair took root and grew from his flesh as the last of Cain's humanity disappeared and the wolf took control. Yet even in that moment of terror, as Vlad stood facing the oncoming storm, he found himself shocked at the colour of Cain's fur: pure-white and gleaming in the low light.

'Now that *is unique,'* he mused automatically. Vlad spread his arms wide to shield the Support Group, the dark protector.

Cain rolled onto his front and shattered two more connections in showers of silver shards, leaving only his left ankle bound, and he pitched up onto all fours as his back arched. His spine convulsed downwards and surged as the bones cracked sickeningly and reordered themselves, expanding so torturously the werewolf roared. His face jutted forward and his nose and mouth elongated with a horrid suddenness into a long and powerful muzzle, eyes sinking back into his skull as they narrowed and yellowed into gleaming points. His hands and feet splintered and regrew and twisted into huge paws, and a long tail erupted from the end of his spine. It whipped the air dangerously as the werewolf thundered in fury.

The beast-formerly-known-as-Cain staggered forward, his gigantic white body tremoring as he unleashed an ear-splitting howl. At the sound, Vlad felt every single ounce of his power try to escape, his control the only thing holding back the vampire beneath as he defended those cowering behind him.

Vlad evaluated the werewolf and estimated him as fifteen-foot long, snout to tail, formidably larger than any specimen he had met before. His dazzling white coat glinted in the basement's soft light as Cain turned and locked eyes on the Support Group. Jagged, hairless lines marked the hollow points where Cain's human-form scars were, his skull criss-crossed with livid tracks.

Cain's pitch-black nose sniffed the air, the points of his foot-long ears twitching to every minute sound. Vlad wreathed himself in darkness entirely.

"I said go and I meant it, do not make the mistake of staying for Cain!" Vlad called back to them. "He is gone, he is just a beast. RUN!"

They reacted too slowly.

With another roar, the werewolf battered the concrete with his huge paws and darted forward with titanic speed. Instantly, Vlad swept his arm round in a wide, graceful motion, drawing a thin veil of darkness in a cloak of shadow. It rose and breathed out across the basement, forming a shroud of confusion across the werewolf's eyes, blinding his view. In that same movement, Vlad enveloped Lucy, Fable, and Jacob in a curtain of power and swept them silently aside as if yanked by ropes.

The gigantic werewolf ground to a halt, claws tearing the floor in horrid screeches of stone. He stared wildly, eyes gleaming, wide nostrils flaring and scenting the air. However, Vlad's shroud of strength was delicate and impenetrable by all senses. The werewolf gazed round in futility and Vlad held onto the threads of his darkness, pressing everyone flat to the wall and knowing Cain's hunting eyes could discern nothing but a slight shading across the stone.

The werewolf took three breaths, then snarled and stalked from the basement, his bulk only just squeezing through the entranceway as old timbers heaved and creaked in place, tail lashing three lines into the walls.

Vlad focussed on his senses and waited, wrapped in that darkness for longer than his gut told him to. When at last he dropped his strength, he did not stop to assess the group. Jacob and Fable stepped away and looked at the entranceway in terror, however Lucy followed Vlad as he crossed the basement and pulled on a pair of thick leather gloves from the canvas bag sitting by the wall.

"What are you doing with those, Vlad? Where are you going?" Lucy demanded of him as the vampire grabbed hold of all four ends of the silver chains and hauled them up from the ground. "You can't go after him, he'll kill you!" Lucy cried but she stepped too close and immediately stopped, her face screwed up in pain. She leapt back quickly and pointed at the chains. "Oh God, those are monstrous!" she said hurriedly. "How can you stand them?"

There came a howl in the distance, far beyond the church grounds, and Vlad pointed at the entrance, face set like pale marble, hair-thin black veins already appearing across his flesh because of the silver.

"You hear that? That is the sound of a sapte-level werewolf racing across Ellin's Island, heading for the only light source he can see: the closest town. And that light happens to have a great deal of meat living in it. I stand the silver because I must, Lucy. There is no-one else that can. If he kills me then I die knowing I tried to stop him."

"But you said it yourself: you don't know anything about his type of wolf," Lucy tried arguing, her leaching worry strangling her reasoning. "He could tear you apart!"

"He could but hopefully he will not," Vlad said as he hefted the silver chains, their influence devouring his strength. "I do not have long before I can no longer use these. Lucy, remain here with Jacob and Fable, make sure they stay out of trouble. And keep Sarah calm, she is most dear to me. Like you all," he added quickly as he re-awoke his darkness. Vlad failed the first time, the silver having already removed a large portion of his strength, so he removed more of his control on the power and swept from the room, the electric light flickering ominously, the chains glittering in silver streams.

THE WASTELANDS AND INDUSTRIAL COMPLEX, ELLIN'S INDUSTRIAL ISLAND, NORTHERN ENGLAND.

Every colour and structure of the neglected landscape blurred as Vlad soared low, fangs gleaming in the chase. The silver chains trailed behind him in four shining lines, draining his power even through his thick leather gloves.

The beast devoured the distance faster than any lower clan werewolf could and Vlad was thankful the island was so vast and confusing for a creature unaccustomed to the old paths and sunken roads. The terrible blue moon's bright light glinted off shining pools of muddy water, vast beams of white striking the wasteland flats in columns and sheets.

Through the gloom, Vlad saw the hulking werewolf moving far ahead and forced more of his power past the siphon of the silver chains, increasing his speed at the cost of his reserves. Cain's heavy paws pounded the island as he headed towards the shores, his direction off-bearing from the single bridge lying northwards. One thing linking all werewolves was that they avoided water. The river would buy Vlad time.

Cain slowed at the bank and Vlad dropped, his feet hitting the ground hard as he kept his darkness wrapped about his form, staving off the silver's gnashing hunger. The werewolf padded the shoreline, watching the lapping waters suck the rocky banks, and growled like a distant storm. Pure, venomous rage emanated from him as he prowled. Vlad felt flickers of fear sparkling within himself: almost every encounter he had had with werewolves of any clan had ended unpleasantly.

"You are trapped, Cain," Vlad called out. "There is no reason to continue. Remember who you are."

The werewolf stopped and turned with deliberate slowness. Vlad twitched for he saw the calculation in the move, the careful consideration; most other animals would react quickly to the noise, turning swiftly to face a potential threat, but this beast was intelligent, high above the wild mindlessness of lower clan werewolves. Cain's wolf was well aware of his vast, raw power, and he clearly was not above giving a show of dominance as he moved lazily round then set his weight on his front paws. He leaned towards Vlad in challenge.

That intelligence concerned Vlad more than anything else.

The vampire seemed miniscule compared to the gigantic transformation, and in the deep moonlight Vlad *felt* small, too. It was not often that another could cow him but the turmoil of his depression, coupled with the frightening strength of the silver, clawed at his every sensation, dragging everything he was into a drowning pit of despair.

The cursed creatures of the night stood and stared at one another upon that arena of mud, like some gothic oil painting.

'This will have to be quick,' Vlad told himself. *'Or he will kill me, followed by everyone else. Do not let that happen.'*

The werewolf growled in warning and took a step forward. Vlad set his stance and shook the glimmering silver chains out before him, two per hand, rattling them loudly and bolstering the effect with a shower of darkness. A rain effect of shadow fell about the wolf's heavy shoulders, rupturing his glare. Cain stared round in confusion and when he looked back, Vlad was gone.

Suddenly, he vapourised from the air and collided heavily into Cain's huge white body with almost every ounce of power he possessed. Vlad cried out in pain as Cain howled and rolled over, the vampire tumbling with him until he was crushed beneath the beast. Before Cain could react, Vlad dropped his control, sending a colossal blast of power into the werewolf's chest, punching him fifteen feet into the air and sending him sprawling across the mud in a heap of writhing limbs.

Half a second later, Vlad was attempting to find a purchase and bind the violent creature in chains but Cain thrashed and roared too much for submission. The werewolf's strength was phenomenal, close even to Vlad's when unaffected by silver. That was a horrible realisation.

"Stay *still*, Cain!" Vlad cried but the werewolf only grew wilder, lashing savagely with his massive paws. An iron-hard claw met Vlad's flesh and tore his abdomen, sending lines of dark blood dancing through the air, spattering the muddied ground. Vlad grunted in pain as his dead nerves fired deep, lancing signals. Humans would have been killed by the injury, but vampires used pain to bolster their strength, and Vlad's power rose within him until it reached a fever pitch. "I said STAY STILL!" he roared and Vlad wrenched the werewolf up by the fur and leapt into the sky.

Cain bayed and screamed against the moonlit night as Vlad held back his snapping jaws, the silver chains whipping the werewolf in the wind. He aimed for the industrial complex and landed in a crushing pile upon the highest metallic platform. Several struts collapsed and disappeared into glittering puffs of nothing, fading from existence, illusion magic disintegrating around them as Vlad rolled from Cain and the werewolf struggled to rise, his paw evidently hurt.

"I'm trying to help you!" Vlad called. "Do you not see that? You are no beast but a man, a man trying to break free of these wicked bonds…"

The white werewolf took a struggling step toward the vampire and then he suddenly bent over and convulsed. Vlad thought he was about to howl but he instead threw back his massive, shaggy

Blood and Biscuits

head and unleashed the most violent sneeze. If the situation had not have been so disastrous Vlad would have smiled at the sheer absurdity.

"You see? That is your human form struggling to break free, Cain! Come, let us be rid of this terror, let us work together."

Vlad had put little faith into the suggestion but he thought it worth the attempt. Lower werewolf clans were sometimes impressionable but it seemed the sânge-sapte group would not listen to reason.

The pale werewolf set his gigantic body against the exposed steel supports and beams of the industrial rooftop – the spell that held them there threatened to buckle and fade away. Then Cain charged.

"Oh bugger," Vlad muttered.

The werewolf struck him with such force the very air compressed, and the two tumbled through the factory, bodies striking every skeletal strut, bursting them apart in showers of light and dust, the magic binding them to reality failing in pieces. Mid-flight, Vlad wrapped what he could of the silver chains about Cain's shaggy form. His jaws snapped, tried to clamp round Vlad's face, but the vampire was too quick, the tattered remains of his power ensuring his head and body continuously glimmered out of place so Cain caught nothing but air between his fangs.

With a calamitous cannonade of noise, the beasts of darkness crashed through twin sheets of corrugated iron, which disappeared at the rupturing of their magic, and slammed into a stone shelf. Vlad hauled Cain off as his paws scrabbled and tore at anything within reach, but as the vampire rose in graceless exhaustion one of the werewolf's claws dragged down his back and rented apart the dead flesh, dragging it wide open, painting an arc of crimson through the air. Vlad screamed and his veins pulsed black beneath his skin, silver chains rattling and shining as he shook them free.

The werewolf drew himself up as tall as he could, silhouetted by deep moonlight, his matted fur drifting heavily on the rising river wind. Vlad dragged himself upright and leant against a metal strut, eyes locked onto the horrifyingly enamouring vision of the muddied white werewolf, his golden yellow irises staring down at the small vampire before him, judging him worthless.

Cain's beast threw back his grizzled head and gave a most terrible roar that shook the foundations of the factories, shimmering its magic and sending shockwaves of fury and spite up Vlad's spine. Power streamed back into him as he steeled himself and faced what was to come, blood leaking from a corner of his mouth.

In that fraction of a second, Vlad felt a single spark of fear. It did not send his body into expected tremors and weakness; as Cain began his charge, his white jaws slung with silver droplets, Vlad's fear manifested as survival, his need to linger on. And for the briefest of moments his despair lifted entirely and he was free from the shackles of his depression. He *wanted* to live; he *wanted* to see the light of day again. Ironically, these were not things any other vampire would long for.

Every ounce of Cain's mass fell upon Vlad but the vampire's hands rose to meet him and caught the upper and lower jaws of his muzzle in the grip of a man determined to survive. Hot, sweating breath beat around his face as his knees threatened to buckle but he channelled more of his ragged, frayed power into his legs and back and pushed until the werewolf was hauled up and away. Vlad bellowed war into Cain's face, darkness billowing out and turning the sound to a demonic hell cry, and he forced the werewolf backwards, claws dragging deep trenches in the stone shelf, chains hanging about them in a curtain of shimmering silver, ever drawing their strengths away.

Vlad grunted and found his voice.

"This…brings back…memories…Cain…" he muttered. Then, with a guttural snarl of effort, Vlad mangled the werewolf's jaws together with a sickening *crunch* and threw him bodily from the shelf.

Down Cain fell, through metal and stone, for five hundred feet until he struck the ground, coming to rest at last in the wasteland muds far below. Shaking, Vlad crawled to the lip of the shelf and peered down. Cain did not move.

Sorrow returned instantaneously. He had killed his friend, senses too dulled by exhaustion to perceive any signs of life in the werewolf. The vampire rolled onto his back and looked into the eye of the sated moon, and he hated it with his every fibre. It had brought nothing but misery that night.

"You are nought but a mirror for the sun, you horrid rock," he grunted bitterly.

Something stirred upon the wind and Vlad *heard* movement, heavy and laboured. With a rope of resignation knotted inside him, he peered back down the vast height and saw Cain's shuffling body heaving itself upright. The werewolf shook himself down like an oversized dog and sniffed the air, his breaths struggling against damaged bones. Vlad watched the beast curiously, his mind too tired to conjure any useful thoughts. Then he sighed in dismay when Cain howled once more and took off across the wastelands, limping for the lights of the town across the river.

"Oh for God's sake," Vlad muttered.

He rolled off the shelf and fell five hundred feet to the ground, silver chains held behind him like shining standards. His flagging darkness captured his body a second before he struck and carried him on the wind in pursuit. Vlad did not know if he would outlive a second encounter but he saw no other choice.

Suddenly, the wind compressed and burst over them in a deluge of wordless noise. The sound of a single, piercing scream exploded across vampire and werewolf and altered the energy of the island. Cain skidded to a halt and looked eastwards, then he sprinted off towards St Ellin's Church so quickly that Vlad flew straight past him. The vampire cursed himself and reset his direction but Cain ran too fast for Vlad to hope to catch up in time, his destination now a lone figure stood before the glowing basement entrance of the church ruins.

Vlad concentrated through his waning strength and saw Lucy, her mouth wide in a blood-curdling scream, pale palms facing the oncoming white storm. Her hair streamed out from her head and black flames wreathed her, shimmering and beautiful.

'*So you* have *been practicing. Another interesting thing.*'

"Lucy, move!" Vlad boomed but she did not hear, or she ignored him. The banshee remained steady, face determined, hands never wavering as Cain pounded across the mud flats, eighty feet from her.

Yet the many centuries of work he had done could not prepare him for the most unexpected encounter.

Rather than descending upon Lucy and tearing her apart, Cain slowed and walked to her with an almost gentle curiosity, and Lucy stemmed her scream. The werewolf halted before her, deep-yellow eyes tracking her face and hands calculatingly. Vlad felt flashes of recognition emanating from the beast, a silent stream undercutting his rage as Cain studied Lucy's passivity, her body cast in black fire. Vlad hit the ground and tore two long furrows of dirt, and he watched Cain bend his head and lower his muzzle into Lucy's outstretched hand, his great eyes closing for a moment as her fingers spread into the long, white fur, hair matted with blackening blood, her dark flames gone now.

Lucy held him for a time as Vlad moved round to her side and watched with energised fascination.

"How is this…how is this possible?" he whispered, shock clear in his voice. "How did you know to do this?"

"I didn't," Lucy whispered back as Cain, his lower jaw dripping with gore, moved so that her hand traced lines of comfort up and down his snout. "I thought you were going to be killed…I…I'm so tired…"

Lucy suddenly failed and her hand dropped. Cain stirred irritably. His eyes snapped open as she fell backwards, and Vlad caught her easily. He lowered her carefully to the ground as the werewolf reared up on his hind legs and howled, towering twelve feet of pure muscle and ire, claws shining in the moonlight, and Vlad stared in horror at what was to befall him on that chilly night in northern England.

'I never would have thought it would end like this,' Vlad told himself. His mind worked with surprising clarity, as if looking his true death in the face might bring relief. *'Too many centuries gone by, perhaps too many to count now. This might grant me peace after all.'*

Vlad saw a light from above as the werewolf bore down on him, as if the sky itself opened and swallowed him in its everlasting embrace, and the vampire enveloped its warmth as his skin burned. The demon of his despair that hounded him would finally be sated.

The burning of his skin grew terribly painful and Vlad suddenly realised the light was coming from behind, not above, it was not the calling of the heavens but the black and shrivelled hands of Fable standing firm by the church entrance, a grim look etching her face. Jacob stood by her side as Fable's hands reached towards the werewolf, bittersweet Light flickering and pulsing from her body in weak shafts, framing the darkness, casting thin bars of brilliance. Cain roared and where Light touched his flesh pure white fur faded and human skin appeared beneath.

The true form of Cain was revealed by the faerie's Light.

Vlad stood in wonder, a thousand questions scrabbling for attention at the shores of his mind, yet none would be answered. All he could do was watch as dozens of moments happened at once, crashing together as the influence of the silver chains brought Vlad to his knees and bound his body in exhaustion. A pair of hands met his shoulders and dragged him over the mud, his head lolling back as he stared into Jacob's desperate eyes, the wraith's decomposing face twisted in a gaunt mask of fear. He was shouting something but Vlad could not hear over the sound of rushing blood in his ears, the chains wrapped about his ankle and gathering dirt across the ground.

A flash of white circled overhead and Vlad saw Sarah flying down from the church rooftops. She passed over Cain's head and he swiped at her viciously, to swat her from the skies. Sarah screeched – Vlad thought it was in excitement – then flew round again, slowing enough to allow Cain the chance to slash at her. His heavy paws passed straight through her pearlescent form and the werewolf roared in frustration.

'She's acting as a distraction,' Vlad thought mildly in his almost hypnotic stupor as Jacob hauled him away. *'Now that is interesting.'*

"Get *up*, Vlad!" Jacob called and the vampire gazed into his face.

"Hmm?" He asked pleasantly.

Something snapped inside him and he clutched hold of his fracturing mind and divided powers.

It was not the terror in Jacob's voice nor the sight of Lucy's unconscious body upon the ground. Nor even was it the faltering desperation written across Fable's face. It was the group itself, their fight in the face of adversity, their unification not only to defend Vlad but to bring back their friend from the very brink of destruction. In this realisation, Vlad returned to reality, and he stood, smiling, with much recovered strength, Jacob by his side.

He handed the wraith an end of a silver chain.

"I think we are going to need these," he said quietly, his voice echoing like Sarah's. Jacob smiled and took the proffered chain.

"You go left?" he suggested and Vlad nodded.

"A fine decision, my friend. Aim for the legs, that will bring him down far more efficiently and protect us all from his claws. Are you not afraid of him?" Vlad asked of Jacob, looking at the gigantic figure of Cain as he grabbed at Sarah.

Jacob laughed throatily.

"You forget, I've already died once. And in life I made it my purpose to *protect* animals, even when I failed to protect myself. Vegan, remember?"

Vlad nodded again. Without another word, he and Jacob seized up the silver chains and sprinted towards the gigantic beast,

Blood and Biscuits

his shaggy snout spinning in every direction. With the distractions of ghost and Light set, Vlad darted left and ducked beneath a flailing paw as Jacob ran right, and both men hauled all four lengths of silver round the giant werewolf's long shins and wrenched as hard as they could.

With an earthquake rumble, Cain tripped and tumbled to the muddy ground, paws and drooling muzzle smashing into the dirt hard enough to loosen a grunt of pain. Without hesitation, Vlad leapt forwards and lifted the werewolf with every ounce of strength he had – Cain's transformed body easily weighed more than a thousand pounds – and Jacob threw the ends of his chains underneath the beast. Vlad took them and passed the ends back over and Jacob wound their links through one another as the werewolf howled in bitter aggravation.

Jacob stepped back with a ragged sigh of relief as Vlad pulled the chains tight and dragged Cain back towards the basement entrance of St Ellin's Church. The werewolf was properly incapacitated by silver now; he would not be able to escape again.

"Jesus Christ, that took some work," Jacob muttered as he lifted Lucy and carried her in his arms. Fable, her Light exhausted, staggered and leaned on Jacob as well, the wraith bearing her weight with ease. He followed after Vlad as the vampire dragged the werewolf back down into the basement's depths, claws scraping and catching on the stone steps as Sarah passed overhead and disappeared through the solid church.

"I am going…to need…some blood…" Vlad managed as he positioned Cain so he would fit through the small stairwell before dragging him back down. "But first…a coffee…"

RUINS OF ST ELLIN'S CHURCH.
NORTHERN ENGLAND.

Blood and Biscuits

The werewolf slid into the basement and growled as the electric light and sanctified ground worked in unison with the silver chains to subdue him, if not undo the blue moon's influence on the sânge-sapte's blood curse. Cain's eyes rolled back in his head as the result of the fight with Vlad took its toll, and he fell into a pseudo-stupor, conserving energy and biding his time.

Vlad dragged the werewolf the last few dozen feet to the mattress and sought the dangling ends of the silver chains, their lengths binding the werewolf's body fully instead of simply his wrists and ankles. Vlad reconnected the chains to the iron pegs still embedded in the ground.

"Will he stay like that?" Jacob asked worriedly as he lay Lucy down near the coffee table, Fable leaning against the wall. "He broke free easily enough the first time…" he trailed off.

"It will not be so simple for him a second time," Vlad explained as he stepped away from the werewolf, and the influence of the silver, then moved to the far end of the basement. "Just as I am, he will be utterly spent and resting to preserve what he has left. I suspect the worst of the blue moon is over now and we shall be better off for it. My goodness, I need to sit down."

Jacob hurried over and helped Vlad onto a chair. He peered into the vampire's eyes a moment then glanced all round his face.

"Your, err…your skin's gone a bit…veiny…"

Vlad felt his cheeks and brow then rolled up his muddy sleeves and looked at his arms. Great black lines tracked his flesh, pulsing with fury and vigour.

"Well would you look at that," Vlad said with interest. "No need to worry, Jacob, they are simply my blood supply pushing out the last of the silver poison from my body. I would imagine my face looks a bit strange?"

"Yeah, like some oily roadmap," the wraith said with a sly grin.

"How remarkably sensitive of you," Vlad chuckled.

"Sorry, couldn't help it, I'm still shook up from earlier. Here, I'll get us some coffees while Fable and Lucy recover."

He moved over to the refreshments table and returned a moment later with a steaming coffee for the vampire.

Vlad looked it over then glanced at the table absentmindedly.

"Technology has come a long way," he murmured as he sipped his coffee and felt the warmth of it slide down his cold throat.

"What do you mean?" Jacob asked as he looked at Lucy. He nodded tightly, most likely confirming she was fine.

"Well, four hundred years ago a simple device such as a thermos or coffee decanter would have been grounds for witchcraft accusations, and now we do not even consider them as we use them. We take for granted all that long ago would have been considered kingly. I wonder how the world will view *us* in four hundred years' time. Perhaps there will be no world to speak of, perhaps we will be the only ones left... My apologies," Vlad said quickly. "I was rambling again. When I am tired I say silly things, my mind wandering like animal trails through the woods."

"That's alright, I understand," Jacob said encouragingly. "My partner, Luke..." He hesitated a moment, as if he had not meant to say that bit. He gazed pointedly at Vlad but the vampire said nothing. Then he looked himself down and shrugged, satisfied with something. "He was from before I turned...he's long gone now. Luke thought a lot like you. He was eccentric, to say the least. And he taught me so many things, and not just about things that can be *learned*, like from a book, but about feelings and what it means to hold love so dearly in your heart that it hurts."

"Did you find the greatest lesson in love was learned when he abandoned you?" Vlad posed. It was not a question designed to be rude or mean-spirited, simply an observation.

Jacob nodded sadly.

"I'm afraid so. It isn't until we lose something we realise just how much it meant to us."

"Well said," Vlad acknowledged.

He glanced at the slumbering form of the gigantic werewolf then at the unconscious stillness of Lucy, and something clicked in his mind. The scents of a single hair drifted across his mind's eye again, that image of a wild man and the second foreign odour passing before him, borne on the memory of wind, and Vlad knew to whom the floating hair at Lucy's mansion had belonged. He could smell that same man buried in the slumbering werewolf, that second, unknown scent overpowering now.

Vlad stroked his chin thoughtfully.

"Perhaps there was more to that moment of hesitation between Cain and Lucy."

"I don't follow," Jacob said before drinking down his black coffee quicker than a human could have managed. Vlad heard it sloshing in his stomach.

"It is just…I have never known a werewolf to stop for anything before, least of all a woman screaming. Werewolves despise noise and are quick to destroy the source of it. It does not make sense, so I must be attempting to make the *wrong* sort of sense from it. I have not encountered Cain's clan before, his is entirely new to me; I thought his wolves were legend, rumour, yet here he sleeps before us, smelling the way he does."

"I think he smells like wet dog," Jacob grunted.

"Clan?" Fable asked quietly.

"Remind me to explain werewolf lore to you both another time," Vlad sighed. "For now, just accept that Cain is an anomaly, white fur and all. And that is another thing: white fur? Werewolves are brown or grey or black but never white! I could understand it if he was albino in his human form but he is dark of hair and skin."

"You're just making the wrong sense of it," Jacob repeated and Vlad smiled.

"That about sums it up, I fear. Look, you both take yourselves back to your place. And Jacob, make sure Fable has not damaged herself any further channelling her magic like she did. Her hands have suffered more than enough harm; you were both extremely brave to take on the werewolf but I would not have Fable extend her injuries because of it." Fable stirred in embarrassment as Jacob opened his mouth to protest. Vlad held up his hand. "It is fine, Jacob, do not object, I can finish up here and wait this out. Cain needs a guard until the morning; he will be too weak to overcome his silver bonds now, and I am recovering quickly – look, the black veins are already receding."

Vlad indicated his arms. They watched as the thinner dark lines disappeared back beneath his flesh.

"Are you sure you'll be alright?" Jacob asked.

"More than sure. Lucy is unconscious, which I believe exploits a certain loophole in her binding curse, putting it into a sort of freeze as she recovers. I have never known if it was accidental or not, as if the original lyrical curse architecture was mispronounced or had poorly written spell lines, but it is a boon to Lucy. The blue moon happens only the one night – it is a normal full moon tomorrow night and the chains will no longer be necessary. Please, be on your way, I greatly look forward to seeing you next week, Jacob. You too, Fable."

"Shame, I was hoping to say bye to Sarah," Jacob said sadly, looking up at the ceiling pointedly. Fable answered, voice reflecting her tired thoughts, fresh pain lancing her hands.

"She will be confused and overexcited," she explained. "I suspect you'll find her as normal next week, Jacob. Come, I need rest. As Vlad said: I may have worsened my condition and I would tend my wounds before this potentiality sets in."

Jacob and Fable packed up their belongings and walked purposefully from the basement, as if the battle with the werewolf had never taken place. As they came to the entranceway, Vlad called after them:

"Thank you, both of you. For your assistance with Cain, I mean. I doubt I would be sitting here if you had not put yourselves in danger. So…thank you."

Blood and Biscuits

"You're most welcome," Fable said, inclining her head regally. Jacob simply smiled.

Then the wraith and faerie were gone, leaving a vampire watching over a banshee and a werewolf.

Vlad sensed Jacob leave the church grounds, still unable to attune himself to the faerie's presence, and begin his steady walk across the wastelands. He sighed and finished his coffee, placing the cup carefully on the ground so the pottery rang across the concrete slabs clearly.

"They have gone now, Lucy, you may awaken."

The banshee stirred and raised her head. She did not seem well but she managed a watery smile for Vlad.

"How long have you known?" she asked shakily.

"A few minutes. As soon as you awoke," he replied easily. "It is a good thing I know about the loophole in your curse, I am too weary to think of a lie-by-omission to satisfy the sanctified ground's hold on my curse. But why pretend to be unconscious?"

"I didn't want to get any questions," Lucy admitted as she stood slowly, brushing off her knees. "And I wasn't sure about the loophole, by the way, so that's another thing confirmed." She glanced at Vlad awkwardly. "You, err, probably have a few questions…"

"One or two, yes," Vlad replied wearily. "I guess the biggest one, though, is your scream."

Lucy nodded and dropped herself heavily into a spare chair.

"I wasn't going to try practicing it at first – the idea of exploring my power is frightening to me, as you already know – but then…I don't know, I guess with seeing Cain's condition worsen I wanted to find some strength in the world I could control. I tried performing a banshee scream at the mansion, like you suggested, but it wasn't that loud and I didn't know how it would go tonight."

"Apparently it severed your consciousness for a time," Vlad pointed out in amusement. Lucy laughed nervously as she stood and poured herself a black coffee. She grabbed six chocolate biscuits –

they were the thick-layered kind, Vlad had heard they were most satisfying. "Severing consciousnesses is not usual for people of our types of curse, Lucy. We are designed to remain one with our minds, even through sleep, and so learning this skill may very well prove several other things we did not know. But that is not enough to warrant not being questioned. I for one am extremely proud of what you achieved, for it shows what hard work and courage can accomplish in the right hands."

Two spots of colour appeared on Lucy's cheeks as she carried her coffee over.

"Thanks..." was all she managed as she sat carefully and drank, the basement strangely quiet in the gloom, as if a hush had descended with everyone gone and the werewolf now truly slumbering.

Vlad took the measure of her, the way she held herself, the small glances she made to Cain. Vlad knew for certain what it was now, the thoughts filling Lucy right then, he had seen it countless times throughout the centuries. Yet the admission was hers to make alone, Vlad's capacity was listening and observing.

That did not mean he could not test the waters, however.

"The way you stopped him was nothing short of remarkable," he noted quietly. The giant white werewolf's breaths came deep and strained. "It goes without saying this is simply not normal. Never in my time have I encountered a werewolf that could choose to stop. Free will is our most valuable gift, Lucy, and to remove it is a heinous crime. Hence my hatred of mastery."

Vlad let the comments sit for a time as Lucy visibly mulled them over. Cain's huge eyes shifted and twitched beneath his lids, his breathing growing deeper as he slipped into new forms of troubled sleep. Lucy made a short noise and shrugged.

"The scream was me trying to stop him from escaping, and that certainly had an effect. I suppose I had a feeling it would work."

"And indeed it did, and the townships beyond the river will forever be in your debt for this act. As for his ability to think beyond his rage? It must be something to do with the sânge-sapte blood curse. Though I have observed some lower-clan wolves respond to a little coercion, usually involving food, they do not listen to base-level reasoning, their human minds buried too deep within. With Cain, it was almost as if he recognised you through the fury that blinded him and chose to stop because *of* you."

Lucy sighed and shrugged again, an accepting sort of motion.

"I feel like you're getting at something," she said quietly. "And that feeling tells me you already know the answer. So, go on: say what you think."

"Are you sure?" Vlad asked carefully, allowing the opportunity for her to change her mind.

"Yes. Otherwise it'll eat at me."

Vlad pointed at Cain.

"You and he have shared something beyond these walls. I know not what, precisely, but it speaks volumes of the foundations of affection. When we met at your mansion, I smelled the hairs of a man on the grounds and on your dress, hairs I now know were Cain's." Lucy breathed a sigh but Vlad smiled encouragingly. "This is no matter of embarrassment or shame, this is no secret you need hide. Whatever you have built with him, that human emotion reared its head when he charged at you and fought the werewolf side of him, causing him to stop and consider his actions. Something in either of your curses has allowed that to happen. So yes, I theorise based on observational evidence."

Lucy smiled lopsidedly.

"You are eerily perceptive, Vlad," she muttered. "I can't believe you smelled his hair, that's really scary. I guess that's what a thousand years of age will do to someone."

Vlad's blood ran cold – cold*er* – for a moment.

"A thousand years…" he repeated softly.

"Mmm," Lucy said with a deeper smile. "It's my turn to shock *you*. Several weeks ago, you mentioned you had been in Ireland – in Wexford, you said – during the time of Henry's invasion.

Blood and Biscuits

I happened to already know this piece of history, and all I needed to do was a little confirmation at the library. Twelfth century, that event was, but you aren't Irish, you're ancient Romanian, and so I added an extra hundred years for good measure. This puts you at a thousand years."

Vlad said nothing and Lucy seized on this.

"Why hide your age, Vlad? I don't get it! I understand that vampires can grow incredibly old but you are miraculous!"

"I hide it for the same reasons you hide your attachment to Cain," he replied smoothly. "I do not wish for people to know the true me. Not yet, anyway. A thousand years means I have seen enough to destroy a normal mind – many vampires have been broken by their age, but not me. Most others are eventually killed by some means, usually magic or a stake through the heart or sunlight. But not me. Why is that? I may never know and so I prevail, determined to change what I can, *who* I can, to avoid history repeating itself, over and over again. A catalyst wandering here and there, making the smallest nudges, starting people down different paths, showing them *all* choices available, not just a select few others would have them make.

"But that is nothing, it means *nothing*. What is important is the here, the now, what is occurring between you and Cain, Lucy. You said nothing about it when we went for our walk and if it had not been for a few stray hairs I never would have thought it possible, given you were at each other's throats last week over the matter of Alizon's treatment…"

"Cain apologised to me the day after that. Sent me a text. Before that, though, he invited me for a drink and I told him I had to get back because of my binding. But then I…asked him back. Not sure why, really. And he agreed. We only had a cider, nothing more; I'm not sure I *can* have anything more. I just showed him round the house, especially the creepy parts. It was nice. We met up again after that. Twice, actually. Again at the mansion and another at his favourite bar."

Blood and Biscuits

"Well whatever those moments were, they meant a great deal more to Cain than you possibly considered. It stopped him from losing his mind during one of the worst moments of his life. Not to add pressure to you," Vlad chuckled and Lucy reciprocated. "If you want my advice, I would treat yourself and Cain gently, and be honest. It is not my business to probe or make assumptions on what you want from this but I am a romantic at heart – I think all vampires are, that seems to be the one aspect the stories get right. A facet of the mastery, I think."

"God knows where we go from here, if we can in any capacity. Maybe it's best we let it lie for now."

"Look, you are both headstrong and intelligent, independent people, with minds and hearts that suspect what they want. It is a beautiful thing to observe, and despite my 'advanced age', as you call it, the powers of the connections of the heart still marvel me and fill me with wonder. Look at what happened tonight with Cain after only a tour guide around a haunted mansion, and a walk in the woods, and some apple fermented by-product."

Lucy laughed openly. The sound was infectious.

"Anyway," she said, pushing off her legs and standing tiredly. She checked her watch and nodded. "It's time I left before I'm dragged back, kicking and screaming. Are you going to be alright here?"

"Remember you actually have an extra twenty-two minutes for the time you remained unconscious, so make sure you stroll leisurely home. This unconsciousness business with your curse, it does rather make one wonder about the theories of thought, does it not?"

"Yeah but that's got nothing to do with me and my curse," Lucy said, brushing a hand through her wild hair.

"If you say so. As I said before, I have my own doubts about the matter, but the fact that your lack of conscious thought could produce such a powerful negating effect on your curse does give one pause. Anyway, I shall be fine, I will sit and think for a while, as it were, and ensure our hairy friend remains stable. Go on, I swear you will see me next week with the right number of limbs, and in the right places, too."

Lucy chuckled again and walked to the door. However, she rested a moment against the entranceway and looked back.

"Vlad?"

"Yes, Lucy?" he asked without looking at her.

"Before, when we were here alone a few days ago…you mentioned you'd seen the face of evil…"

"Indeed," Vlad intoned darkly, five hundred memories passing across his eyes. "You wish to know what that means."

"No, I want to know if you think Cain's inherently evil."

Vlad glanced back in surprise.

"Certainly not! Choice, Lucy. It is all about choice. Cain cannot help his nature any more than we can. He would choose different if he could."

Lucy breathed in relief and smiled.

"Oh good, I didn't think so. It's just…we may well have had very different definitions and I just wanted to check."

"I suppose that does make sense," Vlad said. And then Lucy disappeared, a sort of pleasantness following her as Vlad sat back in his chair and considered all that had transpired.

After a long while, most of the black veins had sunk back into his body and Vlad felt a great deal recovered. Now all he had to do was wait until the blue moon had slunk down beyond the horizon.

Four hours later and the moon did precisely that. As Vlad felt it slide beneath the reaches of England's gaze, the werewolf began to twitch. He snarled and then roared as his body convulsed and contorted violently. Vlad watched it all, the limbs contracting, the musculature shrinking like water rippling beneath a sheet, bones re-cracking, reshaping, claws retracting back into hands and feet. The man returned once more, his lupine voice strangling into human again.

Blood and Biscuits

When all was done, Vlad stood and walked to the coffee table, solace guiding his thoughts. He made a particularly strong coffee and picked up two whole packets of Jaffa cakes, and then he went to Cain's side as the naked man tried to slow his rapid breathing, his skin shining with a thin layer of sweat.

Suddenly, Cain sat bolt upright, the silver chains sliding off him easily now his frame no longer supported them, and patted himself all over, eyes searching frantically for something.

"You are fine, my friend," Vlad said softly, crouching beside Cain, offering him the mug of black coffee, the silver's influence once again drawing poisonously at his reserves of darkness. "You have hurt nobody. Any traces of blood are your own, I can assure you."

Cain looked up at the vampire then lay back with a groan.

"God, that's a relief. But why'd my ribs feel like they're on fire?"

"Because I went full vampire and hit you in them," Vlad responded breezily and Cain barked a laugh. Then he hissed and pressed a hand to his right side, two flashes of pain igniting in his leg and arm.

"Jeez, and the bruises here?"

"I threw you five hundred feet to the ground."

Despite himself, Cain gave a long, low chuckle. He sneezed and cursed many things in a surprisingly inventive line of expletives.

"At least you kept your promise," Cain muttered and Vlad nodded.

"I did my best, though I required some help. You have a lot of care around you, Cain, did you know that? Lucy was particularly astonishing, I might add. Anyway, here," Vlad said as he held out the coffee again. "I feel like you need this."

Cain took the drink this time and glanced up, worry and warmth warring for dominance in his eyes.

"Lucy. Is she alright?"

"She is fine, though a little shaken. She had to leave a few hours ago on account of her accursed binding. Nevertheless, you are safe, we are all safe, and there are no more blue moons for quite some time. So rest, we shall have much to discuss next week. Or earlier, if you wish to contact me for a chat, as humans say. But I will ask you one thing, on the subject of Lucy: before all of this happened, and you came to this basement in search of salvation a few days ago, how was your week going?"

And Cain, despite everything, ignoring the agony throughout his body and the post-transformation fears, smiled as if the entire world was shining down upon him. He was happy.

THE INDUSTRIAL COMPLEX, ELLIN'S INDUSTRIAL ISLAND. THREE CONSECUTIVE NIGHTS FOLLOWING THE SUPPORT GROUP.

The next day was spent recovering Cain's strength and ensuring he was well enough to take a few walks around the island with Vlad for company, commenting on the coldness of the air and the human-dug river leading into the sea a mile away. There was one more full moon to endure but its blue counterpart was behind him and Cain managed to remain in human form during that night, sleeping soundly on the mattress in the church basement as Vlad watched over him silently.

For several nights after Cain left, Vlad took to the battlements and turrets of the factories of the wastelands, staring out across Ellin's Island at the ancient church grounds and wondering. He knew she was in there though she did not show herself until the very small hours of the mornings, her shining spirit spinning and twirling to music box. Vlad watched with sadness and joy as the ghost flew through the shattered archways and danced through the graveyard, feeling a strange mixture of pride and a kind of remorse.

Only he could possibly understand his own mind. The further down the road he got, the harder it would be to explain.

And when the time came, Vlad was not sure he would be forgiven.

Week Six
The D.I.Y of Exploding Banshees

**RUINS OF ST ELLIN'S CHURCH,
19:03**

"How was everyone's week?"

The sense of the room deepened as everyone glanced between each other. Where once there flitted awkward, furtive looks, there now hung a feeling of togetherness, the fondness for shared company. Fable was still laughing at a joke Fable had explained to her. Sarah chatted warmly with Lucy about the weather, the merits of dandelions and if they were worth the bother, and their pastimes since last seeing one another. Cain sat with his arms crossed over his chest, though he was no longer impassive and stoic. His hair was trimmed again, face clean-shaven, a smell of washed clothes and aftershave emanated, overpowered by the huge sense of proud gratitude flooding from his soul. The werewolf felt something so powerful it gripped Vlad's dead heart and gave it jolts of heat.

Cain smiled.

"Thought I'd start this one," he said easily. He shifted and pulled a short face of pain as his side twinged: his ribs were still bruised. "Look, you know what? My week's been a damn sight better since that bloody blue moon's gone. Not only that, I've somehow kept my job *and* I've found a new bedsit to live in for a little while. I'm killin' it right now."

"What's the new place like?" Lucy asked, concern lining her voice. "I know Jay's wasn't fantastic before he moved in with Fable, so I'm just making sure."

"No, I steered him clear of that one," Jacob said, leaning forward. "Managed to get him a better place on the south side of town. Overlooks the river, it's much nicer."

"Yeah my room's got a good view," Cain added. "I didn't realise how big Ellinsgate was, can't believe I was thinkin' of moving on again. It's quite pretty, in places."

"The town has its charms, especially down near the harbour," Vlad said cheerfully. "I have seen it at various times throughout history and it is currently at its finest. That might not say a great deal to you all, considering the work that still needs to go into renovating the sixties throw-up blocks, but it is much improved from the days of yore."

"I don't think I've ever heard someone genuinely use the term 'days of yore' before," Jacob grinned, teeth glinting in tight, rotten flesh.

"Well keep listening, I am full of old phrases, my friend," Vlad replied dryly. "Anyway, Cain, I can *feel* you are brimming over with something else. Can you share with the group? Or is it just happiness hungover from last week?"

Cain shrugged, a smile spilling onto his face. He was a rather handsome man, when not cast in gloom, fearing the future. Scars lining his eyes and cheeks added a certain roughness to him, Vlad thought.

"It's partly that," Cain said. Then he shook his head. "No, it's *mostly* that, I haven't felt this relieved in years. Another blue moon gone and I can sit back, knowin' I didn't hurt anyone. Thanks, Vlad…"

"Do not thank me, Cain, thank your friends here. Lucy stopped your crazed charge towards town. It was Fable and Sarah that distracted you. And Jacob helped me stand and take up those silver chains. I did nothing but sink a few good hits into you, no doubt enraging you further and making matters worse."

Fable hissed disapprovingly and Jacob snorted derisively.

"What?" Vlad asked.

Lucy shook her head. "Don't be so humble, you idiot. We watched you from the church: we saw you fly him to the top of those old factories and fight up there, I'm certain you exhausted Cain so we all had a chance to overcome him."

"Is that true?" Cain asked interestedly. "I flew?"

"In a manner of speaking," Vlad replied slowly. "I was trying to get you high enough so you would grow cold and slow – my apologies for this – but your jaws veered me off course. We, um…smashed into the factories and made quite a mess of things."

"Yeah, like punching holes through steel," Jacob noted.

Cain sat back, arms crossed interestedly.

"Now *that* sounds fun, but God I hate heights. Terrify my trousers off. I need a coffee to handle all this," he said wryly. Something else scratched his tone and the scent of him, Vlad knew immediately he was diverting conversation from his inner monster. He watched as Cain stood, deliberately favouring his injuries, and moved to the table. As he poured himself a strong coffee, he muttered,

"Vlad."

"Yes, Cain?"

"There's no biscuits."

"Oh dear, did I forget them?" Vlad asked worriedly. "I am so sorry, situations took my mind this past week and I completely misplaced the need to restock. I got new tea but no biscuits…"

"No, I didn't mean it like that," Cain stammered, turning to face them, a hint of red at his cheeks. "I wasn't being ungrateful or nothin', I was only sayin'. Jus' wonderin' if you had anymore elsewhere, that's all."

"Dammit," Vlad cursed himself. "I should have written it down somewhere."

"You should set yourself weekly alarms," Jacob said, pulling out his battered smartphone, waving it pointedly. "Certainly keeps me alert with my internet sales, which are going swimmingly, by the way."

Vlad continued to fuss and Cain walked back quickly.

"I said it's alright, Vlad, I don't need biscuits to survive."

"I know, and I know it is only a small thing but it really gets on my mind if I do not get the details right." Vlad patted himself down as if he had a spare box of Jaffa cakes on his person; he could not shake the failure he felt in himself.

"Vlad," a misted voice said dreamily and the vampire looked up suddenly. Sarah gazed at him, her veil never once lifting. He stopped and listened. "They are only things. Just things. Don't trouble yourself over material possessions. They come and go, like people. And *like* people you can't take things with you when you leave your world. I'm somewhat of an unwilling expert."

Vlad instantly calmed himself, commanding his desperate brain into silence, berating his sense of idiocy as he straightened his shirt and altered his face, appearing humbled instead of ashamed.

"You are right, Sarah, I was wrong to despair. I think a facet of my depression sometimes turns into a neurotic fixation if I fail something, regardless how small. Thank you for clearing my mind."

Sarah inclined her veiled head.

"That is quite alright. We all suffer one way or another. Let it not be over something as frivolous as biscuits, though I do miss their flavour. Perhaps one day I'll be released from my torment, free to dwell on life's pleasures once again."

She whispered the last sentence so quietly Vlad was convinced she meant it only for him. Indeed, Jacob was already talking, indicating he had no idea Sarah was still speaking.

"My week was up and down. Haven't thought about the awful things I've done for a good few weeks, now I've got focusses. Fable and I have managed a couple night walks, which we started after last week's session. Wanted to clear our heads. It's quite liberating being out when hardly anyone's around. I can lift the balaclava and breathe a little; not that I *need* to breathe, but still..."

"That's brilliant, Jay," Lucy said encouragingly.

"Indeed, a most rewarding outcome," Vlad agreed. "What things are you focussing on that have produced such positivity?"

"Well like I said earlier, the internet business has improved, so that's a major bonus. Also, Fable's been teaching me the complexities of French – I know a fair bit but I wouldn't say I'm fluent in any way."

"You have been a most studious pupil. Very receptive to my teachings, considering I thought I had forgotten a good deal of the language," Fable said, her black and shrivelled hands rubbing together, a motion clearly paining her skin yet relieving the muscles beneath. Vlad suspected this dichotomy and empathised heavily, knowing all too well the necessities of hurting the self to heal the greater whole.

"Well French is Latin-based, like Romanian," Vlad offered. "So, it never took me long to learn it. If there is anything you are missing, I am sure we could figure it out together. Online translators are not the most reliable sources; they are decent for single word searches but not sentence structure, grammar's finer subtleties. Sorry, I digressed. You were saying, Jacob?"

The wraith shrugged and smiled awkwardly.

"That was pretty much it," he admitted. "It was a week, all things considered. Had its moments."

Vlad felt Jacob hid something but he would not bring it up if the wraith wished it private.

"Good," Vlad said. "You do seem brighter with newer prospects." He turned to Fable, who spread her damaged hands.

"There is not much to say for myself. I have been in greater agony from the wounds of my magic but that is the consequence I must face for channelling Light when I am banished from such things."

"Ahh," Vlad breathed, "I was just thinking I was glad you had not been damaged by last week. Perhaps I was mistaken."

"The damage is mostly internal. It hasn't spread to the skin so I should be able to recover."

Cain shuffled in his seat, his coffee hiding a grimace of shame.

"God, I'm sorry," he muttered with a wolf-like growl. He looked away, refusing to meet Fable's gaze. "I didn't mean for that to happen; I didn't want you guys to suffer. You shouldn't have thrown yourselves into that crap last week."

Vlad smelled inner pain emanating from Cain now, his earlier elation revealed as a mask for buried guilt. That happiness peeled away quickly, a shallow scab from a raw wound, and Cain bled before them. Vlad stemmed the flow before it could drain the man's reserves.

"Be quiet," he hissed, compassion submitting to an uncompromising tone. The others of the group looked surprised but Vlad knew Cain would respond better to command and firmness rather than sympathy. There was a time for commiseration and the charity of kind remarks but not to bolster another's self-pity. It was a form of 'tough love', as it were, and it was exactly what Cain needed to hear. "We have already told you what we did was our choice and ours alone to make, Cain. You could not help yourself and so we helped you and all of Ellinsgate, but it was *not* your fault. Nor, however, is it yours to dwell on and be sorry for, so I do not want to hear you again apologise for what happened last week, the same as none of *us* apologise for the foibles of our curses. We prepared and, save for some ribs, a couple of faerie hands, and a few egos, nothing was hurt."

"Crikey," Cain blurted, shocked. Vlad read his mood and found it had elevated significantly, a spark of respect igniting in the man. "Didn't expect that," he said.

"No, I suspect you did not. This is a support group, Cain, for real *support*. That means we shall and will do all is necessary to help

Blood and Biscuits

whomever we can in whatever *way* we can. Though we are not counsellors we are still bound in honesty and privacy, and often what people *need* is not what they *want*, yet is necessary all the same."

"Got it," Cain responded. "No more apologies. Accept it and move on. Stop feeling sorry for myself."

"Exactly. If you wish to know the precise details of last week then by all means ask away. And reflect on it, certainly, but let your thoughts reside more on what you have gained from it. Like the trust of those here, for example, and perhaps a slight fear, too?"

Cain smirked as Lucy suddenly jolted in her seat and gave a small "Oh!" of surprise.

"Is everything alright?" Vlad asked as she leant down beneath her seat.

"Yeah fine," she said, her voice muffled as she reached under then pulled out a small plastic bag. "I completely forgot I actually have some emergency snacks in here. You'd think I'd have been reminded when Cain whinged about having none here; memory's always been all over the place."

"I don't *whinge*," Cain grumbled quietly.

"Well wonderful" Vlad said delightedly. "If you are happy sharing with the group, of course."

"They're here *for* the group, idiot person," Lucy explained, reaching into the depths of her bag and pulling out a few packets of crisps and biscuits. "Brought salt and vinegar, ready salted, got some ginger nuts, custard creams...got fig rolls here."

Everyone made a noise of satisfaction. All except Cain, anyway, who folded his arms and made a disgruntled sound. Lucy looked at him pointedly.

"What's up?"

"Fig rolls, that's what's up."

"You don't like them?" the banshee asked, handing round the large bags of crisps. A strong waft of salt and vinegar hit the room and Vlad thought of the seaside.

"There's nothing to like!" Cain exclaimed.

Blood and Biscuits

"There is a lot to like about figs," Vlad cut in indignantly. "Not just for their wonderful flavour and health properties but for their history, also." Jacob rolled his eyes and tutted, but Vlad ignored him. "Did you know figs are counted amongst the very first plants to be cultivated? And that they are possibly the very first thing to have been domesticated?"

"Like cats?" Cain asked.

"Um, agriculturally speaking."

"'Course you'd have a historical knowledge on figs, of all things. How many facts about ancient fruit do you have?" Jacob asked in disbelief.

"Thousands," Vlad stated with a note of pride. Jacob sighed.

"Figures. You were probably there when figs were invented."

"Perhaps," was all Vlad said.

Cain looked at Lucy.

"Lemme' explain, 'cause I'm still, obviously, thankful for the food. Figs have gotta' be the worst fruit in existence and the biscuit itself is weirdly soft *and* crunchy at the same time. What's that about?"

"They're just snacks," Lucy said, shrugging.

"No they're not, they're lies."

Lucy scoffed. Her attitude had definitely changed towards the werewolf, her sharp edge blunted, her drive to scold him reduced, but a hardness to her said she would be a formidable opponent to Cain's temperament. That was a good thing, in Vlad's eyes.

"Don't be so dramatic," Lucy berated. "If you don't want them have a Jaffa cake instead." As she said that she pulled out a long, thin plastic package and Cain's ears pricked. Lucy smiled thinly. "Yeah, thought that might get you interested. Here, fetch." She threw the Jaffa cakes across the circle and Cain made to grab it but Vlad was far too quick. He barely had to lunge as he reached out and grabbed the packet before Cain. Vlad looked at the cakes interestedly as Cain sat back, deflated.

Blood and Biscuits

"I wonder if I could eat all of these in one go," Vlad said absently. Then he looked at the crestfallen man-wolf and let out a loud laugh. He held out the packet to Cain. "I am joking, my friend, I could not possibly deprive you of these. For one thing, I would be instantly sick." Cain took the cakes happily as Lucy chuckled. Fable leant closer to Jacob.

"I don't understand," she whispered.

"I'll explain later," the wraith whispered.

Cain tore open the packet and devoured three in one go. His face lit up, his body visibly relaxed. Jacob looked at Vlad. "Didn't think you'd be one for playing a practical joke."

Vlad feigned a hurt expression.

"How dare you, I should have you know that back when I was a young man, I was quite the prankster. Having a permanently dour mood can really give you a strange sense of humour," Vlad finished slowly.

Cain suddenly stopped chewing, his face screwed up in thought and, through a mouthful of orange and chocolate, he said,

"Oi! Did you just tell me to *fetch*!"

Lucy howled and rocked back in her chair as Jacob slapped his legs in laughter and Vlad covered his mouth to hide his traitorous grin. Even Fable sniggered quietly as Cain continued.

"I cannot believe you told me to fetch. Evil sod. Wadya' want next, your bloody slippers? Want me to bring the paper for you then chew on a nice bone?"

"I was wondering how long that'd take you," Lucy said, her eyes flashing so deeply that Cain sat back, a warm look growing on his face. Vlad coughed pointedly, though he had no need to clear his lungs.

"Still, let us continue onwards. Who is left...ahh, Lucy. Setting aside canine jests, how was your week?"

"Fine, thanks," the banshee responded brightly as Cain grumbled harmlessly. Lucy considered her answer. "I've...yeah, been a bit happier this week. It started heavy but once that ordeal with the blue moon was over, I focussed on trying to be happy again. According to online forums for trauma sufferers, I've actually been coping with my anxieties quite well. I've even found various ways to pass the time without dwelling too much on my, err, unique situation. Don't know if there's any more banshees out there feeling the same as me – I'm not even sure if they *can* feel the same, I've never looked it up." She paused then changed subject. "Anyway, I've practiced that scream a little more and I think I've gotten some way to mastering it without passing out afterwards."

"I must say," Vlad added, "judging purely from outward admission, you are quite different now from the banshee that first took step down into this charming basement five weeks ago. It is extraordinary, the person hidden beneath that exterior you cast about yourself shines through and I, for one, think you have journeyed further than you give yourself credit for."

"Damn straight," Jacob said, clapping Lucy on the back as Cain nodded thoughtfully. Fable flashed her an encouraging look.

"You all have," Vlad said to the group. "Do not think yourselves the same as when you first met one another. I sit before you all a humbled man, who counts himself amongst the lucky few that has witnessed such astonishing people become utterly different by simply allowing themselves the chance to know they are not alone. It gives me great hope for what might become of this world and the countless secrets it holds beneath its layers."

Lucy smiled awkwardly, evidently not expecting such words about her. The room's lifted atmosphere reflected her deserved pride. Her hair, wild as it often was upon the flux of her emotions, flowed like water. She continued as if uninterrupted, keen to say what she came to divulge.

"Also, I've had a bigger look round my mansion to see what else is there – there's some really cool stuff, you guys should come up some time. For one thing, I'd actually be able to stick around without running off, what with my binding and all."

Blood and Biscuits

"Oh yeah it's pretty fun up there," Cain said after he swallowed his mouthful. He stiffened slightly and Vlad smelled a trickle of embarrassment. He had clearly not meant to admit that piece of information.

"You've been up to Lucy's mansion?" Jacob asked curiously. Cain burbled but Lucy shrugged it off.

"He has. I invited him up. I hoped it might take his mind off the blue moon fiasco before it happened. We had a drink and a wander round."

"Oh right," Jacob responded measuredly, slowly. "Well I hope you kids had fun."

"Ahh the blooming flowers of attraction, how fondly the petals grow." Sarah merrily bobbed nine inches above her chair. "Though be wary of the pale rose for her thorns grow sharp and she would draw blood if shown ill respect. Should the wandering man wander too far, too freely, his redness would mire the purity of the ground."

There was a stunned silence and two spots of colour reached Lucy's cheeks. After a few seconds, Cain leaned towards Vlad and the vampire tried hard not to smile.

"I think...I think the ghost just threatened me," the werewolf muttered.

"I believe all she did was suggest a metaphor," Vlad clarified. "Show caution to both her and Lucy and you will be fine, Cain. Alternatively, stay away from white roses. It truly is impossible to discern what Sarah means."

Cain nodded and sat straight again, and Vlad stood to make himself a coffee, hiding his sudden inability to mask his mirth from everyone. His mind was acting up again; it sometimes did after extreme events of stress. He supposed it was some strange defensive mechanism to counter the enormous fight with a fully transformed werewolf. A warping of his brain formed by depression, causing panic over the mildest discrepancies, finding humour in the strangest places.

Blood and Biscuits

Vlad tried reigning in his rising and falling thoughts but, as he so often did, he was unsuccessful. Instead, he simply walked away from everyone to give the appearance of keeping himself busy, when actually he was too scared to show his vulnerabilities. Vampires could not afford to appear weak, that was what he still told himself sometimes.

Suddenly, through the mists of his thoughts, Vlad felt his senses twinge and he knew someone rapidly approached the church. Had he not immediately recognised their breathing pattern and the sound of their boots he would have flown from the basement to confront them. As it was, Vlad turned neatly with his coffee as the person slowed cautiously outside then descended the entranceway stairs. They did not immediately make themselves known so Vlad crossed the basement, hoping not to catch them unawares and frighten them.

"Are you there, Alizon?" he asked quietly.

A timid hand thrust out from behind the wall of the stairs and waved nervously.

"Yes," came a small voice and Vlad moved round to see the witch properly. This week she wore a midnight blue short tunic with a belt round her waist, dark trousers and boots. Vlad gave her a deep smile and she almost looked him in the eyes. Almost.

"I am so glad you decided to join us again. I know it has been two weeks, and please do not take this the wrong way, but I am also rather happy you did not appear during the last session."

"Oh," Alizon said in surprise, her round face falling briefly. The Support Group muttered behind them, evidently pretending to mind their own business. "Why's that?"

Vlad leant in closer and whispered:

"We had a rather large werewolf on the loose."

"Ahh, *that's* what that was," Alizon said and Vlad looked at her in confusion.

"What do you mean – were you here?"

Blood and Biscuits

"In a sense." Alizon's eyes wandered with some indiscernible memory. "I felt a huge disturbance on this island from the river waters; I can attune myself quite well to the imprint of the rains they once were. Water bears witness to much, and like heat it retains the imprint of memories, which I can fuse with and discern."

"A fascinating concept. Whatever kept you away from here. Things got a little…out of hand, shall we say, but all is well now. Welcome back, it is good to have you here again. I trust you had a pleasant fortnight?"

"They have been difficult," Alizon muttered as she shuffled into the room and circled round to the coffee table. Everyone watched subtly, though Cain stared the hardest, a thin, palpable layer of shame peeling off him curiously.

Vlad sensed thin sheets of surprise and relief lift from Alizon as she noticed lemongrass and peppermint tea.

Vlad rejoined the others with his coffee. He smiled at them all.

"So, who else had a good week?" he asked optimistically, creating a general murmur of assent. All except Jacob, whose already dilapidated face fell as he remembered something. Vlad felt an icy spear stab the wraith's heart and he leant towards him automatically, showing understanding before Jacob had spoken.

"Whatever it is, you can tell us. We will listen."

"What? No, it's stupid, never mind."

Lucy shook her head and Sarah hovered lower above her seat. Vlad smiled grimly.

"Nothing you say here will be considered as such. Come, we have known one another for six weeks, I would hope by now you accept we will not judge you."

On the fringe of his senses, Vlad noticed Cain glance again at Alizon worriedly, the enchantress still brewing her tea. The werewolf was agitated.

Jacob sighed heavily and leant back in his chair, an innate response Vlad supposed was due to the pressure he put on himself.

Blood and Biscuits

"I've spoken to my ex-partner, Luke…" The name dragged out of Jacob as if cutting stripes from his flesh. Vlad knew the feeling. "Well, he called to speak to *me*, actually. Said all kinds of things, not really sure exactly what, now I think about it."

"Kinda' blurs into one, doesn't it?" Cain suggested and Jacob nodded. Vlad was surprised by the werewolf's input; it was only six words but it revealed a lifetime of information about him.

"Yeah it does – it did," Jacob corrected. "He just rang up one day, somehow got my new number, and asked if he could meet. I told him I didn't know, thought it was a bad idea."

"What was it he wanted?" Lucy asked.

"God knows, I never met him," Jacob sighed again. "I bottled it and bailed. He was asking to meet publicly and I couldn't bring myself to do that. It's hard enough leaving with the balaclava and gloves on as it is but to face that turmoil in front of strangers was asking too much."

"Most understandable," Vlad agreed, rubbing his chin thoughtfully. "And there is no discerning his purpose in all of this?"

"Nothing springs to mind. He took all of his stuff when he walked out, and he said enough to me that made it very clear at the time things were over. Don't know if it was the skin falling off or the brains that did it."

It was a feeble attempt at a joke, aimed at deflecting Jacob's obviously lowering mood. Lucy put her arm round his shoulders and the wraith leaned into her a little, taking some comfort in her mere presence.

"It's horrid, Jay," she said.

He nodded miserably.

"Aye. Was such a short call, too, and a few texts following. A bit of conversation, handful of messages, and now I feel like a whole world I'd put behind me's come crashing back down. All I've done these past few months to forget him and move on with what life I have remaining seems like it was for nothing. Why would it make me feel like that?"

The question was rhetorical but Vlad could not let it go. He could not.

"Often that is all it takes for the worst of our previous lives to make themselves known again: a simple conversation," Vlad offered. "But in that moment, you recall their voice, their mannerisms, the memories of joy and sadness you formed, a lifetime together with a shared bond. You do not even have to see their face yet you remember their eyes, the shape of their mouths, their hand gestures, body language; you envision all the minute imperfections that made the largest perfection you ever beheld. And it all comes back to you with such a shock you reel for a long time after, wondering in heart-breaking detail what they could possibly still want from you after ripping so much away. Your mind invents all manner of meanings, tries to reason it out logically and emotionally until all you can do is assume the very worst and the very best simultaneously. We conjure so much and so little all at once."

Vlad turned the words over in his mind then finished. "The emotional intelligence we have retained from our human selves is both a gift and a curse, I often feel."

"You speak from agonisingly beautiful experience," Sarah noted deeply and Vlad nodded.

"Centuries of it, unfortunately. Whether or not you actually meet Luke is beside the point, Jacob, for you recognise how it made you feel and act upon it. You did not wish to suffer that same pain and humiliation again and so you chose not to meet him. If you ask me, and I am well aware you have not, I would say you being a wraith was circumstantial in this decision."

"I think what Vlad's sayin' is rather than let your, err, situation guide you, you made a rational decision based on your feelings. That's brave. Very brave. I struggle with acting rationally – always have – so I admire that in you," Cain added and Vlad tipped his coffee cup in recognition.

"A wonderful summary," the vampire said quietly as Lucy delivered Cain a smile filled with a dozen things.

"You think I was right in not meeting him?" Jacob asked. Vlad shrugged.

"I do not think it is about right or wrong, only what is best for yourself. Life is survival and if this protects you then *that* is surviving. If you change your mind and feel you can meet with Luke, then perhaps suggest a neutral location. I recommend you find out what it is he pursues beforehand, otherwise you might be caught on the back foot, to use a cricketing idiom."

"I'll bear that in mind," Jacob replied stoically.

"'On the back foot' is from cricket? I always thought it had something to do with horses," Lucy said.

"What on earth kind of horse-related activity would make you think that?" Jacob asked, surprised. Lucy grinned lopsidedly.

"I don't know, dressage?"

"Jesus Christ," Cain laughed and Lucy shot him a playful look. Vlad felt the tension ease again.

Sarah spoke next, her voice echoing as it always did.

"Don't be burned by love's cruel flame, Jacob, you are too wonderful to suffer so. I once beheld such love in my life, only to have it all taken from me by teeth and by water. I would give all I have, and all I am, just to hold him once more. To stroke his face, to feel his body and his soul entwined with mine, and to tell him that…everything's alright. I'm back now, I'm with you."

"Thanks, Sarah," Jacob replied quietly, the shock of her deliverance burying into his empathy and sorrow. "If there's ever anything I can do for you, you'll let me know, right?"

"Right," Sarah said with an odd giggle and she drifted higher once more, her burden evidently lifted for a time.

Vlad took a deep breath, the air travelling to his obsolete lungs. He ran his hand through his dark hair and leant back, mulling over his many thoughts. Sarah usually dominated his mind but Jacob's predicament needed care, too.

"Why not suggest you bring your Luke here?" Sarah asked innocently. "It's peaceful, out of the way, and neutral. I could always play you a song from my magic music box for some ambience. I'm thinking Black Sabbath."

Jacob's eyes grew wide.

"My sincerest gratitude, Sarah, but I think Luke would probably be a little more than confused. If it *does* happen then I'll probably meet him…I don't know, somewhere closer to town. Sorry, Sarah, I do appreciate the offer."

"That's perfectly alright, the basement still smells of sweaty werewolf anyway."

"That was uncalled for," Cain muttered as Alizon finally came to the circle and took the empty seat between Vlad and Lucy. She sipped her lemongrass tea and said nothing, simply listening and avoiding all eyes.

Then Vlad came to a decision and realised it had been a surprisingly easy one.

"If you want, Jacob, you would be more than welcome to use my home in town. It is out of the public eye and will go unquestioned if you explain it as a rental. I will make sure there is tea, coffee, et cetera."

"I couldn't ask you to do that," Jacob said quickly though Vlad caught the scent of hope. *That* was his answer.

"And you never did. I offered it and you shall have it, for as long as you wish."

"But…but where will you be?" Jacob stammered.

"Elsewhere. I have other places I can go, errands to run, things to sort out, as it were. I might be a recluse, and a vampire, but I still have a life to lead. In a manner."

Jacob sat speechless and Vlad clapped his hands together.

"Then it is decided. All you need do is send me a message – you already have my mobile number – and I will vacate as necessary. Please stop trying to say no, it is done."

Jacob threw his hands up exasperatedly.

"But I don't even know what I'd *wear*!"

Vlad looked at him pointedly.

"You wear whatever makes you feel strong, my friend."

"Vlad..." Jacob began. Then he sighed a third time. "Thanks."

"You are welcome. That is why I am here. Now then, who else would like to offer up insight into their week?"

It all went by smoothly after Jacob had poured out his worries. Lucy detailed the time she spent showing Cain round her vast mansion. Fable spoke of the small amount of money she had made from the internet business buying and selling car parts.

"It has transpired I am fascinated by human machinery," Fable said, her black, puckered hands gesticulating enthusiastically as she spoke. "Though I come from a world of magic and wondrous delicacy, there is something unique and utterly mystifying about these clunky pieces of metal driving around, polluting everything. I find bewilderment in myself at this sense of intrigue, but there we are."

Vlad felt like laughing.

"That is good!" he said happily. "However strange it might seem, you found an anchor in this world you can hold onto and focus with. But do not stop your fascinations and studies with cars, there are many ingenious creations of humans that could do with an intelligent mind like yours to help improve and develop, you need only apply yourself. Would you like to borrow some books on mechanics and engineering? I know the internet is as vast in its breadth as it is deep in its subject matter, but books will always feel a tad more tangible in the quenching of knowledge's thirst."

"You have books on this matter?" Fable asked strangely, one eyebrow arching beautifully on her perfectly formed face, androgynous features somehow finding the absolute balance between facial symmetry and sharp distinction. "I would not think this to be of your tastes."

"I am too old not to have interests in every topic of this world," Vlad pointed out easily. "I am well versed in the creations of man; you might not know it but I lived through the evolution of simple machines and, later on, I came to be quite the researcher during the industrial revolution."

There was a stunned silence and Vlad looked round curiously.

"Is everything alright?" he asked worriedly, thinking there to be some sort of problem. Cain shook his head.

"No, it's just…is there anything you *haven't* seen or done, Vlad? This is a massive chunk of history you're talkin' about here and you seem to be buildin' a serious portfolio of involvement. Will you ever tell us how old you are?"

"Perhaps one day. But you have to admit, it is a lot more fun this way around."

"I've resigned myself to just turning the things you say into a sort of jigsaw game," Lucy said. "I think I've got all the corner bits now so I'll be looking out for the edge pieces as the weeks go on."

"I like that analogy," Vlad admitted. "My life as a puzzle, all the pieces scattered about. Anyway, that concludes question one and we have a few things to take home. Quite literally, for Fable; Jacob, if you make a decision then please do not hesitate to message me."

"Righto," the wraith replied. "Never texted a vampire before."

"It is good to try new things," Vlad commented and, despite his low mood, Jacob laughed. It was a nice sound. "So, shall we move on to question two?"

Everyone nodded but when Vlad moved to speak, he felt a little tap on his arm. He looked round and saw Alizon whispering something behind her hand.

"Can I say something?" The sound was so small nobody else heard.

"Of course," he whispered back, his hand covering his own mouth. "To the group?"

Alizon shook her head, her eyes glancing everywhere but at Vlad. The vampire smiled and looked to everyone else as he announced,

"I suggest a ten-minute coffee break. You can gather your thoughts and think about what you want to get off your chests."

"Oh good, I always feel bloody awkward leavin' for a brew when people are talkin'," Cain grunted as he shifted himself up. "Like I'm bein' naughty or summat'. Anyone that wants a Jaffa cake I'd suggest you get there quick. Then put 'em straight back down and step away and think about your mistake."

Vlad watched as instead of heading straight for the coffee table, Cain waited three seconds for Lucy to cross the circle and draw level with him. Then they both paced across the wide basement floor together, fists clenched and arms held firmly by their sides in an unnatural way of walking, evidently not knowing what to do with their limbs, looking unfortunately amusing in the process. Vlad snorted quietly.

'People and their desperate attempts to avoid their feelings,' he mused.

As everyone retrieved snacks and drinks, Alizon led Vlad to an empty space and fidgeted with her fingers. Vlad felt a spark of magic between them before it dissipated. Channelling as an act of comfort. Only true observation could reveal this.

Often, profound moments are lost in words, for the more spoken the less there is *said*.

"Is everything alright?" Vlad asked quietly as the others talked pleasantly. He saw Cain laugh about something with Fable while Jacob and Lucy conversed with Sarah over some matter of grave importance. Knowing Sarah, it was probably *literally* about graves.

"Ev-everything is fine, why d-do you ask?" Alizon responded.

Vlad raised his eyebrows. "Oh, I…never mind. So, what is it you wanted to say?"

"I had a g-good week."

"You said earlier you had a difficult time of it," Vlad pointed out.

Blood and Biscuits

"The last two weeks *have* been difficult but that doesn't mean they've not been good."

"Ahh, I see. What was difficult about them?"

Alizon hesitated, fingers twining and moving amongst one another as the electric heat *smell* of magic crackled between them again. Vlad knew she would not use her power inside the basement, he could sense her intent.

When Alizon spoke, her voice cracked against the strain of communication.

"They were d-difficult be-because I struggle…every day with talking. To people, I m-mean. People that aren't my guardian. And it's hard getting myself even out the d-door. I'm struggling right now, and m-my magic tells me you already know this. Your vampire senses are so in-tune with everything around you. That's not fair; I d-don't ask to have my mind invaded."

"I am sorry," Vlad said genuinely, containing his senses behind the walls of his control. There was a sudden drop like a chasm as every heightened sensation fell away, leaving Vlad with the simplicity of normality. He felt surprisingly alone. "They slip out naturally, allowing me to read a room and maintain concentration of my surroundings. I was not invading your mind, that is the worst power a vampire can have, but I will keep my senses well away from you, as is your wish."

Alizon brightened.

"It is, though if it weren't for m-my m-magic I wouldn't mind. But that isn't why my weeks were difficult…it's as I said: my brain, it…struggles with c-c-communication."

"Look, Alizon, if this is hard for you to discuss I understand. We all struggle contending with the many aspects of our existence. Our lives, or deaths, are consistently attempting to drag us down when we least expect it. I have always asked myself the same question: I am a damned vampire, a lord of night, why should I have to suffer from depression?"

Blood and Biscuits

Despite her odd mood, Alizon smiled and her gaze almost found Vlad's. Then it darted away again, terrified to connect on such a personal level. Many cultures of the world consider looking another person in the eyes rude, whilst many others believe precisely the opposite. However, Vlad knew neither of these were Alizon's way and commenting would most likely exacerbate her fears.

"Oh, vampires are wonderful creatures," she said in honest fascination. She looked over at the other Support Group members. "But then, everyone here is wonderful, in their own right. Even your white werewolf, mopey as he is."

Vlad looked at her again.

"How do you know mopey turns white upon transformation?"

Alizon raised her hands and looked at them strangely, as if reading lines of scripture on her palms.

"My eyes of my magic…they tell me many things. One of the side effects of being a weather witch is I find connections with the strangest aspects of our world. Right now, a vast storm batters the Pacific and a heat wave decimates parts of Central America. If I wanted, I could use these extremes to begin unravelling the mysteries of life they are affecting, but that would cost me dearly."

Vlad noticed that Alizon's speech improved when talking about her capabilities.

"Instead, I sit with my magic's quiet sides and let them tell me what they wish." Vlad said nothing. It was important Alizon said whatever she needed to feel comfortable with the group, even if she talked about herself with no real direction. "That's why I had such d-difficult weeks, I was re-reeling from my first time here, especially with what the g-g-grumpy werewolf said, and then I used the night's calm air last week to read what this island played host to. The stiller the weather the more difficult it becomes to fuse with so I spent a lot of energy obtaining information. I don't know if *you* know but the moon and the nature of the night and its weather have a unique connection, and some say they can influence the curses of this world. I learnt that from my foster carer, Aunty Windwater."

Vlad inclined his head and thought of werewolves.

"I have heard that in passing," he replied in a withdrawn way. He raised his eyebrows. "Aunty Windwater, you say? You speak as if she raised you rather than somebody that took you in for a year or so."

"Yes, outside of boarding school, in holidays and later on after I left education. She's been a rock for me, the only person I can really focus on properly. My foster carer, yes, but really more of a mother. Certainly more so than the woman who calls herself such."

"Emotional anchors keep us grounded when all about seems put to storm. Your Aunty Windwater sounds very special." Vlad did not wish to push the matter and so stayed on Alizon's conversation. "What did you see when you read the blue moon night?"

"I saw violence. Bloodshed. A powerful white werewolf battling with a gigantic force of pure darkness – I assume that was you."

"A rather accurate description of the monster within me," Vlad said plainly, emotionlessly. "I hope you were not recovering alone since you joined with the atmospheres above Ellin's Island."

"No. No, I was with Aunty Windwater for the blue moon. She's Wiccan, she raised me in her ways without being pushy about it. Though the word 'witch' exists in her beliefs I'm not Wiccan myself, but she respects and guides my ways as well her own. I couldn't miss a blue moon on Halloween, it's so important her – to all Wiccan, actually."

Vlad thumbed his forehead.

"Of course it is, I utterly forgot you might derive significance from its presence. Did you do any rituals for the moon?"

"Oh yes, we lit white candles for divination and peace and filled bowls with moon water Aunty Windwater had left out to charge up over the year. She's been looking forward to this for a while."

"I can tell," Vlad said amusedly. "It sounds like you made the most of it, such an event is special, regardless of one's beliefs. To spend time with those we consider family is, and always will be, special. Even when we argue at Christmas."

"I love Christmas with Aunty Windwater! Every year we chop down the tree that's closest to death; she taught me if we must use a living thing for food or ornament then let them have had a life first. Then we decorate the tree with dried fruits as we sip hot spiced mead, ahh," Alizon mused quietly, her eyes rolling back a little at her memories. "We planted a crystal as well, an amethyst, so we could make a wish for the future. It's the fulcrum of the ritual, making plans for what's yet to come."

Vlad placed each piece of information Alizon gave him in the vast, deep vaults of his mind, listening as he stored this woman's life and times.

"I am enamoured by the memories of your life, Alizon. You have such structure, such form, to the curves of your existence but you are not one to be shaped by others, by their events, to be moulded by how others see you. Like Ellin's Island itself, *you* are the shaper. You are the one that *brings* form; you are the rock in the river that creates the paths, where others diverge around or batter uselessly against." Vlad took a deep breath and *smelled* the scents of the church, his blackened lungs desperate for the life they could not attain. "Such history in your threads. I thrive on the tales of others for their lives and their loves."

Alizon's eyes flickered and her mouth twitched in almost-embarrassment, and then a tiny amount of her changed, as if she calculated something, her intelligent brain firing in countless pathways Vlad could never hope to understand. "Ellin's Island," she repeated slowly. "That's always struck me as interesting. There's never been anything of this land belonging to a famous Ellin. No mayor or governor or architect. I thought an explorer from here but there's nothing online."

"The nearby town is Ellinsgate," Vlad suggested.

Blood and Biscuits

"And the two are linked but I know these parts well, and their histories, and I've never found someone by that name of note."

Vlad shrugged.

"I do not know what to tell you; this place was named by an old mayor ages ago."

"And I wonder when *that* was," Alizon said suggestively. Vlad registered how forward the enchantress could be but he had no time to dwell as the group began shuffling back to their seats.

"Ahh," Vlad breathed. "It would appear to be time for question two. Come," he said to Alizon, "would you care to join us for the rest of the evening?"

"That would be lovely," she responded, surprising the vampire once again. He had wholly expected Alizon to deny and leave. Ever since meeting her at the folk festival, the enchantress continuously changed how she presented herself, how she dealt with scenarios. So much so, Vlad had to alter how his own mind operated just to keep up.

"Very well," he said simply, noticing her fingers had halted, no longer seeking her magic's comfort. He crossed the basement to re-take his seat as Cain pressed a black coffee into his hands. "Oh, thank you, Cain," he said, and the werewolf smiled.

"No problem, mate. Least I could do for all the Jaffa cakes, support sessions, and rib breaking."

Vlad tipped his head in acknowledgement as everyone reclaimed their own chairs. He lowered the smallest sliver of his control and allowed a minute amount of power to seep out, directing his senses towards the entire room and beyond but keeping them well away from Alizon. She had not said she did not want him monitoring everything else of the island.

"So, who would like to get anything off their chests? Anything at all, good or bad. I, for instance, have found my depression has resurfaced somewhat following the events of last week. Dark thoughts have invaded my mind, threatening to suffocate me. Once or twice I have been tempted to hurt myself again."

Cain shifted awkwardly in his seat but Vlad ignored him. Alizon looked round the room aimlessly, a pleasant smile on her face.

"I have done what I can to keep the demon that hounds my steps at bay – keeping myself busy is a very good way of doing that, though I am forever in search of more things to do. I have no job, not needing one in any way, and I have no living family to occupy my time with."

"You have us," Lucy suggested and Vlad smiled.

"I do, and this place – all of you – are a wonder to me, but I must still trudge through a whole week before I can return here for a few hours every Monday night. Which, I might add, is *still* the most utterly depressing day of the week, even dead."

"I agree. Maybe it's a social hangover from our human days, or perhaps everyone else's sour mood infects us as we walk around town," Jacob offered. Cain indicated the wraith enthusiastically.

"Mondays suck! I *do* have a job and the first day back on's horrendous! Today was particularly bad: the weekenders buggered up the entire warehouse layout and the canteen had run outta' chips. On day one! Who runs out of chips on day one, for Christ's sake!"

"At least you can eat chips," Jacob pointed out as Lucy gave an exasperated look and Sarah began humming a rather joyful tune to herself. "If I try any potato-based foods I vomit horrifically."

Cain snorted.

"Aim it onto a canvas and call it modern art, then sell it online," he suggested unhelpfully, and Jacob, to Vlad's astonishment, looked for one single moment to be considering it.

"I could call it 'Zombie Rejection'," Jacob grinned.

Cain looked shocked.

"You said we couldn't say that word," the werewolf admonished.

"*You* can't, *I* can. I'm taking it back."

Blood and Biscuits

"That's double standards, mate," Cain muttered as Lucy shook her head. Interestingly, Vlad found, Sarah rose higher. She was finding the whole exchange amusing.

'It is good to see her enjoying herself. I know she becomes miserable during her time alone. Anybody would, trapped inside the crumbling ruins of a church nobody knows. To be free is her ultimate cure, that becomes clearer by the day.'

Cain feigned an annoyed expression as Alizon leant towards Vlad and whispered something.

"I think I understand th-this conversation a bit better than last time," she uttered.

"Do you indeed?" Vlad asked gently. "Do you think you discern the social subtleties of the mockery and jesting?"

"Perhaps," Alizon said proudly. "The werewolf pretends he is annoyed when actually he's only prickled at most, turning it into a show. The wraith baits him in what I assume is friendship while the faerie displays indifference. Correct?"

"That is a rather clinical approach to observation but correct, nonetheless," Vlad whispered back.

He meant to say more but something suddenly changed, some part of the room caught on his senses and *tugged*. An electric shock arced down his spine. His proprioception had snagged on an unknown force, like moving a hand through the dark and catching it on a single spider's thread. Nothing ever disturbed his senses like that.

He turned toward the direction of *pull*, to where Lucy sat. Her back held ramrod straight, narrowed eyes staring dead ahead, unfocussed. Conversation continued for a while until Cain noticed, then Jacob, Fable. Vlad watched Lucy – he knew she was not thinking about the Support Group.

"Lucy, is everything…" Jacob began but Vlad cut in.

"Hush," he said quickly and the wraith silenced.

Suddenly, Lucy's eyes grew wide and she opened her mouth. For one horrid second, Vlad thought she would scream, but instead she spoke five simple words in a voice not of this world. The banshee's true voice.

"My house is under threat."

Without another sound, Lucy's body erupted in black flame and all except Vlad and Sarah leapt back in fright. The sight was incredible, thick tongues of dark power enveloping her entirely as she tilted her head back and accepted the fires. The flames engulfed her and in the next instant, Lucy was snuffed out of existence.

All about them was silence for nearly five seconds, then the room descended in panic and shouting.

"Jesus, Vlad, what the hell was that!" Jacob cried, rotting hands clenching and unclenching wildly. He stammered on as Cain stepped forward, rage and terror warring for dominion on his face.

"She just…she exploded! She just exploded! Where's she gone, Vlad? Tell me right now what happened to her!"

Alizon started worrying, wringing her hands desperately. Fable stood behind her chair, nothing on her beautiful face betraying a single hair of emotion.

Vlad shook his head.

"I do not know, Cain. My best guess – calm down, Jacob, you will do yourself an injury – my best guess is Lucy has been taken by her binding back to her mansion. Alizon, everything is alright, you can take a deep breath now."

"She said somebody was threatening her home," Fable added thoughtfully, a blackened hand pushing her golden hair back fluidly. She maintained a brilliant level of calm. "Her binding could be compromised so the magic seeks to protect itself *and* Lucy by drawing her back."

Jacob stared around the basement madly as if Lucy would appear from the doorway. Cain started wrenching on his coat angrily, resolve carved onto his face.

"Exactly," Vlad confirmed. "Contrary to what you all think, I do not know everything about everything. This is a new occurrence to me, too. She has been taken by her binding and I do not think she will find anything pleasant at her house."

"What're you saying?" Jacob asked, worry stretching his ruined features as clear as the tendons beneath his fractured skin.

"I am of the firm belief, Jacob, that we need to go after our dear friend Lucy and assist her in her time of need. Will you join me?"

"Hell yes, I will!" Jacob exclaimed indignantly, as if Vlad had suggested he would do the exact opposite. "But I'll be damned if I can remember where the place is... Jesus, this is happening so quickly, she's only been gone a minute."

"These things must be acted upon swiftly," Vlad said.

"I know where that bloody mansion is," Cain muttered angrily, wrenching his coat on. "I can walk us there right now."

"I know perfectly well where the mansion is, Cain, and there shall be no walking. Grab hold of my arms and I will fly you all there."

"You're not serious," Jacob said in disbelief.

"I am deadly serious. Walking is too slow – whatever Lucy has been taken to confront it will not be long before both forces meet. No, you will be carried through the skies. It will not take long, I am sure."

Cain looked anxious and Jacob's face fell at the prospect. However, Alizon and Fable both brightened.

"Ooh, I've never seen the town from above," the enchantress said happily, eyes looking up at the high-vaulted ceiling. Fable echoed her sentiments.

"It has been many decades since I last flew upon anything, and I have yet to add a vampire's flight to that list. You might call that excitement?"

"Good woman," Vlad said. He looked to the men, they put on the bravest faces they could.

"Let's get this over with," Cain muttered as Jacob nodded. Cain glanced down at him. "I don't know what *you're* scared of, if you fall you can just slot yourself back together! Me, on the other hand…"

"*You* got tossed around that arsing factory out there like you were made of rock, so don't you come at me with that 'you're already dead' nonsense. Be a werewolf and hitch a ride on Vlad."

"We say some really weird stuff here," was all Cain grunted as they approached the exit.

"Bring my friend back safe, Vladislav!" Sarah cried as the group prepared to leave. He turned and looked at her, his face as kind as he could make it.

"We will, my love, we will."

"I would be lost without her," the silver ghost continued as she flew back and forth agitatedly. "Seeing her gone would make me hate this existence more than I already do."

"We will bring her back, Sarah, and when all is said and done, I will discuss with you your situation to see if there is some way we might end your misery. Is that a deal?"

The ghost halted. Everything about her went utterly still.

"You could do that?"

But Vlad was gone before he could reply, before he could think on her sorrow anymore.

THE SKY

"Oh Christ, this is high up! I'm gonna' die, I'm gonna' die, I'm gonna' die!"

"Stop struggling, I need to concentrate."

"AAGGHH WHAT WAS THAT!"

"Cain be quiet, it was a pigeon. Jacob, calm down or you'll fall."

"Good *Lord*, this is fascinating! Books on engineering pale in comparison."

"Thank you for that optimism, Fable."

"Bloody hell, I don't like this! Aagghh, summat' went up my shirt!"

"Cain, for God's sake, it's only wind. Vlad, are you going the right way? Watch out for the cloud!"

"Over the top we go!"

"Not over the trees! They've got pointy bits! Oh, bloody hell!"

"Weeeee!"

"That's the spirit, Alizon."

GALLOWAY'S MANSION, MEADOWROCK HILL, A MILE NORTH OF ELLINSGATE.

Vlad landed as carefully as he could and his four passengers disembarked in a dishevelled heap. Cain was sneezing and shivering from head to foot, and he wandered off quickly to regain much of his constitution without embarrassment. He did not need witnesses in case he vomited. Jacob stepped away and shook himself down, making a 'Whoo!' noise of excited agitation as Fable rubbed her injured fingers together. Alizon smiled at the sky, her hands on her hips.

"Well *that* was interesting," she said happily. "I did a lot of weather reading up there and the night sky is truly joyful at the moment. There's rain to the south that will miss us, but it's happy rain, good rain. It doesn't need us underneath to appreciate it."

Vlad suspected the words Alizon offered were most likely an unintentional misdirection from other conversations she found too personal to discuss, matters that would otherwise seem rather trivial to others, matters taken for granted, such as emotions or opinions.

Cain returned, his feet pounding the ground with distress.

"Why aren't we already inside? I know this place, might be able to figure out where she is. But this mansion's huge, it's gonna' take serious time. Vlad, if somebody's hurting her-"

Blood and Biscuits

"-You will do whatever it takes to protect her, I know," Vlad cut in gently. Cain took a deep breath and Vlad counted that as an indication the werewolf put more of his trust in Vlad's guidance. "And to protect her we must do *all* we can. We know not the nature of this threat," Vlad finished.

There were precisely eighty-six windows upon the front, eerily gazing across the dense-grown woodlands, some of the town's lights visible through the trees. Deep-purple paint had once adorned the walls but it had long-since faded, peeling in strips from lashes of weather. It was a beautiful thing, Vlad told himself, though to most others it stood ominously, a foreboding tombstone of time and creeping period décor.

"Can you sense where she is?"

Vlad saw desperate pain shading Cain's eyes, Jacob's hand on his shoulder, looks of worry from Fable and even Alizon. This was more than he ever thought possible from such a group of supernatural strangers.

"I will find her," Vlad said, an inelegant yet profound statement of sincere truth. "There is very little that can hide from me."

The vampire lowered the walls of his control and shaped the darkness within, moulded it quickly from its terrifying force, altered it with every ounce of experience from centuries of hardship and toil. He forged its intent and hammered it into his own design, and he channelled a hundred arrow-straight senses into the mansion, delving deep into the rooms and halls and its very soul.

He *smelled* must and dampness in corners and rotting walls, the *feel* of dust and eddies of a thousand drafts seeping through a thousand cracks. He mapped the warped, looming walls, *felt* the scratch of every exposed brick, the passage of every chimneybreast whistling coldly until, at last, his senses came to a maze-like network of tunnels lying beneath the mansion. Vlad *smelled* ancient drips of wine and festering wooden boxes. He *felt* feet scrabbling, the hurried breathing of somebody he knew, and three soft heartbeats of people he did not.

Foul blood urges rose hungrily at the sensation of life but Vlad quashed them firmly.

"Found her," he uttered and a sliver of relief passed across Cain.

"Where?" Cain asked, every ounce of sarcasm and dark humour set aside, the sensibilities and natural temerity of the emboldened man emerging, resolve found, determination clear.

"There is a labyrinth of underpasses beneath the house," Vlad explained. "She stalks those ways, confronting three people. Human. I have hope we might yet rescue our dear friend."

"Then in we go," Cain announced, striding purposefully towards the mansion's vine-rimmed double doors, his moment of fear in the skies forgotten. He threw the doors wide, hinges gliding smoothly and noiselessly, and Vlad felt just the smallest amount of disappointment they had not sounded like those gloriously cliché ones in horror films, with a whining groan sending shivers down the spines of the audience.

'Life is not like the movies,' he told himself as he ensured Jacob, Fable, and Alizon were perfectly fine with what they were about to do. The latter seemed oddly comfortable with the situation; Vlad thought she would struggle with sensations of threat. However, it was becoming clear Alizon's difficulties lay primarily in social interactions. She most likely found great mental stability in keeping herself busy, whatever the task, as long as it did not include direct conversation with strangers or discerning others' emotions.

'Perhaps,' Vlad thought, *'such absence of care for how others present themselves allows for a more clarifying outlook on the harder facts.'*

Cain led them through the doors into a vast atrium of lavishly decoration, complete with a delicately carved grand staircase, many of its stairs smashed and splintered. However, much to Vlad's continued disappointment, they were not to explore the mansion's inner workings but instead descend to yet another basement. He sent such selfishness fleeing from his mind and scolded himself for his impetuous thoughts.

"The wine cellars lead down behind the stairs," Cain announced. He walked past the wide staircase to a small side door of thick oak and curved, willow embellishments. "It's dark down there," Cain muttered, "really dark, just watch your step."

"We'll be alright," Jacob said firmly, his own attitude improved by Cain's strong will.

The door opened quietly and Vlad immediately smelled a tang of fear escape the musty depths. It was not the fear of a banshee. Vlad kept his thoughts to himself, he did not wish to damage anybody's determination if Lucy was in peril.

Distant voices could be discerned as they descended the deepening darkness of the wine cellars. That stimulus of sound did not belong to Lucy but three people. Vlad *felt* their human hearts quickening and *smelled* the cheap alcohol and energy drink caffeine on their breaths. He recognised something about them but could not place what.

Vlad's feet hit the cellar floors and he directed them west, towards a sharp cry of pain. A human had torn their hand across something rusted. The taste of blood iron splashing the ground struck the air like a blinding flash of light dancing before the vampire's eyes. It sent wonders scurrying through his mind. His lusting darkness smashed against the steel-hard walls of his control; Vlad very nearly dropped every inhibition and rushed towards that scent of life.

There was something else in the blood, too.

"They are male," Vlad whispered.

"How can you tell?" Fable questioned through the gloom.

"The *stink* of testosterone on the air. It festers on my senses," Vlad practically spat, trying to shake off the hormone's stench. "They are not far, I will guide as best I can, given your lack of senses."

Blood and Biscuits

"Oh, I can help with that. Should've thought about this earlier," Jacob said and a moment later a torch illuminated from his hand. He held aloft his smartphone, a tiny white light shining brightly through the murk. Vlad stared at him for a moment.

"You know, I often forget those things are so multipurpose," the vampire noted honestly. "Up until, perhaps, ten years ago I would have been making you all rely on burning sticks to light the way. Technology truly is phenomenal."

Jacob shrugged awkwardly and held his phone forwards so everyone could see through the winding corridors. Vlad took the lead, hurrying along with his mind conjuring eight thousand awful scenarios befalling Lucy as he followed the rising sound of panicked voices.

"Shh, I think I hear something," one of the men whispered up ahead.

"You heard nothin', just find a damned ladder and get us up to that room. It's bad enough we're stuck down here as it is, but with Jack gone…"

"God, don't mention him, it gives me the creeps, the way he went. I didn't know he was that bad, what'm I s'posed to do, know how he's feelin'? Ugh, trains are s'posed to be quick, but still…"

Vlad turned a fifth time and the hot scent of blood multiplied in his senses. The men were close, Lucy not far from them. The shape of her form outlined in the vampire's thoughts, crouching low, pressing against something. Vlad was starting to think Lucy was not hurt at all. He was certain the men had no clue she was there. The humans spoke again, their voices harsh with anxiousness.

"You sure this is where that crazy girl came?"

"I told you, idiot, I followed her back here that same night we found her and that…that demon. She disappeared soon as she walked through the doors but I know this place now. She'll be here still. We can kill two birds with one stone gettin' this done, all we needa' do is find that room then that girl, got it?"

"Yeah, but…"

Vlad heard a sudden noise, one that made his blood colder than it already ran. It was the keen, metallic sheen of a knife drawing from a leather belt loop as one of the men brandished the weapon through the darkness. Vlad accelerated, almost gliding across the cellar floor as he contained the war of his power. All his urges bade him to charge the men threatening his friend, to wrap them up in darkness, drain them of blood, and leave their emptied bodies draped across the trees as a warning to all others that dared step foot on his protected ground.

'I am the darkness,' Vlad said to himself. *'And I will not…'*

His racing thoughts drowned entirely when, without warning, Lucy stood from where she crouched and stepped before the men, the overpowering flames of fury and outrage burning through the tunnels and striking Vlad with a monumental strength.

It did not take long for the men to notice her.

"Oh Christ, Seb, there's someone else here!"

"What, where? I can't see nothin'!"

"No but I can hear 'em and they're breathin' hard, mate. I'm leavin', Seb. Move!"

'She has not screamed yet,' Vlad noted internally. *'They cannot see her.'*

Vlad turned the final corner and Jacob's torchlight filled a cavernous wine cellar, illuminating a scene of complete chaos. Instead of rescuing Lucy from the clutches of evil, she was instead advancing slowly upon a group of men desperately racing around the room, knocking into barrels like drunken mice, trying to find a way out through the sudden light.

Before Vlad could do or say anything, Lucy spread her arms and unleashed a scream so deafening, so full of thunder, even the vampire pressed his hands to his ears. The walls shook thick streams of dust free and the long-since dried wine barrels rocked in their rusted stillages. The humans' panicked faces turned ashen, mouths opening wide in terror absolute.

"Jesus, what the hell is that!" one yelled.

Blood and Biscuits

"Move, move, move! Outta' the way!"

Lucy's feet left the floor, hair and dress billowing in a devilish gust of wind rattling every brick and bone, and she screamed ever louder as her body of dark fire dove towards the men, their cries of horror completely unheard by all except Vlad. His darkness reacted to the banshee's fury, whipped at it aggressively, defensively, and then it stepped back and began to *learn* from it, as Vlad's power had done every time it had encountered something new.

With a series of dull thuds, every last one of the men dropped to the floor and became still, eyes and mouths still gaping in deathly visions of terror. They had fainted out of pure terror.

Lucy lowered to the floor gracefully, arms returning to her sides as her scream silenced so suddenly it seemed to drag everything inwards. The wind howling through the cellars ceased and Vlad removed his hands from his ears. He looked round at the Support Group: they all seemed fine, if a little shaken. Alizon looked at nobody, her hand gripping Fable's arm tight enough the faerie's face was screwed up in pain. Alizon looked down and hurriedly removed her hand.

"I'm s-so sorry, I didn't mean..."

"It's quite alright," Fable said almost pleasantly, brushing down her arm. "You meant no harm. I'm just glad we're all fine."

Lucy turned at the sound of voices, eyes filling with more anger. However, when she saw who it was her face broke into an exhausted smile and she stumbled forward. Vlad made to catch her but Cain darted forward and took her up in an embrace. Her pale arms fell round his wide shoulders and they held one another so tightly Vlad thought they would squeeze themselves into oblivion.

Lucy leant back after a moment, a stern look lining her face.

"You nearly kill us all last week and now you expect me to just *fall* into your arms like some helpless princess?"

Cain hesitated.

Blood and Biscuits

"Well you nearly got yourself killed just now," he offered hopefully but it did not seem to satisfy Lucy. "No you didn't," he added hurriedly, "you had this handled. I didn't, not last week, but I didn't know you were worried about the others so much."

"I was scared for *you*, Cain. I was terrified the army would be called, or something, and you'd be shot to pieces!"

"And I thought one of them guys was gonna' kill you – I was *terrified* you were gonna' die!" the werewolf growled and even Lucy seemed shocked. The layers of Cain peeled away, exposing him as just as vulnerable and frightened as the rest of that group in the wine cellar. "You disappeared in smoke and I didn't know where you'd gone. At least *I* had the decency to keep to a bloody lunar timetable; you were just *poof*! Then you give *me* crap about bein' a threat when we've got a vampire who can fly while holding four people like they're made outta' pillows, and turn chains to dust like it's nothin', and…"

Cain's words cut short when Lucy's hands left his back and dragged his face down to hers. Vlad raised his eyebrows and made a low whistling sound of surprise; Jacob gasped and Fable let out a quiet "Oh bravo" as the banshee and the werewolf became one – they seemed just as shocked as each other.

Vlad's face cracked a deep smile as a tiny sniffle sounded nearby. He saw Jacob wiping his eyes and making no show of hiding it. The wraith glanced at him and Vlad saw his tears shining black, just like Lucy's.

"Oh, it's just so lovely, isn't it," Jacob muttered as Fable put her arm round his shoulders tenderly. "Everyone needs a bit of that in their lives."

Jacob crumpled and leant against the faerie. Vlad reached out and gripped his shoulder, and said quietly,

"When you are ready to call Luke then do so. We stand with you and your decisions, as always. I think you must settle your soul's imbalance."

Blood and Biscuits

Jacob's dead, motionless heart skittered a little and he buckled into Fable. She gathered him up, the man breaking down in sobs as Vlad went to stand beside Alizon and wait for her to ask why Jacob was crying. When she finally did, Vlad explained as he beamed from ear-to-ear. He had not felt quite like this for a very long time.

"But I still don't understand," Alizon said as Cain and Lucy separated and embraced for a while longer. "They hardly know one another."

"It has been six weeks, Alizon," Vlad said as Jacob and Fable made to start leaving the cellar. "That is more than enough time for two people to realise a shared bond, however tenuous the connection. And these two have been through far more together than most will in their lifetimes. There is strong research into human behaviour describing the pressures of highly intense situations forging stronger relationships in shorter timespans when compared to standard couplings. Perhaps those findings hold water for people such as us, too."

"I suppose that makes sense," Alizon admitted, though her tone conveyed no such conviction. "Not that I'd have much experience in this matter."

Vlad detected a depth the enchantress would probably not care to admit. She would speak when ready. The vampire made sure his senses circumnavigated Alizon as he took his cue from Lucy and led the way from the cellar pathways. When at last they returned to the mansion proper, full night had stolen the light through the cloth-covered windows. Vlad sighed, satisfaction flooding his blackened veins.

"This has been…an interesting time, to say the least. Lucy, what would you like done with the three trespassers once they recover?"

The banshee grinned wickedly.

"Leave them. They found their way down there, they can get back out again. I doubt they'll go snooping round for anything after what they saw."

Cain looked at her strangely.

"What they saw? You mean an angry hell-banshee flying right at them?"

"In a sense. But I've found some online blogs about banshees and it turns out when I – we – scream, sometimes my victims witness the totality of pain they've inflicted on others. Perhaps it's part of the premonition of death imprinting of them…life flashing before your eyes the moment before you die, only sort of in reverse. Wait, that didn't make sense."

"It is called the 'Banshee's Confession'," Vlad intoned. "I had thought it only legend, given my limited dealings with your people. Yet legends can become, once more, fact."

"Well, that's the best I can come up with. Nice name, by the way, I'm glad you know something about it as well, even if it's superficial. So yeah, that's probably what the men saw."

"Years and years of trauma they've inflicted on others screamed back at them in one go?" Cain reaffirmed.

Lucy nodded. "I think so. That explains why they fainted."

Cain mulled the notion over and evidently decided on something.

"Please never scream at me. I think I'd explode."

"It's *intentional* harm, Cain, not accidental. Not pain you've given against your will."

The werewolf brightened.

"Oh! Then I reckon I could handle a good shoutin' at."

Lucy smirked.

"Don't tempt me."

Cain blushed a little.

"So, you definitely didn't need our help after all, then?" Jacob asked, his voice strong again. Lucy shook her head.

Blood and Biscuits

"Not in a physical sense, no. But I appreciate you all coming anyway, it makes me feel wanted."

"It is always in my nature to help wherever needed," Vlad commented easily.

"So we've noticed," Cain muttered.

Vlad pushed the mansion's double doors wide to the swallowing night. He always felt stronger beyond the confines of walls; even though vampires requiring invitation into homes was a myth, Vlad still always felt a powerful sense of foreboding when he was surrounded on all sides. As a human, he had suffered from mild claustrophobia so he supposed it had carried over with his depression when he had turned.

The waning moon shone glistening upon the hilltop and Vlad stepped out into the deeps of the night.

"Should we call an end to our session and go our separate ways?" he asked them.

Vlad had expected all to agree and ask for a lift back into town but nobody moved, even Alizon.

"Is everything alright?" the vampire questioned. Fable rubbed her arms awkwardly and Jacob kicked his heels.

"I dunno'," Cain said quietly. "Feels a bit cut short."

"Cut short?"

"Yeah, like we're not done. I got a few things to get off my chest and I'm sure other folks do, too. Normally I'd wanna' leave and get back to bein' alone but…I guess I don't. I can stay late, I've got a bit of lieu time at work and my boss is fine with me textin' last minute to be late in the next day – got a good rapport with him. How about you lot, got anythin' on?"

"No," Jacob said. "I fancy talking a bit more, clear a few things." The wraith indicated the mansion. "This was just a break from the real work of getting to know ourselves, not to sound corny."

"That did sound corny," Fable said, her astonishing face ignited by a jagged smile. Jacob glanced at her.

"Now when the hell'd you learn to joke?"

Fable made a gesture.

"It's taken some acute observation, let me assure you."

Vlad looked at Alizon, the enchantress standing apart from everyone else and pointing to the mansion in a slow sweeping motion. He thought of approaching but decided she would not appreciate that.

"Alizon?" he asked gently from afar. "What are your thoughts?"

She took a moment longer with her task then turned to Vlad, a look of contentment about her.

"Yes?" she asked. Her attention had clearly been too preoccupied with the house to know what anyone had been saying. Vlad tilted his head thoughtfully then looked up at the peeling paint and exposed masonry of the mansion.

"You were counting the bricks," he stated.

Alizon nodded as the others looked on in confusion.

"Indeed. The front face has fifty-nine thousand, five hundred and eight bricks. Simple mathematics, multiply columns by rows then subtract any singular bricks missing."

Vlad smiled darkly as Jacob's mouth fell open.

"Why'd you need to count *that*?" Cain asked incredulously.

Alizon smiled strangely. "I like to know details." That was all she said on that matter. As the others fell into conversation with one another, talking on matters of mansions, intruders, and wellbeing, Alizon glanced up at Vlad's face, gazing somewhere around his chin, and said, "Lucy and I have chatted, by the way, and she's mentioned you've got knowledge of thought and how it manifests outside the body and mind. I'd forgotten to say this."

"Now that is a strange segue," Vlad commented. "Lucy said this? I am surprised, I will admit, I was not expecting her to mention such a thing."

Alizon shrugged.

"Well she'd been asking me about my magic and then I described how I'd been struggling to get to grips with a particular brand of cloud spell because I couldn't get my thoughts in order, and then she came out with this stuff about you."

"That seems fair enough. Now, I do not have knowledge, per se, but I do take interest in the theories, which is what I was trying to convey to Lucy. How did you get to there from bricks?"

"It crossed my mind as everything does. I only say this because if you're interested then one day you should meet my Aunty Windwater. I'll take you to her cottage some time, in Kent, she'd love to meet you, too."

"Why, is she a researcher of thought?" Vlad asked. "Strange, considering most theories died out a century ago."

"No, she's not a researcher, really. She just has insight I think you'd be interested in. That's the best I can describe it as. It'd be nice, you could come for coffee and see the place where I grew up. Have a think."

"I will certainly do that," Vlad said pleasantly.

"I need a drink," Jacob muttered from where he stood beside the mansion's open entrance. Vlad clapped his hands together.

"An excellent idea! You all make yourselves comfortable at Lucy's behest, I shall go and get the beverages. No, do not try to stop me, Fable, I will bring the hot water for your special tea, also. And yes, Cain, I will bring Jaffa cakes and some meat, I can hear your stomach and you need sustenance rather than sugar. Cooked or uncooked?"

Cain glanced down at Lucy and grimaced.

"Best make it cooked," he said. "Don't wanna' put her off me yet. Not 'til I've got credit saved up."

Vlad nodded then spread his arms, letting his darkness wrap him up and carry him into the sky, the faces of the Support Group far below all staring as he departed.

"Alizon? Can I, err, apologise for what I said two weeks ago?" Vlad heard Cain nervously say upon the wind as he picked his direction and flew.

"Yes, of course," she matter-of-factly replied as Vlad disappeared amongst the clouds and finally lost hearing of the Support Group.

Vlad concentrated on the forest grounds until he heard two rapid heartbeats skittering amongst the low brush and ferns. He dived and a moment later twin shrieks rang out across the night.

THE INDUSTRIAL COMPLEX, ELLIN'S INDUSTRIAL ISLAND.

Vlad stepped down into the humungous stone kitchens and stood for a moment in the cold air. The fires in the hearths had not been lit for many years and the long larders stood empty of food. His old home was a monument to a time long-since gone, when he was free to live a life of his choosing.

Passing the washbasins, Vlad dropped the two fresh rabbits he had caught on the tables. For a moment, he considered using his darkness to strip the rabbits of their skin and their flesh, but before he reached into his mind to lower the walls of his control he stopped himself.

"No," he whispered, replacing the walls. "I will do this the old-fashioned way. I shall feel alive again."

Vlad slid an old hunting knife from an array of blades, sharp and glinting. Slowly, methodically, he skinned both rabbits and cut the meat into strips, simply enjoying the time and the visceral energy it took, a grim smile reminding him of hunting as a man rather than chased screaming prey down darkened alleyways, haunting the streets as a faceless beast. Many lives and many more years had passed since Vlad had turned from the monster that still roared within the prison of himself, and since that time, he had been free to redeem, to release the caring person he had once been. A lover of all things good.

Blood and Biscuits

Opening a deep drawer, Vlad took out a propane burner and a stack of pans. He set aside the one he used every week to boil water for coffee and tea and took out a shallow cooking pan. He lit the burner and tossed the meat strips into the pan with a dash of oil from the side. He added cracked black pepper and a crushed sprig of rosemary. It *smelled* like it would be delicious.

Vlad hummed a small tune as he flipped the frying meat, keeping it from catching, then switched off the burner, leaving a little blood for Cain's palate. The meat cooled as he went into another cupboard. He looked at the vast stacks of biscuits and Jaffa cakes, teas and coffees stored within. There were some plastic containers, too. He took down three packs of biscuits, two boxes of Jaffa cakes, and a container, then he returned to the burner. Vlad tipped the meat into the plastic container and sealed it.

He crossed the vast kitchens and picked up a sturdy, leather rucksack. Looking into one of the pantries, he viewed the stores of alcohol inside. The vampire smiled thinly and removed a bottle of red wine, two bottles of cider, a medium flask of whisky, two ales, and a martini pre-mix. He put them all in the rucksack and returned to the long table. He placed the container and snacks inside the bag and tied it shut.

Lastly, Vlad wiped the cooking pan clean and restored everything to its proper place. He left the kitchens and quickly walked the ancient corridors leading to the entrance, the deep-red, enchanted rug beneath his feet muffling his steps as tapestries hung all around him, detailing centuries of battles and mysteries Vlad had yet to uncover. He supposed there had once hung vast portraits upon the walls, also, but they had been torn down long ago.

Vlad marched through the vast doors and left the stone walls behind him as the entranceway closed automatically, the abandoned factories empty and alone once more, the secret hidden. He crossed the wastelands to the basement of St Ellin's and recovered the last of the biscuits, hot water, coffee, and tea. He did not wish to disturb

Sarah and so he made to leave quietly, but a thin voice wisped behind him as Vlad put his foot upon the first step.

"Did you rescue my friend?"

Vlad turned and faced the ghost, her veil as impassive as ever.

"We did. They await my return. It seemed she needed no saving after all. She has grown strong, my love."

"Under your guidance," Sarah noted, drifting down into the room and hovering three feet above the concrete. Vlad shifted the rucksack on his shoulder and shook his head.

"I have done nothing but listen and provide advice where I can," he said. "Nothing more."

"That's simply not true, Vladislav. You're more than that to us; you stand as strength and determination, wisdom and nurture of fathers and mothers to us all. The mere fact you stand for us at all means more than somebody that simply listens, my own love. For all the hundreds of years I know you've lived, I doubt you've found a more caring circle than those awaiting your return. I wish with all my heart I could join you, I really do. But that's not my fate, you know this. I'm only a memory, and memories are always forgotten, sooner or later."

A single tear escaped Vlad's eye and tracked a crimson path down his cheek. Yet he cried not for the things Sarah said about him. Vlad did not even cry out of sadness. He felt joy in his dead heart, deep and sincere and profound. Joy for Sarah and the closeness she showed him, a true feeling of happiness at how much she recognised beyond the emotion of her soul. And relief for the acceptance she finally showed.

'*She is writing her own destiny,*' Vlad told himself. '*Sarah forges her own path to a destination she knows is coming.*'

"When you pass from this world you will go knowing you will never be forgotten," Vlad said quietly. "That is the honest truth of it, for as long as I remain upon this earth and long after I, too, walk the halls of the afterlife."

"Would you be the one to do it, Vlad?" the ghost asked, approaching him so fluidly it was as if she passed through water. "To be rid of these stone chains, to be gone from this torment…though your group meant well there has been no saving me. The last bastion of hope, gathered in this room as the last petals of my heart bloomed in phantom for another world. Would you be the one to end my suffering?"

Vlad faced her, standing as straight as he could.

"Though it would take a ritual I am not even sure could come to pass, I would do it if that is your wish, Sarah. If you asked me to send you on, to move you beyond this world to the oblivion that awaits us all, then I will make it so. And damn the consequences."

Sarah inclined her head in sorrow.

"That's what I wish, Vladislav. I've had two hundred years to bring myself to this point and I am certain. You will kill me, to float once more in freedom, as a bright flower taken by a new wind. This is what I wish."

And with that she drifted away, through the ceiling and back up into the only home she knew. A moment later, Vlad heard the strains of Moonlight Sonata floating down to him and he smiled a watery smile. The vampire left the church grounds and took the alcohol, meat, and snacks back to the mansion upon the hill, to be with friends in a circle he had made, a circle of friendship, not of destruction.

And as he flew all through his mind spun the same thought, over and over again:

'Her choice is to move on, and I know how to do that. But would the others ever agree? Would they ever understand?'

THE PARROT AND CRACKER,
ELLINSGATE.
TWO MILES FROM ELLIN'S INDUSTRIAL ISLAND.

TWO DAYS FOLLOWING THE SUPPORT GROUP.

"Did you bring it?"

"I did," Cain muttered. He put down his dry martini and reached into the folds of his coat. His face was shadowed and tired, but his eyes told the real story: he no longer suffered. He seemed better, despite his ordeal last week. The matter at Lucy's mansion had done him good. "You sure you want to do this? Not convinced any good'll come of it." Cain said cautiously.

"It is the only way I will learn," Vlad replied quietly, putting down his whiskey tumbler and stretching a pale hand across the table. They were sat in a corner down a flight of steps where hardly anyone else ever ventured from the warmth of the hearth upstairs. They would not be disturbed, nor overheard.

Cain placed a glass vial in Vlad's hand, a tube with a bronze stopper and delicate gold filigree tracing its length in beautiful patterns. It was an old thing, staggeringly valuable. The bronze kept magic contained nearly as well as brass. "Thank you," Vlad said, staring at the vial a moment, and at the dark contents within. "Was it difficult to get?"

Cain pulled back his sleeve and showed a bandage wrapped round his forearm. He grinned.

"Nothin' like a little scratch to keep you alive, eh?" he growled. Vlad smiled at the morbidity of the comment. The man was not wrong. "Lucy wrapped it up for me, she did a good job," Cain added. "Didn't ask any questions, too, wouldn't want her to worry."

"She has an eye for intricate work," Vlad agreed absently as he looked into the vial's depths, the fluid moving with wondrous flow as he turned it round and round, letting the bar's low light catch its angles. "I am very fond of this newfound kinship between you both," the vampire added.

"You approve?" he asked, sipping his drink. Vlad detected a genuine sliver of hope, something he immediately quashed.

"Does a full-grown man require my approval?"

Blood and Biscuits

"S'pose I don't," Cain said slowly, "though it's good to know you do, either way."

"It is always uplifting to understand those you confide in find your personal choices agreeable," Vlad admitted as he gave the vial a small flick. He drank the last of his whisky and let the burn disappear down his cold throat.

He observed the blood with avid interest, his keen academic eye overriding his innate hunger. It seemed different somehow, its physical properties acting strangely compared to the other fourteen werewolf curses he had encountered. "This is fascinating," Vlad murmured, tipping the vial upside-down and watching as the blood ran down the tube. "It seems...thicker than normal in some orientations and then thinner in others. It is also *very* dark, almost black. Cain, are you certain this is your blood and not some trick?"

"I wouldn't try and fool *you*, Vlad," Cain said with another sip of his martini. "Not after everythin'...not after you've shown you can beat up a twelve-foot, angry monster. Definitely twelve foot?"

"You were abhorrently huge, my friend," Vlad replied, looking at Cain seriously. "The largest specimen ever recorded, and I consider myself an expert on your kind – no offence intended, I mean not to trivialise you." Cain waved the comment away absently as Vlad said, "There were many traits and aspects to your transformed self that require further study, but first I start with this sample and perhaps answer a few questions."

"I thought you said you can only drink human blood," Cain pointed out.

"A grand point. However, this is neither human *nor* animal. I can imbibe werewolf essence and learn from it but it will not sustain me. On that note, I *can* taste most bloods in small amounts, rather like humans and their poisons, but never to replace that which I sorely need to live in this guise of death. The closer to human the animal is, such as other primates, the more I can taste before I succumb to sickness."

"Please…don't tell me how you know all that," Cain said, drinking his martini to hide his pallid expression.

"Quite," was all Vlad replied with.

The vampire stared into the vial again, a millennium of questions and legends, rumours and myths from the darkest corners of the earth suddenly brought forth, distilled in that single amount of blood. All that effort and research, the travelling and toil, all of it had led to a small glass tube resting in Vlad's palm. He could almost have laughed had his mind not become eerily quiet, the usual storm of thoughts quelling to nothing, like a sudden drop of all sound in the middle of the ocean, as he unlatched the bronze stopper and opened the vial. A hundred scents emanated immediately from the contents, the smells of the wildness of nature and the fury of life cascading magnificently across him. And the scent of that strange addition in Cain's blood, back again to haunt Vlad's mind. His fervour was almost too much to bear as he brought the vial to his lips and drank the blood down in one short draught. He left one single drop.

Instantaneously, the deliverance of knowledge flooded him and every one of Vlad's senses came alive in a rush of fire. He gripped the table's edge as the curse of a sânge-sapte's blood filled him, and he closed his eyes against the tide of essence. When at last he spoke, it was barely a whisper.

"Cain…there is much to discuss…"

Fig. 10. The Door of Lucy's Mansion.

I do not know why but I am fascinated by doors and doorways. Perhaps it is the belief that vampires cannot go through them without invitation (an egregious lie most likely put about by student werewolves). Or perhaps it is because that behind every shut door there is the promise of something, the potential of something. There is mystery, intrigue, sometimes cleaning cupboards... yet that potential is always there, inviting you to brave the handle and unlock possibility...

Week Seven
White Fire Eyes

THE PARROT AND CRACKER.
WEDNESDAY.

Cain's drink stopped halfway to his mouth.

"What do you mean 'discuss'? I thought you'd just down the stuff and be happy with it. You wanna' know more?"

Vlad shook as the powerful blood took hold and throttled his senses. It was absorbed and pulsed through his veins as all others had, but this was different. Vlad felt alive and like he stood upon the very brink of death. Slashes of black night warred with radiant basks of burning gold as his darkness railed against his control, desperate to rush to his aid and overcome this foreign poison. It all happened in a moment but seemed as if an hour had passed before Vlad regained his composure.

The vampire finally allowed his power to rid the blood and the werewolf curse, and Vlad's senses returned.

'It does not feel altogether like a curse. I cannot discern what that is, or what that means. I felt the strange scent of his blood in my own – is that possible? This is entirely new; like no other werewolf blood I have tasted.'

"Of course I wish to know more," Vlad said measuredly, receding tidal waves of biological curse still trying to overcome him. "And you should, too, if any part of you wants to learn who you are, Cain."

Vlad thought Cain might simply walk away, or even throw his martini in the vampire's face, but instead the werewolf nodded and bit his cheek.

"Fine. What d'you wanna' know?"

"No specifics, just something to combine with the imbibing of your blood."

"Christ, that sounds weird," Cain muttered.

"Yes, I rather appreciate that. So, why not start with what age you were bitten?"

"Bitten?" Cain asked, confusion crossing his face. "Age? What're you talkin' about?"

The vampire put it in more simple terms.

"You know, when you were attacked. I have tasted an astonishing amount of strength in your curse, it must have been a horrifying werewolf that transferred the virus to you. It is unlike any I have tasted before – Lucy knows what I mean, I told her quite a bit while you were unconscious before the blue moon."

"Oh right," Cain said in disbelief. "Did she…understand you better than I do?"

"Very much so," Vlad said with a smile. "But she was worried for you, open to anything to try and help. Anyway, this is about you: how old were you when you were bitten?"

"No, I wasn't bitten," Cain replied, shifting his shoulders awkwardly. "Is that wrong?"

"No, not wrong, but it is *usually* a bite. So, yours was a scratch, then, meaning…"

"I wasn't scratched, neither," Cain said matter-of-factly, taking another sip of his drink. "Is *that* wrong?"

Vlad hesitated, his turn to be confused.

Blood and Biscuits

"I – yes, it is. That cannot be possible, there are only two methods of successful viral delivery and both have been mentioned."

Cain shrugged easily.

"Can't say anythin' other than what I've given you. I wasn't scratched nor bitten. Always been this way, always will be."

"Ever since you remember?"

"Well, it came out when I went through puberty, which was a massive shock, as you can imagine. But I thought that was normal for werewolves; least, I thought that once I knew werewolves existed. Which, by the way, happened when I *became* one. Funny old world, innit?"

"Funny is definitely one word for it," Vlad said, rubbing his chin thoughtfully. "I am sorry, Cain, but this simply cannot be. I accept you did not turn until you reached adolescence…"

"Puberty," Cain corrected and Vlad tilted his head just a fraction. "Adolescence came at the normal age. I hit puberty early."

"*How* early?" Vlad asked worriedly.

"Four," Cain said simply, taking another sip of his drink. "Four years old."

"Good God!" Vlad exclaimed. "I have heard of this rarity but the consequences can be quite severe if gone untreated."

"I got no treatment, far as I remember. No doctors, no hospital trips, no nothin'."

"No hormonal treatment…"

"Nope, always tried to stay off the stuff," Cain jested lightly.

"And you are outwardly very healthy," Vlad said.

"No tumour to have caused this – none I can smell on you, anyway…"

"No way, you can smell cancer?" Cain asked, impressed.

"Believe me, I have never wished to, it is a truly horrid smell, and a horrid realisation to make," Vlad admitted mournfully. "But that is beside the point. You experienced puberty at four years old, I struggle with what your life must have been like as a child."

"Hard," Cain admitted heavily. "School's a nightmare. Don't matter if you're bigger than everyone else, a man's voice comin' out won't stop 'em ganging up and bullyin' you. However, by twelve I was gettin' into bars and clubs so I stopped gettin' problems when the sods realised I could get 'em booze. And when I started standin' up for myself," Cain added darkly, his fists clenching unconsciously.

Vlad imagined bones cracking against those knuckles, hard years of harder lessons.

"I am sorry to hear that, Cain. I have studied the virus' latency in many respects and it does have a little influence on a child's development, hormonally, but it is not all that much. You are far beyond this threshold. So why should you be any different?"

Cain spread his arms and shone a cheeky grin.

"Here I am: medical miracle."

Vlad's eyebrows raised.

"That you are, though I am old enough to tell you with some confidence miracles do not exist. Where phenomena occur, they can be answered in some way or another, science or magic. 'Miracle' is just another term for the as-of-yet unexplained."

"Honest, Vlad, I dunno' what to tell you. I've always been this way. If I'd a mum or dad I'd ask them."

Vlad made a noise in his throat.

"You are an orphan? You never mentioned this in the support sessions."

"Never needed support with it," Cain said. "I had foster parents, here and there, and then life settled down with Jan and Pete."

"How did you circumvent the matter of the werewolf transformations? No average foster parent would cope with such extremes."

"No kidding. I had a handler, some guy comin' every month, couple days before every full moon. He'd take me off, up-country, and sit me in a small, shiny room, give me food and entertainment and whatnot. Wasn't too bad, felt like a second home. Then he'd take me back again. 'Pparently, it was all in the foster agreement, signed off by some Cambridge court, I heard him say. Foster parents'd never say nothin' about it."

Vlad considered matters of Cambridge. This did not come as much of a surprise. At the end of the day, werewolf children still needed care; it made sense having a system to protect them during their monthly cycles.

Cain grunted in his throat.

"Jan and Pete were different. They really cared about me, showed me love. They home-schooled me from thirteen, got me happy. Far as I was concerned, life was pretty easy until I *turned* every month, as you and Jacob call it. Jan and Pete knew, and they protected me – one of 'em would come with that guy every month, never left my side, but I still ran away, in the end. Terrified I'd do 'em harm. I was only a child, man. They'd taken me on outdoor trips and gotten me into survival techniques. Taught me enough about self-sufficiency, anyway, so when I eventually left I actually kinda' knew what I was doin', you know?"

Vlad nodded, feeling something rise in him. It mattered not how old they were or how capable they seemed: children were too vulnerable to be unprotected. Vlad had always struggled with the notion of children being harmed and thoughts of Cain fending for himself against all manner of ills throughout his young life brought a great deal of sadness. It was a by-product of having once had a child of his own; even though he had *long*-since outlived them, being a father altered the brain permanently.

"What I *do* know, Cain," Vlad managed, "is whatever the complexities of answers are to the grand question that is *you*, I am convinced all of it lies in your blood. I will figure this out and, if you wish, tell you precisely what makes you who you are and why. Deal?"

Cain proffered his hand and flashed another grin, and this time Vlad saw just how exhausted the man still was two weeks after the blue moon's vengeance.

"Deal. Now let's drink."

AN EXCHANGE OF DIGITAL WORDS. THURSDAY.

Jacob. Hi, is this Vlad?

Vlad. Yes this jacob?

Jacob. Oh good, was worried I'd text the wrong person. Yeah it's me, are you free?

Vlad. Yeh. doin nuthin @ th mo. Went 2 town now watchin film. U

Jacob. Similar. Fable out, mind's racing. Decided to message Luke and meet up, see what he wants. Won't wear balaclava, I'm not hiding anything from him. Is it still cool to use your place?

Vlad. Gr8 news! N yes. ill send address. u send time 2 meet.

Jacob. Thanks, Vlad. Why are you writing like that?

Vlad. Like wat?

Jacob. Like a teenage girl from the 90s.

Vlad. I thort txt speak was wat peeps did. Rong?

Jacob. Haha! Oh dear lord, that is outrageous! I'm genuinely crying with laughter! No, Vlad, text speak hasn't been around since smartphones took off. It was to combat character limitation. Pretty much relegated to Twitter now.

Vlad. Oh thank God! That was driving me insular!

Jacob. Huh? Insular?

Vlad. Ugh, autocorrect. *insane.

Jacob. I'm so glad I messaged you, you've really brightened my day. I actually taught YOU something.

Vlad. Glad I could be of service. If you still want the keys to my apartment, I suggest you mention this to no one at the Group.

Jacob. I'll be telling EVERYONE at the

Group, Vlad. Your threats don't scare me.

Vlad. Bugger. It was worth a shot.
Alright, tell me when you need them and I will meet you there. I am happy for you, Jacob.

THE LIBRARY AND ALCHEMICAL WORKSHOP, THE INDUSTRIAL COMPLEX, ELLIN'S INDUSTRIAL ISLAND. SATURDAY.

Vlad delved the library maze, under archways of books, between towering shelves, round three tight corners, and down a shallow set of stairs, until he found the 'P' section. Darkness enveloped him and he passed into the higher reaches, deep smells of oak and mahogany drifting on currents of air. Under bridges and through giant cones of books, he arrived at a small division on Practical Gardening Spells and stopped at 'Personal Medicines', ignoring the sound of a bookworm shuffling deep within the waves of tomes. It tried to crawl onto his shoulder. Hovering upon wings of shadow, Vlad carefully brushed the bookworm away and selected a title.

'𝕭𝖎𝖔𝖑𝖔𝖌𝖎𝖈𝖘 𝖆𝖓𝖉 𝕮𝖚𝖗𝖆𝖙𝖎𝖛𝖊𝖘 𝖔𝖋 𝖙𝖍𝖊 𝕰𝖆𝖘𝖙𝖊𝖗𝖓 𝕽𝖊𝖆𝖈𝖍𝖊𝖘.'

He turned the thing slowly, feeling its heavy weight and age.

Next, Vlad retrieved three dense books on the subject of engineering and human machinery dating from the 1970s. To Vlad they represented a wonderful turning point of mechanical evolutions and revolutions. He tucked them under his arm and thought of Fable. If she wanted more all she need do was ask.

Vlad weaved between the shelves and walkways, exited the tunnels, and returned to the laboratory beyond the library, set up in the huge space once used for lectures and readings. He placed the book down with a satisfying *thud*, dull echoes booming through endless halls of wood and stone. Opening it gently, the spine creaked satisfyingly. Dust shivered free and Vlad, his touch as light as air, leafed through the beautiful pages of painstaking handwriting and watercolours, his brain reeling off random chapters.

'*Essence of Night Spirit, Rock Troll Ward, Charm of the Fae, Forest Fungi in Battle Wounds…ahh, here we are. Revelations of the Werewolf.*'

Vlad himself had added this page long ago at the height of his scientific and supernatural discoveries. He poured over the details and, when happy, moved to the laboratory and proceeded to gather materials.

'*Blood, blood, blood.*'

The stimulating thought danced round his mind as he worked, hands moving so delicately his fingers hardly moved at all, opening jars, pouring fluids, combining it all together. Hunger grew once more in his stomach as he removed his long red coat, the twirling cloth irritating him more than anything, and moved across to a long workbench. A vast array of equipment was arranged carefully, most items sitting cold and lifeless. He had not performed any experiments for a long time; in fact, this would be his first in over eighteen years.

Two mornings prior, Vlad had meticulously cleaned every surface, washed each flask, and sterilised every instrument. He detested working with compromised tools.

Vlad picked up a borosilicate flask and swirled its contents. The large volume of fluid within spun almost iridescently, its colourless form splitting the cascading light, creating rainbows across the workbench. Vlad smiled and set the flask down, then opened a jar of long-since browned leaves, labelled: 'Leafe of Wolfsbane: a one-fourth leafe for eache sânge incremente'. Vlad removed two leaves, put one to the side, and divided the second into three quarters. Seven fourths for the seventh clan. He placed one quarter back in the jar and sealed it. He dropped the one-and-three-quarters' wolfsbane leaves into a jade mortar and ground them into a fine dust with a smooth, marble pestle before adding the powder to the flask of colourless fluid. Instantly, the dust dissolved, reacted, and turned the fluid a fascinatingly deep lilac.

'How pretty,' Vlad thought as he pulled a glass vial from his pocket, the one given by Cain. A single drop of his blood remained. Vlad unfastened the lid and tipped the blood into the lilac fluid.

There was a sudden hiss and the flask grew noticeably heavier, and a moment later the fluid swirled of its own accord. It turned a blinding white.

Vlad leaned in closer.

"I have more to work from than initially speculated," he spoke softly as he watched the white liquid dance within the flask. "Which is good, as this will take quite some time. It is not time for the Grampians yet…"

Biologics And Curatives of The Eastern Reaches

This is simply a book from my library. You may marvel or stare in confusion at the odd flower on the front; I usually do the latter.

RUINS OF ST ELLIN'S CHURCH.
THE START OF THE SUPPORT GROUP.

"Discovered anything yet?"

Vlad and Cain sipped fresh coffees, the rest of the Support Group filing into the basement pleasantly. Lucy embraced Jacob as Fable went to greet Sarah and Alizon.

Vlad tried not to look at Cain. Unexplainably, he could sense the man's feelings, determine the werewolf's sense of his own body. He was *aware* of him more. It was not strong but certainly tangible enough to distract him.

Vlad shook his head, ignoring the awareness.

"Currently no. Despite what people think, matters such as these take a long time. Humans have their genetic processes and DNA sequencing; vampires have the even more complex task of using their senses and natural skillsets, processes the simplicity of machinery could not hope to match." Cain glanced away a moment and Vlad realised he had been hoping for more than he had let on back in the Parrot and Cracker. Vlad nudged him encouragingly. "It is ok, my friend, we will find something eventually. Take heart, I have never failed before. I will not fail you now."

"Thanks, Vlad," Cain said simply and then he strode off to greet Lucy properly. Vlad smelled the relief in both of them as they approached one another, an animalistic scent that had long-since changed from wariness and annoyance. But it was more than that now, the two felt solace simply *being* with one another.

'How soft the pale rose can grow,' Vlad reminded himself. The increased awareness of Cain pulled on his mind as the vampire waved at Alizon and Fable, the former still not meeting his eyes.

Vlad sat in his chair – he gave off the appearance of relaxation but his mind was a hive of activity, his senses constantly searching Ellin's Island for anything out of place. However, all was still on that rain-soaked night and Vlad felt relieved, glad to be in Lucy's company. He longed to hold her again.

Blood and Biscuits

Vlad caught himself and mentally shook off Cain's thoughts before beginning the session.

"How was everyone's week?" he asked easily, the phrasing ringing nicely throughout the basement, as if the high-vaulted room was designed to house that very question. "I have seen a couple of you since last week's session but I can only know so much. So...Fable?"

The faerie looked up and smiled, her face still finding the most astonishing beauty in the darkest of places.

"Yes? Oh, you wish me to start."

Vlad made a passive gesture.

"Only if you want, there is no obligation. I am simply going on a rough rotational basis and I cannot remember the last time you began a session. Are you ready?"

"I am. Hmm, how to summarise...I suppose you can all guess my pain is as prevalent as ever, though its acuteness has lessened somewhat since the incident of the blue moon."

Cain shifted as if he was about to lean forward and apologise again, but instead he glanced at Vlad awkwardly. The vampire knew he recalled being explicitly told not to say sorry for things that were not his fault. Vlad *felt* this through the new awareness of the werewolf. Fable continued, unaware, and a pang of hunger struck Vlad's stomach. He ignored it, knowing he had more than enough time to complete the session *then* seek out sustenance.

'I managed to last longer than expected after the encounter with Cain,' Vlad thought quickly. *'I thought I would have three days before requiring a feed but it has been two weeks and I am only just hungry. Perhaps it is these sessions: they occupy my mind and fill me with purpose once more. It has been many years since I have felt such alleviation.'*

"Other than my hands," Fable said, glancing at her palms pointedly, "I have kept my mind busy. 'Hanging out', as you Earthlings say, with my friend Jacob. Oh, and I have read an absolute *wealth* of mechanical history from books Vlad very kindly passed on to me so I could study."

Vlad waved away the looks people gave him.

"Like I told you, think nothing of it. Gathering dust should be the fate of no book, all should be treasured and cherished. Aside from 'The Nine Loves of Adrian' by P. J. Smith. Now *there* is a book that can rot in a lavatory for all I care. It is loose stool water of the highest calibre," Vlad added disgustedly.

Jacob groaned.

"Absolute crap," Lucy said putridly, feigning spitting on the floor. "Glad I charity shopped it."

"I appreciate and respect many things of the human world but that book is not counted amongst my long list," Fable stated, her blackened hands wringing slightly as if she wiped slime from herself. "Just…disgusting."

"It didn't make any sense at the end," Alizon said. "Were the grammatical errors intentional? There were commas everywhere! I found it tiresome, more than anything."

"Couldn't *reach* the end." A grimace twisted what remained of Jacob's part-rotten face. "That bit where Adrian and Natalia go to the swimming pool?"

"Oh don't! Too many references to floats and moisture," Lucy grumbled, pretending to be sick. "And who the hell even thinks of using chlorine sensually!"

"The book wasn't *that* bad. I actually really enjoyed it," Cain suddenly added and all eyes swivelled to him in shock. He shrank immediately, embarrassment pouring from him to the point where Vlad felt ashamed, too, through their unexplained link. Cain looked at them all indignantly. "What? A man can't read?"

"Of course a man can read, but sometimes he must consider his choices carefully," Vlad muttered.

"You like romance novels," Lucy stated, a devilish look in her eye. Cain grinned.

"You expecting horror, were you?"

Blood and Biscuits

"More action thrillers," she shrugged.

Vlad snorted. "It would seem we all have divided opinions on the novel, if you can truly call it that. Perhaps 'cess pile' would be more appropriate, or 'foul arrangement of words unfortunately vomited up, compiled, and published'. Shall we move on before Cain finds himself admitting, perhaps, a little too much?"

Everyone laughed, including Alizon and Fable, and the room fell once more into a naturally settled state. Vlad observed Cain a moment and decided on something.

'He is a large man, far beyond what the awfulness of extreme early puberty would allow. Though this could simply be genetics or an environmental thing, or even luck, I should try the blood analysis with a tincture of moonglow stem then distil the solution through a steam filter, just in case. If there is grey powder residue the resultant distillate will be colourless, perhaps that might reveal a little more about our lupine friend's curse.'

Vlad closed down his thoughts of research and turned his full attentions to the Support Group. There was time enough for the science of magic later.

"Just to finish," Fable said, steering the conversation from divisive literature, "I have learned many things on the basic principles of vehicular locomotion and dealt with the particular subject of diesel combustion. I eagerly await to see how that develops." Fable gave an enthusiastic smile.

Vlad spread his hands encouragingly.

"Wonderful! Hobbies and occupations of the mind are the best distractions. They provide personal growth whilst letting ills of the body and spirit heal. I am very happy for you, Fable."

Next came Lucy. She had researched banshee legends and begun comparing the myths to what she knew of her capabilities. The longer Vlad had known her the less fearful Lucy had become of herself, displaying signs of self-control, of finding strength. That was always a good thing.

Blood and Biscuits

"It's just...I guess I have been struggling a bit with what happened last week. I'd no idea that could happen – me exploding, I mean. Obviously, I'm used to the six-hour time limit, that's expected now. Predictable, I guess Vlad'd call it. But being taken like that?"

"It was a surprise to everyone. I didn't know how to react; I don't think anyone did. You must've felt terrified."

Lucy grimaced at Jacob.

"I was forced against my will to travel through darkness and protect a house I hate. I wasn't terrified. From the moment I was taken, I was angry. *Really* angry. I guess I got over it when I arrived, though, like I could focus that anger on the problem – those three idiots – and take it out on them. But yeah...I struggled with that this week."

"Thank you for sharing. Nobody should be forced to do anything. Unfortunately, we get no such agency over our deaths. We will persevere, Lucy, you are not alone."

"It's nice to be reminded of that occasionally," she said, crossing her legs and leaning back a little.

When Cain spoke next, he was a man of few worries. Aside from his own concerns for Lucy's wellbeing, the werewolf described what in all essence seemed to be a perfectly sound week: he was getting more sleep, his job was not taking a physical toll, and his transformation worries disturbed his daily thoughts less frequently than expected.

Sarah was perfectly content with simply floating and saying nothing and even Alizon gave a little wave when her turn came. She remained silent but Vlad thought the small motion was, in fact, an improvement.

"Jacob, how was your week?" Vlad asked. Jacob wrung his decomposed hands a little and looked in every direction except at Vlad.

"I'm still organising my thoughts. You mind skipping me a sec?"

"You could always combine it with question two, if that would be easier?" Vlad suggested and Jacob thought about it. He smiled a little and nodded.

"That'd be better. Have my cake and eat it, and other idioms like that."

Vlad sat back and listened as Jacob began, red-scorched eyes shining with hurt and pride.

"Yeah, I, err…I had an interesting time of it. Can't describe the week, was just a blur of new brains and French lessons to begin with. Thanks, Fable, for that."

"You are very welcome," Fable replied pleasantly, inclining her head.

"Yeah. So anyway, as you all know my ex, Luke, rang me last week and properly caught me off-guard. Was a massive shock, to say the least."

Despite the sombre mood Cain chuckled. It was clearly accidental and he looked positively ashamed when he realised the sound had escaped him. Jacob looked at him in question.

"You laughed. You just *laughed*," he said, more out of surprise than anything else. Cain glanced at Lucy and the others then nodded.

"I did, yes. I was just thinkin'…how funny it was that out of everythin' we've been through, and given the kinda' people we are, the fact it's everyday stuff that upsets us is really…funny? It is t'me, anyway. Sorry, Jacob, I didn't mean to interrupt you. Move on, everyone stop lookin' at me."

Cain waved them away and Jacob smiled.

"I know what you meant, and I guess it is kinda' dumb. Still, that's the way it is. So, Luke rings me and I tell him I don't want to meet. Then last week happened, with Lucy and her mansion, and seeing her with the inappropriately timed Cain made me rethink my position. I wanted to hear him out, at least. Unfinished business, and all that."

Blood and Biscuits

"Every person that is important has unfinished business, Jacob," Sarah echoed tunefully across the group. "If it is strong enough it can tie us to this world for eternity until it is complete. I, for one, would love to see people populate this island again. Long has it stood as an empty memorial for what was once vibrant, an astonishing kingdom of love and laughter. My family were once counted amongst them."

All looked from Jacob to Sarah, and then to Vlad.

"Is that right, Vlad?" Lucy asked. "Did people live on this island once?"

Vlad rubbed his chin thoughtfully and nodded. His hunger returned with a deep, sharp pang but he set it aside.

"Indeed, they did," he replied slowly. "Many thousands. It was a vast place to behold, when the river was not redirected. This island was, by many definitions, a *happy* place."

"And now it stands as a reminder of what might happen when good things come to pass," Sarah finished. "And I am trapped here by some cruel twist of fate, waiting for this, too, to pass."

Vlad turned a hundred things over in his mind as Jacob took up the reins again.

"We all feel in some way trapped," he offered and Sarah rose a little silently. Jacob pointed at Vlad. "Though I didn't the other day when our vampire friend here offered me his apartment to use in case I wanted to change my mind and meet Luke – oh, Vlad uses text speak when he messages, by the way."

"No way!" Cain exclaimed, his eyes wide.

"Oh my God, that's hilarious," Lucy said, her hands over her mouth to cover her laughter.

Fable and Alizon looked confused but Sarah rose so high she was in danger of disappearing through the ceiling. Vlad made a defeated gesture.

"I understand your amusement but that was simply unfair, Jacob. English took me a considerable amount of time to master and I have always tried to do the best I can to use it correctly. However, it keeps evolving and there have been simply too many cultural shifts to deal with over the centuries for me to keep on top of. I am afraid communicating via mobile phones was never an important point for me when I can cross whole countries in minutes to see somebody I wish to speak with."

Lucy held up her hand.

"Vlad, we're just having a giggle. We all think you're bloody amazing."

Vlad reeled.

"Oh! I...thank you, Lucy. That means a great deal to me."

"Yeah," Cain said. "Even if you *do* text like a little girl."

Lucy looked indignant.

"*You*, mister fuzzball, use too many emoticons to qualify judging someone else on their mobile habits. So zip it. But while we're at it, I've got to ask: on the Nine Loves of Aidrian," and here Cain rolled his eyes, crossing his arms defiantly, "what was your take-home of that awful shower scene?"

"Oh, for God's sake," the werewolf muttered, "why won't people leave that bit alone? It's always *that part* specifically, too. People are obsessed! Look, Adrian called out his mother's name as him and Natalia were steamin' it up to highlight the turning point in his mental state, that's it. No more abuse, just the end of an era for him. It's obvious if you read it properly!"

Lucy blinked several times as she evidently re-evaluated the werewolf. Fable made a twisted face of horror and Vlad grimaced. The vampire spoke as if through thick mud.

"I have seen many terrible things in my life but none – I repeat, *none* – have come close to every horrid word in that book. Might we please move on from it before I am liberally sick across the floor?"

"Oooh, I wouldn't wanna' see a vampire puke," Jacob said.

Vlad nodded.

"It is most vile, I assure you."

Blood and Biscuits

Cain made a motion of self-silence and flashed a grin at Jacob, who returned it despite his mood. The wraith twisted his tongue, visible through the holes in his cheeks, as he thought on what next to say.

"Sorry for throwing you under the bus, Vlad. Deflection, I guess. Still, honesty's the best course. I met Luke at your apartment – awesome place, by the way, you guys should see it some time - and we talked. Actually, that's *all* we did, just talked."

"That's great, Jacob, that is quite the first step," Fable said. She looked puzzled for a moment. "But I knew none of this. We live together and you did all this without my knowledge."

Jacob nodded.

"Yeah, sorry about that. You said you were going to go chat with the guys down at the local garage about the history of spanners and I thought that'd be a good time to go and see Luke."

"Spanners?" Cain grunted and Fable smiled.

"Fascinating tools, they are. The truest application of force and leverage in one simple extension of metal. Humans really do just get along without magic, don't they?"

"They do, bless their little cotton socks," Jacob said.

"So, what did you talk about with Luke?" Lucy pressed, clearly trying not to laugh at the absurdity unfolding all around her.

"Oh, this and that," Jacob responded airily. He held something back. "Alright, it was more than that. He apologised for what he said to me when we broke up, and he knew he was in the wrong. I didn't expect any of that, nor do I expect to get back together – I mean look at me, I'm hideous."

Jacob motioned himself up and down, the visible tendons and muscles of his face pulling taught as his yellowed teeth gritted firmly. Fable hissed and Lucy tutted at him.

"Isn't it enough that you let others put you down? Do you have to be so hard on yourself as well?" Lucy asked irritably. Jacob shrugged.

Blood and Biscuits

"Well I'm not exactly palatable. But again, Luke didn't really mention that. He was just apologetic, heartfelt. Said he couldn't believe what he'd let get between us and how if he could take it all back, he would."

"And what do *you* believe is his purpose?" Vlad finally asked.

"He said he wanted to know the new me, to understand me. Does that make any sense?"

"It's a real head scratcher," Cain said. "To *understand* you. What the hell's that s'posed to mean?"

"My point exactly," Jacob said. "It's got me stumped, kinda' left me a bit stunned in that massive flat. I just drank spinal fluid coffee and didn't say much. Luke tried to make small talk, asking me if I was still vegan despite everything, but it all just sort of felt…forced. He asked if he could hug me goodbye when he left but I said no. Then he went. Does that all sound nuts?"

"Not even slightly," Lucy said. "Not from your side, anyway. Physical touch is a powerfully personal thing, I think just standing there listening was the best course. All in all, it seemed a good idea to get it over and done with, and now you can stop worrying about what he wanted from you. You can go back to being a full-time wraith."

"Yeah," Jacob agreed, though Vlad was not convinced he was entirely sure. "So that's my thing to get off my chest this week. Not sure if it was positive or negative but you can't have everything, I'm afraid."

Jacob reached down beneath his chair and took a small box of brains from his bag. He popped open the lid and began eating quietly, a look of contentment passing over his rotten face.

"Who's in the mystery box for tea this time?" Sarah asked with ghostly interest.

Through the mouthful, which threatened to squeeze out the holes in his cheeks, Jacob said, "No idea this time. It's mostly unidentified grey matter, but there's a lovely garnish of abducent, facial, and olfactory cranial nerves on top. I made a protein sauce out of spinal fluid and soya curds with a sprinkling of rosemary to finish – adapted it from a Nigella recipe."

Lucy accidentally made a retching sound as Fable nodded in consideration. Cain simply looked away and Alizon fidgeted with her fingers. Sarah, however, seemed overwhelmingly positive.

"Wonderful. To attune yourself with food is to connect with the earth herself, and your daily regimen of brains really ties you completely to the truth of life: thoughts and feelings. Well done, Jacob, my daffodils will be most proud when I tell them."

"Umm, thanks," the wraith managed through another mouthful of brains. A strong odour of pride emanated off him, the secret behind the emotional mask he wore.

In amusement, Vlad looked round the circle until Alizon raised her hand, her round face earnest and determined.

"You really do not have to put your hand up, Alizon," Vlad said calmly. "It is sort of a, how should I say it…free for all, I suppose."

"I like organisation," the enchantress said plainly. Alizon suddenly realised all eyes were on her and she visibly melted in her chair, her flash-in-the-pan moment of courage quenched. "I, err…I-I-I…"

"It's alright, Alizon, don't speak if you don't wanna'," Cain grunted gently. "There'll be plenty opportunity when you're ready."

Alizon nodded, almost meekly, and sank back into herself, her moment gone. Vlad was confident they would hear her story eventually, all she needed was to feel strong enough. That would only happen if she felt part of the group.

"Anybody else?" Vlad asked calmly. "We could always try a coffee break; I have new biscuits I want some opinions on. I cannot taste them, as my body only accepts blood and the odd spot of alcohol for my pleasures, so it will be interesting to see what you all think."

Blood and Biscuits

"Yeah alright, it'd give me a minute to see what I've gotta' chat about," Cain grumbled. He stood, hands pushing off his thighs, and the group rose with him automatically. Vlad watched curiously: it was as if Cain had some pull that made everybody unwittingly align with his motions. It was quite the thing to observe, Vlad wondered on it as the Support Group dispersed.

"I'm going outside for five minutes," Alizon told Vlad as she aimed for the stairs. "To read my magic. When I last fused with the rains here there was a strange feeling, something really strong and old buried in the mud. I'd like to explore that again."

"I hope you find it," Vlad said encouragingly. "See you in five minutes."

Alizon disappeared. The vampire watched, thinking her reconnection with her magic comparable to humans taking cigarette breaks. Although, Vlad further supposed, Alizon's magic would have far fewer damaging effects on the body.

"Is she alright?" Lucy asked, concerned, a fresh black coffee steaming in her mug. "She seems more talkative and less self-assured rolled into one. And I'm a banshee suffering from entrapment, anxiety, and isolation, I know a thing or two about self-assurance issues."

"I would imagine you have become quite the expert," Vlad noted dryly. He felt the electric heat of distortion beyond the church grounds and then the explosive power of strong magic channelled with great skill. "Alizon is a troubled mind, like all of us, but what ails her, I think, lies deeper than the sorts of things that have happened to *us* to make us feel certain ways. I speak, of course, of the mental ailments we all suffer from, some of which might yet be cured, like with your anxiety. Yet with our beloved enchantress, I feel her mind operates differently on a fundamental level, the foundations of her cognition wired from birth and giving her worries, social difficulties, and setbacks we might incorrectly associate instead with trauma."

Blood and Biscuits

"You're concerned she might not be curable," Lucy concluded without question, sipping her coffee, looking almost *beyond* the basement limits as if she could empathise enough with the walls that Alizon might yet feel the support outside.

"If she wishes to be cured at all," Vlad said. "If somebody is born one way is it right to assume they need *fixing* so they align in some other way? That is not fixing, it is *changing* them to suit our needs, not theirs. That is superficial, a move of vanity. In such ways we forget those of social impairment often excel in other areas. Who are we to presume they would wish themselves like us? Alizon is simply different, like we all can be, though she is so gifted in magic it makes me pity any that stand in her way should she choose to turn her powers to the offensive."

"I doubt she's capable of that," Lucy said, though a hint of apprehension lined the softer tones of her voice. "There's no violent bone in her body."

Vlad tilted his head.

"Upon surface-level inspection, you could say that about any one of us. Even Cain, if he were not to speak for five minutes, might give off the appearance of a pacifist rather than a beast adept at tearing people apart."

"That's *not* his fault," Lucy almost hissed and Vlad nodded.

"Indeed, and we all know this better than perhaps himself, yet we also know that keeping any one of our hidden monsters restrained can be extremely hard. I have shown enough of who I am to you all that this should come as to no surprise."

"And what are your thoughts on Alizon's hidden beast?" she asked. Lucy was intrigued, her inquisitive mind always seemed to be. "What's lurking inside her that might one day break free and unleash itself upon us all?"

Vlad sighed.

"I honestly believe there is nothing."

"But you just implied she could harbour aggression!" Lucy exclaimed, careful to keep her voice down.

"I did, but that was mostly to cover myself in case I am wrong. However, I truly think our enchantress friend hides nothing. What you see is entirely what you get, which is, in this modern world, something of a rarity. She is a natural-born witch capable of extreme power suffering from something vaguely akin to what humans might sometimes describe as Asperger syndrome, though in Alizon it could well be anything or, indeed, nothing. She is who she is, beautiful in every way."

Lucy reeled, shock plain on her face.

"Vlad, you...you can't just say that."

As the others gathered their drinks and snacks, Vlad knotted his eyebrows.

"I thought it was the closest I could diagnose-" he began but Lucy suddenly grew angry.

"No. Vlad, just...no. You can't go around telling people what might be wrong with others. It's not right. It's one thing listening to us and helping us through things, but diagnosing somebody? You don't *know* what Alizon's got. You're just basing your opinion on stereotypes but that's older thinking, nowadays it's not so simple. Whatever Alizon says or does is her business, it's not yours to tell me what you think is *wrong* with her."

Vlad folded his arms, darkness filling his veins at the admonishment. However, he beat it back, tamping down the latent rage, choosing instead to accept the punishment.

"I am sorry," he muttered, staring at the ceiling. "Of course, you stand in the right. I should not have assumed."

"No, you shouldn't have." After a moment, Lucy calmed, knowing the matter was over. "It must be tough for her, being in this group and not knowing how to act, what to say." Vlad shook his head.

"It is tough but more than that she is incredibly brave, overcoming an innate desire to run away at every opportunity when surrounded by people. Though you required no saving, Alizon was ready to join us last week in the charge to the mansion. She needed no input from us."

Lucy's look of surprise deepened.

"Oh, that's amazing! She must be very proud."

"I certainly hope so. I, for one, am proud of every one of you, although you need not my validation. You require only approval from yourselves: it is this acceptance that will finish your road to recovery, at least for the psychological side of things. I have faith you will all get there."

"I certainly hope so," Lucy repeated with one of her contagious smiles. Vlad reflected it.

"Come," he said quietly, "I can sense Alizon is done with her magic and the night is wearing on for your binding. Incidentally, how long do you have left?"

Lucy glanced at her watch.

"Three and a half hours, give or take. I aim to be back early, just in case of delays with the train."

"I understand. Pragmatism is something to be admired." The others returned to the circle and Vlad spread his arms welcomingly, his eyes on their biscuit prizes. "Ahh, I see you have all found the new stock. What do you think?"

As Alizon trudged back into the basement, Cain sat back in his chair and looked at his handful of biscuits. He gave a short, appreciative smile.

"Oh yeah, jammy dodgers. They were the best as a kid. But what are these little things?" the werewolf asked curiously, picking up a strangely shaped mound with three almonds buried in it. "They smell damn good, whatever they are."

"Ahhh, Bethmännchen – before any of you say 'gesundheit' be warned, it is a tired joke and stopped being funny thirty years ago." A small smile played on Vlad's lips as Alizon took her seat, her eyes nearly meeting his briefly then looking away. "Over one hundred and fifty years and the biscuit has never changed. I bought those in Frankfurt several days ago, I thought you might like to try them. I am well-informed they are very satisfying."

"What the hell were you doing in Germany?" Jacob asked, peering at a biscuit before passing it on to Lucy.

"Picking up some chemicals and herbs only found there," Vlad replied.

"Oh right," Jacob said slowly, clearly forming a question. Vlad answered it before he could ask it.

"It is nothing to worry about, Jacob, merely a few experiments I am trialling." Vlad glanced at Cain and the werewolf nodded knowingly, sipping coffee and biting into a Bethmännchen. A sensation of absolute pleasure emanated from Cain as the taste filled him and relaxed his nerves. Vlad focussed on that tremor of sensation for a half-second and thought back through the centuries to what it was like losing control to powerful emotions driven by such simple stimuli, when the electric input of phones and video games did not exist. New tastes enacting such pleasure, to close the eyes and open the mind to everything around it, to stop time itself. Vlad missed those days. "Anyway," the vampire continued, bringing all attention back to the group, "we have side-tracked. We should move on if we are to see question three. Who was next?"

Cain raised his hand and Alizon chuckled in the corner.

"You're not supposed to raise your hand," she muttered and Cain snorted.

"Bugger, forgot that," he said, lowering his arm again. Vlad looked between them. The move was possibly the most deliberate act he had ever seen, and because of it, he *smelled* the thinnest cord of tension ease in Alizon. Cain spoke on. "If I'm honest, I *am* still worryin' about the next full moon. Not 'cause I don't think I can handle it – Christ, with this church I think I'll feel safe for a long while when my time of the month rolls around – and not 'cause I'm worried what you guys'll think of me, but because…actually I dunno' why. I really don't. I think I'm just scared, truth be told. Now why the hell'd that be?"

Blood and Biscuits

"You've spent your entire life terrified of who and what you are, and what you're capable of through measures far beyond your control. Just because there's some shade of protection against it now doesn't mean you'll be any less scared. As a common phrase goes: it's a force of habit," Fable said constructively and Cain nodded.

"I guess. There's probably more to it but for now, thanks. I 'ppreciate it."

"Think nothing of it. That's what we're all here for."

Vlad accepted all information then moved on to Lucy, and then Fable, and then Sarah. Each had weights to lift from their chests, each had pains to remove before they could breathe again, physically and *meta*physically. Sarah did not mention anything of her private discussion with Vlad the week before, instead spending her time relaying her disappointment that many of the cemetery's flowers had passed away, gone with the cold winter days and leaving her once more without memory of petals. Lucy spent a few minutes happily describing what daffodils looked like as Sarah bobbed up and down, listening intently to every word as she hummed with increasing volume. The others watched admiringly. It was a strange thing, to observe a banshee outlining minute aspects of nature to a ghost, and yet it happened all the same. Sarah had to correct Lucy and say the flowers growing round the church were marked with pink spirit roses, too, and Vlad smiled at the conundrum.

When all was done, Vlad looked at Alizon and gave her an encouraging smile. His stomach clenched in his hunger but once again he set the sensations of it aside. He had a few more days before it was too late, he could afford not to feed right now.

"Anything to get off your chest, good or bad?" he asked the enchantress.

Alizon went to shake her head and then stopped, evidently deciding on something.

"I've spoken to the waters of this island and they've revealed some interesting things," she said.

"Oh yes?" Vlad asked, his intrigue piqued.

Blood and Biscuits

Alizon nodded, hands fidgeting nervously from speaking in front of everyone.

"Y-yeah. It seems this island w-was indeed a lot b-bigger, as you said, up until about a hundred y-years ag-ago. There are still molecules of water from over *four* hundred years ago, according to oxygen depth-memory and obstructions of stone foundations lying in the dirt layers. Fascinating."

"Can you get anything else from the water?" Fable asked, interest in someone else's magic seeping from her. Alizon's face lightened and she almost smiled as the subject turned to her abilities. This was where she excelled.

Vlad suddenly felt a cold shock in his heart like an icicle stabbing him as he suddenly realised something. It could not be stopped.

"Oh yes! I derived many interesting things, from the types of crops grown to the amount of people that walked upon the soils. It's not just the water I read but the earth and the dirts, too, and through this I think I've discovered a fact about our friend, Vlad."

All heads turned to the vampire, his back ramrod straight, face utterly impassive. There was no way out of this sudden situation.

"And what might that be?" he asked neutrally, his tone betraying nothing.

"You've been here before, Vlad."

"That is very true, I have visited this island a few times in the past on my travels across the world. And I have a home in the town."

"Not just visited or lived nearby," Alizon continued. "The waters are too strong in several places. There is an overwhelming sensation of darkness in the ground, a darkness I recognise from your kind. It's still leaching out as we speak, like oil from a sunken ship, a thin trail of power. Hundreds of years of activity still coming back out the soil…there was a vampire circle here, wasn't there?"

Blood and Biscuits

Vlad hesitated, centuries of history crashing back down in one gigantic weight. When he finally nodded, he did so with utmost care.

"Yes, there was."

Lucy glanced at him.

"Was this *your* circle, Vlad? The one you had with your creator, er…?

"Izanami," Vlad said measuredly. "And she was no creator but a monster. Purest evil."

"But you were in her circle, right?" Jacob asked and again Vlad nodded.

"Indeed, but centuries before the UK was even an established kingdom," Vlad said. "And not in this country at all but across huge tracts of Asia and in many Eastern European dominions, too."

"Then what's this power Alizon felt?" Cain asked interestedly, arms folded, biscuits forgotten.

Vlad had planned to eke his secrets out over many months so his friends could properly absorb the information. He had not counted on Alizon's sheer strength reading back through the histories of *mud*. It was too wild a variable to predict.

'Then again,' Vlad thought as he made to speak, *'situations with Sarah have moved on quicker than anticipated, too. I cannot lie on sanctified ground and I will not betray their trust. Besides, they would have found this all out sooner. Why not now?'*

"It was indeed a vampire's circle but not one of mine," Vlad said measuredly. "It was what I called a 'Grim Circle', designed to combine strengths of vampires to harvest humans. To turn them into cattle, essentially. They were devilish; this particular Grim was one of the more revolting. They would use mastery as easily as breathing, like some God-given gift they were duty-bound to use on humans, make them slaves for all manner of unspeakable reasons."

"Power shouldn't be used like that. That's bloody gross," Jacob hissed. "Vile."

"Putrid, it was, and you only have to *hear* about it. I am cursed to remember every detail with vivid clarity. This Grim Circle was a plague on the land and it was my job to rid them from existence."

"Jesus, Vlad, what were you, some kinda' hunter?"

"Though not a word I would use, it is as accurate as can be. I hunted for a time, anyway," Vlad said honestly. "I was angry. Very, *very* angry. For one hundred years on this island during the seventeenth century. I could not deal with my depression, I struggled to balance the opposing forces of my nature with this need to protect those unable to protect themselves. So, I took my rage out on those causing the harm."

"What did the humans think of you?" Lucy asked. "They must have suspected you weren't one of them."

"Many folks knew what I was but once I proved I was no threat they asked for my help. As you might imagine I cannot possibly say no to a request for aid, and when there are particularly vulnerable people involved, such as children, I feel no remorse when I remove the threat to them, one way or another. I was and will always be a husband and a father, and that will never leave my blood, however poisoned by curse it is."

"So perhaps a better description would be 'protector'," Fable offered and Vlad nodded.

"Yes, that is my preferred nomenclature. I was known as 'the Sentinel Unseen' and 'the Shield from the Skies', though I had many other names in many other countries. My payment was precisely one pint of blood from a healthy, adult volunteer and no more. Do not think me pure of heart, however, for if I was offered money, I would gladly take it."

"Hey, a bloke's gotta' get paid," Cain said quietly. "But seriously, this is some dark stuff. What the hell'd you do to the Grim Circle when you found them?"

Every face was rapt with attention, every eye trained on Vlad as he bared more and more of himself. He relayed centuries of information in mere sentences, showing little justice to the rich tapestry that was Vlad's eternal life.

"I located the Circle and descended amongst them during one of their nightly rituals. When they finally noticed me, I allowed them to attack first. That is when I drew my weapon, not before. From there it was a simple matter of aiding their shoulders part ways with their heads."

The room reacted accordingly.

"Whoa!" Jacob exclaimed.

"Bloody hell!" Cain blurted.

"Good lord," Fable said.

Sarah's humming stopped and Alizon's eyes grew wide. Vlad shook his head.

"I am not proud of it but that is what I was and what I did. You do recall I am a vampire, correct? A lord of darkness, one determined these past three hundred years to change. Though seemingly, the ground is still stained with the memories of all those dark deeds."

"Indeed," Alizon finally said. "But that's not everything. From what I discerned you were around for a long time after that, weren't you?"

Once more Vlad sat in surprise.

"I feel you do not give yourself enough credit, Alizon," he sighed coldly. He spread his hands openly. "Yes, it is true, I made this island my home for a long while. However, after my first century of protecting, I was so disgusted with myself, despite all the good the humans said I had done, that I left for America. I...travelled, I suppose, and saw the new world for another hundred years before returning to provide protection again in a different capacity, seeing new generations of people living here as I sought to defend them using only my words. Strangely enough, it had a greater impact than the sword ever did, for no evil ever returned to this island. And here became my permanent residence, the longest I have ever taken root in one place. That does not mean I never left but I spent a good amount of time in the company of many generations of fine folk. I was their dark protector and they were my friends."

"And walking feedbags," Cain muttered.

Vlad shot him a look.

"That too, though they only ever willingly gave. Our relationship was symbiotic. Religion factored far more heavily in those days, it took a lot of building of trust and respect before I convinced them I was the Lord's messenger, sent to watch over them for a small price. I would only take what I needed and would see to their aftercare."

"Jeez, and there's me thinking you were a nice, sweet vampire incapable of violence," Jacob said, aiming for jovialness but not quite reaching it.

"There are many facets to my history even I am still coming to terms with," Vlad admitted. "But know this: I am glad they all led me here, to this moment, this single point in temporal and spatial dimensions – oh, do not look at me like that, Cain, I *adore* physics. And I can honestly say I am at peace with what I have done if it means I have helped people live the lives they wanted to live."

"And to honour their wishes to see them on from their deaths. To find a way to release them from their spiritual bonds and send them on from their earthly prisons. To see them gone to the next life."

Vlad looked up and saw Sarah no longer hovering above her seat. She sat upon it as if made solid. Neutral. Emotionless. She was utterly impassive and opaque.

"Indeed," Vlad nodded.

"Wait, what?" Jacob asked, confusion rising. "What did she say – see her on from what? Vlad, what'd she say?"

Vlad swallowed against a mound of pain in his throat as he stared them all down, each coming to the realisation of what Sarah had muttered in their own time. Lucy remained silent, her face a story of heavy understanding. Fable grew agitated, as if the world was about to fall in on her. Alizon blew out her cheeks and stood for

Blood and Biscuits

the coffee table as Cain crossed his arms and looked away, a man refusing to acknowledge what he felt.

Jacob, however, grew angry.

"Vlad," he demanded. "Vlad! God damn it, what did Sarah mean? What did you mean?" he growled, turning suddenly to the ghost sitting stoically upon her chair.

Her veiled face took in Jacob and Vlad could have sworn he felt a spark of sympathy jolt from her. It was the first and only feeling he had ever perceived from the ghost, and the vampire was in no way certain he had truly felt it or if he had imagined a projection of his own hurt.

"It's as I said, Jacob," Sarah spoke, her echoing voice kind but firm, "I'll be granted salvation from this prison. I cannot be remade solid, it's not the way of things, so *my* cure is ethereal. He's told me he knows a way and I would see it done, if but to rid me of my incarceration. I'm sorry, my friend, please don't cry for me. Be joyful, for I will be with my family again soon. The afterlife awaits me."

"No," Jacob said, standing abruptly and shaking his head, the rotting flesh of his hands tightening to pale strands as they balled into fists of rage. "No. This isn't the way we do things. We should be helping her, Vlad! You said you could cure us, cure us *all*. This isn't cure, this isn't bloody help. This is suicide!"

"This *is* helping her, Jacob," Vlad said, forcing his own pain down as he stood calmly, his hands up. "This is what Sarah wants. There is no other way, I have searched. For the rest of you there may yet be some answer to the curses that haunt you, but for Sarah she *is* the haunt. What cures her lies beyond this world only. Sarah is not cursed; what binds her is not some evil lyric in a spell of dark magic, it is a facet of nature itself. Sarah is dead, like all others from her time, except her soul cannot move on. It must be allowed to leave for the afterlife."

"You're wrong," Jacob hissed. "It's easy, you're wrong. She can be cured, just like anyone that's died like Lucy or me. Just wait

Blood and Biscuits

it out, you'll find something! Keep researching," he pleaded desperately, "maybe there's an answer in the Bible. Maybe God knows, if I could just ask Him…"

"I am sorry, Jacob, but God would not want this for Sarah, this existence of nothing. The Bible teaches ways to live your life and honour the soul, not how to resurrect the dead." Vlad kept explaining as Jacob shook his head angrily. "Sometimes human souls can be bound to the mortal plane if their bodies are bound in iron but with ghosts they are bound by hugely powerful emotions. It is sometimes crudely known as 'unfinished business'. Jacob, I am sorry but I can promise nothing else because there *is* nothing else. Every lost soul must be accounted for in the afterlife, one way or another. To leave a soul trapped outside the gates of oblivion is a travesty of life, a mark of gross disrespect to death, and Sarah's soul is long overdue. The afterlife *must* be paid."

"And how would we even do it? Huh? Do you even know, Vlad? There's no way you can just open the afterlife, what you're talking about is ridiculous."

"Yes, it is! It is exactly that but there, I think, you already know the answer. I have researched enough to believe I have the best answer for her. But it would require every one of us, for this is old magic, and-"

"Fantastic," Jacob spat, the layers of self-confidence and strength he had built about himself over the weeks shedding away as the pain he felt for Sarah, and the clear betrayal he felt at her choice, ground him down to the rawness beneath. "You must be really proud of yourself, Vlad, having changed so much, to go from a hunter to a great protector then back to a hunter again, searching for the next kill. And how long have you known Sarah was here?"

"Many years. Two centuries, to be exact," Vlad replied quietly. "Two centuries of servitude to her death. Countless cycles of visits and explorations of memory, yet she forgets my every time. I have watched her for so long she is a part of my blood, though Sarah does not know it. I doubt she has even truly heard me now."

Blood and Biscuits

All glanced to Sarah but she was hovering freely again, humming and drifting around a ceiling vent, fingers trailing the rusted ironwork patterns.

Jacob shook his head again, his dilapidated face a picture of absolute fury, and he snatched up his bag.

"Is this all this group has ever been to you? Just a way to get us all together so you can carry on killing? Rearranging other peoples' lives to your ends…you've been watching her for two *hundred* years just to end her existence, Vlad. It's sick, that is sick. This is all a bloody joke."

"I was trying to cure her, not *kill-*"

Jacob made to leave but Cain stepped before him. Their eyes met, rage meeting placidity, and right then Vlad saw the man Cain had become. He was who he wanted to be, for better or for worse. Choice had once more set somebody on a different path.

"Don't do this," Cain said, low voice rumbling. "Please, mate. We need you here, we all do. This ain't right, you walkin' out. Sarah needs you."

"Move," Jacob hissed. "Move or I move you."

"Please," Cain said again but it was too late.

From a place of horror and deep tragedy, Jacob's sunken brown eyes filled with white fire and became the wildness of the true wraith. He roared a terrible sound and Vlad became paralysed with the fear Cain felt, the sensation keen through the link they shared. Cain could not react fast enough as Jacob seized him up and threw him bodily as if he was only balled paper. Alizon screamed and Fable cried "No!" as Cain soared across the basement and struck the wall with a sickening *crunch*. He collapsed to the floor as dust and pieces of masonry dislodged all around him.

Lucy gasped in shock and ran to Cain's side as Vlad stared at them all, unable to do anything, motionless just as Cain was. Through his strange awareness, he felt the man's agony lance down his spine and leg.

Blood and Biscuits

Before anyone could say anything, Jacob ran from the basement and disappeared, and Vlad *felt* his presence diminish the further he travelled from the church. Fable turned and followed after.

"I cannot let him leave me," she announced. "It will only hurt him more."

And with that Fable disappeared, too, and the basement fell eerily empty with both gone.

"Oh God, Cain, are you alright?" Lucy asked, her panicked words falling heavy. Vlad had never heard her so worried. "Cain? Cain! Talk to me, tell you're ok."

"He is alright," Vlad said as he limped over, sharing the werewolf's pain, breathing hard with his beating lungs. He stopped himself immediately. "I can feel his heart and mind. Just give him a moment, his back is injured. Ironically, the full moon would cure him of this. Sorry, that was insensitive."

Lucy sat back on her heels, hand twining through Cain's hair, stroking his head, and finally the man stirred. He groaned and placed a palm on his back, voice shuddering in his throat. He shook his head and eased himself upright.

"Ow," he muttered dryly and despite her worry Lucy smiled.

"Oh, thank Christ you're fine," she said, holding his face as she looked him over. A little blood ran from Cain's mouth but only from where he had bitten his cheek. Nothing internal. "You hit that wall hard. I thought you were a lot worse off."

"Well I don't *feel* terrific," Cain growled as he tried straightening his back. He failed. "Jeez, that guy can pack a punch. What the hell *was* that?"

"*That*, I believe, was the Latent Wraith, the real beast Jacob has hidden for fear of losing control. It is the beginning of what happens should he accept his natural rage or go long enough without eating. It will have terrified him beyond all else."

"Good, I hope he's scared. Little git caught me off-guard with his weird eyes goin' on," Cain snarled as he made to stand. Lucy pushed him back down gently, her small hand easily overpowering his large bulk as he flopped down again.

"Just…take it easy," she said. "I don't think Jay meant what he did."

"Yeah, I bet he's all twisted up full of regret right now," Cain said spitefully. "Next time I see him…"

"You will understand the position he is in, and that he will soon enough feel he has lost everything by losing the self-control I mentioned. He will begin feeling his whole world, his new existence he has been building, has been torn apart by his own hands. You more than anyone else present might relate," Vlad pointed out and Cain looked up with depthless gaze. After a moment he nodded wordlessly and looked away. A sense of acceptance filled him.

Vlad tried to shake off the awareness he had of Cain again but once more he failed. He felt a pang of empathy towards Jacob and then a flash of anger as he thought of him; a myriad of complex imaginings ran through him, from potential loss of friendship to what it meant to be alone. Lucy threaded her slim fingers through Cain's hand and Vlad felt overpowering relief and affection empowering him. Guilt flooded Vlad at trespassing on another's thoughts, an intoxicating sense of intrusion, and he realised this was what empaths lived for, the ability to share in another's intricate, intimate emotions and feed off their strength.

Closing off what he could of his mind, Vlad concluded that what Cain felt for Lucy were the embers of love.

"This is not a time for dwelling on what has happened," the vampire stated, "rather a time to move forward and reach out to those that have put their trust in us. Jacob is not lost, simply displaced. He will need space from us and this church, but mostly he will need the company of only Fable for a time. I see she harbours great affection for him, he needs that closeness right now."

"This is awful," Lucy said quietly as Alizon circled the room, the witch's agitations evidently stopping her from clearly processing what had happened. "What would make him flip like that?"

Blood and Biscuits

Before Vlad could answer, Sarah suddenly descended between them all, her form hovering close to the ground.

"Why has my friend run away? Does Jacob not like me?"

"Oh no, Sarah," Vlad tried to say comfortingly. "It is not that at all. He is struggling to, err, think through what has been said regarding your choice."

"He does not wish happiness for me?" Sarah asked and the almost child-like pain in her questioning nearly broke Vlad's cold, dead heart.

"That is not it either," he attempted to reassure her. "He does not understand why you are choosing this. I think Jacob struggles with the thought of people deciding to end what they have, to..."

But Vlad could not finish for Sarah, beginning to cry, suddenly flew through the ceiling and was gone. Vlad sighed as Lucy gestured towards where she had disappeared.

"And now Sarah's upset. What the bloody hell is this all about, Vlad? First Jay's all happy and smiles and making jokes about awful books and then he freaks out and attacks Cain. What's this *about*?"

"A feeling of betrayal, mostly," Vlad surmised. When all looked at him, he pointed to himself. "I am only guessing but what Jacob is experiencing might be a resurfacing of his darkest thoughts. He made attempts on his own life before, this will bring that guilt and shame crashing back down. He has spent months trying to work past what he tried to do, and *why*, most importantly, and here is somebody else embracing the act. Jacob is being confronted not only by somebody essentially choosing suicide but he also faces a group of friends, people he considers his one support network and his peers, actively encouraging it. When you frame it like that does it not seem downright disturbing to you? This is precisely why I did not wish to discuss this yet, I feared something like this would happen."

Blood and Biscuits

"Yeah but that's not right," Cain said, propping himself up on his elbows and wincing at the agony in his back. "Sarah choosin' suicide, I mean. She's already dead, for one thing, like you said."

"Yet she has lived longer than any human should, in constant emotional distress and loneliness. Sarah is, after all, the closest to human out of all of us, and the pathologies of the mortal mind still hold for her. It is too much for human thought to endure, especially a mind governed by a soul still bound to this earth by one hugely powerful emotion, as in the case of ghosts."

"But you're way older, *and* you've got depression," Cain pointed out. He hissed in pain as he moved and Vlad put his own hand to his spine in their sympathetic connection. "Ow, jeez! If I find Jacob, I'll…never mind. Point is, you've gone through worse than Sarah – well, maybe not worse, but the same. How come *you're* not clawin' at the afterlife tryin' to get in."

Vlad raised his hands then let them fall in defeat. There was no higher reasoning to this.

"I am not imprisoned," he sighed, indicating the church all around and above them. "I am free to move and learn and grow at my own whim, plus I have my memories and I have learned to regain all emotions whereas Sarah simply cannot do such a thing. I am *cursed* and dead, she is only dead. Simply dead. Two hundred years bound to one place in emotional disturbance is enough to drive somebody mad but Sarah has lingered, her sense of loneliness and isolation growing as she yearns for kinship. She cannot leave, she cannot learn, she cannot grow, she cannot even escape into her own mind in the sweet illusion of true madness. She only exists, desperate for salvation. And when companionship finally reaches her, with our Support Group, I think she has found it has compounded her issues. Now she seeks the final comfort of true release. We cannot take that choice from her, Cain, we would condemn Sarah to an eternity of misery."

Blood and Biscuits

Vlad heard a sob from behind and turned to see Lucy standing with her arms hugged tight across her chest, black tears cascading down her cheeks.

"This really has been your plan all along, hasn't it?" Her voice wavered. "To get us together under the pretence of a support session to use us to release Sarah."

Vlad shook his head.

"No! No, not exactly. What I told you was true: I honestly wish to help people, and the only way I thought I could start making a difference was to begin with people like myself. But I have watched Sarah for over two *hundred* years," Vlad emphasised, his own voice cracking with the strain. "She has become the very nucleus of my intent to turn all evils of this world into good. Death is just another facet of life and if I can prove ghosts can find the peace all living things deserve then I can prove, once and for all, life is not pointless, that life has some bloody meaning! And with that meaning, death becomes just as important. I will prove we have worth if it ends me."

Vlad realised, then, that he was shaking with blinding rage. Quickly, he smoothed out his darkness and calmed his blood. He sighed and released his fury.

"Death cannot be overcome but it can be met as equals, and reframed to justify us, just as life brings everyone to their knees. This is the path I have chosen but I cannot walk it alone."

The past two centuries of careful observation and attempts at keeping safe what he cared for came barrelling from him, secrets laid bare before them. He was the Support Group's instigator but he needed to make admissions, too. This was what he needed to get off his chest that night.

There was silence for a moment and Vlad thought everyone else would storm out of the basement, too. And then, like a ray of hope, an answer came from the most unlikely of people and it brought with it the realisation that what Vlad had been doing those past seven weeks had not been for nothing.

Blood and Biscuits

"But life *has* meanin'," Cain said from the floor as Lucy hugged herself tighter, refusing to look at Vlad. "Y'see it every day. Just look at Lucy and I, for Christ's sake. A month and a half ago you could never say a banshee and a werewolf would ever *sit* in the same room, and now look at us."

Vlad sighed and clasped his hands to his hips.

"You are right, of course you are right. If there is one thing to be taken from this group it is that you have changed so much as to sway me, Cain. You all have, in such a short space of time. Yet there is still that feeling inside me, that everyone must find peace in the end, one way or another."

"Because you never have?"

Vlad glanced at Alizon and felt a sliver of shock at her willing involvement.

"Perhaps," he admitted easily. "Surprisingly, I have not given it much thought. Depression has a way of making me feel selfish at times but in other ways I will not dwell on thoughts of myself at all, and so I avoid thinking on my existence as a point. But if you want the honest truth, I think a lot of this stems from my family. Rather like Sarah in that regard; my wife and my child woke up one day to find I was gone with no explanation. Though I spared them learning of the monster I had become, I was still left with the harrowing knowledge that they were alone, and they died without me by their side. Never going back to explain is my greatest regret, to offer them the choice of accepting me or rejecting me. The latter would not have mattered as long as they knew I had not abandoned them. But I was a coward."

"And now you seek to turn this around by helping others live better lives and find better deaths," Lucy said, her arms loosening slightly. "A protector of all things, not because you like humans or supernaturals but because you respect the sanctity of the soul and will protect and guide its passage through time. Magic, faith, and science, all in one. A shield to the vulnerable and a sentinel of death, a watcher of all passing in and out of this world. I get it now."

Vlad bit his lip painfully and looked to the ceiling to avoid Lucy's piercing gaze.

"In its very essence, yes."

"But why Sarah?" Cain asked. "Outta', what, thousands of ghosts? Out of everyone that ain't found peace, why her?"

"Because…" Vlad faltered. He cursed himself a fool and he let it all go, surrendered to the same trust the others put in him. He could not protect them from what was just, he had no right when they were more than capable of making their own courses. Besides, he could not lie when stood on sanctified ground.

Only, Lucy answered first.

"Because she's your family." Her voice was thick with realisation.

Vlad smiled grimly.

"Though Sarah does not know it, she is my last descendent."

"Wait, wait, wait, what?"

Vlad did not look at them, he could not. Lucy sat upon the floor next to Cain as Alizon busied herself making mint tea, most likely finding it calmed her shaking hands.

"No," Cain said, the word cutting through the air. "That's not possible. Last week you said you had no family."

"I said I had no *living* family. I never lied to you, I cannot in this place."

"How do you know?"

"Excuse me?" Vlad asked, politeness once more retaking his whole being.

"Well, you know…you're ancient, as you put it before, but Sarah ain't. She's two hundred years old, somewhere abouts. That's not ancient, just old. And she's English whereas you're Romanian, so how'd you know you're related?"

"You will have to just believe me when I tell you I have traced my family for as long as I have been dead, starting with the birth of my grandson after my daughter married a soldier."

Blood and Biscuits

"You said you never went back to your family," Alizon said matter-of-factly, her back still to them all as she made her tea.

"They were not aware, no, but when I had chance, I would return to my homeland to watch from afar. My wife remarried six years after they declared me dead – it is good she found love again, I am sure she hated me until the day she died. My daughter, however, was widowed after her husband was killed in war, though think not upon her suffering for she threw herself into raising her child and her grandchildren, and she cherished and nurtured the connections with her community. For this, I take at least a *little* comfort in thinking she may have gotten that from me. I believe when my daughter died, she found peace, never knowing her father watched through the window as she lay upon her death bed. The love beyond the glass. She breathed her last breath surrounded by new generations of her family, all smiling and crying. Surrounded by love."

"Christ, you've been through some stuff," Lucy said. "I'm sorry for you."

Vlad shrugged, pretending he no longer felt the keen blade of anguish knifing once more through his heart, the old wound re-opening fresh as if he was back there, through time and distance, seeing his daughter's tired eyes closing for the last time. He bled his sorrow anew.

"Do not be. Not many who see their children die do so at the end of their long and happy lives. Perhaps I am lucky," Vlad sighed heavily. "I got to see my daughter become an astonishing woman, to bring life into the world as her own mother had done before her. I watched when she married, I watched when she was told of her husband's passing, and I watched in those quiet moments when she felt alone through the years. She will never know but I saw her entire life, start to conclusion. I am proud of the person she was. And now…"

Vlad faltered and knew he was crying blood. He did not stop. The tears were a gift from his sadness, a release too long held back.

Blood and Biscuits

"And now, on the brink of my family's final closure, I am the one ensuring it ends on its own terms, that the woman I never told was my sole heir all those years ago, can *finally* rest long after her soul should have made its last journey, can *finally* find peace. The last of my line, another person I failed in history's cruel torment. If my blood is to be undone, then I will see it undone."

"And you will be the one to deliver it." Lucy intoned, her denial not forgotten but set aside to be dealt with later. That was her own hurt, her own problem to work out. "That's what Sarah's asked and that's what must be done."

Vlad nodded, face shining crimson.

"Thank you. To know I have friends beside me means the world. Not many vampires can say the same."

"Speaking of friends," Cain rumbled as he made to stand. The pain obviously cost him. "Didn't you say to mardy-arse before he body slammed me and stormed out you'd need *all* of us to release Sarah?"

"I did," Vlad said.

"And how'd you plan on convincin' resident zombie to play nice if he's dead set against it?"

"No zombie references, please, no matter how rightfully irked you are. I think in time Jacob will acknowledge this is Sarah's choice, for better or for worse. He will react strongly to the notion of suicide, with his beliefs and his own struggles. However, I hope he sees this will not be the case, that Sarah deserves to die."

"That doesn't half sound odd."

"I feel like we say that a lot," Lucy muttered.

The others helped Vlad stow the chairs against the basement walls then piled the things on the coffee table neatly, telling himself he would return for it all later when he was rebalanced. Vlad joined Lucy, Alizon, and Cain at the stairs, feeling the ambivalence of relief and burden in equal measures.

"How long do you have, Lucy?" Vlad asked and the banshee checked her watch.

Blood and Biscuits

"Another two and a half hours before I should head back to the mansion. Why?"

"If you make it two hours and twenty minutes, we should all go get a drink."

"You serious?" Cain asked.

"I am indeed. I do not wish to be alone tonight and I feel as if we have more to say to one another, as long as I have read your moods correctly."

Alizon twitched worriedly.

"I kept my senses from you, do not worry," Vlad assured her. "I was going by general mood alone."

"A drink sounds alright," Lucy said nonchalantly. "Not sure what else I'd be doing otherwise. Can't exactly force Jay to come back and talk everything through tonight and I don't want to just sit around figuring out how to undo my curse. How'd you feel about a drink, Cain?"

The werewolf nodded, ignoring the pain still shooting up and down his back and leg.

"I can ring in late tomorrow morning so I can squeeze in a few before I turn in. Not martinis, though, they'll just bugger me up. Though they'd probably help with the pain."

"I could drop you *both* at the mansion if you would prefer?" Vlad suggested as they moved outside.

"Oh," Cain said slowly. "I mean...Galloway's is *technically* closer to work..."

"If you're looking for an answer then of course you can come back to mine," Lucy said quickly. "As long as you don't mind a thousand drafts and the feeling of being watched all the time."

"Have you *seen* my bedsit?" Cain retorted. He groaned through the agony in his back and put his arm round Lucy's waist as they stood outside the church for a moment, looking up at the pale sliver of moon hanging far above them all.

Vlad smiled and looked at Alizon.

"And what about you, enchantress? Care to join us for a drink?"

"I, err..." she stumbled, looking away. "I wouldn't want to impose."

"It's not an imposition if you're invited," Lucy responded with a smile, her own arm finding its way round Cain. "Besides, you don't *need* an invitation. We're a group and we stick together."

"And that is the way of it," Vlad concluded. "Once Jacob and Fable return I am sure that statement will be more convincing."

As they walked, Cain and Alizon fell into conversation, musing on their childhoods in foster homes and laughing at unexpected moments, and Lucy fell into step with Vlad. After a moment, she asked,

"Were you ever going to tell us? About Sarah and you, I mean."

"I was, I swear it," Vlad admitted. "But I needed more time. After we triggered her renewed sense of loneliness with our presence in her church, I thought Sarah would last a few more months before coming to me for help. I wanted to use that time to build relationships so something like tonight with Jacob would not happen. The ritual I spoke of can only happen under particular circumstances and I am afraid we might miss the closest one; this was not a problem before Sarah's mind changed, as there is another alignment of forces next year, but now I feel we might drive her vengeful if we fail to send her on soon. Ghosts might not be able to change emotionally but they can still become furious forces of nature should they be denied an end to their suffering."

"Didn't think there'd be so much pressure," Lucy said quietly and Vlad nodded. "I really hope Jay comes back to us," she muttered.

"I am sure he will," was all Vlad said.

THE LIBRARY AND ALCHEMICAL LABORATORY,

THE INDUSTRIAL COMPLEX.
TUESDAY, ONE DAY FOLLOWING THE SUPPORT GROUP.

Vlad's phone began ringing. He answered it immediately, thinking it to be Jacob. However, it was just a cold caller trying to convince him his recent car accident was not his fault, despite Vlad's insistence that he did not have a car nor a driving license. Vlad bit back the string of curse words he wished to assault the caller with and hung up angrily, finding frustration coming easily to him at the moment.

'At least the mast on the high tower is letting signals through the magic around this place,' he mused.

As distant sounds of wordpeckers squawked and flapped in the library, Vlad poured over his book of old medicines again, intent on finding something else from his historical writings as another concoction bubbled gently over a paraffin burner turned down low. He had removed one fluid quarter-ounce from the large amount of white solution and poured it into a second flask. In turn, this passed down a steam filter tube with surrounding cold-water jacket, but not before Vlad had added five drops of moonglow stem tincture and stirred the new solution sixteen times precisely; the resultant steam slowly condensed down into another flask.

Vlad glanced up from the book and rolled his eyes as he saw the colour of distillation.

"Still white," he muttered, wiping the flask to see if it was an illusion. It was not. "That means nothing to me at all, the fluid should distil colourless. Well," Vlad told himself, his voice bouncing through the cavernous library tunnels, "that means there is no residue remaining. I must try again once the boil is done. Also, I am talking to myself, that is never a good sign."

Vlad set aside the book and turned his attentions to studying the minute detail of another volume of lore, entitled '𝕿𝖍𝖊 𝖂𝖊𝖗𝖊𝖜𝖔𝖑𝖋𝖊: 𝕾𝖙𝖚𝖉𝖎𝖊𝖘 𝖆𝖓𝖉 𝕻𝖗𝖔𝖔𝖋𝖊𝖘 𝖔𝖋 𝕮𝖑𝖆𝖓𝖘, 𝕮𝖚𝖗𝖘𝖊𝖘, 𝖆𝖓𝖉 𝕭𝖊𝖍𝖆𝖛𝖎𝖔𝖚𝖗𝖘; 𝕭𝖊𝖆𝖘𝖙𝖊𝖘 𝖇𝖞 𝕹𝖆𝖙𝖚𝖗𝖊 𝕺𝖓𝖑𝖞, 𝖇𝖞 𝖁. 𝕰𝖑𝖎𝖆𝖉𝖊.'

It was not a slim thing, weighing at least seven pounds in

parchment inserts alone, and was deeply concerned with long essays of legends and narratives, of explorations of different lands and landscapes for any information on werewolves, historical accounts of Vlad's escapades across the earth in his searches for truth. The heavy book also contained vast numbers of scientific studies and experiments, laced with lengthy descriptions, diagrams, annotations, and personal speculations. Vlad had spent decades putting together the volume as he studied werewolves predominantly across Europe and Africa, finding dozens of commonalities, making groundbreaking discoveries where many others had failed. One of the first realisations Vlad had made was that the werewolf curse was unaffected by one's skin colour, something other academics centuries ago had failed to acknowledge in the blindness of their worldviews.

The book was extremely well kept – he had had an Icelandic chemical enchantress apply several layers of protection lyrics over the tome to stave off the ravages of time and misuse. Flicking carefully through the leaves, Vlad read title after handcrafted title.

'*Isolation of the Lonesome Wolfe*', '*The Broken Man, and How to Bring Them Backe from Darke Thoughts*', '*Clans and their Sub-Divisiones*', '*Curse Alchemistry*' *– Ahh, now that is what I need.*'

Vlad skimmed the detailed pages of ingredient lists, simple spells, and natural incantations, desperate to find something he had missed. He reeled off the information as he read.

'*Root of ironwort, silver or bronze daggerleaf, pillar-salt pulp…no. None of these for Cain, he is too high in the hierarchy. I am at a loss.*'

Vlad paced the laboratory, hands behind his back, and thought on the sensation he felt directly after drinking Cain's blood, that balance of curse against something else. It warred with his reasoning, chipped away at his knowledge. Werewolves were bound by a curse invading their blood, yet Cain's blood did not quite feel that way. Fleetingly, Vlad thought perhaps Cain's early puberty had influenced his virus type.

'But then, Cain was not bitten or scratched so there was supposedly no viral transfer. He is definitely a werewolf, I have witnesses and damage to my illusions as proof. What on earth does this all mean? The man is an enigma.'

A sharp thought arose and for an instant, Vlad looked to a doorway at the side of the vast library, to the chambers lying beyond, the image of a vast black sphere swirling and whirling in his mind as he considered stepping back into the throes of the darkest magics. However, the risks were too great, he would be foolish to attempt for such a simple matter unless he had no other choice.

Life was full of choices. Vlad had not spent all of his yet.

Impatiently, he considered the original flask of pure white fluid, the first he had made as stock, and something clicked into place in his mind, a thing he had struggled with since realising he was keenly aware of the werewolf's mind.

"I was linked to his blood," Vlad whispered with a smile. "Goodness, a new discovery! I have not made one of those for a while – nothing to do with answering his curse, but still! Drinking Cain's blood bound me to his mind. My God, what an awkward thing to explain."

Flushed with at least a modicum of success, Vlad sat down again at his workbench and took out a fresh piece of parchment from a drawer and found a clean quill and inkwell, keen to begin construction of a new page of notes. He would commit his thoughts and hypotheses to paper then begin a more thorough study later.

As he worked, Vlad glanced briefly at the boiling flask of white fluid and something caught his eye. He peered closer, careful not to disturb the distillation apparatus.

"Now that *is* interesting," Vlad muttered. "Grey powder residue on the inside of the flask. Visible now enough has boiled away. But that is not possible if the resultant maintains its white colour. What does *that* mean, I wonder? I can avoid it no longer, I must take him to the Grampians. He must feel the connections there."

Vlad's stomach tightened with pangs of hunger again and he acknowledged it finally.

"Very well," he muttered. "I will feed again." He retrieved his phone and scrolled through the contacts. "Now who would be willing to give a pint? After all, it *is* nearing Christmas. 'Tis the season, and so forth."

Vlad stopped the moving screen and pressed the name 'M'. The tone rang for an Iridum satellite phone based in Antarctica and a small voice answered on the other end. Immediately, at the simple sound of their light Jamaican accent, Vlad was transported back sixty years. He remembered the precise way their eyes moved, the shape of their mouth as they spoke, the subtlety of their hand gestures and the perfection of their body language, and he smiled as he asked how they were.

Clifftop Enlightenment

"Excuse me, is this seat taken?"

She was reading a book, one he did not recognise or understand the language of, but when he spoke her golden head looked up, sunlight glinting on her shining hair, and a broad smile stretched across her beautiful, androgynous face.

"Vlad, it's nice to see you, thanks for coming! Of course this isn't taken, sit beside me."

"Terribly kind of you," Vlad jested lightly, perching beside Fable on the bench and staring out to sea. "A wonderful choice of spot, especially in early evening. You would have thought that after the night I became a vampire I would shy away from cliffs but I really do not. I adore the salt, the crash of the waves…for a moment I forget my anxieties and depression, as if the world falling away at my feet is all that matters."

"I'm glad I chose this place, then," Fable said deeply, "if it gives you peace from your thoughts."

"A moment to delve into yours," Vlad replied. "Oh I got you tea, I thought you might care to try Lady Grey, I gave her a slight twist of lemon to compliment the flavour."

Vlad pulled out two cardboard cups with a café brand embossed on their sides, *Sally's Vegan Steamers*.

"Oh thank you, Vlad, this is exactly what I needed. It'll go well with the salt on the air." Fable took a sip of her hot tea, aromas of orange peel and bergamot emanating from the cup. She closed her eyes in pleasure. "Now that's delicious, a real treat. I've never heard of this cafe, are they in Ellinsgate?"

"Down Seafarer's Way, yes. Owned by a woman called Sally, lovely person. She is between those two trinket shops, *Tit for Tat* and *Knick-Knack Paddy Whack*. She is exclusively vegan, apparently, and her special drink is the oat milk 'Frothy Toffee

Coffee'; I do not know what has happened to coffee in four hundred years but it has been abused by humans, that is for sure."

"And so I stick to tea," Fable chuckled. "You can't decaf, skinny, half-froth a cup of hot water and a bag. Simplicity."

"Don't forget the twist of lemon," Vlad added.

"I shan't, if you acknowledge that contraction of 'don't' you just let slip," Fable countered, smirking.

"Bugger."

Fable chuckled and sipped her tea again.

"You doing anything nice this week?" she asked pleasantly.

"Well, actually I am going north tonight to see a friend. I spoke to them last night and decided to go as quickly as possible."

"Does this have anything to do with Sarah?"

"It does, yes. And I am hungry. Very hungry."

"Ahh, one of your donation contacts. Remember the silver amulet so you do not lose yourself, my friend."

"I never do."

For a moment, the monuments of dark and light sat upon that bench together and looked out to sea, enjoying the warmth of their drinks and of each other's company. Eventually, however, Vlad remembered all moments must end or else new moments must serve as forfeit. He leant towards Fable ever so slightly.

"In your message you sounded distressed. I was happy to meet anyway, I enjoy visits like this for a chance to speak individually – such intimacy is rare nowadays, but you gave me the impression of urgency."

"No I'm not distressed, or urgent, perhaps a little worried? Ahh, Jacob told me tone is very difficult to convey via text, maybe you interpreted my words differently to how I meant them."

"Yes, perhaps that was it," Vlad muttered, thinking on his own foibles with digital messaging. "I am worried about Jacob, too, now you mention him. He did not react how I thought he would after he heard what I had to say about Sarah. How is he?"

Blood and Biscuits

"He is well enough, very angry but otherwise healthy. For a wraith, anyway. We were all shocked, Vlad, but Jacob took it hardest. I don't know what to say about the matter, all I want to do is take him in my arms and...I don't know, hold him, I suppose."

Vlad glanced at Fable. He probably just misunderstood. Fable cleared her throat.

"Either way, if you want to get through to him I'd suggest you speak to somebody that knows ex-human minds better than me. I won't be much help, I'm afraid. That's why I came here to read, I can't do anything else for him and his mood is upsetting me."

"I was not seeking to burden you with my own worries, it is my fault this happened at all. But I shall take your advice on seeking counsel, I need him to at least understand, if not accept." Vlad sighed and tapped the bench agitatedly. "Well here *we* are anyway," he said, wanting to change the subject. "After I got your message I managed to organise a free hour or two before we, um..."

"Before you start planning to open a rift between this mortal realm and the afterlife," Fable finished neutrally, sipping her tea pleasantly as if what she said was normal. "You know, usual stuff for November."

Vlad gave a grim smile, thoughts of events yet unpassed grappling with his every doubt of success, siphoning the strength from his very bones and leaving the weaknesses of self-scrutiny and anxiety, making him glad of the bench beneath him. Vampires do not enjoy admitting weakness.

"Let us hope whatever happens, Sarah finds her peace," Vlad finally said, sipping his coffee and enjoying its sensation. He could not taste it at all, save for the slightest bitter tang of iron, but he imagined it was wonderful. "However, coffee and the afterlife were not why I came; if you are not distressed then why am I here? Are you alright? Not that I do not enjoy your company, you understand."

"You are here because I wanted to tell you a story, a story about this day but from years ago. I thought if I do not tell you now, and something happens to either one of us at the ritual, then I think it would be a terrible waste for us not to get to know one another better. I know how fond of stories you are."

"You do?" Vlad said in surprise.

"Of course, even in my first week with the Support Group you were detailing matters of the soul in an excited retelling fit for a storyteller. And because of this, I thought you would enjoy a tale from the Eight Realms, Vlad, though I am no master teller myself."

"I would very much enjoy that, and I am sure you are perfectly brilliant. What is the theme of this story?"

"Downfall."

Fable drained her tea and folded her fingers. She cleared her throat, eyes drifting in memory, voice finding itself. She took a deep breath as the sea breeze caught the light strands of her hair, emblazoning her head in trails of pale fire, the evening sun glinting off the sharp angles of her face.

"Once, there was a world, a most illustrious world, of gold and clear water and trees of immaculate colour. It was a place of the legends of Songlight and the chasms of air, forests of bronze, and seas of endless deeps. Once, there were faeries, constructs of song itself, sung from the threads of life like weaving a web from fine strings of voice, connections of the soul from mountains to living things, from soils to living things, from fires to living things.

"Once, in this world of perfection, there came an understanding, a great treasure of knowledge revealing the true calm of harmony, the equilibrium of the five opposing forces, each counterbalancing the others, pressing their Weights down upon this perfect world to bring about a stability that could not be undone, of Magic, Life, Death, Mass, and Truth. The Five Weights, all held in balance by the World Songs, strict melodies counterpointing one another that wound the ropes of reality about the centre of harmony itself. And with this knowledge the faeries knew the importance of the ballads within them.

"Once, there was a cave, a most extraordinary cave, at the centre of all things, a realm outside of realms, a place outside of

Blood and Biscuits

places. The Midpoint Cave, the start and end of things. The waypoint for new spirits and old ballads to fuse into Songlight, the faerie name for souls. Spirits given by the trees bind with ballads given by the balance, and they find life together."

Fable wrapped her fingers round her mug and stiffened her back.

"Upon this very day, many years ago, there began a new song in the Midpoint Cave. Its melody lilted sadly at first, for the ballad was salvaged from the ashes of another, a faerie ballad that ended and travelled back to the Midpoint Cave. Shed of its spirit, the visage of another gone to the afterlife, the ballad was bathed in the pale waters of the pools within, cleansed of any remaining memories of its former existence and made anew. Ready to harness Magic and Life and Truth for the next Songlight, Weights of the soul. Death and Mass are Weights of the body.

"The ballad found new life in the balance and was born again, to be sung into its next existence by the faeries guarding that place. And they sang a World Song, the Weight of Life, and the ballad found a spirit, forging the Songlight. They sang the Weight of Truth and the Songlight discovered knowledge. They sang the Weight of Magic and the Songlight's connection to nature was formed. Then they sang the Weight of Mass and the Songlight was made real, and they sang the Weight of Death and the eventual ending of the Songlight's spirit was created, for all things must end, energy to be returned, energy to be reused. These last two Weights were set in place for when the body came, the housing of the Songlight, the conduit through which magic would be channelled."

Fable peered into her cup but realised she had drunk it already. Vlad noticed her gloved hands shaking, he knew not if for the burnt flesh beneath or the tale she spun.

"On this day, years ago, the sun shone on the Midpoint Cave and the new Songlight was taken into the sky. The draw of Magic took it to the Forests of Berrúnhëre, one of the eight countries of the Eight Realms, and the shimmering clouds charged and changed. The eyes of the sky opened and ten thousand tears fell from her, a great sadness drenching the world for the loss of life before and great joy for the new life made.

"Amongst the tears there fell a drop of liquid gold. It poured down the branches and into the trunk of a Ginn-Satŷry tree, cooling and turning into the ground as another World Song of the forest faeries, the Ballad's Goldening, shaped it, moulded it, gave it form and purpose, guided it back up to the ground above. It was gifted a body by the world, grown from soil and water and energy's purest forms. The gold reached the surface and was pushed forth from the tree, its hand first, then its arm, a face, a head, the wings, and the rest of the body of a baby. Many years ago, today was this new child's Birthing Day.

"Light bathed this new life as it was taken into care, raised in the image of their parents and peers, crafted by time and experience, gifts and learning, until they were their own person, given over to begin raising another. Only, this matter never arrived, for when this faerie came to sing a new ballad into the world, on a new Birthing Day, they did not complete their voice of the Ballad's Goldening correctly. The wrong words came and the new baby never formed. Their spirit and ballad were retaken by the Ginn-Satŷry tree, drunk back into the balance so the ballad was not lost and the world remained true, the spirit taken back to form a new faerie. Except, the heart of the failed adult was soured and undone, harrowed and hollowed out by the loss of the child, maddened by their inadequacy. Angry beyond anger, sad beyond sadness; this child had never been theirs, they had never known the child, yet the loss cut them as cleanly and deeply as the sharpest knife. There is nothing sadder than a song unsung."

Fable smoothed back her hair and tapped her fingers on the bench, her eyes avoiding Vlad's. He asked no questions, only watched and listened, refusing to acknowledge every thought selfishly vying for his attention.

Blood and Biscuits

"You see, in the faerie world there is no space for emotional reflection, no idea of rectifying what's wrong in your mind. Adults die to feed their energies back into the balance just as children are born to continue singing the Weights of that balance and keep them true. The belief in the almighty equilibrium of the Five Weights is so great, the belief that all answers are given by the natural constructs so strong, that nobody ever acknowledges their own faults. *The truth hurts*, as they say here, and it's best faeries don't accept our shortcomings, else risk unbalancing the harmony in our hearts."

Fable sighed.

"It's the greatest tragedy of the Eight Realms, to deny our own emotional turmoil, as if our haunted, suffering minds were a hidden sixth Weight, one we ignored and shunned so we could praise and sing for the other five. And the faerie that sung the song wrong? They could not abandon their wayward imaginings, of abject failure, nor accept emotional suppression set down by society. They gave to temptation, to self-treachery, and travelled to another country of the Eight Realms, learning in secret a second discipline of magic, a discipline that could erase heartbreak from the Songlight, seeking to turn back emotional time."

Fable shuddered to a halt, eyes shining with gilded tears, and gazed out to sea, the story over, the link to her past revealed and raw. After a pause, Vlad finally spoke, his interest too great to let the moment become silence.

"And what happened to this faerie?" he asked with care.

Fable twitched off a glove.

"They discovered some rules should not be broken," she said quietly, resting a burned hand upon her leg, the flesh as black as the coffee Vlad no longer wished to finish. "Where once there was loss and sadness there came pride and arrogance. Not to replace but to paint over, to hide the turmoil. Emotions too powerful for faeries to understand yet expcrienced every day by most on this world. Such feelings turned the faerie into a pale imitation of what they once were. And with the attempt at learning more, the faerie burnt almost all magic from their veins and was exiled for their trouble, the droplet of gold, the vessel of ballad and spirit, the *Songlight*, cast out of the world that never tried to understand how they felt after their failure."

Fable gazed at her hands.

"These are monuments to what I was, not who I am now. Vlad, you will never know what it meant to me when you asked how I would like to identify, as a man or a woman. I gave no thought to the notion until you suggested it, giving no thought yourself other than how you might address me, and I panicked. I chose woman because of the maternal bond but I never stopped to ask myself why. *Why* did I choose this path? Why maternal? Well, now I know."

"Now I know, also. I am staggered by this revelation, my friend, and saddened greatly by your pain. It is beyond incomprehensible that your subconscious mind looked to heal itself by assuming the role of mother you felt you were denied. I…" Vlad pinched the bridge of his nose in thought. "Has your identity helped you come to terms with what happened?" he asked slowly, measuring caution with care.

"Yes. Yes, it really has. I no longer seek shame but to move on, to better things, and for that the Support Group has been invaluable."

Fable pulled on her glove again. Vlad simply watched the sea calmly, never taking his eyes from the foam and the waves, gazing over the rim of his cup.

"Thank you for telling me this story," he finally said. "Was it truly for me or did you wish to tell it for yourself?"

"A little of both," Fable admitted. "It is an amalgamation of stories and an old moral of faeries restructured together, I thought it would be enlightening for you, because…"

"Because stories help us understand one another. Through them we disguise our deepest emotions as morals so others can listen and appreciate more clearly, unpacking the meanings later."

𝔅lood and 𝔅iscuits

"Precisely. And I have been sat here with the one thing I brought with me from the Eight Realms trying to decide how to approach this matter with you."

"I never wished to force anything from you. You did not have to tell me anything."

Fable held up her hand.

"Except I *did*, I would not be true to myself or my denied heritage if I didn't tell you. It's what defines me, moulds me. I am defined by my grief."

"No. You are defined by your choice, Fable, and whether accidentally or not you *chose* to identify by how you perceive your grief. This perception makes you a person. You understood on an *emotional* level what it would take to move on from your grief, and that is by understanding the loss mothers feel when they are denied a child. You above all other faeries realised the hurt they feel. You are, it would seem, capable of experiencing much more than your fellow faeries. Your mistakes define you."

Fable's shoulders sagged a little and she looked away, sorrow misting her eyes.

"This is no bad thing," Vlad said quickly. "It is actually the most normal way of life. Learning from your mistakes is exactly what makes you a fully-fledged person on this world, and I should know, I have made *many*. Your choices define you because they are made with experience, experience gained from mistakes." Vlad hesitated, a question at his lips. "But I do have one thing to ask, if you would permit it?"

"Go ahead," Fable sniffed.

"If the Five Weights of the Eight Realms rely upon absolute balance then surely people *part* of this closed system, the faeries, unravel this harmony when they are exiled?"

Despite her mood, Fable gave a wonky smile.

"I thought I knew you quite well, Vladislav, but noticing that conundrum, and so quickly, is impressive, even for you. Yes, by taking the conjoined Songlight of spirit and ballad and body, such as myself, out of the balance the two sides to *your* equation would no longer add up. But this is not a two-sided balance, Vlad, it is *five-sided*; there is no left-equalling-right but Five Weights supporting one another, Five Weights counterbalanced around the fulcrum of the Midpoint Cave. If you take my affiliation to magic out then the other four Weights would theoretically become unbalanced, too, yet with my removal from the system, you also take my Life, my Truth, my physical Mass, *and* my payment to Death. I'm a perfect system in and of myself, so my removal from the balance, with complete severance, doesn't disturb the harmony of nature. I cannot give, I cannot take. And when I die, I do not join my brothers and sisters in the afterlife but instead go to the human afterlife."

"Whoever figured that out was disturbed," Vlad commented sickly.

"Indeed. And so I walk upon foreign lands comforted only a little by the thought that my exile, at least, did not damage my homeworld further. To channel my Light, to draw on the balance from across worlds, is too much to bear yet bear it I must sometimes. My pain is payment for the magic drawn. In minute doses it is sustainable, barely, as you have already seen, but one day, I am sure the Light that formed me will also be the death of me."

Vlad said nothing else on the matter, instead he pointed to the book folded over Fable's finger and asked,

"What are you reading?"

"Oh this?" Fable replied softly, looking down at her book. "It's the one thing I was permitted to bring with me to Earth from the Eight Realms. We're allowed a single set of clothes and one personal item. This was my choice. It's a book of Light magic, given to me by a friend from a Realm not of my own. A book containing secrets addressing issues with how to cast my Light whilst on Earth."

"Good Lord," Vlad whispered.

"Oh yes, my final ruse and a little 'screw you' to the faeries that exiled me. Cain taught me that phrase, I rather enjoy it. It has a good feel to it."

Blood and Biscuits

Vlad only nodded and tipped his coffee cup to the faerie. "Happy birthday, Fable," he said.

Fig. 11.
My Demon, Cuthbert.

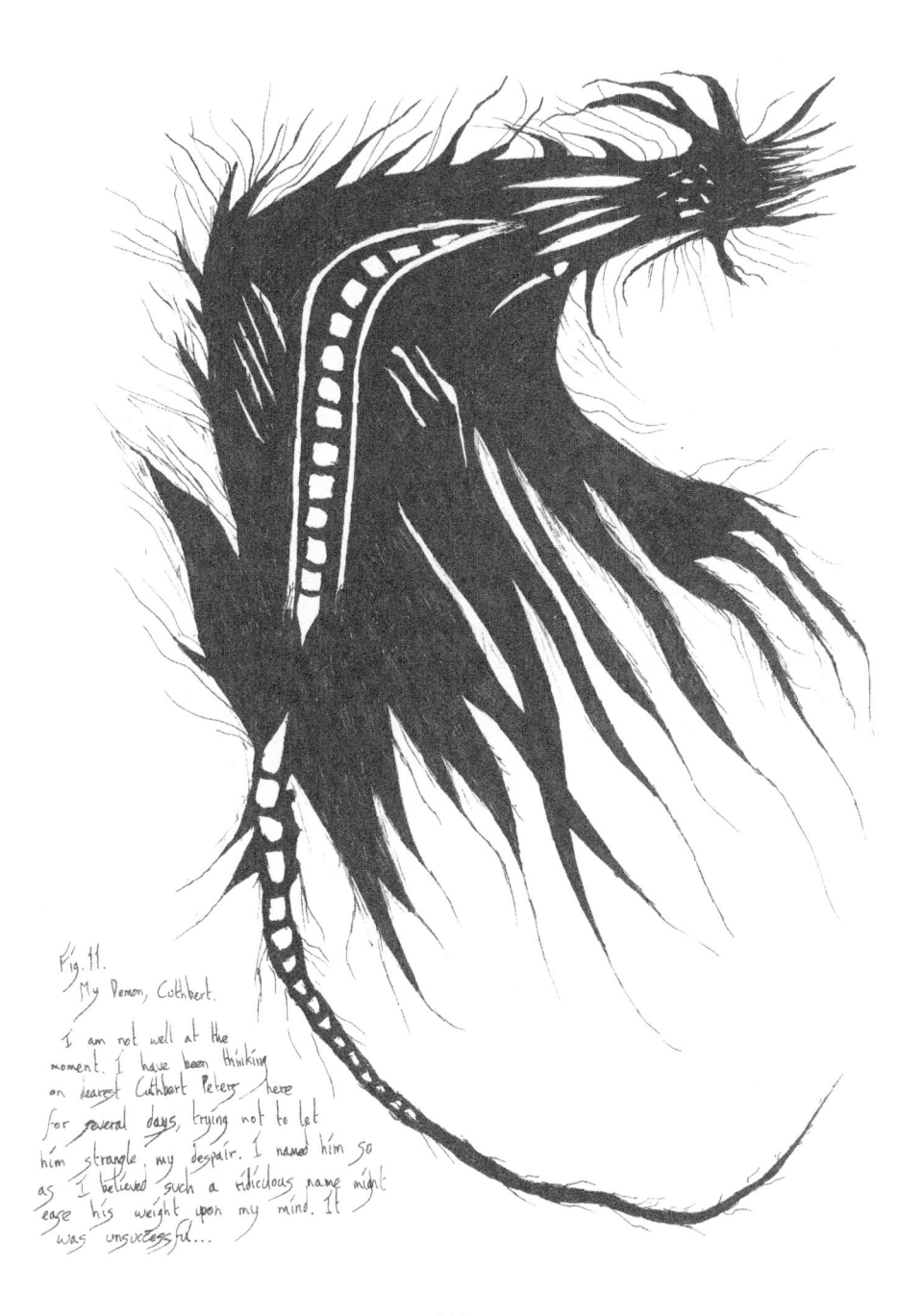

I am not well at the moment. I have been thinking on dearest Cuthbert Peters here for several days, trying not to let him strangle my despair. I named him so as I believed such a ridiculous name might ease his weight upon my mind. It was unsuccessful...

Fig Roll.
I could not help myself, this amused me far too much. Cain is mistaken: fig rolls are delicious. I like to imagine Cuthbert hates fig rolls, too.

Week Eight
The Stone of the Damned

THE SKIES AND HIDDEN RESEARCH FACILITY OF THE SOUTH POLE, WEDNESDAY.

'Now where did I leave that station?'

Across the freezing sky Vlad skimmed, his shadow trailing behind him, onyx-glowing eyes searching the ground. Every sense penetrated the deep ices and snow banks, tuned to find some trace of the place he had made years ago.

'I am usually very good at finding things but the magnetic South Pole has shifted four miles since I was last here. It has moved over six-hundred miles in the last century, it is hardly surprising I struggle...'

Something *caught* and Vlad changed direction immediately, the wind howling as he bolstered his echolocation. He gently weaved round a lone wandering albatross, its gigantic wings hardly moving at all, and spied a line of chinstrap penguins far from the shore. Vlad had always enjoyed observing animals in their natural habitat; they were amongst the purest forms of life, untouched by the faults of humans and their supernatural evolutions. Nature's wildness had always been a calming point for him, willing serenity back into his veins should his depression rise again.

Vlad flew alongside the albatross for a while, the cold air passing round them, before his senses twitched and he dived towards the vast expanse of ice below. Cracks and fissures and a huge plain of white dust appeared, and a dark speck in the snow. The hidden facility, two hundred miles from the true South Pole, completely

Blood and Biscuits

undetectable by the U.S-led Amundsen–Scott station there.

Vlad landed in a flurry of powder and noticed the spider's web of thin cracks patterning the impact. Vlad reproached himself.

'Next time control your landing, foolish man. What kind of a vampire lands with a thud!'

Vlad walked to the small station, the summer sun hanging just above the horizon, his pale skin shining like the snow in the glint of light. He hitched his heavy rucksack on his back, thinking on the contents.

Approaching the station's steps, Vlad took a moment to appreciate the dark facility. It was not huge by most measures, but was still a good ninety feet wide, two hundred long, with two floors and an underground complex for heat generation. Vlad felt the hum of power beneath his feet as he ascended the steps and rapped smartly on the door.

Somebody scrambled within. They would know who was at their door; nobody else would be wandering the frozen south. The rubber seal popped open and the door swung wide, revealing an elderly human, a woman. She smiled, the black skin of her face crinkling kindly, and stepped aside to permit Vlad.

"Mrs King, I trust I find you well."

"God, you make me wanna' jump in a hot shower just *lookin'* at you," she said enthusiastically, a light Caribbean accent filling the room musically. She slammed the door and sealed the hatch wheel. "Cup a' coffee?"

"Go on, then," Vlad accepted, *thumping* his heavy bag down, stamping his boots against the thick mat. He followed into the room, making for the kitchenette along an inner wall. Every time he met Moira, she always made him happy, no matter his mood. Moira just had that effect on him. "Do you still have the Columbian stuff?" he asked.

Moira smirked at him.

"You tellin' me you can taste the differences, now? Sounds like a new power, and also a lie."

Moira emptied water from the tap, which fed from a huge bowser in the floor above, into an electric kettle. Vlad leant against a work surface and grinned a vampire's smile, four fangs extended fully. Moira glanced up in the silence and jolted at the sight, and Vlad laughed heartily.

"Don't you do that, you terrible man!" she exclaimed, hand pressed to her chest. Vlad heard her hammering heart. "You know I jump easy. I don't see you for months on end then you come here, outta' the blue, no warnin' save a phone call, and scare me! For a joke, no less!"

Vlad laughed again, the noise a healthy sound.

"I am sorry," he said, holding his sides. "I am so dour all the time; it feels good to release it occasionally. I need more experience at bringing joy to myself."

Moira slapped him playfully on the arm as the kettle finished boiling.

"Well don't practice on me, you hear? And don't apologise when you don't mean it. You're not on holy ground so don't expect me to believe a word you say."

"Noted," Vlad said, taking the proffered coffee. "Thank you, Moira." He took a sip and sighed, the *smell* of Columbia in his nostrils. "So aside from fools making you jump, has all been well out here? How is John?"

"He seemed good, last time we spoke," Moira shrugged nonchalantly. "I'll be back when the sun starts losin' its power around mid-autumn, after I do my star experiments, and then John'll have me for four months again. He'll be out every day havin' lunch with one of the kids when they're not workin', I expect, or writing his novels in hip cafes – always his favourite, he loves young people's energy. Probably enjoyin' some peace and quiet without his demandin' wife around."

"Oh, I do not think that for a second," Vlad chided pleasantly. "You both raised wonderful children but I would imagine it is *you* taking the opportunity of peace and quiet now they are adults and you are 'free'. Nevertheless, John is a wonderfully caring man. He probably misses you greatly."

"I know he would like to see *you* again," Moira said quietly as she sipped her coffee. "He considers you a dear friend, you know."

"That is touching to hear," Vlad replied simply.

As they spoke, Vlad glanced at a framed picture on the side, near the microwave. It was a grainy, faded photograph of Moira at twenty-four years old on her wedding day, her arm round her smiling new husband, John, faces beaming with pride. His parents flanked him as Moira's mother stood beside her, an empty space where Moira's father should have been. Illness takes too many lives.

"Isn't that what we all need from someone else?" Moira asked pointedly and when she looked at Vlad, she evidently saw consideration lining his face. "You found anyone yet, you lonely man? Even vampires need love, y'know."

"*You* have been watching too many films," Vlad commented.

"Maybe, but that don't make it any less true. Now answer me: anyone to call your own? You deserve happiness, same as anyone else. More so, if this Support Group you've been tellin' me about is as successful as you say."

Vlad grimaced and Moira caught the look.

"What? What's happened?" she asked worriedly. She gestured to the wide sitting area surrounding a huge flat screen television and home entertainment complex. "Come, take a seat. Tell me about it."

Vlad followed and they sat opposite one another. He glanced around the facility, and at the wasteland wilds of icy snow outside.

"Any problems with the place? Need any upgrades or maintenance?" Vlad asked casually, hoping to delay the conversation.

"No, everythin's fine. I get my helicopter'd fuel and handymen in, once a month as always. They keep me runnin' tight. But don't avoid the question, Vladislav. What's on your mind?"

Vlad sighed. With pains, he explained the situation he had

caused with Jacob and Sarah. He told Moira everything, her face never wavering from a mixture of concern and understanding. He did not stop until everything was out, a puzzle emptied from its box. Moira sat back in her seat, evidently gathering the pieces to form the full picture.

"This wraith – Jacob? He sounds like a nice boy."

"He is," Vlad said, "but full of worry, absolutely con*vinced* he is worthless. He has taken great offence at the notion of Sarah finding peace in moving on. I suspect the reasons why but I cannot hope to bring him back to us, for his own sake and for the sake of the group."

"And this is why you flew ten thousand miles? To ask me how to get this young wraith back into your flock?"

"By and large, Christian metaphors aside. Though I also wondered how your research was coming along. You mentioned great activity with the Blessed Emerald, is this still so?"

"One thing at a time," Moira urged. "You might well be twenty times my age but I'm older than you in years remainin', so show some respect. Look, I say you go to Jacob. I know you struggle with the one-to-one stuff sometimes but that's alright, you can be *bad* at things, too, Vlad."

Vlad made a noise of humility only a vampire could make and sat straighter.

"I will try your suggestion. I hope Jacob realises he is not wrong for feeling what he feels, nor is he right in thinking we all believe him a fool. Does that suffice?"

"He cannot be made to feel happy but he can hopefully be convinced this is the best course. I think you'll need to be the one to do that, your connection was stronger than you anticipated because his reaction was such a surprise to you."

"Evidently, things still slip through my fingers," Vlad said quietly.

"You might not be human now but you were *once*, and for all your amazin' qualities, Vladislav Eliade, you still have these tired old mortal drawbacks runnin' through you."

"Hmm," Vlad agreed wordlessly.

"Anyway," Moira said, slapping her legs and glancing at another door. "You came for two reasons, did you not?"

"Well I asked about the Emerald…"

"Balls to that, you didn't come all this way, crossin' sand and sea and God knows what else, just to talk about a green rock pointin' at the stars. You're here because you've read my report and because of your Sarah. You've come to see the Necrostone."

"However did you guess?" Vlad asked seriously as he finished his coffee and stood, brushing himself down and walking towards the door leading from the housing quarter to the main facility.

"You know, you're not as adept at keepin' your feelin's hidden from those that know you, pale man," Moira said affectionately. She groaned as she made to stand and instantly Vlad was back by her side, gently holding her beneath the elbow so she could rise with dignity. "Thank you, Vlad. I'm gettin' more tired every day. I forget for all my years you've stayed the same age; you dunno' how long it took to accept that." She peered up into his face a moment and sighed. "Still so beautiful, a man of myth to behold and wonder upon. Still so vibrant and charming." She sighed. "Anyway, can't stand around musin' on the past – work to do and all that."

Moira moved away, her shoulders slumped more than before. Vlad changed the subject rather than face old memories.

"I hired you because you are the best," he said as they moved towards the door. "It was not out of pity or charity, nor favouritism, though you have earned *that*, at least. I hired you because I trust you with these tasks."

Moira looked up at him, amusement glinting her eye.

"And there's me thinkin' it was for me good looks."

As Vlad failed to think of something to say, Moira pressed her finger against an electronic reader and a lock *clunked*, permitting them into the facility. Lights blinked on automatically, illuminating a long, sterile corridor lined either side with doors, the gentle hum of power beneath them more prominent. Moira led the way, pointing out doors as she went. "Room of Ashes – had some issues with the lyric work for ogre and wood nymph but there's promise for forest troll with more research. Artefacts Chamber – haven't been in there a while, since that bloody amulet tried settin' me on fire. Toilet – there was a plumbin' issue but Jerry sorted it." Vlad snorted at the levity. "Ahh, Stone Room. Come on."

Moira opened the door and walked inside. Vlad followed, his eyes taking in the large space beyond, walls lined with hundreds of shelves, each row filled with thousands of sparkling gems and shining precious rocks. Every item was intricately labelled, representing weeks of categorisation work alone.

"Every time I see this place it brings such a feeling of being so very small. Though my life has changed throughout the centuries this is one place proving to be quite the constant."

Vlad let the poisonous threads of his despair pass him by rather than choke him. Cuthbert, his demon, always tried suffocating him when least expected.

"It makes me feel warm and fuzzy," Moira said as she walked into the open centre and stopped beside a bronze device sitting upon a tall stand. The elaborate machine was rather like an upwards-facing hand with ten fingers, each bent inward. Sat within its grasp was a rough and unremarkable stone, jet black, twin white veins running parallel around its middle.

As Vlad looked down the shelves of rocks, he caught sight of a ruby-red gem and a flash of Lucy's face struck him.

"Such a shame your Stone Theory never went anywhere, Moira. I would have believed the Scarlet Eye of Withering Hill the perfect candidate for proving the tangibility of thought."

"Vlad, sometimes you've just got to let things go. Ain't ever going to find an answer to that other than Forestein and Rosetta were wrong. I've tried tellin' you before."

Blood and Biscuits

"Indeed, you have. Yet my doubts remain."

Vlad approached the black stone on its stand and stared down at the thing.

"Hmm...You know, I always thought the Necrostone should be utterly flawless but it is rough and unremarkable. It should be perfect in every way."

"Why should it? It owes you nothing. Nothing worth having is without fault. Often the greatest things exist *because* of their imperfections. Some owe their greatness to the problems they faced, like the movie Jaws."

"It is the roughness that defines us," Vlad finished and Moira smiled deeply. Vlad sighed. "You say you are nearly there?"

"I am so close I can practically feel it when I say the right lyric," Moira explained.

"Are you confident I taught you the magic well enough?"

"Yes, there's no doubt there. But it's not enough, it's like the stone needs somethin' else, somethin' *more*."

"Well I scoured the legends and the texts after I found the damned thing in Egypt..."

"Yes, yes, you broke open a tomb outside a'Cairo, you're very powerful," Moira said dryly, waving away his words.

"Alright, there was no need for that. "What I meant was there is nothing else on the matter. The texts are clear: the stone will only awaken for something that 'lives as in death then dies as in life'. That is the magic I gave you, the lyric for the Spell of the Living Dead. There can be nothing else."

"Well, I dunno' what to tell you. The spell makes the stone shake a bit and then it stops. And I don't wanna' go stompin' around gettin' uppity when that thing could open a new dimension and pull me into the afterlife!"

"No, that is most understandable. Look, I will keep trying and you focus on your wordmanship, perhaps the lyrics are just too old now, language having changed so much. Many of the spells of Ellin's Island have gone funny over the centuries, their meanings changed as the words of their languages have altered in meaning also."

"Aye, but them are lesser spells. This is complex, dark magic; no matter how hard you try, its meaning is solid. Can't change. I've read that enough times in my books."

"Then perhaps it is a matter of enunciation."

"You'd better not be commentin' on-"

"-For the last time, Moira, I am not commenting on your accent. You have been making that joke for fifty years."

"And you've been scarin' me with your fangs for sixty!"

"Fair enough," Vlad chuckled.

They left the Stone Room and walked out the main facility. As they re-emerged into the living quarter, Vlad offered Moira another coffee.

"Why not," she said, settling once more on a sofa. "And you can tell me what's in that bag a'yours while you do."

"Oh, I had completely forgotten," the vampire remarked as he tipped granules into two mugs. "That is your Christmas bonus."

"Well isn't that nice," Moira practically purred as Vlad made the coffees and joined her by the television. "What be it this time? Gold? Frankincense? Myrrh?"

"I get it, I am old and I probably met Moses when I was a teenager, you make *that* joke a lot, too. And no, the reason I brought the bag is because of a chance."

Moira stopped for a moment and stared at Vlad.

"A chance?" she repeated and Vlad smiled. He nodded and Moira's eyes shot open. "You have found my replacement?"

"I may well have," Vlad said. "But only if you want it. I know you enjoy it out here, and I admit the money is good, but I thought perhaps you might wish to simply settle down, finally leave this all behind. Before you say there is nobody as good as you then I do not doubt that, however you must be allowed to retire at *some* point and seventy-six years is more than enough, do you not think?"

"But what about Frank?" Moira asked, hopeful voice

Blood and Biscuits

measured against potential dismay.

"Your shift cover for winter? He knows nothing, only how to keep a place from going under and what not to touch. He will continue in that vein, but there might well be someone else to take *your* place if they are willing. If re not, I will still see to it you retire, and handsomely, too. You deserve rest."

"Sounds like I've been forced to work here. You know I chose this, right?"

"Oh, I am very aware but it has been too long and I know when somebody must concentrate on themselves and their lives."

"Hmm, always one for givin' out the advice but not for *takin'* it. That a vampire thing?"

"No, it is in fact a male thing," Vlad smiled. "That will never change though I am working on a solution to our sex as an entirety. There is no hope for convincing us to ask for directions, however."

Moira sat for a long while in quiet happiness, a feeling of satisfaction emanating from her, washing over Vlad pleasantly. He felt good about himself for the first time in days.

"So what's *in* the bag?" she asked eventually. "It looks heavy! It certainly doesn't contain no replacement scientist."

"Oh, a frozen turkey," Vlad replied, half-grinning. "Big enough for all your family for Christmas. That is what I meant: the chance will begin with you reintegrating back into your family properly."

"But," Moira stammered, "I'm *here* for Christmas."

"Not this year. Nor will you ever be again."

Moira clasped her hands together in delight and then, to Vlad's surprise, she slid her sleeve up and revealed her wrist, a slight scent of the same perfume she had worn for decades not quite masking the swell of blood beneath the skin.

"Are you hungry, Vlad?" she asked easily, seductively. Vlad's senses nearly burst, her heart still strong for this.

"Famished," he muttered. "Remember your silver amulet…"

"You'll not need it, you never have done," Moira said, her

hand already on the back of his head.

AUGUST LEAVES APARTMENTS, 54 ASHFORD LANE, ELLINSGATE. THURSDAY.

On a heavy fire door at 22:00 precisely, a fist rapped politely. Someone shuffled inside and the door opened. In the frame stood Jacob, head and face covered by a balaclava sporting the Union Flag. His bloodshot eyes, the sclerae pale-yellow, widened in surprise.

"Christ, Vlad, what the hell are you doing here?"

The vampire stood straight, a smart, black trilby twirling artfully between his long, slender fingers.

"I have come to you in deepest respect and with the heaviest of apology," Vlad began.

"Oh God, don't start talking like that round here. It might look nice but there's druggies three doors down and I think the old lady up at 49's in some sorta' knitting gang."

"Would you like me to have a constructive chat with them?" Vlad enquired.

"No! God, no, just get in, quick."

Vlad moved inside and Jacob shut the door. He removed his balaclava and Vlad surveyed him automatically: the man had evidently spent a lot of his time angry, the remaining skin of his face hanging lax. The visible tendons beneath seemed tight as his muscles clenched.

Vlad caught sight of an iron crucifix about his neck but said nothing. Crosses and vampires were another myth though some members of the undead did not take kindly to reminders of their blasphemous existence.

Jacob paced the darkened corridor and into a bright room and Vlad followed through to a kitchen. It joined an open-plan living and

Blood and Biscuits

dining room – quite spacious, given the area and apartment block layout. The furnishings were light and colourful and Vlad suspected a lot of the artwork of abstract machines were Fable's. Jacob's touches were obvious in the smaller details, the subtler things, all of the same type of subject. Sculptures and oil prints of faces, each displaying powerful emotions. Though the artist had deliberately warped them, the faces nonetheless depicted such raw feeling they seemed enhanced by the distortion.

Vlad peered at them curiously, the images of a young man trapped in eternal horror and a bare woman feeding a baby capturing his attention the most as Jacob grabbed the kettle.

"Coffee?"

"Only if you are making one for yourself," Vlad insisted. Jacob shrugged dispassionately and turned the tap on. Vlad looked around again and pointed aimlessly. "You have a nice place. You and Fable must be happy here."

Jacob shrugged again, a habit of his when uncomfortable.

"It does us well, when she's actually here."

"Ahh yes, where *is* our faerie friend?"

"Sheffield."

"Come again?"

"Sheffield," Jacob reaffirmed as he poured the coffees, keeping both black. "She read your engineering books and learned all about 'intracity locomotive transportation', as she put it."

"So now she is in Sheffield riding the trams?" Vlad asked with a slight smile.

"So now she's in Sheffield riding the trams," Jacob repeated, his low mood unable to stave the smirk from his bloodless lips. He handed Vlad the coffee and walked across the open-plan to a low sofa. "She's sent me messages about how much she's enjoying it and getting to grips with the timetables; I've never really gotten selfies before but now I'm getting flooded with tonnes of Fable and bloody trams. There's one with her standing in front of a ticket office that might actually make you laugh 'cause she's pulling this ridiculous face."

"Whatever keeps her happy," Vlad responded neutrally, perching opposite Jacob and remaining passive. "But the discussion of Fable is not what brought me here tonight."

"No, I'd imagine it wasn't. So why *are* you here, Vlad? This some way of convincing me everything's alright? That what you did was fine?"

"I was considering starting with something to that effect, but at the Support Group and would have been considerably more selfish, with platitudes of hopelessness and Sarah's woes, et cetera. I have since realised you wish to hear none of this."

"Oh right," Jacob said idly, rubbing the rim of his mug, removing some imaginary speck of dust. "That's not a realisation you come to on your own. I know you well enough to think you might've been speaking to Lucy about all of this."

"We had a brief chat over a few drinks but I did not go into details, that would not be right."

"So who was it, Cain? Jesus, what the hell does *he* think of me after I nearly brained him against the wall? Is he alright?"

"Our werewolf is absolutely fine, if still nursing a slight headache. He harbours no ill will, I should not think; he has come a very long way from the man that stumbled into our midst during that first session. As have you," Vlad added. "But to answer your question honestly," he continued before Jacob could interrupt, "I went to Antarctica yesterday to seek advice from a very old friend."

Jacob spluttered on his drink and coughed loudly as coffee sprayed out of every hole in his face.

"Oh God, that's disgusting," he muttered, wiping the mess off the coffee table with a tissue. "Sorry about that. You were in Antarctica! – oh of course you were, why am I even questioning that? So what's down there, then, more silver chains? Some ancient bog brush capable of turning back time?"

"A research facility of my own creation," Vlad answered, the breeziness of his tone catching Jacob off-guard.

Blood and Biscuits

"Right, well that...that makes sense. What's it researching?"

"Some of the *many* magical phenomena of this world and others," Vlad replied, leaning back and drinking his coffee, the warmth of it heating his dead throat pleasantly. "From the powers of sunlight on vampire skin to pressure forces influencing the rotational dimensional symmetry of certain spells – this concerns geometry in Euclidean space affecting magic – from celestial alignment patterns to the strengths of magic-infused gemstones. That latter one is an area of particular interest for me."

"Ok, number one: I don't even know what Euclidean space *is*, so you didn't need to confirm that, I was just gonna' believe you unconditionally. Secondly, magic stones actually exist?"

"Oh yes," Vlad said excitedly. "I have collected near-countless over the centuries to discover their properties and observe their interactions with nature and with each other. Indeed, many are little more than propagators for something else rather than conduits of actual power themselves. Catalysts or starter motors, if you will. The stones range from the almost benign, such as the Rock of Epotha – a dark-green orb of bolstered granite used to add flavour to soups, so far as I can tell – to the extremely powerful."

Despite his sadness, Jacob's interest sparked.

"I can't believe any of this is actually real. Then he looked Vlad up and down and evidently re-evaluated. "Well, I suppose if people like *us* exist then I guess magic pebbles can, too. But none of this explains you being here, nor does it make me feel any better about the situation with Sarah."

"Quite, and I would not expect it to. However, I have a friend at that facility, Moira, a human I have employed for over eleven years-"

"A human?" Jacob interrupted suddenly, sitting straighter on the sofa. "You have a human working for you? Does she know all about who you are and *what* you are?"

"Of course," Vlad said off-handedly. "She is one of my ten donors. The individual I used a few weeks back was a middle-aged man called Geoffrey in Liverpool. I have known Moira since she was sixteen years old. She became a very dear friend of mine, a very intelligent one who, after forty-two years studying and working in science sectors, decided to work for me instead. To study magical phenomena and open her eyes to a wider, deeper world of such mystery mere mortals unable to comprehend such vastness ignore it. I mean that with respect, obviously."

"Yeah, sounded respectful," Jacob grinned. "So, Moira…"

"She gave me a human's approach and told me to be honest with you," Vlad admitted, "and come to you personally rather than let you believe I abandoned you. The rest I figured out myself. You are not alone, Jacob. You never were. We are all the same, in the end, suffering as we do in our own funny ways."

"Funny's one word for it," Jacob grunted but Vlad smiled.

"See, I said that exact same thing to Cain last week. He has a very similar outlook on life as you do."

"I realised that a while back," Jacob said with another half-hearted shrug. "*God* I hope he doesn't hate me. Maybe he'll forgive me; Lucy's done him the world of good."

"And long may they last," Vlad said. The point is, Jacob, what you felt when you learned of Sarah's intentions, and how you reacted to the reason I *originally* set up the Support Group, were perfectly understandable. I am sorry it did not come to you in an easier, more delicate manner. I am not saying this because I want you to help Sarah enter the afterlife, I am saying this because I want *you*, my *friend*, to make peace with this decision. It is not one made lightly, Jacob, it has taken Sarah two hundred years to come to terms with."

"I just…" Jacob began, looking away as both hands gripped his mug, most likely a self-defence mechanism. Vlad held up his pale palms.

"I know. I am not pressuring you, I am only doing what I should have done weeks ago and explaining the real situation and how we have gotten here. Sarah is the last of my family, Jacob," and

Blood and Biscuits

here the wraith's eyebrows shot up.

"Ok, I didn't expect that."

"Yes, you left before I had chance to tell you that part. Sarah is my daughter's ever-so-many-greats granddaughter, and therefore directly related to me, however diluted that bloodline is now. She is one of the reasons I came to the north of England to begin with, after I learned of her. I wanted only to see her, to visit her, to let her know I was somebody she could trust, but she died tragically before I could know her. Sarah does not remember me at all, she knows only the kindly vampire trying to send her from her doom, her fate undeserved. Sarah should be able to choose her future, something I hope you might relate to."

Jacob breathed through his teeth as he heard it all, shoulders heavy with the weight of pure feeling. When he spoke, the words dragged from his throat.

"She is such a strong, delicate soul," he said.

Vlad nodded.

"Brittle, I think they call it."

"Only to a point. Seeing her turn to this answer…I can't bear it, not with everything I've been through. I've never gotten past trying to kill myself, Vlad, and confronting my faith again – like when you found me in Ellinsgate, in the church, it's got me feeling like that again. I can't just sit by, let alone *help*, when somebody wants to end their existence."

"I know you are hurting, I truly do, and I understand why. I cannot imagine the pain you must still feel from your past and from this new challenge. But this is not the same, Sarah is two centuries old and she is not alive; she has every right to choose the manner of her second ending and we are obligated to assist because she cannot do it herself. Her suffering will only worsen if we stand idle. It is possible-"

"-but Vlad, it's not-"

"-no, please let me finish. The soul can poison without the body and mind. We must all carry this burden if we are to help our friend move on. This is her conscious *choice*, the thing separating us from beasts. Her choice must be respected if we are to end her suffering, and she *has* suffered, Jacob. For two hundred years of complete isolation and loneliness. That is more than enough, would you not say?"

"And we can't break this bond like we might for Lucy and her binding?"

"This is no spell, nor is it this curse. This…is natural. A facet of two worlds, Earth and the afterlife. Sometimes souls do not make it through, lingering until their emotional turmoil, their unfinished business, is satisfied."

"And what *is* Sarah's unfinished business?"

Vlad sighed and shook his head.

"To see her family again."

"Christ. So she's stuck here for eternity since they've all passed on."

"Precisely. And because she never knew who I was before she died there is no hope I, as her ancestor, could satisfy this matter. She would learn who I am then forget it again. It is simply natural. Therefore, we must *break* this cycle for her. Confront the afterlife and force the damned thing open. Allow Sarah to be with our – *her* - family again, and sever this bond of hers. That *is* the only way. To free *and* cure her."

"Please," Jacob grated, "let me be alone with this. I need time. It's too much after everything."

"I understand," Vlad said respectfully. He drained his mug and placed it on the coffee table neatly. "I shall leave you with the peace you need, this is awful enough without my presence infecting the atmosphere."

As Vlad exited, a call from Jacob halted his hand upon the kitchen door.

"You're the best thing that ever happened to me, Vlad. I want you to know that. I guess you'll always be my saviour."

Vlad did not look back. Indeed, he almost fled the apartment at the strength of Jacob's admission.

RUINS OF ST ELLIN'S CHURCH.
THE START OF THE SUPPORT GROUP.

"It's quiet here, I don't like it."

Vlad looked at Lucy and noted the two empty chairs where Jacob and Sarah normally sat.

"There is a horrid sense of something missing, I agree, but we can do nothing about it. Jacob has very strong personal reasons and Sarah, I would imagine, is coming to terms with her decision. She says her goodbyes to the church she reluctantly called home for two hundred years."

"Well Jacob's still at the flat, as far as I'm aware," Fable noted solemnly. "He's hardly moved for days. I tried convincing him to come tonight but I feel he'll skip it. I'll let you know if he messages me using these ingenious communication cameras." Fable waved an old refurbished smartphone proudly. "I can even do some of my internet trading on here, absolutely delightful engineering."

Cain sighed as he sat down, his back now healed. He sniffed loudly, pointing at his nose.

"Bloody allergies're flarin' again. Haven't done a *big* sneeze yet but it won't be long before that bloody full moon's back and I'm honkin' everywhere like some mad, snotty foghorn."

Lucy grimaced.

"Tactful as always. I'd rather you just sneezed and got it over with, you kept me awake all last night with your sniffing."

"Yeah, sorry about that," Cain replied sheepishly. "I'll go and sleep in one of them other creepy bedrooms 'til it's over."

"You'll do no such thing!" Lucy exclaimed. "You're my hot water bottle! I might technically be dead but I can still feel chilly. Cold resistance seems solely Vlad's gift, lucky sod that he is."

"You know, I sometimes miss a good shiver," Vlad said

calmly, trying to remember exactly what feeling cold was like. "I can detect warmth and I know when it is *supposed* to be cold, but as for when I should be freezing to death, I feel perfectly well. To escape environmental ravages of life, I think, is one of the few bonuses to being a vampire. Anyway, we are here for a reason, despite recent events, so let us begin: how was everyone's week?"

"Not good," a small voice said and all looked to Alizon. She shrank a little in her chair but did not shy away entirely. Vlad said nothing, he opened his hand welcomingly and Alizon took some strength from the motion. "My mother came and found me," she muttered, scratching her arm awkwardly.

"Your real mum?" Cain asked. "But you were fostered, how'd she find you?"

"She is p-part enchantress, too," Alizon struggled, "and that small core of magic was enough to guide her back to me a f-few years back. It was the fact I'm magical that made her unable to deal with me as a child, which is why I was s-sent away to Aunty Windwater's. Since I came back from school in Wales she finds me occasionally, always randomly, and she always shows up drunk."

"Oh crap," Cain muttered, folding his arms across his chest as he always did when faced with darkness. "She make much trouble?"

Though Alizon's face did not change, the tendons of her neck tensed slightly and her eyes shook. It was answer enough.

"Yes," she whispered. Without warning, Alizon reached down and rolled up the bottom of her tunic. Upon her hip, stretching across her abdomen, was a long, dark bruise. Livid purple, blackened edges, jagged in ways that could only be agonising. Vlad felt rage spark, catching alight within him, his next thought of hellfire vengeance.

Then the last piece of the puzzle fell into place, the jigsaw of Aunty Windwater. The woman that had unofficially fostered Alizon, the person the witch escaped to whenever her mother sought to abuse her. Her safety net, her port in any storm. Her real mother when her biological failure was incapable of love and protection. The idea of a young, terrified Alizon suffering at such torturous hands made Vlad feel venomously sick and the old urges to kill rose within his blood again, something he struggled to keep buried all too often.

Lucy practically hissed. "She did this to you, your mum? Jesus, that looks painful. Alizon, I'm…I'm sorry."

Alizon looked away, biting her trembling lip. Vlad's internal flames fanned hotter by the hurt on the witch's face and it took everything not to lose the grip he had on his iron-hard walls of control holding back his power. Fable smiled encouragingly at Alizon, finding care where Vlad suddenly found he could only muster white-hot burning retribution.

"It's alright now, Alizon, you are not with her anymore. You may lower your top; we've seen your pain and we see you. You are beautiful," Fable said, her hand held out softly.

Alizon lowered her shirtfront, wincing as her fingers grazed her bruised skin. Vlad felt the raw connection through his senses and he almost stood to leave and find this mother of Alizon's to exact the same pain upon her. Instead, however, he breathed calm into himself and sat back in his chair.

"Thank you for sharing with us, Alizon." He gave every outward measure of a serene man, the illusion masking his boiling fury. "If you permit me a moment, I may have something for the pain. I have no herbs to heal a witch's ailments but you will not suffer discomfort for a time."

Alizon nodded and Vlad stood. He left the basement and returned within a minute, hand clutching a fistful of dark-red herb, their long-ago desiccation losing none of their potency.

"I will make you a tea with these, a rather potent Chinese leaf known as 'hóu zi de yá chǐ'. It translates loosely as 'the monkey's teeth', for some ungodly reason, despite involving neither monkeys nor teeth."

"Oh, that's nothin'," Cain said, leaning forward jovially, evidently keen to rid his mind of Alizon's bruise and perhaps make her smile. "When I was outside Beijing, I saw an English translation on a sign stickin' out some memorial garden that said 'The grass is smilin' at you. Enjoy the beef.' Go figure."

Lucy burst out laughing and Vlad asked, through a chuckle, "You have been to China? That is quite surprising."

"Why? I've been all over, just to get away from faces and people I know. When I left Jan and Pete behind at my last foster home, I took trains through Europe and rode the Trans-Siberian to Asia. At fifteen I was about six foot, six-one, and looked mid-twenties so wasn't bothered much. Worked my way across Mongolia, down through Huabei, Huadong, gotta' job at sixteen as security in Shanghai, diddled around in Huazhong…sightseeing in Hong Kong. Vietnam was fascinatin', Thailand indescribable, Kazakhstan mindblowin'. Yeah," Cain added when Vlad raised his eyebrows, "there's a tonne to me people don't know. Most just assume things but I'll tell you this now: I've seen some stuff, mate."

"I bet you have, I hope you wrote it all down," Vlad added simply. He turned to Alizon with the steaming tea in his hand, holding the boiling hot mug easily as he proffered her the handle. "You will find comfort in this, I assure you."

"Thank you, Vlad," Alizon said, clasping a hand to her side, massaging the muscles there. "I'm sure it was an accident, really."

"Sure looked it," Cain growled, hands clenching, knuckles gleaming bone-white. "She say sorry after, I reckon?"

"She did, yes. She always does," Alizon said easily.

"Ahh, well that makes it all better, then." Cain's square jaw clamped on the words. Vlad *smelled* his anger, knew it had nothing to do with the upcoming full moon. This rage was Cain's alone. Vlad said nothing; he could see this was not incidental for Cain. Something personal drove him to empathy. Vlad *smelled* worry and fury mixing in Lucy, the same outlining Fable's face. "What was it," Cain asked, "didn't mean to throw the bottle at you? Got confused when pushin' you down the stairs? The drink made her do it?"

"Yes, she struck me because of the wine she'd had."

Blood and Biscuits

"And how does that make you feel, Alizon?" Vlad asked quietly, politely, neutrally, disguising the dark disgust wrenching his blackened heart.

Alizon cocked her head, evidently thinking about the question, as if she even dared have an opinion on her own mother.

"Not great, I guess," she finally said and Cain, despite himself, snorted.

"Don't mince your words," he muttered. Vlad was thankful Alizon did not respond as he suspected she would not understand the layers of his meaning.

"But my thoughts don't matter," the enchantress continued. "I was a mistake. She had to get rid of me when I was young, I get that. I think what she feels is mostly because I can get quite frustrating a lot of the time." As if her mother was not to blame at all. "That's all. Just too much alcohol and me being me."

"*No*," came a sound so slick with ice the entire basement shuddered.

All looked to Vlad and Alizon's gaze nearly met his own, his eyes full of centuries of withheld vengeance and barely contained ire, the force overwhelming Cain's entirely. The vampire shook his head, fighting his fangs trying to burst from his jaws.

"That is simply not excusable. Whether or not your mother raised you is inconsequential: you did not choose to be born nor did you choose your parentage, but you deserve to live your life as you see fit, free of abuse. You are to be protected by those claiming to love you, not hurt in any way. You matter, Alizon, you are unique and incredible; you must *never* allow anyone to make you believe or feel otherwise. You are not frustrating, not in the slightest. That reminds me, have your tea," Vlad bit off. "You will feel better."

His control steady despite the rage coursing his veins, Vlad watched Alizon with the cup of monkey's teeth tea, its steam a powerful cacophony of dates and almonds. She raised the drink gratefully and sipped, and after a moment she smiled.

"It tastes very nice, thank you," was all she said.

Blood and Biscuits

"Hopefully it shall block some of your pain," Vlad said quietly. "Do you plan on seeing your mother again?" he tested.

"I hope not," Alizon responded shakily. "Not that I ever have a choice in the matter. She always seems to know where I am."

"Isn't there some spell to shield you from her?" Lucy asked vaguely but Alizon shook her head.

"No, weather magic doesn't work like that. It's more for manipulating base elements and revealing what exists already, reading signs created by the world, and the imprint channellers of magic or power leave behind, like Vlad and his tramping around Ellin's Island for decades. I can't just form new lyrics out of nowhere and apply them to myself."

"Have you ever tried?" Fable asked. "Because my own magic, though admittedly from another world, *does* work a little more along those lines. It's creative from the forces of the trees, rather than bending existence, so I could potentially aid you. That is, if I wasn't relegated to the most basic of Light production only, and that causes me enough harm already."

"*That* is the real frustration," Vlad noted. "But if your mother comes for you again, Alizon, then you will let me know, will you not? Make an excuse then go to the toilet or something similar, and message me. I would love to pop over and have a little chat with her, maybe straighten a few things out."

Cain smirked in satisfaction, catching Vlad's meaning. However, Alizon missed the edge to his voice and the depth to his subtlety and she nodded.

"Yes, I'm sure that could be arranged. She likes a bit of gossip."

She sipped her tea again and Vlad sensed a small measure of pain slip away from her deep bruise. The Chinese leaves were working, calming Vlad's mind a little. Lucy glanced between him and Alizon but Vlad shook his head; this was not their fight. It was not his, either, but he knew Alizon believed her mother's words and felt herself as useless and frustrating as she claimed. In reality, a half-enchantress, like her mother, would not have any chance against a full-blooded witch, regardless of age or bloodline, and this most likely played a large part in the woman's disposition and choice of self-destructive pastimes.

"Alizon, you are not alone," Vlad said with heavy finality. "I want you not to just bear that in mind but to truly *know* it. If you feel you cannot escape then message me and I *will* come for you, wherever you are, at whatever time. No one should suffer in silence; you are all too precious for that."

Alizon nodded slightly, her tea clasped firmly in her hands to stop her fingers from shaking, and Vlad noted the similarity to how Jacob had sat in his apartment, too. People often reacted the same when unable to express themselves, and it was the one time Vlad had seen Alizon perform conventional body language.

Keen to move on and not embarrass Alizon by dwelling on her pain, Vlad asked the first question of everyone. Each said their piece, describing their weeks and how they felt about them. Fable was positive she had mastered the Sheffield tram systems and was now quite fluent in how they all functioned.

Lucy and Cain had eaten takeaway pizza and explored the grounds of Galloway's Mansion, tearing away at the thickets of overgrowth and trying to reach the deeper parts of the extensive garden structures. Lucy detailed how excited she was to finally see the observatory while Cain expressed interest in the notion of the vast greenhouses and how the old machinery within all worked. To finish, Lucy acknowledged she and Cain had tried to locate the secret room the three humans had broken in to uncover but they were unsuccessful.

Vlad realised it had only been half an hour and they had already finished question one. Without Jacob or Sarah present, they had stormed through the first section, yet the brevity seemed weighed by gravity. Vlad sighed inwardly and approached question two – do you have anything to get off your chest? – hoping Alizon had something joyful she could cling to.

Blood and Biscuits

"I don't have anything to vent," she stated almost pleasantly and Vlad knew the Chinese tea had removed much of the pain without her knowledge. "Nope, everything's quite alright now."

"Well good," Vlad said. "But if you do think of something please do not hesitate to let us know. There is no strict code to this, or a timetable, simply a set of guidelines. Fable?" Vlad asked.

The faerie looked up from analysing her blackened hands. "Yes?"

"Do you have anything to unleash?"

Fable evidently filed back through her memories.

"Aside from the trams I've been quiet of late. The pain in my hands has lessened further so I'm getting more sleep, yet to counteract this I have a worrying sense of disturbance, as if the balance of our group, and across the worlds, is off. I cannot explain it yet I dwell on it often."

"That's understandable," Lucy said and Vlad nodded. "What with Jacob not here and Sarah yet to join us."

"Indeed," Fable agreed, "though it's more than that. I feel in my core as if something greater is amiss. It annexes and dominates my mind."

"Is it an encroaching sense of doom, or does it manifest akin to general anxieties about nothing in particular?" Vlad asked.

Fable made a gesture.

"I...don't know. It could be both, I suppose."

"Then I suggest you concentrate on what is important and, when moments allow, give these thoughts more time for consideration. Something may hide in them. Though they are often untrustworthy, worries from magic should not be dismissed."

"As you advise," Fable said delicately and she sat back in her seat.

There was definitely a strangeness in the air, as if two absent members caused rifts in conversations. The dynamic had sapped and people were uneasy, unsure how to continue without what was quickly becoming apparent were two emotional nuclei of the group.

Blood and Biscuits

Vlad drank his coffee, watching people eat their biscuits quietly, eyes flitting around the basement aimlessly.

In the end, Vlad managed to extract small answers from Lucy and Cain regarding theirs struggles. Lucy's fears for Cain and his attitude of self-destruction had waned with his personal growth, only to be replaced by anxieties on his safety throughout his transformations. Cain, meanwhile, was growing more and more agitated that Lucy would never be free of her binding.

The fact both now worried for one another instead of themselves was not lost on Vlad.

He almost reiterated his promise to find a cure for them all but it would not help. People knew he was trying to save them yet continuously reminding them of his lack of success was tantamount to admitting failure – not something to repeatedly drill into people.

Vlad sat back and let them talk, a dozen matters on his mind. He knew not the appropriate time to discuss the ritual for opening the afterlife, nor did he quite know how to mention it would only be possible next week. These things warred across Vlad's mind as he watched and listened intently, trying not to seem like a man worrying upon deep things.

When at last they ended question two, Vlad suggested a ten-minute tea break. He needed to stop and think. Enthusiastically, Cain led the charge to the coffee table, hands immediately ripping apart a fresh pack of Jaffa cakes before anyone else could even sniff at them. Lucy grabbed four fig rolls and some prawn cocktail crisps while Alizon hung back so as not to bother anyone until they were all satisfied. Fable, meanwhile, was content with pouring herself a rosehip and fennel tea and taking four bourbon biscuits; Vlad noticed she now put away quite a few of them since learning they were animal friendly.

"How's Jacob?"

Vlad looked down – he had decided simply to lean against a wall and focus his thoughts to try to solve the conundrum of Sarah's departure. Lucy stood there, coffee in-hand. Cain glanced over and

Blood and Biscuits

she flashed him a smile full of warmth.

"He is…" Vlad hesitated, a hollow sigh whispering from his dead lungs, "not great. I went to his apartment to speak with him and though I think I made things a *little* better, I do not believe him convinced by our venture. I fear we must continue without him and hope, one day, we might see him again."

Lucy's face fell further with every word.

"Poor Jay, this must be so hard for him. It was a shock to us, too – Cain and I spoke about it a lot during the week, but that doesn't stop us from seeing that it's right. However, what Jay's been through perhaps tops us all, aside from you, Vlad."

Vlad waved the comment away.

"I have not assumed, and never will, I am any different from you, or that I have suffered any more. I have had *many* years to come to terms with my life and my choices in death. I do not expect those far younger than myself to do the same in far less time. My immortality has unshackled the man I once was from his long imprisonment within this monster before you."

"For what it's worth, you've helped us all through so much already and I, certainly, will never leave your side. And I don't see a monster, Vlad, I see *only* a man. A man full of guilt and pain, yeah, but goodness, too. You've given us somewhere to come and complain and get to know others like us. You've shown us a wider world already and made us believe we're not freaks, we're *not* monsters, that we can control who we are and really contribute something to our existence if we actually try. And, if you'll let us, we can do the same for you should you ever wish to include us in your extracurricular activities."

"I would like that very much. There are certainly a few more things I wish to show you all, should the time allow."

Vlad squeezed her shoulder affectionately. Lucy put her arm round his side and hugged him close, her cold palm hot through his shirt.

Lucy smiled again, her sharp-features beaming and glowing,

Blood and Biscuits

and Vlad mirrored the look.

"Come on," he said eventually, "let us return to our group and see if we might finally let question three see the light of day. It has been, what, eight weeks now? It is time to – oh! Now that *is* a surprise!"

"What?" Lucy asked anxiously. "What've you sensed?"

Vlad's power narrowed on a figure stepping within the boundaries of his awareness, their hurrying feet light across the wastelands of Ellin's Island. He recognised them and smiled a knowing smile.

"You will see soon, they are nearly here. If you would like a clue, it is Jacob."

"Wait, what?" Lucy exclaimed, her face a mixture of emotions. "That's not a clue, that's just the answer! How crap are you!"

"I know, I am no good at guessing games and I felt as if the moment needed no drawing out."

"Oi!" Lucy called over to Cain, Fable, and Alizon, her face beaming. "We've got a visitor!"

Everyone looked to the entranceway and sure enough, twenty seconds later, Jacob stepped down into the dim-lit basement, an extremely uncomfortable look upon his dilapidated face, balaclava twirling awkwardly in his grasp. Lucy marched forwards and hugged him before he could do or say anything, his mouth caught in a small 'o' of shock as his arms hugged her back, eyes squeezing shut a moment.

Then Lucy stood back and assessed him happily.

"It's good to have you back, Jay. Just don't hit Cain again, he moaned all week about it."

"Oh God, I'm so sorry," Jacob began as Cain walked up to him, face hard as rock. Vlad took a step towards them, wondering for a half-second if he might be required to halt an altercation before it had even begun. Yet he found surprise again as Cain took measure of Jacob then held out his hand.

"No hard feelin's, mate. I know you weren't yourself."

Jacob, clearly relieved more than anything else, took Cain's hand and shook three times, almost solemnly.

"I really am sorry, Cain. I was angry."

"That you were. But you're not now and that's what matters. It's good to have you back."

His tone was clipped and short but his manner was friendly even if he *reeked* of absolute restraint. Cain gave a tight smile and walked away again, and Vlad heard Jacob say to Lucy,

"I thought he'd be furious with me."

"Oh, he was," Lucy replied carefully. "But he's done a lot of soul-searching since then and came to the correct conclusions just in time."

"I'd imagine he had some input from you," Jacob commented and Lucy nodded.

"He wouldn't be able to cope without it, unfortunately," she smiled.

"So you two are doing well, then?" Jacob asked cautiously and Vlad smelled more than hope in his voice.

Lucy looked over at Cain and heat emanated from her, waves rising from her bones and blood.

"We are," she said simply. To a normal man that would have sounded curt but Vlad was not normal, and when he focussed his mind, he felt precisely what Lucy felt. Vlad's awareness of Cain had diminished entirely since drinking the werewolf's blood but he was still capable of understanding the emotions people gave off.

A glint of silver appeared from the ceiling and Vlad saw Sarah poking her head through the concrete. Nobody else saw her. Vlad gave her a thumbs up and she nodded, then she was gone again, to the church above to continue whatever she felt needed doing. Vlad guessed she was quite seriously saying a personal goodbye to every daffodil left in the churchyard.

Jacob approached and the vampire looked at him warmly.

"It is good you came back."

Jacob shrugged, as he always did.

"It was the right thing to do," he said simply. "But thank you."

"You are most welcome. The pleasure was all mine. Come," he said – the atmosphere of the room had improved with Jacob's arrival as the wraith retook his usual seat. "We are more complete but there is still yet ground to cover before we retire for the evening. If you would like, Jacob, we could let you tell us how your week has been and see if there is anything you might wish to get off your chest before we finally unlock the secrets of question three. Would that be acceptable?"

Jacob looked round at everyone and they all peered back at him. He gave off a scent of worry and then it was gone again, quenched by courage or something similar. Vlad watched the wraith sit straighter and face the room, hands clasped tightly in his lap as he spoke.

"I'm not here for that."

"No?" Vlad asked curiously. "Is that not what you wished for from this group? The peace and predictability of normality. To find strength in vulnerability."

"It was – well, at least…I thought it was. But I've had time to think, and with Fable's positive outlook on life suddenly gone this week – "

"I can only apologise a thousand times," Fable interjected but Jacob shook his head.

"That's not what I meant. It was a compliment, of sorts; you're brave to go out and see what you like of the world, even if it is just trams." Fable made a noise in her throat and Jacob reacted. "My bad, I meant trams are cool. Look, my point is I've had time to think it over, and without a force of absolute cheerfulness around it was easier to sort out the thoughts in my head one by one. And I think – *think*," he emphasised, "I've come to the conclusion that what I reckon about Sarah doesn't matter."

"Oh, but it does," Vlad said and Jacob glanced at him. "We

are emotional beings, this is important for what we do here. You, Jacob, I have found are a very emotion-based man when you want to be, and this is precisely what Sarah needs."

"It is?" the wraith asked curiously and Vlad nodded.

"Indeed. If we always let facts guide us, we would get precisely nowhere. Sarah has made her decision emotionally and, in that manner, we must respond in kind. Yet we cannot lose sight of morality, of what is right and what is easy, and I think that is where you have struggled."

"I guess that's right," Jacob agreed slowly. "It just really hit me hard, and it came outta' nowhere, too."

"That is my fault," Vlad said. "I should have been forthright from the beginning, I see that now."

"It's alright, you were only protecting Sarah. I see that, too. Still, I haven't fully come to terms with this but I think, in time, I'll walk the right path, the hardest one. I called my dad, actually – don't worry, I didn't speak about us lot, and he doesn't know about *me* yet. I just gave him a basic description, no ghosts, and he had some advice. Told me what mum would think, too. And yes, before you ask, I'll help you do this. That's what's right."

"Thank you," Vlad responded gently, a flush of gratitude flooding his cold, dead veins. "I think there is somebody living above us that will appreciate this very much. Sarah was quite upset when you left suddenly last week; she will be thrilled you are back amongst us."

"Yeah well…this is for her anyway."

"This is for all of us, Jay, it always has been," Lucy added. She reached across, as if bridging a yawning chasm between them, and took his hand. The act was only small yet it made a very real impact in Jacob's mood as he gave off a hundred scents. "Sarah is just a conclusion, I guess, to us all and how we came together. This is where she finds her peace, like we all will some day."

"This is her acceptance of who she is," Cain offered. "From what I've realised, that's all Vlad ever meant for us: to find a purpose

Blood and Biscuits

and follow it. Sarah's is to move on, that's all. It's beautiful, really."

Jacob sniffed loudly and looked away.

"So how do we do it?" he asked, his voice firm and strong, bolstered by determination. "You said you know a way."

"I do but it is far older than I am by several millennia, from the time of the building of the pyramids and beyond. And I am not sure yet as to how exactly we are going to get the catalyst started."

"The catalyst?" Alizon asked.

Vlad nodded and began his tale of Moira and the research station at the bottom of the world. He explained the Necrostone and how close Moira had come to unlocking its potential with the Spell of the Living Dead. Jacob crossed his arms heavily as everyone else listened, rapt with interest and filled with confusion, until Vlad reached the end of his story and sat back, preparing for the onslaught of questions. But they never came.

In fact, the only person that spoke was Alizon, and it was not what Vlad expected.

"Thank you for sharing, Vlad."

"You are...welcome?" he replied curiously.

"But you're wrong," she said firmly.

"Excuse me?"

Where the room was quiet before now it fell into a dragging silence, the intake of a deep breath. Alizon noticed none of it, her determination set.

"The Spell of the Living Dead, it doesn't mean that," she said.

"It is the closest approximation I have ever been able to find for what the stone texts describe," Vlad said. "I assure you, it-"

Alizon interrupted, no note of apology in her voice. Not that Vlad would have foreseen or needed one; apology is simply a facet of more regular conversational techniques. Alizon was not 'regular'.

"No, that lyric is different, subtly so. You said the texts state the Necrostone can only be awakened by something that lives as in death and dies as in life."

"Yes, so a lyric giving the illusion of life by conjuring the reanimation of death. Not to cause any offence but that does describe a few of our group."

Lucy cleared her throat and Jacob shuffled in his seat. Vlad inclined his head towards them both.

"As I said, I mean no offence."

Alizon shook her head. "Again, no. If there's one thing I know, spell lyrics are notoriously misleading. They're like a genie's wish from those old stories: you must be absolutely precise in your meaning, leave nothing open to misinterpretation. Otherwise, you'd wish for a tonne of gold and a block of it appears above your head and squashes you. I'd say these ancient texts will be exactly the same: misleading."

Something stirred in Vlad, a spark of hope burning the failure awakened by the demon of his depression.

"Go on," he measured.

Every face watched them avidly. Alizon cleared her throat and continued, nervously.

"Well…it's as I said. That spell name gives the impression of what you said, so I'm not surprised you didn't notice the hidden meaning. From what I can tell, though I've never heard of this Necrostone or its texts before, the meaning's actually something that's *almost* like life that then dies *almost* like normal. A bridge. Then, you see, you don't have spell lyrics to misinterpret, just cold hard facts of life and death. That, I'm guessing, is what this Necrostone's about, really, whatever it is."

Vlad pondered Alizon's words as they echoed in his mind, turning over again and again, trying to make sense of them.

"Wonderful," he finally sighed. "Now we are further than ever before and the one hope I had for freeing Sarah is gone. No, Alizon, it is not your fault, before you try and say anything to that effect," Vlad added as the witch opened her mouth to speak. She sat back again, a scent of relief spreading from her. "It is just…I cannot see what else might be the answer. The texts were so old already that much of them had faded, and to translate I had to recall quite a significant chunk of middle Egyptian language I thought lost to me so I could use *that* to translate further back in history from stone records."

"I mean, *you're* kinda' like that," Jacob muttered as Vlad continued.

"Indeed, I was not fluent when middle Egyptian was still being *spoken*, so imagine how hard it was…to…"

Vlad stopped and looked at Jacob suddenly.

"What did you say?" he asked quickly.

Jacob looked up in surprise. He had not expected a response.

"I, err, meant *you're* a bit like that, Vlad. You know, dead but not dead, alive but not alive. You said it weeks ago, at least in essence."

"Did I?" Vlad queried.

"Yeah, something to do with souls. You said you don't have one. But you didn't mention Lucy or me, so really if we've still *got* our souls intact inside us then surely we're not altogether dead. And since you're already pretty old who's to say vampires don't hark back from way before *you*? I mean, nobody really *knows* the origins of humans so they definitely won't know people like us, will they? Vampires could have been around since the dawn of humans, meaning you guys are intrinsically linked. That make sense?"

"Yes, I have always argued for the case of vampires as guardians of humans, but…" He stopped, considering matters thoroughly. He tilted his head, analysing minute aspects from different angles, mouth twitching wordlessly as he processed everything. "I suppose that is factually correct – that you are not altogether dead, I mean. The beating of the heart does not define life, it is just a pump for the body. Many things are alive without hearts, after all. Many things that are dead still have moving blood. *My* blood courses through my veins through the magic of my curse, something that would drive scientists to insanity, I am sure. Hmm…"

Vlad paused, every eye and ear trained on him. He was the

centre of the room.

"Banshees and wraiths *do* need a certain period within which they – sorry, *you* – can be created, else their bodies simply become corpses. Your curse does that for you. After death, the soul does not leave the body immediately; it takes a little while before it can properly coalesce every experience and emotion in life before departing this world as a single unit, to put it clinically. If not cursed, then a soul needs to wait until the mortal world aligns with the afterlife, at either dusk or dawn. To reanimate a true corpse, one without curse or soul, is to create a Furie, a mindless drone driven by rage and hunger only. This requires magic of a different kind."

"But vampires are different," Cain pointed out. "You guys run around without souls but you're properly dead."

"True, so far as I have surmised from my studies," Vlad agreed. He felt as if his mind had been hurtling at top speed but was now mired in mud, sticking at every functional opportunity. "So that would mean vampires…live as if we are dead. Our bodies do not live at all! Your bodies are still fuelled by food and your souls whereas ours are by blood, by darkness. Every thought and experience you have still builds your souls whereas vampires simply move and think as if we are alive but are, in fact, dead…And, therefore, we live as in death. *True* death. And if we were to die it would be as if in life, as our bodies turn to the dusts of time. Oh my. Oh my indeed."

Vlad smiled a strange smile and peered at them all.

"You think you've got it?" Lucy asked excitedly.

"I believe I have, or rather Jacob has," Vlad said, hardly able to contain the bonfire growing in him. Then he faltered. "But it could not work, surely. I cannot simply *die* to unlock the Necrostone, that is ludicrous! There was no mention of a trade in the ancient texts, no statement of one life for a death. That makes no sense! But still, one does have to wonder."

"You're starting to ramble," Lucy said. "And I think we're all confused."

Vlad did not respond but instead turned to the faerie.

Blood and Biscuits

"Fable, how willing would you be to channel just a little of your magic? If you still can, that is."

Fable was clearly taken by surprise.

"Um, I suppose I could, though it might set back my healing again."

"And I would not wish you to suffer any more than you have. However, this may be the only way. If it helps, I think I might be able to find something similar to Alizon's tea that could aid you."

"If I use my magic now will it help further our cause?"

"I cannot give you certainty but I am confident it is the answer, yes."

"Then I see no choice but to oblige," Fable sighed, lifting herself from her seat heavily, damaged hands pushing from her legs determinedly. "What is it you need, precisely?"

Vlad walked into the middle of the circle. He found a spot in the floor that dipped inwardly and lowered a section of his control. Immediately, a sliver of power pushed into his veins and Vlad extended an iron-hard claw. He pressed the nail against the cold skin of his wrist, felt the pinch. He had been here before. Mouths fell open, horrified, as Vlad pushed the nail into the flesh of his forearm and scored a thin, deep gash. Cuthbert, his demon, lashed out and Vlad felt the sickening sensation of being in control of his pain. He was the master of himself, the wound proved that.

Dark-red, almost black, blood poured from his arm and cascaded to the floor as Lucy and Jacob gasped and Cain swore loudly. Fable and Alizon watched, fascinated, as Vlad directed the blood into the dip then stood back. His darkness sealed the wound in his arm as Cuthbert roared in his head. He hated it when Vlad controlled his depression.

The blood stopped. No scar, no physical memory defining his despair.

"There, that is the essence of the vampire," he said quietly, indicating the pool in the floor. "It is what guides and commands us in place of our soul. Our blood is the very core of who and what we

Blood and Biscuits

are, something that might drive biologists *and* Jehovah's Witnesses mad, forget the physicists. Fable, I want you to channel Light magic into the blood and we shall see what happens."

"But you withstand sunlight," Cain said, sickness lining his face as his eyes darted to the pooled blood. "And you can withstand Fable's magic to some degree."

"Indeed but blood outside my body is far weaker, denied its protection from darkness. It will take little to destroy, I assure you. Against the Sect of Light, it shall be no less vulnerable than a candle's flame suffocated by sand."

Fable nodded and placed her hands together. Her teeth gritted, the familiar electrical sensation crackling into the air. Finally, a shiver of Light appeared, overwhelmingly bright. Fable grunted in pain as she directed the magic down into the pool, and with a sudden flash and an acrid burning smell, the blood burst into black flame and vanished. Vlad smiled darkly as Fable tied off her magic and the Light disappeared. Everyone leaned in curiously, eager to see what remained.

There, where blood had been moments before, was a small pile of pure crimson powder.

"What's *that*?" Cain asked quickly, leaning so far forward he nearly fell off his chair.

"That, my dear friends, is *blood ash*, the remains of a vampire when they are ignited by the sun, in this case Fable's Light magic. Does anyone have a small bag I might borrow?"

Alizon raised her hand then reached down between her legs. She pulled out a dark-green, sequined handbag and emptied the contents into her lap.

"Here," Alizon said proudly, handing Vlad the sparkling handbag. He looked it over and tried to find a sincere smile as Alizon said, "You may keep it. I can always find another."

"Thank you very much," Vlad replied smoothly, bending down to the floor and scooping up the blood ash into the handbag. "I shall take this to Moira tomorrow and test it against the Necrostone.

I hope it works or else we must wait too long to open the afterlife."

"Things seem to have changed a lot in the last few weeks," Cain muttered. Everyone looked at him and he sat a little straighter, arms still folded tightly. "Well it's true. Transforming's one thing but actually openin' the afterlife? *That* is some seriously heavy stuff. I will need a *lot* of Jaffa cakes to get me through it."

The group laughed and the moment's tension dissipated at the familial ease. Though Cain was right, Vlad knew they would get through it together.

Vlad sighed and hefted the small bag of blood ash. He cursed himself for having not worked through the meaning of the ancient texts more carefully, and yet he knew it simply was not possible to know absolutely everything. He stared round the group as they stood and joked in the same manner they always did at the end of a session – even Jacob managed a grin or two – and Vlad knew he had needed them from the start, much as they all needed him. He finished his coffee and thought on the ritual for Sarah, keeping in mind everything that must be completed to bring the gates of the afterlife crashing against this world, and to force them open to permit a ghost.

Things were not going to be easy.

THE RESEARCH FACILITY OF THE SOUTH POLE, TUESDAY.

Vlad touched down upon the shining, shimmering ice with more finesse this time. He shook snow from his eyes. It was nearly a blizzard now, the constant evening sun hardly visible through the thick flurry of flakes pouring from the sky. Snowstorms were rare across the deserts of Antarctica yet there happened to be one then. Vlad felt a muted sense of privilege.

Approaching the facility, he knocked upon the door politely and waited, sensing Moira's hurried footsteps. She opened the door, a shawl about her face.

Blood and Biscuits

"Come in quickly, you're lettin' the cold in!"

Vlad stepped inside and sealed the door. The veil of snow beyond the windows blocked the sunlight, casting the room in darkness.

"I'm glad you're back," she announced happily. "Coffee?"

"A quick one would be most welcome," Vlad replied smoothly, dropping the bag he carried to the floor. It was smaller this time, discrete. "I cannot stay long, I have experiments to return to."

"Ahh, still runnin' that lab o'yours," Moira said interestedly as she tipped water into the kettle and started it boiling. "What's on the agenda this time, troll repellent? Imp bait? Banshee or wraith attractant?"

Vlad shook his head.

"Werewolf blood. I am determining the origins of a new clan I have discovered." Moira made an 'ooo' sound. Vlad continued. "But on the subject of my friends, it turns out all I needed to do was post an online advert and the banshees and wraiths came to me. The modern world has changed things since the old days, everyone came to the Support Group of their own volition. There is elegance in that. I used no guise or pretence."

"Other than withholdin' the true purpose of the group," Moira muttered as she finished the coffees, handing a steaming mug over. It felt like a furnace in Vlad's dead hands. "So did you tell 'em all why you *really* started the sessions?"

"Of course I did," Vlad exclaimed indignantly. "Though Sarah was not my only intention, I was fully committed to continuing the sessions to prove we can all treat each other equally, to co-exist peacefully. It is working far better than I could have hoped. I only hid what I needed until now because releasing Sarah requires everyone's trust, something never thought possible before, not by me and certainly not by the Order of the Obsidian Moon."

Moira shuddered, her hand twitching to where twin point scars shone brightly against the dark skin of her neck. The fangs that had made those did not belong to Vlad.

𝔅lood and 𝔅iscuits

"Don't mention that bloody Order again," she hissed, sipping her coffee. "Some memories never fade, Vlad."

"I apologise, they are still extremely active and I worry about them constantly, but you are right to ignore them. They are gone from your life now, Moira, I made sure of that."

"And what about Jacob?" she enquired. As she drank, Vlad noticed the bandage beneath her sleeve.

"I wish you would let me heal you," he stated but Moira shook her head.

"I said no, Vladislav. I prefer to recover the old-fashioned ways, the *human* ways. You remember them days, don't you?"

"Like they were yesterday," Vlad said coolly.

Moira sucked her teeth irritably.

"And you avoided my question about Jacob. It was a direct one, too, so no runnin' round it with your fancy pants words."

Vlad sighed.

"Jacob has rejoined us of his own choice after I spoke to him personally," he began and Moira smiled.

"Ahh, that *is* good. I know you were worried about him."

"I still am," Vlad admitted. "He seems to carry the weight of everything and everyone on his shoulders."

"Just as you used to – and still do, if you'd ever admit you still need help with your depression. When's the last time you hurt yourself?"

"Yesterday, but that was for a reason."

"I'm sure it was. And the times before?"

"Not for a few weeks now."

"I suppose that's positive, you concentrate on that. The less you punish yourself the better. You know, John really could…"

Vlad held up his hand.

"I know of your husband's abilities and his ways with people but I would not put that pressure on him. He has always been kind yet I know what it is like to face somebody who loved who you love and it is not something I would make him face. It is best I leave your family well alone."

Moira looked at Vlad strangely.

"My God, you men. He would be proud to have you visit us more often than every few years, you know. The kids always love you! And *we* were a long time ago, Vlad, you and I. *And* that was before I even *knew* John! You and I were different back then; we had the whole world at our feet."

"And I could have given you immortality and you refused it," Vlad said, the old wound he thought had healed cracking. "But you were right to choose as you did and you have the beautiful family I never could have given you."

Moira smiled and touched Vlad's arm. She still felt like she used to, the way she held him in that simple way, and for one single moment, Vlad could have sworn he was alive again, *human*. He turned and picked up Moira's wedding picture from the side, and he stared at the smiling people.

"You know, I never once regretted askin' you to give me away, Vlad," Moira said quietly as she peered round his shoulder, her small frame pressing to him as she used to, forming against him. It meant nothing, and Vlad would never once consider acting on his urges, yet that moment of companionship gave him hope for his own future.

"I know," he said, hardly above a whisper. Moira leaned over and pointed at the space in the picture beside her mother, the space where her father should have been.

"It certainly gave people summat' to talk about when the photographer couldn't capture you," she said with a deep smile. "My mother approved of you, you know; her jokes about pale men was just her way, she was very fond of you and your kindness. I was the happiest woman that day when she asked you to pose with her, and when you danced in the evenin'."

"I remember the day to the last flower. You remember the page boy-

"-that tripped over his laces and got my train dirty? I

remember you cleanin' it off for the photo, too."

Vlad smiled. "You know, the photo-invisibility is one of the many things I am still researching." He put the picture back down again.

"Why vampires have reflections but don't appear in photos? Or why their clothes also disappear when they're pictured?" Moira asked with a laugh and Vlad echoed her sentiment.

"Both, I suppose." He paused and looked at the picture again: it really *had* been a wonderful day. "Anyway, it is time I told you why I am here."

"Does the answer lie in that bag o'yours? Because if not, I hope it's stuffin' and sausages to go with that massive turkey you gave me! You know I'm gonna' invite you over for Christmas, don't you?"

"I do and I appreciate the offer. But-"

"But you'll be busy, I know. It's a shame, the grandkids would love to meet you; you've got a quietly funny side to you that's rare in people these days. So brash and loud they can be. And my own kids would appreciate seein' you, too, not just their children."

"Do they suspect anything yet?"

"I mean they're bright, and they're definitely not young anymore. You haven't aged in thirty-five years, Vlad, so I'd imagine they've started suspectin' summat'. I'll ask 'em when I get back home - when *did* you say I can fly back?"

"The twenty-first, as long as this blizzard has disappeared. And no, this bag may hold the secret to all of our problems. Well, the Necrostone's problems. Certainly not any of the other rocks, especially the Volcan Spheres. And definitely not the Steel Fountain, *Christ*." Moira rolled her eyes at the mention of the humungous medieval artefact Vlad had brought back ten years before as the vampire reached into his bag and pulled out Alizon's small, dark-green handbag. He held it out for Moira and she gazed at it with her eyebrows raised.

"Well *that's* a nice purse," she said, her mouth twitching

ever-so-slightly. "You been strugglin' with these feelin's for long, have you?"

"Oh, for heaven's sake! *Inside* the bag, woman! My God, your dryness is exhausting sometimes."

"I learned from the master," she muttered as she opened the handbag. Her eyes reflected the crimson of the blood dust within and she cocked her head. "Is this…vampire ash?"

"From my own veins, yes," Vlad said and he explained what the Support Group had discussed and discovered. "This, Moira, may well be the answer."

"Well it's worth a shot," she said, closing the bag again. "Ain't like the Necrostone can be used up. Come on, let's get it over with. I could do with another disappointment before bed."

Once more, they left the living quarters and entered the glittering Stone Room. Moira went to take the bag to the Necrostone, its rough black form still held in the brass machine's fingers, but Vlad made a noise in his throat. Moira glanced at him.

"What's up?"

"Try the bowl configuration instead of the grasp complex, I feel the stone needs to come into contact with *all* of it."

"As you wish," Moira replied easily.

She removed the Necrostone from its holding and bent the brass fingers down. They clicked smoothly out of the way and a shallow-set bowl rose from beneath, the hidden mechanisms working intricately. Moira placed the Necrostone in the centre of the bowl then re-opened the dark-green handbag. She glanced at Vlad, his arms folded, one hand rubbing his chin thoughtfully.

"The whole lot of it?"

He nodded tightly and watched as Moira upended the purse, the crimson ash settling on and around the Necrostone heavily. Nothing happened for a long moment and Vlad grew impatient. Moira sighed.

Suddenly, the stone texts passed through his thoughts and Vlad made a noise of irritation.

Blood and Biscuits

"I am a fool," he muttered.

He strode across the wide floor and pressed a button on a control panel. Immediately, two hatch doors slid apart in the ceiling and cold air blasted into the room, whirling round the collection of stones. Moira screamed, grabbing an emergency thermal jacket from a hook.

"Give me some bloody warnin', Vlad!" she cried.

He apologised profusely and pressed another control. Four sets of large mirrors angled up from the station's roof and aimed down into the room. Vlad operated a directional control and manually rotated the mirrors until they reflected the sun. Its light was streaked and obscured through the howling blizzard.

Vlad measured a large portion of darkness into his veins and sent out a long shadow of force across the ice, and with a *push* of power, the snow blasted from the skies, scattering across the lands. The sun's gaze bloomed and shafts beamed down into the Stone Room in a cascade of perma-evening, the columns striking the Necrostone in its bowl and disappearing into its black and white-striped form.

The reaction was immediate.

The Necrostone shimmered lightning hot. It dazzled white yet gave off shadow – it was the actual *creation* of pure darkness, just like the power lurking in Vlad's body. The blood dust lifted from the bowl and Vlad approached the brass machine in muted, cautious wonder. Moira joined him carefully.

"In all my days," she whispered.

The floating dust gleamed and winked in the darkness and the sunlight, and then it was absorbed. The Necrostone drank every particle into itself and began to spin, pulsing crimson, shining ever brighter. The stone lifted from the bowl and hovered before them, bathed in light and dark as snow swirled all about it in the returning wind.

"It's so beautiful, yet it makes me so sad. How's this possible with the dust of your blood when the Spell of the Livin' Dead failed?" Moira asked in the storm of light and old magic.

"It would appear vampires may well be the key to the afterlife," Vlad called over the wind. "*One* of the keys, anyway. I honestly cannot give you an answer. It is all merely…speculative, I suppose."

"You know enough from your studies," she began.

"No, this is purely educated guesswork. Maybe, if there *is* a god up there in some capacity, they created vampires to cull the immoral and the weak from the world so the good and the strong may flourish."

"I hope *that's* not from your studies," Moira added.

In the swirl of wind and snow and light and dark, Vlad laughed.

"No, Christ no, it was a joke. Besides, even if that *was* our purpose, we have never exactly stuck to that principle. Vampires are guided by greed and malice as much as humans," Vlad said as the Necrostone slowed, lowering back into its brass bowl. "Ahh, I believe the catalysis is over. Although, perhaps another term would be appropriate as my blood has very much been used up."

The Necrostone halted and returned to its original black form, its two white stripes the last to lose their lustre. Vlad walked to the controls and folded the roof mirrors away. The panels closed as Moira shivered and rubbed her arms despite the thick coat she wore.

She pointed to the stone.

"It still didn't work," she said. "Didn't open the afterlife, I mean."

"No and it will not until we stand at dusk and complete the ritual with my Support Group. The Necrostone is just one part of it – the most vital part, certainly, but one part all the same. We will need everyone if we are to send Sarah to what death may hold beyond the veil."

Moira sighed through her teeth.

"I tell you, Vlad, if you get through all'a this and Sarah's sent to her true death, good and proper, then you're gonna' *need* a Christmas with friends."

"First, I promised to take one of those friends on a little trip north. He does not know it yet but he is about to learn a lot more about his curse."

Mind Over Mountain

The freezing wind whistled as Vlad set his feet upon the rocky ledge and released his cargo. Cain stepped away carefully and shivered, hands plunging into his pockets for warmth.

"Good *Christ*, it's cold," he hissed, stamping his boots, teeth chattering. "Lowlands weren't too bad, managed to keep it together over Edinburgh. I'm normally fine in the cold but this is somethin' else!"

"Really? I cannot feel a thing," Vlad said pleasantly, his knee-length coat of thin, black cloth flapping in the wind, the untied grey belt flowing behind him. He looked at Cain and raised an eyebrow.

Finally, the werewolf sighed and held out a shivering hand.

"Fine, I'll take the coat and hot water bottle, are you happy?"

"Extremely," Vlad said, self-satisfaction brimming over into his voice. He looped the insulated bag off his shoulder and pulled out a fleece-lined, cold-weather coat, a pair of ski gloves, a maroon bobble-hat, and a pink fluffy hot water bottle that radiated heat. "I am not sure why you refused the offer of warm gear, Cain. These are the Grampian Mountains, after all, and it *is* coming into winter..."

Vlad left the statement open as Cain eagerly pulled on the coat and stuffed the hot water bottle inside it, then jammed the hat over his head and pulled the gloves on, dancing around until he started seeming warmer.

"I don't really know, I was in a real bad mood and I was feelin' childish, I guess. Maybe it's an early full moon comin'. S'pose I felt I had somethin' to prove when you offered me warm clothes. I didn't mean to be rude, Vlad, I apologise."

"No apology necessary." Vlad stared at the mountain rising above them, its peak curling over gloomily, gigantic icicles

Blood and Biscuits

glistening in the low sunlight. "How is your back? Recovered enough for the climb?"

Cain pressed his palm against his side and stretched a little. Grimacing, he nodded.

"Yeah, seems alright. Wish Jacob hadn't thrown me but I understand his anger. I'd have been annoyed if I'd been in his position – I'm impressed you got him to back."

Vlad shrugged.

"I needed guidance on how to convince him but, ultimately, the decision was his."

"And was your blood sand a success with that Necro-thingy?"

"It most certainly was." A bittersweet sensation filled Vlad. "The stone absorbed my blood dust and its enchantments were activated. It was breathtakingly beautiful to watch."

"Blood dust, that was it, not blood sand. Good, then, that means we can do your ritual next week. Good, good, good."

Vlad detected a hint of strain in Cain's voice and guessed the man did not actually wish to discuss such matters. There was something else that stuck, though.

"So what was your bad mood about?"

"Oh, err, stuff about my parents."

"What about them?"

Cain's shoulders shifted a little.

"Nothin' much, really - sounds stupid now - I had a nightmare about 'em, couldn't see their faces but I knew it was them. Woke up in a stinkin' mood, like they'd abandoned me all over again. It's nothin'."

"Maybe, maybe not. Unless you are clairvoyant, dreams rarely contain worldly visions, yet they still hold importance. Many emotions can be worked through while you sleep and your memory is stimulated in a myriad of ways. You create stories to sort through problems or understand yourself better. Perhaps your

Blood and Biscuits

unconsciousness was recalling their faces while your emotional mind was attempting to understand why they are no longer around."

"I dunno', all sounds a bit fancy for me."

Cain's blunt response told Vlad he did not wish to continue this matter either, so after a moment's hesitation he changed subject back to the mountain.

"Now you are sated and warm would you care to guess how long it will take to climb to the top of this slope?"

Cain put his gloved hands on his hips, leaned back, and whistled.

"Twenty quid says half an hour. Without darkness, mind."

"Naturally. Consider yourself on, Cain; I match twenty pounds but say *forty* minutes."

They climbed, hand over hand, crampons digging into thick sheets of ice, fingers gripping chunks of snow, as vampire and werewolf scrambled up the vicious rise. Grunting, growling, they threw themselves up the mountainside, faster and faster in the unlikely competition. Their efforts turned to echoing cries of laughter as whole panes of ice dislodged beneath their feet and slid down the mountain's steep sides.

"Nearly at the top now, that twenty pounds will be mine, Cain!"

"Not on your death, pal! Where's this summit?" Cain asked as they hauled themselves through an icy crag then shimmied up a sheer rock wall. "And why'd we climb this last bit when you could've flown us all the way to the top?"

"We are not far, and I thought the exercise would do you good."

"Well that's rude - oof!" Cain gasped, his foot slipping beneath him, fingers catching a frozen ledge. He dangled precariously as Vlad waited coolly, watching him regain his grip. Cain struggled as the clouds parted high above, and then his hand found purchase and he wrenched himself to the mountain's top shelf, crawling over until flat on his back. Cain lay panting as Vlad pulled himself up and crouched beside him, smiling broadly at the werewolf.

"Do you have any idea what you have just achieved?" Vlad asked after a few seconds' recovery.

Cain pulled his wrist up and checked his digital watch with a twisted grin.

"Yeah, I've just achieved twenty quid, mate. Thirty-three minutes' climb, bloody good effort, I'll give you me bank deets later."

"Do not say *deets*, it is beneath you. And you said half an hour, that hardly qualifies as correct."

"Yeah but I was closer than your forty, so cough up, fangy."

"Very well, I shall do a transfer later. That is if I do not lose my patience with the person on the other end of the phone after the bank's online app inevitably fails me."

"Cash is fine, I'll use it for a couple buckets of fried chicken."

"My god, that sounds disgusting. You are going to die an early death one day if you keep eating such disastrous food. Please do not tell me you frequent these places regularly, Cain."

"I...go a fair bit, that's all I'll say."

"Your poor liver. Anyway, the time is not what I meant; look at your fingers."

"Eh?" Cain said, gazing at his hand. "I don't - oh! Oh wow, look at that!"

Cain moved his fingers round in the pale moonlight, staring at the five black claws that had burst out the tips of his gloves.

"Now how in the hell...?" Cain trailed off.

"Stress," Vlad said. "Emotional and physical. Combined with the location, and distance from any electric light or sanctified ground, and given just the right conditions of your strange curse. Come, stand and walk with me."

The vampire held out his hand and the werewolf took it, hauling easily to his feet as they started up the snowy tundra of the sloped mountaintop.

Blood and Biscuits

"This has never happened before, Vlad. What's this place? I don't understand," Cain said disjointedly.

"I never wholly expected you to, even I am unsure on most of it. Until I learn what your blood contains we might only guess at the reasons underlying any of your abilities and aspects. Perhaps your curse is so powerful details of your wolf reveal themselves in conditions less favourable to transformation."

"You're not suggestin' I could turn without moonlight, are you? This is just a reaction, like my allergies! It's just latent from the blue moon." Cain gave a half laugh, though not in earnest. "What you're sayin's ridiculous."

"I am saying nothing. Your blood solution has simply yielded an answer I did not think possible. I combined its distillate with fresh, mature chrysanthemum leaves, famed for light sensitivity, and the poison of sacred datura, a type of moon flower that blooms at night. I consulted a repository of particular knowledge and found a grimoire on chemical potion making lore that instructed me to add powdered salamander claw to bind the flower ingredients in the solution. Your blood gave the slightest change in state of matter, which was enough to tell me all about this," Vlad finished, pointing to the waxing gibbous moon above. "The mountain was my idea."

"Jeez, Vlad, it's too cold up here to start thinkin' about all that language, I can't even understand basic chemistry! How's any of this relate to me?"

"I see your claws have gone again," Vlad pointed out.

Cain glanced at his gloved hands curiously.

"I'm not feeling weird in any way," he said absently. "Maybe it's just a fluke."

"Perhaps," Vlad said quietly, voice dancing along the a shadow's tip. "You find science uninteresting, Cain, but one day it will answer what you are. Leave me to find these aspects of you but there are others only you can explain. There is something you ought to see, it might give you some perspective, and it will answer your queries on this hidden place in the Grampians."

Blood and Biscuits

Vlad did not speak of the slight electrical sense in the air, the lasting remnants of old magic still present in the life of the mountain.

Cain followed the vampire into that twinkling white scape. "I think I see a light," he said. "There someone livin' up here?"

"Nobody has been these ways in over a century," Vlad replied smoothly. "The light is of another kind. You will see."

Dark shapes appeared ahead, solid and tall, and amongst them an arch loomed. Strange symbols marked the stones of its curve, a spiked torch bowl swinging in its centre, a fire in its pit. The bright flames fluttered in the wind, heedless of the mountain's attempts to extinguish.

"There is old power here, Cain," Vlad said quietly as the werewolf stared. "Magic I cannot understand. Flames to outlive all those they once shone for."

"That fire's been burnin' over a century, you say, and it's never gone out. I guess it's to guide people here."

"No, it is to illuminate the warning on the stones," Vlad said, pointing at the symbols curving round the arch. "A warning to stay away, for travellers to keep from what lies ahead. Not that they ever understood the symbols but it is ominous enough to make its point."

Passing under the arch, soon the two men walked into an old ruin, a haunting piece of history broken open by weather and time, Cain's eyes darting to every corner and edge, anything hiding a threat.

"What is this place?" he asked as he turned, his worried, curious gaze taking in the tattered fabrics of tapestries, shards of stained glass still fixed in their frames, upper floors bare to the world, a belfry knocked over, lying strewn in blocks across the mountaintop. More symbols marked the walls and doorway lintels. "Some ancient castle? It'd be pretty low if it was, not like Windsor."

"It is no castle but a temple, Cain, fallen long ago. Its occupants – the followers of its faith and teachings – were hunted and driven out," Vlad explained, placing a hand on a stripped wooden timber poking out from the rock walls and shaking his head.

Blood and Biscuits

"A sad, sorry state of affairs, I am afraid. Would you care to hazard a guess as to the nature of these believers?"

"I wouldn't have a clue."

"Oh I would not bring you here if I thought you *knew* straight off. I am not so unprepared as that. There is the slightest taint of something in the walls, Cain, all you must do is touch them. The answer will come to your senses eventually. I am serious, place your hands on the stone and close your eyes, concentrate your subconscious mind. Do not look at me like that, I have not lost my marbles. Do as I say, what could you possibly lose? Not twenty pounds, that I can assure you."

Cain watched Vlad closely. After a moment, he removed his gloves, closed his eyes, and lay his hands on a column of stone, the freezing surface rough, solid, defying the battering onslaught of wind and snow that had yet to rip it down. He gritted his teeth and pushed his hands hard against the stone, the driving snow disappearing into the background as his heart hammered in his big chest, blood surging through his veins, arteries opening and howling as the wolf buried in his curse came alive in the bright moonlight. Cain's head twitched as he felt four-legged phantoms, heavy and snarling, prowl past him, his teeth bared as a flood of visions of beasts running down a mountainside came to him then. He felt their hunger and their cold, their wants and their urges beating as Cain's own blood beat through his body, thrumming in waves of the hunt, history leaching from that wall.

A distant, guttural snarl from somewhere surprised him and Cain stepped back suddenly, breathing hard, jaw clenched. He pulled on his gloves again.

"What did you feel?" Vlad asked gently.

"I dunno', but whatever it was it was angry," he bit, his tone as icy as the weather.

"I think you *do* know, Cain, but you do not want to admit it. I will show you something else, come."

𝔅lood and 𝔅iscuits

Cain had no choice but to follow Vlad through a smashed doorframe. They delved long, dark corridors until they came into an open room, its roof somehow preserved. In the centre, there stood a tall stone pillar leaning to one side, its angular faces glinting dully. Vines grew down one side whilst a strange language covered another, thin gouges torn in beautiful shapes from the stone. More symbols. Fat, oval stones of different colours were embedded in the pillar and shone with light; the dark vine leaves seemed to grow around them, as if avoiding their beauty.

Cain approached and, despite the cold, stopped and crouched before the pillar, his great shoulders hunched as he looked the stone over. There was longing in his eyes.

"What is it you see?" Vlad asked, his darkness devouring the room.

"I...don't know. These symbols," he trailed off, tracing a finger along the grooves of a few runes. He looked up at Vlad, a strange look in his face. "I dunno' what any of this is but I feel I've seen it before. Vlad, why do I know these symbols? What the hell is this place?"

Vlad smiled.

"They are Scratch Runes, Cain. The hidden language of werewolves."

Cain glanced back at the pillar.

"Werewolf language..." he whispered. "It's werewolves," he whispered. "Werewolves worshipped here. Back there, I felt them...runnin' down the mountain together, like they some sort of...some kind of..."

"Some kind of a *pack*," Vlad finished. Cain's mouth slid open, eyes widening. "Oh yes," Vlad said, pulling his bag back round as he spoke, "a pack of werewolves. The only one I ever heard about, living as humans atop this mountain and changing together every full moon. It is a wonderful thought, is it not?" He reached into his bag and pulled out a thermos. "I have here a different way to ignite the blood - hot spiced rum?"

Blood and Biscuits

"Ooh," Cain said, rubbing his arms to generate heat. "Chuck it here, then." Vlad obliged and Cain caught the thermos with both hands. He popped the lid and took a swig, gasping delightedly at the warmth and taste. "Lovely, that. Ain't a martini but it's good all the same."

Vlad took back the thermos and he drank his own dram, measuring the moment pleasantly as he stared at the pillar in fascination, savouring the *scents* of the rum.

"How'd I sense the wolves that used to live here in that wall?" Cain asked quietly, his words not breaking the silence but enhancing it. "I felt their hunt, like I was runnin' with 'em myself. It was like I was part of their pack."

Vlad patted a nearby wall, one still holding a small fragment of an old tapestry.

"And how did that make you feel?" he asked quietly.

Cain had clearly not thought about it but the answer came easily.

"Like for a moment I *belonged*."

Vlad smiled.

"Do you have a faith, Cain?"

The man kicked his foot out and blew through his lips.

"Nah, not really. I know Jacob likes his Christianity and Alizon's got some Wiccan in her – I think Fable's probably some kind of faerie Buddhist – but I've never given over to all that. Seen too many places and been looked after by too many people to've been raised in one belief, and I don't like the idea that there's a god that chose this life of pain for me. I like bein' responsible of my own failures."

"Very interesting. See I, too, hold that we choose our own destiny. Though religion and predetermination are two separate things, it might surprise you that the werewolves living here did have a faith. They were none of them the same, from all walks of life and religions, yet all were joined in their belief of a *lower* god, a watcher of wolves. Tales differed in origin and purpose of this god, though many agreed He was the servant of a high god of death."

"Why death?" Cain asked, rubbing his chest to restore warmth to his core.

Vlad shrugged.

"That I do not know but it has a nice ring to it, does it not? I brought you here not only to show you what was possible so long ago for werewolves but also because the ritual we have to open the afterlife is Ancient Egyptian in origin. Now you may wonder what this temple and Egyptian history have in common, and the answer is the square root of bugger all."

Cain snorted.

"However, a werewolf is needed in the ritual, it is a categorical fact of the texts I found alongside the Necrostone. We *must* have a werewolf as part of the process of physically opening the gates to oblivion; hieroglyphs contain images of Anubis, a god with a wolf's head, and stories detail His son, a wolf named Wepwawet, as the figurative opener of ways. It is my guess this belief was inspired by the appearance of wild werewolves in Ancient Egypt, and their inclusion in the ritual to open the afterlife. All of this means, Cain, that your kind date back to at least as old as mine, and given how strictly religious Egyptians were it is not difficult to see that they perhaps *revered* werewolves, much as they did cats. The ancients had very real, very powerful connections to death. Many faiths believe in gods watching over specific creatures and all have higher beings watching over people; surely it makes sense to have a god watching over those that are both?"

"Yeah, I guess, as much as faith can make sense."

"That is a very pertinent comment: none of it makes sense." As Vlad explained, they left the pillar room, heading back towards the temple proper. "It is not designed to make sense, that is why it is called 'faith'. You let it make sense of *you*. You put your trust in higher design despite a lack of direct proof. Yet it is the thought involved with faith that is the most important. The *thought*, Cain.

Blood and Biscuits

Memories, conversations, love, sadness, and all others involved with intelligence. It combines in places of faith and soaks into the walls, *literally* soaks in, as if the stone and wood are sponges for the thought energies occurring within them, absorbing and storing for others to find."

"Are you saying - wait, hang on - are you saying this place has memory?"

Cain peered round the ruined temple, almost anxiously, as if he would see ghosts drifting through the shattered halls and peering over the lips of the floors above.

"Every place has memory, however little," Vlad explained calmly. "Weather witches can read history in water, vampires detect history in blood, and places of worship contain histories of faith. It only needs the right type of historian, the right key-bearer, to uncover the secrets locked in the matter, the memories bound within. The faith in the werewolves' thoughts imprinted the memories of their curses into the foundations of this place, the temple acting as a conduit to localise their power; their curses speak to your curse, a communication of the supernatural. I had guessed as much before but you have just confirmed it."

"Do *you* believe in any of that?" Cain asked.

Vlad's lips tightened and he clasped his hands behind his back, snow swirling about his form, wrapping his coat around his body as his wings of shadow often did when he channelled his dark power.

"It is not for me to cast doubt on belief in any way, Cain," his voice echoed. "However, if you ask me directly, then I do not necessarily believe in the finer details. I do think werewolves are necessary components of the ritual but I suspect much of the mythology was added to direct the minds of the masses. Here, in fact, it served well to focus the werewolves of the temple and keep them from humans."

"I guess I'm not surprised, all things considered. 'Spose it's good the people that lived here believed in something, even if it was some massive god-wolf. Least they formed their own pack outside the knowledge of humans. And in rural Scotland, too. Sounds actually kinda' desirable, though I'd be pretendin' with the faith. I'd be addin' nothin' to these walls."

"A man such as yourself adding nothing? Have I taught you nought all these weeks? Cain, you are without doubt one of the most emotionally charged men I have ever had the pleasure to meet - and fight, I might add. Twice. You have a unique curse and a very active mind, one you insist on poisoning with fried chicken, but an active mind nonetheless. You would have made a fine addition to the temple pack here, perhaps even an alpha. Do not do yourself a disservice."

There came a moment of profound silence that muted even the wind. Cain seemed to be considering a hundred things and did not notice when Vlad floated next to him, upside-down, arms crossed and staring intently at the werewolf. Nor did he notice when Vlad began speaking, Cain's eyes pouring over the Scratch Runes on the walls with such feeling all else might as well have fallen into obscurity.

"Cain!"

The werewolf jumped where he stood and glanced round at the vampire, ears twitching wolfishly.

"Jesus Christ, mate, what!"

"My senses tell me you're not far from hypothermia. I need to take you back down the mountain before you inadvertently freeze to death. But I do have one more point to make, before we go."

"Yeah…yeah, what is it?" Cain wondered.

"These runes. They are called 'Scratch' because they are carved from the stone by claw."

"Right, and? They were werewolves, could've split that pillar back there in half, probably."

"Indeed, but can a transformed werewolf write? Let alone with such intricate precision in stone?"

Blood and Biscuits

It was like a boulder falling in Cain's mind, the moment blown apart as realisation dawned on him.

"No. No they bloody well can't! So how was it done, a chisel?"

"You saw those runes, Cain, you know damn well they were not made with a chisel. They were *scratched*, my friend, scratched. The people living here existed for a long time in one another's company, possibly decades. A pack is a powerful thing with wolves and dogs-"

"I am *not* a dog," Cain growled.

"And I am not a bat, yet I share commonalities with them," Vlad retorted.

Cain twitched.

"Look, when I called you a bat, mate, it was weeks ago! I was hocked up on moonbeams and-"

Vlad held up his hand.

"You have nothing to apologise for. But you do have to pay attention otherwise you will die of cold. Those that lived here developed a certain connection to themselves, and with each other. They learnt more about their kind than anyone studying werewolf lore could have thought possible, and it is all in the Scratch Runes."

"I just don't see how you can say that. It's a bunch of symbols on some walls, not a massive history book you can read."

"Oh, but I *can* read it, Cain. I can read all of the language here because objects were discovered. A compass and a translation stone, to be exact, containing pieces of the puzzle to solving the riddle of this temple and all that lived here. But what the academics studying them did not understand, through their hell blazing to read the symbols and decipher the messages, was what the runes truly *meant*. To have been made, this required such intense control over their werewolf curse that the people living here could grow their claws without transforming, without a full moon. Do you see what I am saying now?"

"It's not possible," Cain breathed.

"Oh but it is, you did it yourself climbing this mountain, did you not?" Vlad intoned, walking lightly on the ceiling of the floor above. "And now you know the truth behind werewolves, that they are not the mindless beasts everyone would have them be."

Cain shivered, shaking himself down.

"You talk a lot, Vlad, but sometimes I feel you're skippin' over your real reasons. Why did you bring me here? Really? This ain't you tellin' me about ancient temples and werewolf clans learnin' deep secrets. Somethin's goin' on in that mind o'yours and I want it out."

Vlad grinned a toothy grin.

"Because I wanted to show you that you have the potential to never be alone again. You say you have nightmares about your parents but here, right *here*," Vlad said, patting the wall again, "are the links to your ancestors. Ancestors of curse and pain and togetherness, bonds written in blood just as your parents are written into your genetic code. I am only just starting to learn how powerful thought truly is but right now I see its benefits more clearly than ever. You stood beneath the light of a non-full moon and bared claws for a moment. Your ancestry and your strength are written in history itself and just this once, if we are lucky, for the sake of your curse and your loneliness, history may very well repeat itself."

408

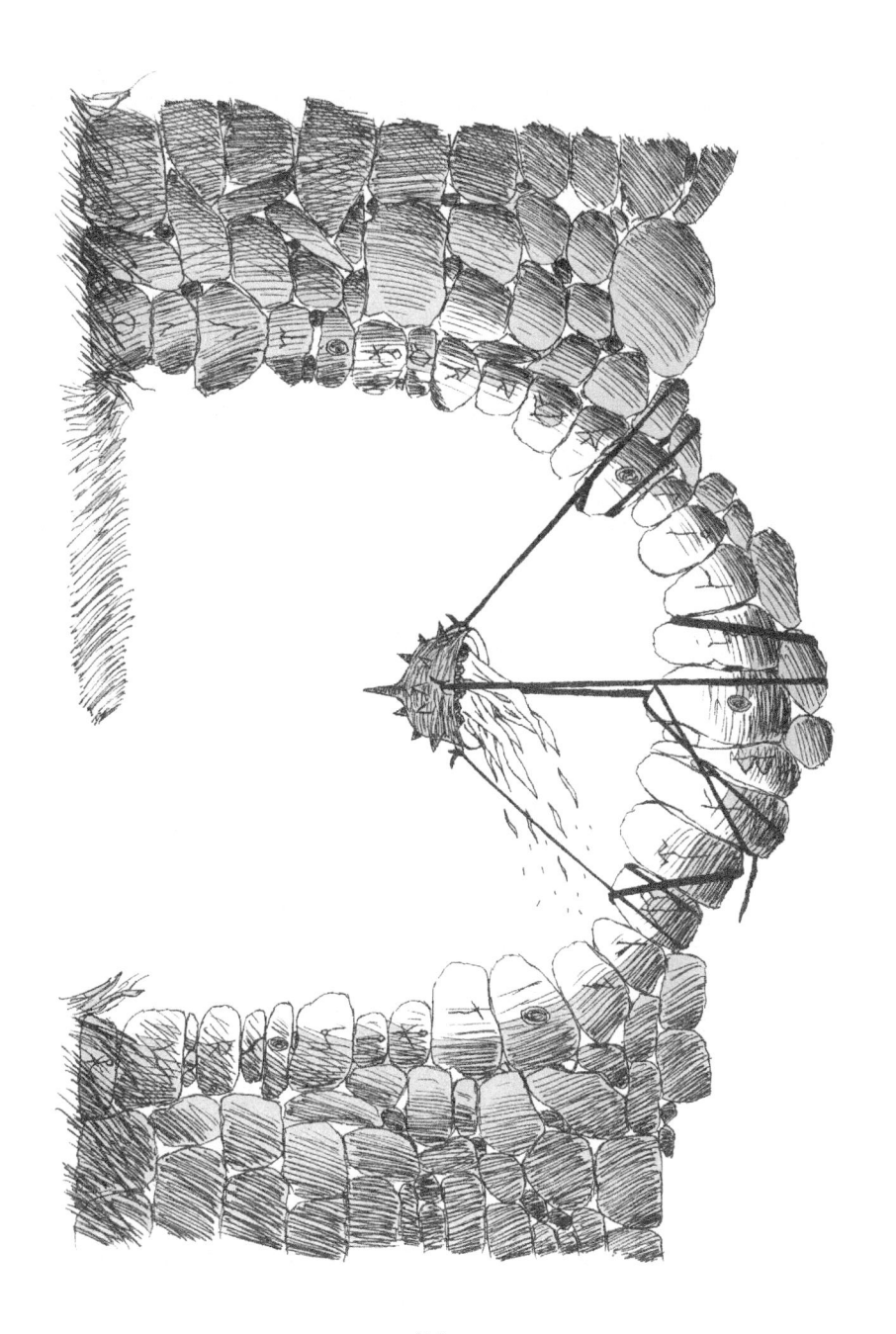

Fig. 1. Temple Arch.

I felt the slightest trails of magic still latent in the air but I could not place its origin. And then we found this torch still burning in its bowl. The wind could not extinguish it, nor could my darkness touch it when I attempted.

The message on the arch stones reads thusly:

"ONLY HORROR LIES BEYOND THIS ARCH".

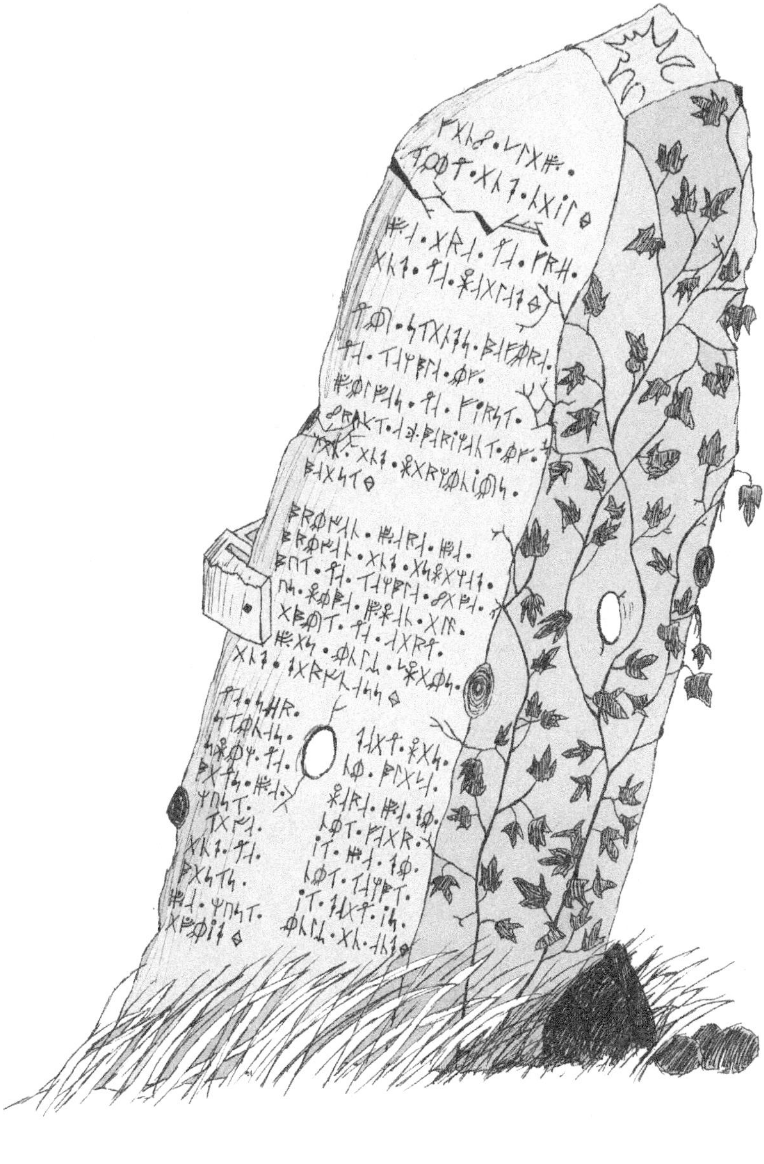

Fig. 1. The Chronicle Pillar

Atop the mountain of wolves we found this pillar, utterly covered in Scratch Runes and overgrown with such beautiful vines. Fluent as I know I am in the old language of the secret wolves, I see sadness in their warnings. I also see great mastery over their curses, for Scratch Runes carved in stone are done with claws. This means a werewolf in human form controlled the growth of their nails in order to create this stunning pillar.

Week Nine
Oblivion Calls

**RUINS OF ST ELLIN'S CHURCH,
FRIDAY.**

"So how'd you feel?" Vlad asked.

"Hic!" Cain said honestly.

Vlad wondered how they had gotten where they were. It had been two months since Cain had tried strangling him, now they had drinks and were talking like old friends. Two powerful beings from opposite sides of a natural blood feud, each possessing an ancient hatred towards one another, sharing an evening of laughter and good will. The stories flowed fast, the whisky and martinis flowed faster.

Both men grew more inebriated by the minute.

Vlad watched Cain for signs of fear but he gave no impression. He *smelled* clean of it, too; only scents of drunken joy.

Cain tipped his glass and grinned.

"Sorry 'bout that," he slurred pleasantly. "Hic! I feel pretty smashin', thanks. Got a smashin' drink, a smashin' girlfriend, and everythin's just…"

"Smashing, I'd imagine," Vlad almost giggled.

"Hic!" agreed Cain.

Vlad shook his head and drained his whisky. He placed the bottle down then grabbed another, a fifteen-year-old Dalmore, highland single malt he had picked up on their return from Scotland. Vlad slipped a darkness-bolstered claw under the foil and tore it off in one as Cain watched avidly, eyes misted by gin and vermouth.

"Wait for the pop," Vlad muttered gleefully, grasping the cork.

Blood and Biscuits

"Hic!" said Cain excitedly.

Vlad pulled and the bottle opened with a satisfying *fuum* sound.

"Whay!" they cried.

Vlad tipped back the whisky then smiled wonkily, fangs bared accidentally, flickers of darkness dancing all over him with compromised command.

"Now now, Cuthbert, calm down in there," Vlad said, knocking his knuckles against his head. The demon of his depression fought enraged against his drunkenness while Vlad baited him. "Naughty boy."

Oblivious, Cain glanced down, eyes growing wide.

"Sweet Jebus Christopher, how many bottles've y'got emptied down there, Vlas…Vlav…Vlasidav? Dasilav? Yeah, that sounded right. Tha's gorra' be fourteen, I'd say. I'm rubbish at sciencin' burr'am good at countin'."

"Seven so far," Vlad noted sloppily, drinking the expensive single malt. It tasted of fire and all things hot though that was as far as his dead tongue would allow, the rest of his senses finding the cinnamon notes.

"Holy crab!" Cain cried. "Sevens? Takes'a lot forra' vampire t'get squitty!"

"Squiffy," Vlad corrected. "Squitty's the other end."

"Hic!" accepted Cain humbly.

"Yes, I 'spose that's true; the bugger is we keep drinking and our bodies keep healing. Got to drink the hard stuff quick if we want inebri-ibenriation. Inebriation. But shh, shh, shush! I'm being sincere," Vlad slurred sloppily, ignoring Cuthbert screaming inside his head. "I've told you the ritual for Sarah and getting the, err…afterlife…thingy…that afterlife thingy open."

"Yeah, yeah, I know," Cain muttered, his drink swinging with his words. "I gorra' get all angry and fluffy again. But how'd y'know I won't run off killin' things like I did last time…s'cuse me," and Cain belched with such frighteningly wet force Vlad feared he might have been a little sick. Cain swallowed nastily then grinned. "Cor, sorry about that, tasted of olives."

"I know you'll be safe 'cause of Lucy," said Vlad.

"Hic!" Cain accepted. He added another 'Hic!' for good measure. Vlad chuckled as Cain rearranged himself and clunked another barely cohesive sentence into place. "You think Lucy'n I're like what you and that Morag lady-person-woman you talked about were?"

"She's Moira but I jus' about got what you meant," Vlad managed.

Cain barked a loud laugh.

"Ha! I just realised y'use word contrictions when you're off your pickle."

"I assume you mean 'drunk'," Vlad remarked.

"Hic!" said Cain, nodding.

"Guess that's right," Vlad agreed. "Use contractions, I mean. I 'ccasionally drop this façade that is all this handsomeness," he added, waving stupidly before his face. "We all gerra' bit strange when we let our masks down – just like you up that mountain days ago! You get your claws back out again yet?"

Cain glanced down at his fingers thickly and shook his head.

"Nah, none of that again. Hey, thanks for takin' me up there, it was proper good to gerra' know all about people like, you know, like me. Still feel like I gorra' wolves stalkin' round me, gets all creepy bein' alone."

"I apologise," Vlad said. "We all got stuff to realise about ourselves. It's why I took you, mostly, to get you opening up. It's good you took something away, though, I'm proud of you. I like to get all sentimental sometimes, let my hair down and all that."

"And warra' lovely thatch you've gorr'up there," Cain commented, pointing at Vlad's head. The vampire returned the gesture.

"And yours is without any balding!"

"To smashin' hair!" Cain cheered, raising his glass.

Blood and Biscuits

"And women that keep us regular!" Vlad echoed. They clinked their drinks. Cain's glass shattered in his hand and he yelped and jumped where he sat as shards and droplets sprinkled liberally across the floor. "Bugger," muttered Vlad. "Forgot to turn my darkness off."

"Ahh never mind, these things happen. I knew a bloke, called 'im Uncle Bacon for some God forsaken reason; 'e used to smash glasses all the time jus' by grippin' 'em too hard when he laughed. You got used to bits in your hair. Your vampire power really works like that? Bein' able to turn it off an' on easily, I mean," Cain added, shaking his hands down and walking to the coffee table. He picked a mug and peered into it with far too much interest, nose practically inside the thing.

"In a sense," Vlad replied. "Well, no...but yes. I can't explain it, stop askin' me difficult questions. Come on, Mr Fluffy, you need another drink. That's an Alizon name, not me. Oi, don't you drop that mug!"

"I won't," Cain announced happily, returning to his seat, mug raised victoriously. Vlad thought hard and lowered a wall of his control, unleashing enough darkness to turn the fine shards of glass scattered across the floor to sand just before Cain clumsily lacerated himself. The werewolf noticed nothing, simply "Hiccing" merrily as he sat.

Cain suddenly sneezed like a small, concentrated explosion.

"Oh soddin' agerllies...allergies. You got any more'n them anti-himstamines, Vladdy Day-care?"

"Was that a film reference?"

"I think it was."

Vlad shook his head and reached into his breast pocket, pulling out a blister pack and handing them over.

"As it happens, I do. Sometimes I forget you're allergic to yourself, Cain."

"Yeah, well..." Cain mumbled, throwing back two pills with a swig of newly mixed martini. Vlad *smelled* his drink and knew it was now mostly gin. It could hardly be called a martini anymore, his olive on the brink of dissolving. Cain sighed heavily, breath close to igniting, and stared into his mug, a heavy feeling becoming him. "Ain't as bad as with that cruddy blue moon. Thought I was gonna' either die or kill everyone, y'know."

"I do know," Vlad admitted. "Well, I guessed it. Didn't count on Lucy having such a strong effect on you, something I won't underestimate this time."

"Now you're relyin' on her," Cain noted. He belched again, undermining the seriousness of the moment.

"Yes. I think the Ancient Egyptians used lower clan werewolves for easier control but you're our only option. No offence. You're clear on the ritual details?" Vlad asked after another swig of whisky.

"Ish," Cain muttered. "Not sure where I fit in before, during, or after I've transformed, however, burra'part from that…"

"So, not clear at all," Vlad laughed. "But that doesn't matter. It's Lucy that needs to know everything. All you need know's that the ritual can't be completed without a werewolf. Oh, and full moon begins Tuesday, not Monday."

"Huh? I thought it was the same day every month," Cain said, confused.

"Lunar cycle's a little over twenty-nine and a half days, so the first night's fallen on Tuesday this week. Make sense?"

"Yeah, I s'pose," Cain said. "You'd think I'd know all that."

"But we can't do it Tuesday," Vlad said.

"Why not?"

"Weather's not right."

"Now what'n the hell's that supposed to mean? Sounds like another Alizon thing."

"It is, partially. I wondered if she could change things about but after reading my old books, I realised it'd be too much for her. We can't do that so Wednesday's what we need."

"That's oddly exact," Cain noted, swinging his drink again.

Blood and Biscuits

"Such matters usually are." Detecting a growing anxiety from Cain, he changed the subject slightly. He pointed to the mattress, the silver chains draped across it ominously, ready to harness a beast. "Happy with that arrangement again?"

Cain nodded blearily.

"I'll have t'be."

"Good. It's not for much longer, my friend, and soon we'll find better accommodation for you during the full moons. I know this isn't exactly…ideal? Is that the right word?"

"Ain't used to you not havin' the right words," Cain smirked.

Vlad shrugged.

"Product of the booze, I'm afraid."

Cain stared into his drink, apparently taking great note of the swirls and the ripples the olive made when it moved. Then he caught Vlad entirely off-guard, which was a rare feat.

"Vlad…why're you doin' this?" He pointed round the basement. "Why're you *really* settin' Sarah free? It ain't just for her. It seems too, I dunno', personal."

Vlad's blood ran colder than it already was but the vampire refused to retreat from the question. It was direct and honest, and Cain needed a little of both right now. Besides, he was still on sanctified ground and there was no escaping its hold, drink or no.

"I've always wished to set Sarah free, ever since I learned her ghost was stuck here. But I suppose you're right: this isn't *completely* for her. You recall we're related?"

Cain nodded thickly.

"Good. Well from what I know of the afterlife – and everything I've learned is divulged from the ancient Egyptian texts I found alongside the Necrostone – I think when a soul reaches the other world ancestors come to collect them."

Cain continued nodding, and then he stopped and raised a single finger in realisation.

"You wanna' see if *your* family's gonna' come, am I right?"

Vlad spread his hands and sighed.

"In some small, selfish way...yes. I wish only to know if they're alright, that they know I'm fine, I s'pose. And that they're all happy where they are. That's all. I'm not looking for forgiveness, I'm not looking for anything other than small closure. After that, everything's for Sarah, and that's the truth of it."

Cain chewed on something as he thought things over, and then he clearly forgot everything a moment later as his drunkenness gripped him harder.

"Hey," he suddenly said, followed quickly by "Hic! Why'd you have such a good English accent? Romanian's nothin' like ours."

"Self-taught, mostly," Vlad replied, half-laughing at the absurdity of the moment. He rubbed his chin. "When you spend so long in the midst of great playwrights and real novelists through the centuries you tend to pick up different cues that set the cornerstones of an accent."

Cain gasped dramatically.

"Have you met old Billy boy?"

"Excuse me?" Vlad said, swigging his whisky.

"Y'know, Shapes – no, that's wrong. Shale – nope, too beachy. Shakespeare, that's the one."

Vlad smiled knowingly.

"Oh I couldn't possibly..."

"Oh, come on!" Cain said incredulously. "You can tell me, I'm awful good at keepin' secrets."

Vlad leant in, pretending other people were around. Cain grinned and leant in, too.

"*I* was the inspiration behind Macbeth."

"That's an outrageous lie!" Cain cried, gesticulating wildly, his drink sloshing.

Vlad pointed at the basement.

"Can't lie here," he smirked.

"But you're not even Scottish!"

Blood and Biscuits

"Whoever said you needed to be?" Vlad asked rhetorically. "I was a lord back then, my title for my hunting duties in the line of salvation of the masses – yes, I did that long before I came here. I offered my services all across Europe from the fifteen hundreds onwards. I spent lots of time out across the British countryside with my monster-slaying weapons…"

"That the official name, is it?" Cain asked with a lopsided smile.

"No but I'm eight bottles down now and at some point even *I* start forgetting things. Point is, people took notice of me when I allowed them. They got really interested in the lonesome man with the big sword that kept bringing heads of evil creatures into town. And when word got out I was dabbling in natural magic that's when story writers started getting funny ideas. Terrible events followed and I still feel guilty about those three women with that cauldron."

"I dunno' how you're doin' it but I know you're makin' it all up," Cain laughed into what remained of his drink.

"As you wish," was all Vlad said.

Cain paused and looked at the vampire seriously.

"You got any more outta' my blood? Speakin' of magic and old science and stuff, I mean."

"An eloquent qualifier and an even more fantastic segue," Vlad said spiritedly. "Unfortunately, no. What little's determined says your curse isn't like any I've ever seen, though you probably already knew that. The mountain taught us enough."

"Hic!" Cain acknowledged.

"Precisely. And I can't find any natural substance or magical property that'll help define the curse. Wolfsbane's the mediator, the, err, thing…the *substance*, that's the word, that splits curse from blood in werewolves, including you."

"So, if I eat enough of it, I'm cured?" Cain asked excitedly.

Vlad shook his head.

"No, you're dead. Sorry. Trust me, the thought already crossed my mind centuries ago and the results were highly unpleasant. Lots of orifices are enthusiastically used as exits by blood, it's absolutely revolting. However, the wolfsbane goes one step further than normal with *your* blood: not only does it split the curse from the virus and the infected blood cells but it also seems to split the curse itself! Now this is highly unusual, I've certainly never seen it before, and what remains of the curse is two things I can't decide upon. We'll have to speak more about your life to develop a greater picture, and maybe one day we'll determine just exactly what makes up…well, Cain."

"You've completely lost me," Cain stated. "I've already said I was no good at science in school."

"And that certainly wouldn't help you here. They don't teach this in schools. I'll show you what I mean when the time's right. But for now, let's enjoy the night and prepare for the week. Our friend upstairs must be given a proper send off."

"I'd have thought she'd be down by now," Cain noted, glancing up at the ceiling. Vlad shook his head.

"I invited her but she politely refused. She had a great deal of vine leaves to say goodbye to and that takes time."

Vampire and werewolf refreshed their drinks and suddenly broke into all the verses of the Drunken Sailor, singing as rowdily as possible as the misty night drew further in, punctuated only by the almost rhythmic bursts of Cain's hiccupping, which seemed to worsen the more enthusiastically he sang.

RUINS OF ST ELLIN'S CHURCH, THE START OF THE SUPPORT GROUP.

"So how was everyone's week?"

There was a general murmur around the basement. Fleeting looks passed between them. Nobody seemed interested in opening up.

"Come now, somebody must have had at least *some* sort of a week? Lucy?"

The banshee shook her head, hair moving independently like it always did when her emotions were free.

"No...no, not really. Usual stuff. Just got a lot on my mind, is all."

"Care to relinquish a few of those worries?" Vlad pushed.

Lucy glanced at Sarah, the ghost humming voluminously and hovering so high above her seat she was nearly disappearing through the ceiling.

"It's...well it's Wednesday, really."

"Ahh, I suspected it might have been that," Vlad said quietly. He repositioned, presenting himself as a vessel into which Lucy could pour her ailments, perhaps emptying herself of sadness.

"I don't want to bring everyone down but I'm dreading it. Have been the past few days once that initial positive reaction wore off."

"That is natural," Vlad commented and Jacob nodded.

"Aye, I think that's what a lot of us got like, too," the wraith offered and Lucy brightened a little. "It's a really difficult thing to come to terms with – trust me there."

"I do," Lucy said quietly. "I can't imagine how you've been doing."

Jacob shrugged.

"Fable's helped me through it. She's got some wonderful insights into the notions of death, made me feel a whole lot better. Thank you, Fable."

Fable reached over and patted Jacob on the back gently, her beautiful face finding the most uplifting smile effortlessly.

"You are all so strong," Fable said, "and I am so proud of you. Let this next step in our journey not overshadow how far you've come."

Vlad sensed a moment of levity. The shared moods of Lucy and Jacob lifted together as a weight bearing them down rolled aside.

"Remarkable," he said. "Anybody else wish to smash through this wall of silence?"

"I had a wonderful week, thank you, Vladislav!"

All eyes turned to Sarah, her spirit bobbing happily. Vlad tilted his head.

"Did you? That *is* good to hear. Would you care to elaborate?"

"I said all my personals to the wall stones and the poor bits of wood lying forgotten after the naughty pew benches dropped them so mercilessly over the years. Then I made sure no graves would miss my company; I'm certain they'll keep up their spirits. I got a good feeling from the Sheridan family in Row D and Mrs. Renshaw emanates wonderful waves of support for my passing. I'm unsure how Mr. Thomas will cope as his flowers never grow quite so well. I think he gets sad down there, under all that soil. Between you and me, he's not been quite since that border collie urinated on his headstone."

Everyone stared open mouthed as Sarah spoke unrelentingly.

"Oh, one night I listened to Vladislav and our werewolf having the most enlightening conversation about William Shakespeare and what it truly means to be inebriated."

"Hey, where was *my* invitation? I could've done with a beer, you know!" Jacob demanded incredulously as Lucy pointed at Cain, a look of annoyance scrawled across her face in angry handwriting.

"So *that's* why you came home completely wasted, clutching a half-eaten Fat Family Cluck Bucket and singing sea shanties!" Lucy exclaimed. Cain visibly shrank back in his chair, looking as if he wanted the furniture to eat him, to take him from the banshee's wrath. "You've got some explaining to do, mister, you told me you were out with work friends."

"I *kind* of was," Cain muttered, never quite meeting Lucy's fiery eyes. Even Vlad looked away just as Lucy glanced at him.

"And *you* needn't try and deny it, you boyfriend stealing corpse. *He*," and here Lucy pointed a pale finger at Cain like she was

Blood and Biscuits

threatening him with a knife, "was in an absolute *state*! Were you aware that after he got back, he spent two hours crawling up and down the mansion on all fours, howling and scratching at the walls? No, I didn't think so," she added when Vlad shook his head, desperately trying to hide how funny he thought it was. "And then he tried barking in different accents and fell down the stairs."

Jacob sniggered suddenly and then looked away when Lucy glared at him. Vlad spoke quickly before the situation worsened.

"I am deeply sorry, Lucy. And Jacob. And to anyone else offended by our actions. The fault was purely my own for I invited Cain to speak on a number of topics that really only he should have been privy to. If he wants to tell you what it was about that is his choice, but it was my duty to inform him privately."

"And the booze?" Lucy continued, her eyes pools of dark fire, hair unnervingly still.

"Ahh, about that. Might I offer you all a nice coffee, free of charge, while I think of a good excuse?"

"It had better be a good one while you get me a strong white with three custard creams," Lucy practically growled and Vlad stood heavily. Without his meaning to, a measure of control slipped aside and he glided to the coffee table as quickly as possible, the electric light flickering as the sensation of Lucy's cold eyes burning into the back of his skull grew hotter.

"Would anyone else like to share while I gather your drinks?" Vlad called over his shoulder.

"I've got nothin'," Cain said quietly, clearly trying to appease Lucy. "My thing's been said already. I'd talk about bein' haunted by a scary woman but I think she'd kill me, so instead I'll just say I'm really glad I found Lucy." Cain looked directly at the banshee, eyes shining with hope as he said: "You make me so happy."

"Hmph. I don't want people thinking I'm a nag, normally I'm involved in a good session, but this time you broke my stairs and had me chasing you up and down the halls," Lucy grumbled and Vlad glanced back. He saw Cain flash a grin at Jacob, who evidently withheld another laugh.

Vlad poured the coffees and turned, drinks in-hand. Controlling his walking, he moved back across the basement. He handed out the steaming coffees and teas, and the biscuits, then sat in his chair to await what the others would tell him.

Alizon had had a pleasant enough week practising her magic and managing to avoid seeing her mother, and for this Vlad sensed everyone's relief.

Fable had spent a great deal of her time focussing her own magic without damaging her hands any more than they were already burned. The constant pain she felt was not diminishing but Fable was certain she could now produce a small shaft of Light magic for a few seconds without causing herself any damage at all.

With the first question done, they slipped into the second easily. Lucy had several things to get off her chest, a lot of which was directed at Cain and his "alcoholic stupidity", as she called it. However, once that was out of the way, Lucy admitted the dread she felt for Wednesday's ritual and how life would change beyond it.

"It's just a terrifying thought, opening the actual afterlife. I've never so much as left the county; I struggle just going outside. What're we going to be like if we fail? What're we going to be like if we succeed? I'm not sure I can wholeheartedly face myself in either scenario."

"I honestly have no idea how we will be shaped, or indeed what precisely we must do, once the ritual is complete," Vlad said. "But whatever happens we are still us, nothing changes that. And for the ritual itself? I will guide you through it. None of you will have very much to do, in the grand scheme of things; as long as we meet a little before dusk, I shall make sure all is in place."

"Shouldn't we go over the basics beforehand?" Alizon asked. Evidently, she found comfort in preparation.

"We could meet here tomorrow during the day and have a practice run. Does that suffice?"

Blood and Biscuits

Everybody nodded as Sarah hummed louder, more melodically.

"Good, then shall we say three in the afternoon? Please wrap up warm, it is December after all."

"That's easy coming from someone that can dive into freezing water and fly across Antarctica in just his knickers," Cain muttered, rubbing his arms automatically at the thought.

The evening progressed and soon everyone had gotten all they needed off their chests, and the basement felt a little lighter because of it. They all needed clear minds for Wednesday and having a haze of self-hatred strong amongst them would not help Sarah.

Lucy checked her watch and nodded to Vlad. He called a coffee break and everyone seemed keen to get over to the biscuits and see what was available.

As was becoming a usual occurrence, Lucy approached Vlad as he watched the group disperse.

"I am sorry about sending Cain home like he was on shore leave," Vlad said before Lucy could chide him again. However, she only smiled.

"Oh God, don't worry about that. He was happy and safe, that's the main thing. I could have done without him digging up the flowerbed but the place is falling down anyway."

"If it helps, he told me to fly him into town and drop him outside a rather greasy establishment filled with other people in varying forms of insobriety. I had only had eight bottles of scotch so I was quite clear-minded by this point, but it was evident Cain was in good, albeit loud, company. He assured me he would find his way back up to Galloway's Mansion after making the necessary purchases."

"What was the name of the place you dropped him off at?"

"It was a tasteful little chicken-based eatery called 'Uncle Pluck's Deep-Fried Clucks'. I am not sure what the proprietor was aiming for because that, to me, makes no sense. Is he cooking the beak and gullet, too? Simply revolting; if I was capable of such things I would have passed out."

"Yeah, Cain loves that place. I'm not surprised you didn't like it."

"Hmm," Vlad said. "It was more physical repulsion rather than dislike. The smell was overwhelming, I detected a curiously high level of testosterone, too. Are they cooking *male* chickens there?"

"Oh yeah, that'd be the Trimmed Cockerel Scraps side order. Cain gets them to stick on his Deboned Cluck Cutlets with Squawk Sauce all over it. Sometimes he gets a Coop de Grâce meal deal with extra Battered Poached Eggs and this nasty drink called a Choccy Splash. They've got a dessert called Lemon Whoopsies that he likes, too. Honestly, the whole thing makes me want to be sick, please can we stop talking about it?"

"With pleasure," Vlad sighed. "I did not realise his issues ran so deep."

Lucy cleared her throat pointedly.

"Sooo…" she breathed slowly as she looked at the group. "We've got everyone now, they seem pretty up on this ritual thing. Does it have a name, by the way?"

"What, the ritual?" Vlad asked.

Lucy nodded.

"The Rite of al-Mawt. The ancient Egyptian process for the opening of the afterlife; *one* of the processes, anyway, I am sure others exist. And now I have very strong reason to believe vampires helped the Egyptians accomplish this, given what we discovered with my blood."

"You know, after I found your online advert I never once thought anything would come of answering it. I honestly thought it was a prank up until the second I stepped down into this basement and realised you were exactly what you said you were."

"And from then on?" Vlad asked curiously.

Blood and Biscuits

"It was quite the wild ride," Lucy admitted. Vlad caught the finality in her tone and addressed it.

"I hope you have no illusions about our Support group, Lucy. This is to continue on, indefinitely, as we search for the answers to ourselves and provide help to any that seek it. Though the road has come to its weary end for one of our number, we must still linger on, continuing into the deep unknowns. Into a brighter world, facing new dusks and dawns together, for that is now my purpose in death. And one day, when you inevitably leave me, as the others will undoubtedly do, I shall have become a more grounded and thoughtful vampire, one that can appreciate all minds and spirits as they are instead of making wild guesses based on my senses."

Lucy made a noise in her throat. "We'll never leave you, Jacob's proof enough for that."

"All things must end, Lucy. Those I come to rely upon will spend their love and vanish away into the dusts of time. I will watch you grow and change into the lives you must accept, one way or another, and then despair as you wither from me and diminish into a new eternity. *Sarah* is proof enough for that. It is my blessing *and* my curse, and that is how it has always been. The Support Group is the only true way my living death finds meaning."

Lucy said nothing. She simply reached round and held Vlad a moment as he sighed in sorrowful contentment. They stood as one, observing the others' new lives as they huddled around a coffee table and unknowingly realised the strengths and deficiencies of their different curses whilst bickering over fig rolls and bourbons. Silent discussions of blood and biscuits.

"Come," Vlad said eventually, and Lucy peeled away from him. "Let us return to our session. There is plenty of time left for us to *finally* start question three and I have a feeling Cain has just discovered I forgot to bring Jaffa cakes again."

Lucy snorted as Cain shook an empty box at the vampire.

"Oi, we're out again!"

Vlad sighed.

Blood and Biscuits

"Bugger, he cottoned on. Look, you will have to make do with the normal milk chocolate wafers for now. I will make sure I restock for Wednesday so you have enough orange fuel to keep you going. That sound like a deal?"

"That sound like a deal," Cain imitated in a high-pitched juvenile way as he grabbed a handful of chocolate wafers.

Vlad let it go. He felt like he owed Cain after encouraging his drinking on Friday night and then leaving him to a banshee's wrath.

Vlad sighed and sat, patting his legs with an almost nervousness. They had come close to question three before but had never had the chance to stretch it out and really put it through its paces. The room descended into quiet again and Vlad decided on the precise wording, feeling as if they entered new territory. Every face looked at him expectantly and he cleared his throat, the old habit somehow still alive.

"Ok," he measured. "Let us begin this third question: if there is one thing today, right now, that could make you happy what would it be?"

Without fail, every eye twitched, every mouth broke into a wide smile, and the basement grew in the senses of comfort and joy. Everyone searched through their memories for what would make them truly happy, truly *satisfied*, in that singular moment.

The person that spoke first was Sarah. She was at peace.

ARCHWAYS AND PRAYER HALL, RUINS OF ST ELLIN'S CHURCH, TUESDAY AT 15:00.

"Crikey, this place don't half look different in the daytime."

"I know what you mean," Lucy said, rubbing her gloved hands together, staring up into the crooked church ruins. "It's really beautiful here, in a strange, old kind of way. I love the dew on the

Blood and Biscuits

vine leaves and the arches; icicles catch the sunlight just right, God, that's pretty."

Jacob, Cain, Alizon, and Fable said words of similar sentiment.

"Indeed, it was always a wonderful church," Vlad said and everybody jumped. They looked up and saw him hanging upside down from an arch, feet bound by darkness, wine-red shirtsleeves rolled back, leaving his forearms bare. "My apologies, I did not mean to startle. I was speaking with Sarah atop the steeple and heard you arrive. Shall we begin?"

"Yeah, once my heart's stopped hammering," Cain muttered. He looked up at the sparkling sunshine glimmering off Vlad. "Aren't you feelin' even a little weak in all that light?"

Vlad shook his head.

"Not for the past eight hundred years. I made a concerted effort to learn how to cope with it upon my skin, now I use only the smallest amount of power to deflect the sun's strength. Fable's magic, however, requires a different sort of power, one I would very much like to master a defence against one day, too."

Vlad floated down to them to prepare for the ritual. They decided on optimum positions for the Necrostone and everyone else during the process using a checklist Vlad had written. He explained everything and as they worked, Sarah descended amongst them.

"The Necrostone weakens the walls between worlds, the sword stroke revealing the gates, and the window to the afterlife is prised apart by a huge force. Then the departed's true name must be spoken so our family can collect her soul."

Vlad noticed Sarah floating before the old, broken altar; positioning herself on the left-hand-side, staring up at the last few shards of stained glass still clinging to the fleur-de-lis frame above. Everyone fell silent, rays of dying sunlight shining shafts through the broken church, bathing aisles and arches in shimmering columns. Slowly, everyone sat upon the old bench seats, hands folding in their laps, and a wordless hush fell over that broken place. Sarah bowed

Blood and Biscuits

her head in sunlight, glittering silver in molten gold.

Those sorrowful grounds, disturbed only by river breeze stirring the vine leaves hanging in thick curtains.

When at last Sarah spoke, she sounded as if talking to someone stood beside her, someone she knew deeply.

"I…have a confession, my love," words drifting into the wind, no longer echoing. "I have not been completely honest with you."

Every eye trained upon her, the minds and hearts of the Support Group captured utterly. Sarah sniffed sadly. Vlad was not sure if she was addressed the church or a memory.

"You've given me joy and you've given me heartbreak, and I have died through both. You've been my anchor and my prison, the home from which I cannot escape; I have survived because of you and despite you, and I am strong. But I'm weak, also, and you have seen all sides of me, in every moment. I have loved you, I have hated you, and we have fallen apart together, forgotten and unloved by a world that has long-since moved on, even as we could not."

Vlad felt everyone's mood shift as a thin vein of understanding bled through them, intertwining all in everything Sarah said. Vlad gritted his teeth, forcing his fangs back when they tried pushing out, his darkness reacting to the powerful regret and longing coursing his body. His old life and his life now were colliding as two worlds might collide, shattering him completely, rebuilding anew from the ashes.

Sarah sighed and held out her hand, her shoulders shuddering as she silently began to cry, fingers meeting only air where there should have been the hand of another to give her strength, to give the love she so dearly craved.

Vlad, unable to watch any longer, stood and approached, and as he walked, he unleashed the power within him, lurking, waiting for acknowledgement. Shaking with raw strength, he directed the shimmering darkness into his hands. Vast black wings erupted from his back in ragged cloaks, shadows of horns sprouting from his temples, fangs finally bursting from his jaws. Sunlight was banished from the church as shade grew through the arches and froze dew upon the stone, droplets turning to ice and striking the ground in teardrops of glass.

The shadowman stepped beside Sarah and held out a hand, his command keeping the claws from his fingers. He took her hand in his, *touching* her skin.

With a shuddering gasp, Sarah's veil fluttered freely, revealing a small and perfect mouth beneath, the first physical contact in two centuries sending shock bolting through her spirit. It took almost everything Vlad had to maintain the connection, the coldness of his emotional core binding with the ghost's soul through sheer force of will and strength of darkness. Nobody had ever done this before. It almost felt *right*. The act drained him even as it filled Sarah with strength, her hand like starlight in his.

Sarah's fingers tightened in Vlad's as he looked to the window, longing to hold her, to show her she would feel no sorrow ever again.

"All I had and all I was, I swear to you. All I have and all I am, I swear to you. And all I will have and all I will ever be, I swear to you here, now. For here, now, will always be my everything, and that is the truth of our time together. You'll be with me for eternity."

Sarah's hand felt so strong in Vlad's, the link of his darkness bridging the gap between two personifications of death, the shattered archetypes of their supernatural paradigms inarguable in that singular moment. Vlad could not tell who she spoke to anymore but it did not matter, it never had. Sarah was becoming one with her passing.

"You never knew why I love daffodils so much," she uttered quietly, unexpectedly. "I suppose I've always been distant with my truth. They remind me of the dress I was married in, so short a union that was. It was so yellow, shining like the sun does now, chosen for me by my mother and grandmother. My veil was…pink, I think. I remember I was so happy; *we* were so happy. So short a union that was," she repeated, looking away from the altar. "But soon we shall unite again."

Vlad's strength faltered and Sarah shimmered away, her fingers falling through his hand, the moment lost to them. He pushed the walls of his control back into place and the power of his strength disappeared, the sun returning to the broken church once more, bathing Sarah in its light.

Vlad stepped away, the moment now a memory forming, allocated to yet another portion of his mind, along with the rest of his life. He sat and Lucy gave a watery smile, eyes shining with black tears. It seemed she had taken much from Sarah's words of imprisonment and sorrow.

They stayed for a long time in silence, the sounds of the breeze running across leaves, whistling through holes in the church stone.

Slowly, Sarah recounted a story from her life, a long and winding tale of childhood and how she had come to live upon Ellin's Island, which had gone by a different name then. She told of the town Mayor and his lovely big house, and how he had known everyone upon the island, how he had shown such kindness to her when she married and started a new life.

The sun lowered dutifully and evening drew in, dusk breaking upon the church as the full moon appeared in the sky. Cain twitched and looked up.

"It's here," he whispered and Vlad nodded, noticing the sheen of sweat on Cain's brow, the rapidity of his breathing. Vlad had been paying too much attention to Sarah, unfocussed on the struggling man beside him.

"Indeed. The sun prevents the moon's power but I see dark clouds upon the horizon. This moon is precisely what we need tomorrow night, my friend, but the clouds will prevent most of its usefulness. For now, you should retire to the basement to remain human. We will see you tomorrow."

Cain stood to leave and Lucy rose with him. She wiped her

eyes, the tiniest black lines smudging her pale cheeks.

"I'll come, too. I've another hour or so before I have to head to the mansion."

Hand-in-hand, Cain and Lucy left the church. Fable and Jacob followed next, accompanying Alizon as she expressed a desire to walk into town and see the evening lights, leaving Vlad alone with Sarah as he had always felt should be the way.

Sarah floated back from the altar and drifted through the church hall. She stopped beside Vlad and gazed at him, veil hiding her face again.

"Come," she whispered, "let us dance one last time."

"As you wish," Vlad said, standing elegantly, letting her lead the way.

Sarah halted by her music box, looking down at it a moment.

"Vladislav, could you hold me again? Like you did at the altar. I wish to feel alive, just one last time."

"I will do what I can," Vlad said and once more, he opened himself to his power, let it flood his veins. His darkness filled him, its bittersweet embrace biting and clawing at his insides as much as it tempted and enticed his mind. Ultimately, that knife's edge dichotomy was the strength of the vampire.

His darkness surrounding and bolstering his body, Vlad took Sarah's hand once again. She felt solid, a human of matter and thought. The energy cost to make that connection, to bring his flesh so close to non-existence he could touch a ghost, was phenomenal, but Vlad did not care. This was far more important than suffering. Sarah shuddered as Vlad drew her close, his arm about her slim waist. She held him as if he was the last thing in her existence, all else but a dream.

Sarah glanced to the font.

"Magic music box: play the Moonlight Sonata, please."

The black box *dinged* softly and its blue light emanated. Within seconds, the two-hundred-year-old song drifted through the gathering evening, haunting vampire and ghost as they swayed in their lonely dance. This was the summation of their lifetimes, every thought and feeling together, every second in each other's company. They fused with the music, with each other, and danced for the last time.

Their feet left the floor, and as they rose moonlight burst across the church and cascaded upon them, sending silver and shadow skittering across the island, twining together, their edges touching, just as vampire and ghost. The song disappeared below as they ascended until they came to the steeple and moved in the air, held together by power so strong it allowed body and soul to meet.

Darkness almost overwhelmed him and Vlad felt as if he could draw Sarah into him, to take that final step and consume her, to become one. They would have what each other craved, a soul and a body, and they could depart this world together. Two perfect parts woven imperfectly to make a living, breathing human. They could die together, live again together, and –

"I don't feel as if I'm Sarah anymore."

Vlad felt a jolt through his emotional core.

He was not human. He never would be.

"It is not your real name," he replied, his words freezing on the winter's air. "Not your given forename, anyway."

"It's not that," she said quietly. "I feel as if my imminent passing is marked by different sadnesses. I look upon the world and see such change, and yet no change at all. The island is unaltered though the lives of people beyond its borders no longer mirror what mine once was. Centuries I've been here yet I know this world less than those who've lived decades. I leave behind a home I don't know…I'm not sure how that makes me feel."

"I know not what to say," Vlad began and Sarah shook her head gently.

"It's alright that you don't have all the answers. You cannot be perfect, though you try so hard to help everyone. One day you'll finally tell yourself, as I have, that it's alright to not be alright. Remember that, before it's too late."

"I will," Vlad said.

The song had not finished when Sarah leaned back and looked up at Vlad. He gazed down and felt shock as clear and pure as a silver knife plunged deep into his heart when Sarah's veil floated back upon the smoothest breeze and revealed her face.

She was so young, her soul captured in time, reflecting the body it had once inhabited, and Vlad blinked with wonder. Sarah shimmered in silver, her eyes searching his own for anything, everything, her grip firm about him as the vampire recalled all of her and held the memories tight. Her sharp features reminded him of Lucy in many ways, though her hair had once been golden, her cheekbones softer. She had lost none of her beauty, nor her fire, Vlad realised, when without warning Sarah reached up and pressed her lips to his cheek.

The kiss was light but it was enough. There was compassion and gratitude in the act and it meant the world to Vlad. Sarah took what she needed from this plane to the next, and her choice was one final act of humanity.

Vlad's darkness fell from him and his eyes opened with a cold snap.

The music had finished and the night was full. Sarah was gone.

Vlad sighed and looked south. There was a Necrostone that needed collecting.

ARCHWAYS AND PRAYER HALL, WEDNESDAY, 16:00.
THE RITE OF AL-MAWT.

"God, I don't feel ready for this. I'm already…ugh," Cain groaned. Vlad sensed splinters of pain stab the man. "Christ, this hurts. I'm already strugglin' against the moon and it ain't even dark yet."

Blood and Biscuits

The vampire looked up as he walked and saw the full moon high in the deepening blue sky, the sun the only thing holding it back.

"You've got this, Cain," Jacob said.

Vlad *felt* them shiver as he approached across the wastelands, sensing Lucy and Alizon arriving a minute later from the west.

Fable cleared her throat and spoke. "We shall *all* be fine. I've never known a stronger group of people than my friends gathered here. Cain, though I know this must be difficult, you'll only transform when *you* decide it, focus on that. I am confident in my Light and in Lucy's command over you; you've shown yourself more than capable in the face of adversity. We all have."

"Yeah but now I'm s'posed to be goin'...ahhh, jeez...full werewolf with all you lot around me and usin' just Lucy to control me."

"Look, I've been practicing all I can these past few weeks and I've got a better grip on my power now. Are you confident in me?" Lucy asked as Vlad shifted the weight on his back, the load's influence sapping at his energy, a satchel bouncing at his side.

"'Course I am," Cain replied, voice shaking with gathering strain, his body's every cell realigning and altering, unleashing the monster within. "It ain't about confidence in you, it's about...trustin' myself. Oh man, make it stop," he panted.

Vlad heard heavy notes of exasperation as he crossed the last few hundred feet, irritated that he was late.

"Jeez, you're really suffering," Lucy said, concerned. "So long as you listen to me now you'll be fine when you transform. Alright?"

"Got it. You're gonna' scream at me," Cain muttered.

"Probably, yeah. Depends how angry you are when you turn white and werewolfy."

"Good," Cain breathed, lungs heaving, wheezing. He snarled: it did not sound human. "I need to be screamed at. Oh *Christ* this better be worth it!"

"It will be," Alizon said simply.

Blood and Biscuits

"This is way beyond anything I thought we'd be doing," Jacob muttered, his feet shifting nervously. "Thought it'd just be coffee and chitchat. Yeah I know, it's my turn to worry. I have feelings too, so sue me."

"I don't think that'll be necessary," Lucy said. "And how're you feeling, Alizon? I love your bracelets, they're fascinating. Oh, did you have a nice evening last night?"

"I'm alright, thank you, Lucy. The bracelets are creations of my own as an extra project for my school teachings; they bolster my power, focus it, help me block out unwanted thoughts…And yes, I had a pleasant stroll with Jacob and Fable through town; they've really put some good money into the renovations, haven't they?"

"Aye, looks a lot better than a few years back. My guess is Vlad had something to do with it," Jacob noted as Cain began audibly pacing the church hall, footfalls reverberating through the stone, awakening the island from its slumber. Vlad smelled the salt of sweat and the rush of deep, hot blood in the man's veins – as the horizon darkened, the great white werewolf returned.

"Speaking of, where *is* our elderly friend?" Cain asked, humour forcing through his pain as Vlad stepped from the shadows and into the last light of the ruins. Cain leapt and spun to meet him. "Jesus *arse*, Vlad, you've gotta' stop doing that!"

"Shall I put forward an advance apology to cover the next fifty times?" Vlad posited. "Because unless you start actually paying attention to your naturally heightened hearing, which you clearly do not appreciate, then I am afraid it is going to keep happening, my friend."

"That sounds like it needs more effort than I can give," Cain grunted through the increasing pressure. Jacob snorted.

"So does having to change your pants every Monday night," the wraith said and Lucy chuckled.

"Welcome, Vlad, it's nice to have you here," Alizon said. She wore a pair of worn, cracked bronze bracelets about her wrists. Inscribed into the dull-shining metal were over a dozen different symbols designed as strange-formed eyes, a type of witch language. Alizon's nails were varnished black and two eye symbols were painted white on the sides of her hands.

"Thank you for welcoming me, it is nice to be here, in a strange way."

"Is this party for me?"

Everyone looked up as Sarah descended amongst them. She floated with jittering motions, excited and agitated simultaneously.

"It is indeed," Vlad replied warmly. The item on his back dragged at him and he removed it. "Have you finished your farewells?"

"Oh yes," Sarah said ecstatically. "Every grave has been informed and all daffodils are accounted for."

"I never asked, Sarah," Lucy began curiously, her eyes darting to Cain anxiously as he pressed his hands against an uncollapsed wall and shook. "Daffodils don't flower until spring so how do you talk to them?"

"I speak to their memory and their hidden faces of gold, their spirits of pink," the ghost replied airily. "Rays of sunshine in my mind as they veil themselves for winter. I shall miss them when they return."

"And they will you," Lucy said gently, looking away, another flash of hurt pricking her.

"What's *that*?" Jacob asked suddenly, pointing at the long, thin, cloth-bound bundle Vlad leant against the font.

"Whatever it is it's making me feel weird," Lucy remarked, taking a step back from it.

"Silver," Fable muttered. "That's what I feel."

"Indeed," Vlad said. "A steel claymore with silver lining the edges. It is not much silver but the effect is still present."

"Wow, where'd you get that?" Lucy wondered.

Vlad grinned.

"Sixteenth century Spain."

"Of course you did," Cain growled as beads of sweat dripped

Blood and Biscuits

down his brow.

"Wait," Jacob said. "Claymores are Scottish – this I know *without* being super old, it's called heritage. Alright, I'm Ghanaian a couple generations back so I can hardly talk. But I learnt medieval weapons in school. How'd you get a claymore in Spain?"

"Good question," the vampire replied. "I brought designs of a rather beautiful sword from a skirmish in the highlands to a smith outside of Barchinona, which is now Barcelona. He was only too happy to try his hand at something new."

"Ahh," Jacob said simply.

"So why've you got this big scary weapon?" Cain asked, evidently keeping his mind from his pain.

"Well," Vlad said slowly, moving away from the wrapped blade to lessen the effect on his blood. "It is part of my hunting arsenal for dealing with lesser vampires. The blade cuts quite easily through the necks of those that choose to abuse their power and accept their greed."

"Oh bloody hell, I haven't had dinner yet," Cain grumbled. "Not that *that* matters, considering…how sick I feel…already…"

"Well you *did* ask," Vlad said, diverting the werewolf's attention. He clapped his hands together and smiled, though he did not feel happy. "Let us begin. The light of dusk is nearly upon us, when the barrier between worlds is weakest."

"That's what you said the Necrostone does," Lucy began, taking a step towards Cain as he whimpered. "Bridge the gap when the barrier's broken, right?"

"Indeed," Vlad said. He dropped the satchel from his side and pulled out the Necrostone, its black and white-striped form rough in his hand. Unremarkable as a seashore pebble. "This little thing is capable of the most wondrous power given the right…persuasion."

"With your blood," Fable said. Her hands clenched and unclenched.

"Right again," Vlad said darkly, placing the Necrostone in

the stone font.

"So why's the sword here if not for killing vampires?" Jacob asked.

"The Necrostone is the bridge between worlds, the catalyst created by Egyptians thousands of years ago, fuelled by blood dust. The half-light of dusk or dawn brings the worlds of the living and the dead in line with one another, like the moon and sun converging in an eclipse – that is the best analogy I can think of. During these moments, the fabrics of realities are weak and a silver sword cuts through the barrier itself, slicing a hole between existences so the Necrostone may bridge them together. Does that make sense?"

Jacob nodded as Cain spoke.

"Surprisingly, yeah. Oh God, I can't cope with this! I'm usually inside at this point; I've *never* seen the sun and full moon out together! Did you say we have to touch each other?"

"Eloquently put. Yes, the ritual laws require touch to bind us in obligation and provide invitation to the afterlife. I wish there was a simpler way of putting it."

"I don't follow," Jacob said as Vlad glanced to the horizon: not long until the sun melted away.

"It is simple," Vlad explained hurriedly. "When we touch, we send an invitation to the spirits of the afterlife to come to the gates. For even if we split apart the walls of the worlds and join them together there may be nobody to greet us – no *one*, should I say. To do this we must have four sentinels of death, one of which is the departed – Lucy, Jacob, and I, and then Sarah for the latter. We must have two sentinels of life – Fable and Alizon. And we must have one sentinel of both, which is Cain. When the gates open, we speak the departed's true name and our family feels our binding magic and hears her calling, and they come for her. It is rather beautiful in its build, would you not say?"

"I dunno'," Cain said, "I don't even know what a sentinel is!"

"Just trust me," Vlad almost hissed in desperation. "We must do this, in the order I specified yesterday, or Sarah cannot cross to the afterlife. We must open it and she must bring our family to her; no one passes the gates of oblivion alone, that is the ultimate law."

"*I* get it, Vlad," Lucy said, "don't worry about idiot over there. He's going dog-form anyway." And as if to emphasise her words, Cain sneezed explosively.

"Buggerations," he grunted. "Fine, let's get this over with."

He stripped his clothes, his spine visibly altered and lengthened, and placed them neatly in a pile near the silver sword, leaving only his pants on. When he turned round everyone looked at him strangely.

"What? Don't judge me, you weirdos. I want warm clothes that haven't been ripped to shreds when I transform back."

"But you…left your pants on," Alizon said in confusion.

"Easy now," Cain grinned, and his teeth looked longer than normal. "A man has limits."

"Come, we must hurry, the moon is nearly alone," Vlad said. "The gates must be opened by one strong enough to tear the cut in realities after the sword cleaves them apart."

"Can't you do it, Vlad?" Cain moaned.

Vlad shook his head.

"No, I will be severely weakened by the sword and the effort of cutting open the afterlife, which requires a sacrifice of pain. The Necrostone needs my energy to maintain the bridge as both worlds move apart. As the sun dips below the horizon, anything binding the worlds of life and death becomes strained. I cannot out-strength the Earth's rotation; I can delay it but I will be vulnerable. You are the only one, Cain, that is why the Rite must be performed beneath a full moon. Do you understand now?"

"Unfortunately," Cain muttered worriedly. He looked at Lucy. "Just make sure I don't go tearin' heads off, alright? Can't have that on my conscience."

"Once Cain's finished having a meltdown we can get into position," Alizon said and Vlad detected a hint of jest. She had come a long way, too. "Are we ok to prepare ourselves now, Vlad?"

Blood and Biscuits

"Please do," the vampire said quickly. "We must be quick to complete the bond. Fable, are you ready to shine your Light?"

"I am," she said easily, stretching her fingers and shaking her shoulders.

The moment grew still, a lull in the seconds ticking away as horizons aligned and worlds joined once more, and Vlad looked to his friends, to these great people of the Support Group, and smiled.

"Where do we go?" he uttered. "What remains of us when we are gone? Though our bodies will desiccate and dissipate, fleshes joining the earth, bones lingering a while, bloods weeping away as tears or river waters, our minds are held aloft in the soul's immortality, the imprints of our earthly endeavours made real in some other place through our body's passing. Our forms might wither and disappear but our minds and hearts that drove them are taken up for preservation, moved to a higher place so we might join all who we learned from."

Everyone looked down, all but Cain. He calmed a moment and sniffed the air.

"Did somebody write that?" he asked quietly.

"Yes. I did," was all Vlad said.

The vampire approached the font, the music box recently removed, and slit a vein down the length of his forearm. The sensation of control over his despair sickened him, his demon Cuthbert snarling in his mind. Dark-red blood spilled forth and spattered the font messily. Fable came to his side and pressed her hands together. The burning distortion of electricity crackled across Vlad's senses as his darkness healed his wound, and Fable sent a surge of Light through the blood. There was a flash, a smell of charring, and the blood was gone, replaced with crimson powder.

"Good, that should be more than enough."

Vlad glanced at the sun, its light blocked by the thick curtains of vines.

"We must act now or else fail," he said as Cain began scratching himself all over, making small sounds of pain. His sweat poured in sheets, the effort of maintaining sanity already taking its heavy toll, body shining in the falling light.

Contact with bare skin would improve the invitation so Vlad removed his shirt and tossed it over a bench, pale flesh glinting in the half-light. Old battle scars lined his torso, wicked marks from his human days carried into his death with his depression. Narrow black veins were already appearing, criss-crossing his flesh from the silver sword.

Vlad moved to the side of the church and wrenched a huge swath of hanging vines, showering the ground in leaves and flecks of dirt. The sun burst through and struck the font in dazzling beams, and just like Antarctica, the reaction was immediate.

The Necrostone shimmered and pulsed and lifted into the air. Everyone but Vlad and Cain stared around in wonder and worry as thin veins of dust shook free from walls, timbers shivering, colours dancing free through the hall.

"Bind with me now!" Vlad commanded.

Lucy and Fable placed a hand each on Vlad's bare shoulders while Alizon placed her palm across his abdomen – even in that moment, Vlad noticed the hand was located precisely where her own bruise was, the one her mother had inflicted upon her. The air pressure changed as the connection built, intensifying as Cain, now tugging at his hair exasperatedly, staggered forward with a snarl and grabbed Vlad's forearm. His already long fingers had elongated beyond normal human length.

The river wind deepened and rattled the church's old bones.

Jacob shifted and rested his hand on Vlad's back as Sarah, humming loudly over the quakes of the church, descended inside the vampire. In a flash, Vlad saw what she saw and felt as she felt: the beauty of a world soon forgotten, the overwhelming joy tinged with loss. Her soul teaching his emotional core.

The very earth itself seemingly rose and fell with the power of death and life united, and the wind became a gale to swirl and roar. Everyone's clothes whipped wildly as Lucy's hair matched her mood, unfettered by the blasts of weather.

'We were missing only an enchantress,' Vlad acknowledged as the Necrostone, bolstered by their link, shimmered iridescently and spun faster.

With demonic force, the Necrostone lashed out and *grasped* him with its deep magic, and he jolted with shock. The stone took hold of his darkness to sap his energy and maintain alignment with the world of the dead, clenching his heart, freezing his blood solid.

The sun's light deepened and Cain roared in agony, the sound dragging from his throat in a horrifying howl. Without warning, the wind fell still and the air became *thin*, as if all weight and pressure pushed it down, leaving only a vacuum. Vlad knew if he were to drop a feather it would strike the floor immediately.

"The afterlife stands before us," he said, voice smooth like ice. "*The connection is made, the invitation primed. To build the bridge the barrier must be broken, the gates cannot open until the act has been made.*"

The vampire grunted and shifted from the others, the invitation written by the ancient magic and awaiting the true name of Sarah. Like ropes held his limbs, Vlad fought the Necrostone and reached out to the silver-tipped sword. His flesh shimmering as if distorted through rippling water, he dragged the cloth from the blade and hilt. The sword glinted in the lowering light; the blade had seen the deaths of a hundred vampires, woken now from its long slumber to wreak a different kind of havoc, to bring chaos from order.

The wind roared and spat and Vlad groaned.

His strength lessened and he looked to the sky: the sun was slipping below the horizon, dusk was moving on. The worlds of the living and the dead were desynchronising. Now the Necrostone needed vast stores of energy to hold the afterlife in place. And that energy came from the source of the blood dust, from Vlad.

Locks of hair lashed his face, wings of shadow beating against the wind, framing his long, pale torso. Even through his waning strength, his slashing darkness keeping his body from failing, Vlad sensed a powerful force unleash upon the world. The church swayed and warped as if seen through old glass, and Vlad saw Lucy holding her hands out to Cain. In horrific convulsions, he writhed and thrashed upon the cold stone floor, limbs and face contorting and elongating frighteningly, the sanctified ground alone not enough to prevent his transformation.

Clutching the sword as a beacon of salvation, Sarah singing wildly within him, Vlad prepared to make the stroke. Cain gnashed his huge fangs and slammed his shaggy paws against the flagstones, enormous muscles shuddering beneath his skin. His white fur glistened in the silvery moonlight and he slowly stood to his full, towering height, looming twelve feet above them all, eyes gleaming, jaws slung with malice.

The werewolf threw back his head and howled a noise so terrible Alizon reacted. She channelled her magic. A series of deep-blue triangular forms burst from her hands and a second later, the waters of the sky dropped into her hands as a clear, shimmering orb. It spread and surrounded herself, Fable, and Jacob. Alizon guided the waters into place as a spherical shield of rushing froth and blue waves, protecting them all.

Without hesitation, Vlad made the old steps of the master swordsman and spun where he stood. Seeking within himself the bridge the Necrostone had constructed, he raised the claymore above his head with graceful precision, centuries of practice returning after so long. Without hesitation, Vlad brought the sword slicing down in a perfect line, and its silver caught the ancient magic of the Rite and *cut* the air itself. His senses felt the molecules cleave apart as the sword struck the barrier between worlds, and left in its wake a long needle of light, a narrow wound, a slice between realities. It would not last long.

"*Lucy, command him! You must make him yours.*"

Cain's eyes shone black in the darkness and his jaws opened, preparing to lunge, but Lucy stepped forward, white hands shaking before her.

Blood and Biscuits

Through the wild din, Vlad fell to a knee, sword point stabbing the muddy ground, and he rested on the hilt, the Necrostone devouring his power. Cain, his mind lost to him, looked between the vampire and the light spilling from the air, confusion mixing with anger as he took a step towards him, mouth slavering, claws unsheathed.

Lucy opened her mouth.

Yet her scream was not the normal cry of the banshee, rather a softer sound, a rounded sound, as if she *sang*. Cain's long ears twitched and his eyes lost the edge of their rage. The great ragged beast stared at Lucy as the Necrostone pulsed stronger and stronger through the church. Slowly, he his head with a deep, guttural growl and Lucy spread her fingers through the fur of his muzzle.

She leaned in close to that huge head and whispered something in his ear as she stroked his long face, and for once Vlad heard nothing. It was not a thing for him to hear.

Cain snarled and rose again, and he stepped towards the wound in the air, Lucy's control over him complete. The werewolf pulled his vast arms back and thrust his giant paws into the split in the air, and with the colossal strength of a creature born from power and curse, wrenched apart the walls of the tear between worlds and forced them aside with a mighty roar of effort.

The Necrostone erupted in raw potential, unleashing a devastating surge through the opening and laying down the foundations of the bridge to connect both worlds across the chasm of the Inbetween, the place within places. The gates of the afterlife gaped open and stood wide; the bridge was made and Vlad was close to collapsing.

"Vlad!" Lucy called through the rush of ancient magic. "What's that, Vlad!"

Through pain, through fire in his blood, through devastation, the vampire forced his head up and saw oblivion, the endless plains of immortality. What met his gaze sent fingers of black ice running down his spine.

Blood and Biscuits

Through the gates of oblivion there sat a vast and beautiful land of pure white light and shimmering silver, a place of serenity and heavenly mountains. White shadows danced and shimmered in their hundreds of thousands. It was too much to bear, too great a thing to witness, its divine purity judging Vlad's blasphemous existence, punishing his eyes for daring to look upon its majesty. And there, sat amongst all that sacredness, its back straight and its piercing eyes staring out at them, was a truly immense wolf. A leviathan of a different plane, its fur shining gold in the blinding white light of death.

The wolf stared through the open gates, face stoic and calm, a depth of infinite knowing in its gaze, and for the first time in centuries Vlad felt truly afraid.

"*I think it is...a guardian...of the afterlife,*" the vampire managed, voice layered with darkness. "*A beast of faith, it stands silently as gatekeeper, and perhaps...I must speak Sarah's name to it. Maybe this wolf is the one to hear.*"

Vlad held Sarah's true name firm, safe from knowledge, safe from Sarah, safe from ruining life further for her should she hear it and remember her own death. Now it was time to release her, to scribe her name back into the world, and Vlad unleashed it like crying the lyric of a spell into a hurricane, calling the words to the great golden wolf of the afterlife. Humbled where he knelt, his voice crossed the bridge between realities, stretching through parallel time and space, to reach the ears of a god.

"*ELLINOR SARAH MORGAN!*"

The golden wolf's face did not alter but Vlad knew he had been heard. The colossus shivered and inclined its vast head, its shimmering fur gleaming strangely as it moved, and then the wolf turned. Its paws struck the ground in deep thunderclaps of doom, and it opened wide its maw. No noise came yet Vlad knew something had changed for a moment later the white shadows of that land fluttered away and hundreds more became solid before the gates of the afterlife. They rushed to the bridge in a sea of movement, silhouettes in oblivion.

Vlad gasped in shock as Sarah suddenly left his body and floated towards the world bridge, the shadows standing upon the brink, the white light of the dead pouring into the dark world of the living. As she drifted her veil unhitched and flew away, caught and disappearing amongst the arches of the church. Sarah came to the gateway and stopped, and Vlad struggled to hold up his head, the sword the only thing stopping him from falling to the ground as the Necrostone drew more energy than any silver could ever manage. His forearms were patterned with thick black veins like tangled fishing nets, his hair hanging about his face in streaks, water vapour condensed on his freezing skin.

He was the only thing keeping two whole worlds bound together, his darkness the source, his resolve the key. He knew he was about to die.

The hundred silver shadows stopped in a vast crowd and three stepped towards the gates, finding solidity. Opaque forms of two men and a woman materialised, each appearing young, *healthy*, and they opened their arms to Sarah. Their spirits flickered and fragmented like white flames but their faces drew Vlad's astonishment for they shone with love and relief. Sarah gave a heart-breaking cry of joy at the sight and the three spirits beamed through the howling gale, the greatest pride evident between them. No words spoken, no sound made.

Sarah simply glanced back at her old Support Group. Her smile carved into Vlad's memories forever, for it was the solace of pure peace.

Sarah stepped into the afterlife and was embraced by the younger man. Her hands reached up to him and they kissed as husband and wife, her parents gazing out at the Support Group with heart-breaking gratitude. Two centuries of separation.

Then Sarah was gone, becoming a silver shadow like her family, swallowed up by infinity.

Vlad stared through the open gates at where she had stood a

second before and saw the golden wolf, its shaggy fur glittering like tongues of bright fire. Its mountainous head surveyed the tear between worlds for a long moment, and then it looked away once more. It opened its jaws and roared silently again as Vlad looked on in agonising confusion, the darkening horizon wrenching his body apart with pain. Again, the silver spirits scattered and two stood out from the crowd that had formed for Sarah. They approached the gates of oblivion. Vlad slid further down the sword, his strength almost gone, and the spirits became solid, smiling at him.

Two women, young and joyful, their hands raised in welcome.

Vlad's heart suddenly *beat* in his chest where it should have been dead and a noise strangled from his throat. He tried to move, tried to crawl to them, but he was paralysed. He felt an abyss take hold of him, and when he thought he could endure no more a third spirit appeared from the depths of death. A man. He became solid and beamed down at Vlad, the two women either side nodding and putting their arms about his shoulders, as real as any of the others.

"That's…you, Vlad!" Lucy cried and Vlad stared at the image of himself with the women in the land of the dead. "What're you doing in the afterlife!"

Vlad saw his doppelgänger, the reflection of himself caught in death, and could no longer put a name to what he felt. He gazed into his own eyes and knew not what he saw. The man staring back at him was Vladislav Eliade, too, but where the spirit looked happy and well, the vampire of earth was spent.

There was no answer for this unnatural happening, Vlad was beyond any knowledge.

As soon as they arrived, the three spirits were gone, leaving the gates of oblivion open, the Necrostone dragging the last of Vlad's energy from him. The vampire fell to his side, his hand dropping from the sword. The last thing he saw was the golden wolf bow its head to Cain before an unknown force slammed the gates shut and the Necrostone stopped spinning. The rock tumbled back into the font and the church fell suddenly quiet; the wind ceased and Alizon released her water magic as Cain leant his huge bulk against a wall and unleashed a single, solemn howl, a sound of lament and confusion.

Vlad lay upon the ground, a thousand feelings pulverising him, and wished to be anywhere else but there. He needed solitude to gather himself but he could not leave them all; Lucy could not control Cain all night.

"Could somebody help me up?" he whispered into the night's coldness.

Quickly, Jacob was by his side. Vlad saw black tears down his rotten face as he lifted the vampire easily and placed him shakily on his feet. Vlad staggered and Jacob grabbed his shoulders, steadying him, holding him until he could support his own weight.

"Thank you," Vlad said quietly. "I am…glad…you came back to us."

"Yeah, and I don't think I'm going to forget *that* in a hurry," Jacob said, pointing at the font and the space of air where the afterlife had shone. "God, you look bloody awful, mate; got all those black veins on you, eesh!"

"Yes, thank you…for that visual…analysis," Vlad muttered. Jacob pulled an apologetic face and leant back to sigh.

"Well it worked. Sarah's gone. That was a good thing to do, she looked really happy. What am I saying, I can't believe we just *did* that! And Alizon, that was serious magic! How come you stood in the afterlife? Mirror image? I don't even understand most of what just happened. I don't understand any of it, if I'm honest."

"That is quite alright," Vlad said. "Perhaps if I get…my *own* head…around the finer points I may be…able to explain enough of it…that we can piece together…the rest. Could you do me a favour?"

Jacob nodded.

"Could you go below and retrieve…those four silver chains, please? We will need them for Cain and I am…too weak to touch them now."

Blood and Biscuits

"Aye, no problem. Won't be a mo'," Jacob said, leaning Vlad against a pew before hurrying to the basement.

"Lucy, do you still control Cain?" Vlad asked, voice cracked with tiredness, body ready to collapse again. Lucy nodded.

"Y-yeah, I think so." She glanced at the white werewolf. He was busy licking under his arm. "I'll get him to comply with the silver chains, maybe they'll just relax him."

"One can only hope," Vlad muttered. "Alizon. Fable. Both well?"

The faerie and enchantress checked themselves over and nodded.

"Good, that is good," Vlad whispered.

He stumbled to the font and peered into its depths. The Necrostone sat just as any other rock and Vlad felt a spark of irritation at it. He did not know why, only that for something so plain and motionless to produce so much power and nearly destroy his body greatly annoyed him right then.

The vampire reached down to pick up the Necrostone but a sudden rumbling stayed his hand. He looked up and saw everyone's faces growing in panic.

"What was that?" Lucy asked as Cain took a few steps out from the wall and stared up at the sky. "I don't…"

The rumble came again, stronger. The ground shifted subtly beneath them.

"Move," Vlad hissed. "Run!"

Without question, they sprinted as Vlad gathered the Necrostone, his shirt, and the silver-edged claymore and followed after, the blade draining what little had recovered of him. He stumbled and fell, sword clattering across the roiling stone ground, then a pair of hands hauled him up. Vlad's eyes blurred and he looked up at Fable, the faerie grunting through pain lancing her hands, her teeth gritted. Vlad heard a screech as Lucy grabbed the sword.

Carrying Vlad awkwardly, Fable dodged between the old

pews ahead of Lucy as Cain launched himself from wall to arch to bench, the ground cracking and shaking, flagstones dislodging through the floor beneath their feet. The Support Group ran from the church as Jacob ran from the basement, four silver chains in-hand, and the roof of St Ellins collapsed in on itself.

"By the Goddess," Alizon muttered, her breath misting as every eye gazed upon the church in its final moments.

Fable placed Vlad carefully on the ground and he knelt. Lucy threw the claymore aside, shaking her hands to rid them of the stinging metal.

The walls crumbled and the dirt around St Ellin's bubbled like boiling water. Arches shattered and tumbled inwards, everything standing for so long becoming ash and ruin as the church collapsed, swallowed by the hungry earth. The noise was immense, the air vibrating with its wrath.

Soon all that remained was a hole in the ground.

Through it all, Vlad watched emotionlessly as the thinnest shadow fell from the sky and fluttered to the ground.

Sarah's veil. The one thing hiding her from the world.

Where it came to rest, it was taken into the soil. A minute later, several points of dirt burst upward and the stems and petals of three pink flowers grew out into the world, the last bastion of a ghost's memory. Spirit roses, Sarah's true flower.

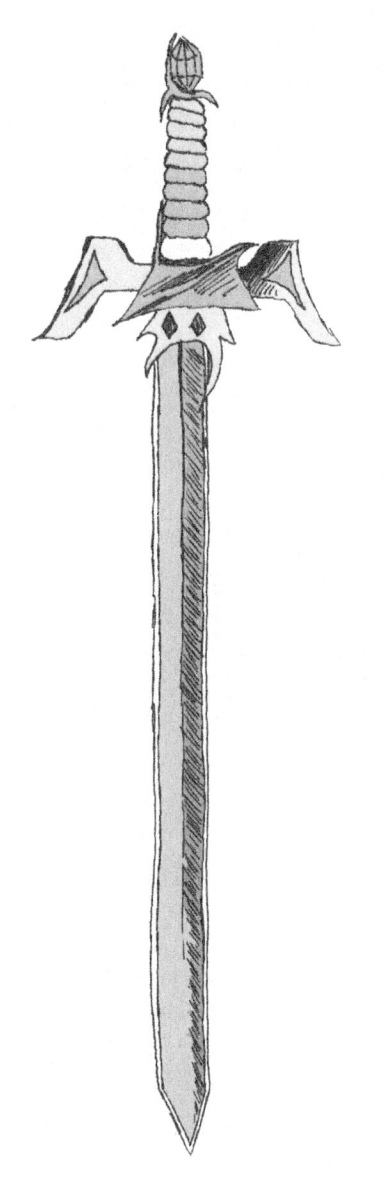

Fig. 1. Silver-Edged Claymore.

I despise using this weapon and yet I must. It is the only one capable of cutting open the window to the afterlife, the gates of oblivion.

I wish very much to throw it in a lovely deep river and be done with the sodding thing. However, I wish not to disrespect the memory of the Spaniard that made it, so perhaps I might donate the blade to a worthy recipient...

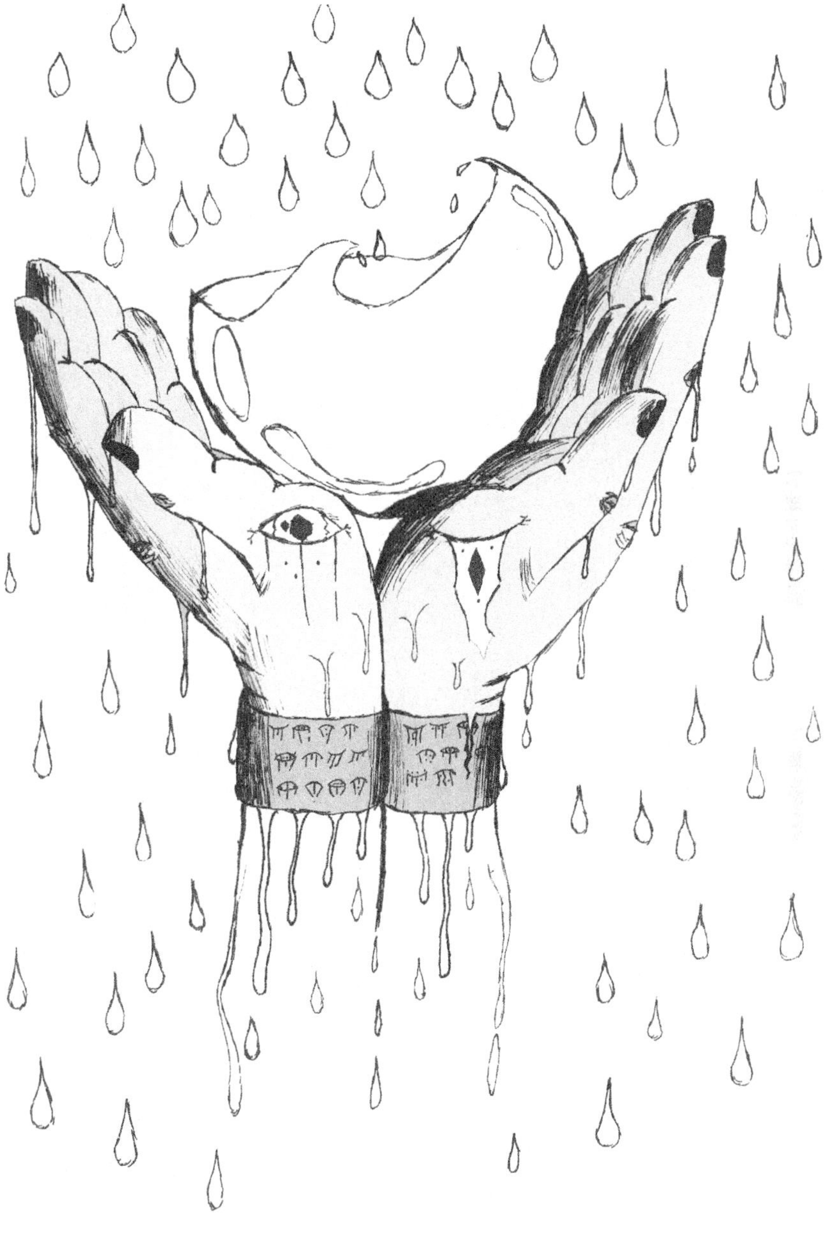

Fig. 15. Alizen's Hands.

The raw power emanating from our resident witch's hands was staggering. The force with which she commanded the waters of the world was awe-inspiring; Alizen did not hesitate to protect her friends, not many would act as she did. The symbols upon her bracelets are of some natural witch language, one, they say, that grew out of the ground and fell from the trees. The words were seen by the eyes of nature and released to those that could shepherd them. Alizen understands them far better than I (little pun there).

THE WASTELANDS,
ELLIN'S INDUSTRIAL ISLAND.

The next hour was a blur.

After the initial panic was over, wherein Jacob and Alizon expressed in varying forms of dismay how their church had been eaten, everyone's focus narrowed on the werewolf.

Through his exhaustion, Vlad directed Lucy to keep Cain calm as Jacob bound him in silver. He was surprisingly pliant; Lucy's strength had grown.

Questions rose about where to keep Cain safe now the church had fallen – Vlad tried reasoning through how the building and Sarah's existence were somehow linked but he was too tired. Nobody was in the right frame of mind. Ultimately, the church was too long for the world; the only thing keeping it standing was Sarah.

In the end, Vlad recovered enough strength to help drag Cain across the wastelands, towards the old, abandoned factories on the south shores. When they reached one of the cavernous holes in the side of the rusting skeletal complexes, he told them all to leave him with Cain there, promising to explain everything tomorrow.

Vlad knew they all needed to recover before he shared the island's greatest secret with them.

"There is sanctified ground and electric lighting within, Cain will transform back in minutes. You have my word, all shall be well. It will be worth it," he said, watching them all leave, exhausted.

OUTSIDE THE INDUSTRIAL COMPLEX,
ELLIN'S INDUSTRIAL ISLAND,
FIFTEEN HOURS FOLLOWING CONTACT WITH THE AFTERLIFE.

Vlad stood before the factory entrance and examined himself. He felt recovered now, every black vein had disappeared.

Cain walked from the depths to stand beside Vlad.

"It is a very good thing Lucy's command over you still had some effect after she left last night or things might have turned out quite differently."

"What do you mean?" Cain asked seriously, rubbing his hands together as the sun broke across the chilly island. Vlad glanced at him.

"Well I was especially weak last night – situations were quite different before, during our fight with the silver chains. Now I had silver *and* the Necrostone draining me. I think I very nearly perished. Subduing you as well would have been too great a task, even for me."

"Then thank God for Lucy, eh?"

"Thank *a* god, certainly," Vlad commented, leaving the matter there. Cain twitched.

"You never *did* tell me if you saw 'em," he said.

"Hmm?"

"Your wife and daughter."

Vlad smiled weakly.

"I believe I did. They were happy. Very happy, actually. It has given me significant comfort seeing their smiles again – you know, I had quite forgotten their faces. To think, I could not remember my own daughter's *face*. Yet seeing her there, young and vibrant, has given me new life in death. And I think I saw forgiveness in my wife's eyes." Vlad hesitated, unsure how much he should burden Cain with. Then he shrugged; the man deserved to know. "Furthermore, I, um, also saw myself beside them."

"Eh? I don't follow. Like a mirror?"

"No, not quite. An image of myself appeared in the afterlife but I am most unsure why. Suffice it to say, the matter is not dropped, but for now, it was wonderful to see my family again. They are, indeed, happy."

"Good," Cain muttered. "That's good, at least. That's decent closure most don't get."

"In all honesty," Vlad sighed, kicking his heels in shame, "I tried joining them. I tried crawling to my family, to be with them in the afterlife, mirror version of me be damned."

"Really?"

"Yes. But I was not allowed. Something held me back, and I am glad it did. I am not done here – I am not done with any of you. I was saved from a mistake, despite what Cuthbert tries to convince me of otherwise."

"Cuth-? Oh, your demon. Good for you, Vlad," Cain said jovially, clapping the vampire on the back. "Honesty's golden and you've got a lot to be thankful for, I think."

"Indeed," Vlad replied simply. Then the vampire remembered something of gold and he nudged Cain. "Another thing about the afterlife? Turns out your lupine ancestors in their broken temple were right: there really *is* a giant demigod watching over death."

Cain looked at Vlad in surprise.

"You're kidding. What did it say?"

"Nothing, it took the form of a golden wolf the size of St Paul's Cathedral."

"You're joking, that's gotta' be a hot lie. Everything them old werewolves in Scotland believed was true? Nah, I don't buy it."

"You know, just because I cannot do it when stood on sanctified ground it does not mean I actively enjoy lying when I get the chance. Cain, I swear it, there was a huge wolf guarding the afterlife. It acknowledged *you*, I might add."

Cain blew his cheeks out.

"That's a lot to take in, just on its own. You really saw a god, Vlad, like an actual god."

Vlad stroked his chin.

"I truly do not know. Perhaps it was an image of magic. I sensed nothing from it, no vast reservoir of strength or anything wolf of it. Perhaps it was less a god and more a guardian and commander, directing souls to the afterlife so we might greet them."

"Either way, I'm glad it's gone."

"As am I. Though thinking on that imposter dressed as myself makes my dead skin crawl."

They stood a while in silence, the good company erasing mental images of giant wolves and evil spirits, enjoying the morning after one of the hardest nights Vlad could remember. Cain shook himself down and sneezed a little, his allergies still present with one more night of the full moon to endure, but the man gave off a distinct scent of satisfaction, as if something had shifted within him allowing a form of happiness.

Cain looked to the rising winter sun and up at the towering factories.

"You think they'll be able to handle this? The afterlife's one thing, but *this* is somethin' *quite* different. What you've got here – well, *had* here – for the past two hundred years, Vlad…it's nothin' short of miraculous. I honestly dunno' how the others are gonna' cope. How's *Jacob* gonna' cope?"

"Everyone performed admirably last night, they shall be fine with this. Jacob is strong in his mind, stronger than you know. And you did your bit perfectly. We would not have succeeded without you, Cain."

"Oh…thanks," the werewolf grunted. Vlad smelled a sliver of pride peel off him. "It's nice to be worth something, I guess."

A river breeze stirred and dried reeds skittered across the mud flats. The sun burnt the last of the night's mist as, finally, Vlad felt a banshee, a wraith, and an enchantress step onto the island two miles away. He knew Fable would be with them but for the death of him, he still could not sense her. Then an idea struck him.

Vlad concentrated and detected the differences of the island itself now others had stepped upon it. He felt the footsteps of four people and the shape of the air moving around their bodies, and suddenly Vlad knew how he could detect Fable's presence without sensing her emotions. He had to read the environment, impressions she left, changes she made upon matter itself.

'It seems so very simple now,' he thought.

"They are here," Vlad muttered. "We should not have long to wait."

"How much will this magic spell take out of you when you cast it?"

"Not much. You understood it as a wolf so it must be simple enough, which is strange, given how long it took me to discover its secrets and lower the enchantment."

"I just can't believe it's been here all this time, right under our noses."

"You may not believe a lot of things about our world, Master Cain, but there are many occurrences hidden from you. However, these are matters for another day."

"Yeah," Cain growled. "One thing at a time."

After twenty minutes Lucy, Jacob, Alizon, and Fable became visible. Vlad and Cain walked out to meet them. Fable placed her hands on her hips and took in the industrial complex curiously. Lucy flashed an encouraging smile at Cain, relief evident on her face.

"Feeling better?" she asked him.

"Much, thanks. Thanks for takin' care of me."

Lucy beamed.

"So what's this all about, then?" she asked.

"This, Lucy, is about the best-kept secret on this island," Vlad responded. "It is about this leviathan of a structure behind me and what it represents."

"Huh?" Jacob said, language failing him.

Cain nodded.

"Yeah, you and me both, mate."

"If you would care to follow me," Vlad said pleasantly, "we need a greater position from which to observe as I perform a little illusion magic."

"Magic!" Fable and Alizon exclaimed in unison as Vlad breezed out across the wastelands.

Hurrying to keep up, Fable said, "But I feel no magic in you! You are a vampire, a creature of darkness, not someone born to

Blood and Biscuits

channel. Darkness counters magic, it's not possible."

"Quite right," Vlad said, smiling, "but like anyone, I can research and study, and I have managed to teach myself an array of useable spells over the centuries with a great deal of hard work and dedication. As you say, I am not born from magic. However, that does not mean I cannot learn a few things here and there, and when I set my mind to something I generally, by and large, see it done. I can hold back my darkness from tainting the spells just enough."

Fable shook her head, unconvinced.

Vlad located a rocky outcrop jutting from the mud, its top relatively flat. It was big enough for all to stand upon and the Support Group followed Vlad onto the dais and stood behind him, the humungous factories sitting in beautiful sadness in the sunlight, a memorial for lives gone by.

"Please note this magic will only work for all here, no others will see what you see or feel what you feel," Vlad explained. "This structure has stood in this same place for many hundreds of years, possibly thousands, and has been covered with an array of different guises to match its place in time. As the master, I can see the guise whenever I wish but for you all, the secret revealed is permanent."

"But it's just some old factories," Jacob said, pointing exasperatedly.

Vlad grinned.

"No, it is not. That is illusion magic masking the true secret beneath, warding off unwanted attention and any possible perception."

"But it can be touched," Lucy added. "I saw you and Cain smash through it weeks ago; it fell apart and everything!"

"It is magic of a different sort to that which you might have heard about in books," Vlad said as he found within himself a reserve of strength. He would use this to supply the spell with energy. "This is a *physical* illusion, the most sublime and unique I have ever encountered. It gives off all the appearances of being real, even to touch, yet it is no more real than a dream. Anything broken is rebuilt

Blood and Biscuits

come the morning."

"I like to think dreams are real," Alizon said quietly.

"Of course," Vlad said humbly, inclining his head. "Well there is really nothing left to say. Shall we begin and see where the rest of our support sessions will be taking place, if you so wish to continue them?"

Everyone either murmured assent or nodded, and Vlad stretched his arms out, shaking his wrists and fingers. He kept all darkness trapped behind the walls of his control, knowing its taint would destroy the magic he was to perform. Vampires could not channel magic, that was the rule, but Vlad broke rules.

"Please, step back and allow me the space required to get this right."

Everyone retreated and Vlad set his body, aligning himself with the industrial complex and clearing his mind entirely, letting only emptiness fill it. He was not a practised sorcerer and he was not born from magic, but he could still do this and perhaps he might finally start bringing some light to the world.

Vlad positioned his hands before him, wrists touching. His fingers were straight, the middle ones bending towards one another. He closed his eyes and breathed, just for the feel of the air in his throat.

The wind stirred a little.

"*Sol et scutum et clypeum lucis. Cadunt. Incidunt et sit nihil. Scutum et lapides de Onyx Castrum, unum ex nihil sunt, conversus ad ruinam.*"

As Vlad invoked the spell, the sun's light grew brighter and all about them the earth shivered. The factories flashed and shimmered. Rusted, skeletal forms reverberated and shone, and started melting in on themselves. The Support Group gasped as the vast, dominating structures loomed over the river simply dissolved away, rendered into nothing and leaving behind something else, something greater. Metal replaced by stone walls, collapsed ceilings by sweeping rooftops of tile, and gaping holes by a grand entrance.

Blood and Biscuits

"*Christ,*" Lucy whispered. "Is that a castle!"

"Yes," Vlad said softly. "A very old and very strange one indeed. Feast your eyes, my friends, upon the Castle of the Black Skies, though I simply call it Laegoria. It is quite the wonder."

Staggeringly tall, vast upon the banks of the river, the castle's every wall and turret shone onyx in the sun. Great halls, huge battlements high above, commanded the eye and Vlad smiled at the sight of home, innumerable shrouds of vines flowering in huge carpets of pink blooms defying the winter cold and framing the darkness. The castle looked almost disorganised, in a way, as if it had been repeatedly built upon over time Layers, wings, towers, and external platforms and staircases constructed to link new additions, each moment creating new elaborations to the roofline.

The central keep seemed endlessly deep, the castle's entire length spreading east and west almost the width of the island. An enormous tower stood at each end, the eastern rise boasting a huge clock face and hundreds of grotesques and waterless gargoyles, the western end reaching higher still and finishing in seven twisting, gnarled turrets, a thousand feet above the ground. More overgrown curtains of large pink flowers, nothing like Sarah's spirit roses, draped from walkways jutting far out over the entrance and climbed up the vast west tower, defining the clock's unmoving face, contrasting beautifully with the black stone.

Even to see now, after so often looking at it, Vlad was moved by its enormity, its complicated beauty. The impossibility of such a place had never been lost on him.

"I can't…" Jacob trailed off.

"I know," Vlad said.

"It's just…"

"I know," Vlad grinned.

"This is…"

"I *know,*" Vlad repeated, excitedly. "That is how *I* felt when I first discovered it."

"Wait, you didn't build it?"

Blood and Biscuits

"*Build* it! My heavens, no!" Vlad exclaimed. "It was always here, this castle, far as I can tell. I simply appropriated it when nobody claimed it in the first hundred years of visiting England. Since then, I have come to call it my home, the place from which I centre myself and my entire world. I have an apartment in town, true, but that is for ease and entertaining company. *This* is where I live and dedicate all research and learning, a place of comfort and mystery, of secrets I still have not identified. You are all most welcome to call this castle your home, too, if you would like."

"Good God, I wish to go in there," Fable said slowly and Vlad laughed, heartily.

"Indeed, after everything we have seen and done, and especially after the ordeal we survived last night, I would recommend we go inside at once and try to find some tea, and perhaps some biscuits. Cain mentioned Jaffa cakes were required?"

"Actually, I was wonderin' if you had anythin' savoury, like that rabbit you did," Cain said sheepishly and Vlad laughed again as Lucy smacked him on the arm.

"I have many things in there, to my embarrassment, so let us go. Come, my friends. Come and see the Castle of the Black Skies for yourselves."

And they set off across the wastelands towards the towering castle of onyx stone and finery and Vlad glanced up at the tallest turret: he needed to sleep at some point, it had been many months since he had last meditated on the island. Now that St Ellin's was gone his metapsychological compass would need realigning.

"You know, I prefer the name Laegoria," Alizon said happily.

THE LIBRARY AND ALCHEMICAL LABORATORY,

THE INDUSTRIAL COMPLEX.

Vlad stared down at the glass slide caught in the metal catches of the microscope before him, his mouth agape. A tiny white dot of purest white powder, almost too bright to look at, sat on the slide. Vlad felt humbled before it, its majesty shaming the darkness within him, his demon Cuthbert withdrawing from the powder as if it threatened by it.

"This cannot be," Vlad whispered. He glanced at the powder again then ran his finger down a page on deiform creatures, angelic and sacred. "This just…I have the answer. I know why Cain's blood acts as it does."

Teaching Lessons

"I'm glad you could make it, I hope your flight wasn't too bad."

"Oh no, I enjoy a jaunt over the hills these ways. I have not flown here in decades, I am strangely glad to see nothing has changed. Same old country lanes, trees hanging over the roads, fields of wheat...you know, I think I am filled with energy by just coming here."

Alizon glanced away, eyes scanning the horizon, desperately trying not to look anywhere near Vlad.

"It was always good for me out here. The open sky, the breeze, the torrential downpours, the freezing snows, the sunshine: all of it was balm to my magic, and living with Aunty Windwater was enough to make me feel loved again."

"Then I cannot wait to meet her," Vlad said, bowing to Alizon a little. As they walked, he thought of the castle. "Tell me, did you like Laegoria? Are you looking forward to the official tour?"

The slightest vibration shook off Alizon, a shiver of anticipation, and she smiled at the sunset.

"It was glorious, Vlad. I've never seen anything like it; the pink flowers remind me of Aunty Windwater's cottage – you'll see what I mean – and those turrets? The Jade Chapel was lovely, Cain seemed happy in the kitchens with his meat and Jaffa cakes. Fable's face when she saw those giant bells! Oh, I can't wait to see more of it."

Down the country lane they strolled, the sounds of sheep and cows in their barns filling the chilly winter's afternoon. They turned down a thinner road, this one hardly wider than a van, and continued in silence.

However, that quiet did not last long.

Blood and Biscuits

Vlad's senses triggered as something approached from behind, fast. He turned and pulled Alizon round with him as a car screeched over the junction and sped down the track towards them. The driver inside could not have been older than eighteen, four friends with him, but Vlad stood in the middle of the lane and waited defiantly.

The driver's eyes grew wide and he slammed on the brake. The hatchback threw up clods of dirt and stones, halting in a cloud of dust. The teenager opened his window as Vlad folded his arms and watched, fingers tapping irritably on his elbow.

"Are you aware you could have killed my friend?" he asked, low voice carrying like a roar, darkness dripping from every word.

"I din't see you, fella', get out a'way, we got places t'be!" the young driver hollered, his friends jeering and swearing beside him. "Come on out the way, don't need no skinny no nothin' givin' me lip. You look like you need some sunshine, mate!" His friends burst out laughing, voices cracking with youth.

Vlad leant forwards and planted his palms on the bonnet, glaring at the spotty boy through the smeared windscreen.

"And you need some manners."

Vlad allowed a glitter of darkness into his eyes. The boy's face paled, his mouth falling open, and he slammed his foot on the accelerator, wheels grinding the dirt. Vlad kept his hands firm as the car tried running him over. The bonnet beneath his hands buckled and caved, plumes of smoke snaking from the rear wheels where they churned uselessly.

With almighty strength, Vlad shoved the car backwards, its five occupants screaming, the hatchback soaring back up the lane. Vlad spun Alizon to the side as the car's still-screeching rear wheels bounced off the ground and the vehicle rocketed off, careering almost completely out of control. The car roared away until it was gone, the struggling engine drowned by the boys' screams.

Vlad flashed a smile at Alizon.

Blood and Biscuits

"Was that really necessary?" she asked, a hint of a sigh about her.

"No, but sometimes certain people need a bloody good lesson drilling into them. They were young, they will get over it. Come on, Aunty Windwater awaits! I do hope she has coffee."

"She has wonderful coffee!" Alizon said loudly as they walked, the moment with the car set aside. "I hate the taste but the smell makes me hungry. Reminds me of nice mornings with bacon sandwiches looking out over the fields. Christmas time and Easter holidays. After what happened with Sarah, I need another reminder of home."

"I did not know you were struggling with thoughts of what we did, Alizon. You should have said something, we could have spoken sooner. I would not have you worrying alone, not unless you wished for silence."

"No, no, you were busy, I couldn't be selfish and take you from your tasks. I was spending a lot of my time ignoring messages from my mother, she's being quite insistent about it. Please, stop trying to convince me otherwise, I don't want to occupy your every second."

"You are *not-*" Vlad began but Alizon cut him off.

"It's alright, you don't have to pacify me. I'm just happy to be here, with you, in the sunshine. One symbol of care about to meet another. It's really special to me."

Vlad bit back his words and inclined his head.

"And it means a great deal to me, too. Thank you for inviting me."

They walked for a while until, at last, Alizon spoke again.

"It does feel right, sending Sarah on."

Vlad sniffed.

"I think that is because it *was* the right thing to do. Nobody can take that from us, as they cannot take her memory."

They walked the last of the lane and came to a small drive, overgrown with hedges and nettles. An open wooden gate sat adorned with sculptures and shells and painted rocks. Beyond was a large cottage, much of it hidden by flowering vines and large shrubs left to grow as they wished. Wind charms hung from branches, doorways, windows, and large red toadstools grew out the garden trees as thin streams wound throughout. Vlad opened the gate and sensed a faint electric hum of magical charmcraft everywhere, a feeling of nature at its purest. Somebody very knowledgeable lived here.

"I can see why you love this place," Vlad muttered as they came to the front door beneath a rickety wooden porch it. He knocked. "This is a haven for natural magic users. Simply magnificent, Alizon."

"Thank you, I'm sure Aunty Windwater would love to hear that."

The door opened and framed an older woman, possibly mid-fifties, of Chinese origin, her tanned skin shining in the low sunlight, a wide smile on her weathered, beautiful face. There was no family resemblance to Alizon at all, that much was immediately evident, but deep affection blossomed in her eyes at the sight of the witch upon her doorstep.

"Alizon! Love, what a nice surprise, I didn't know you were coming over, I'd have put a chicken on or something. I *knew* the Goddess shone brightly last night, she always does before you come. Step in here and give your aunty a squelch!"

Alizon stepped into her outstretched arms and Vlad stoppered a small gasp in his throat. Alizon never gave so much affection at once yet there she stood, channelling her energies into somebody else. Aunty Windwater kissed the top of her head then held her back, peering into her eyes as Alizon stared back, unashamed and unabashed. It was unconditional love and trust, the only eyes Vlad had seen the weather witch look into.

"So what brings you out here again without calling first? Not that I mind, I always told you to get here as often as you could, only I could've been out, girl. You know I'm on my vigils more often than

Blood and Biscuits

not these days. You're not here because of your mother again, are you?"

Vlad instantly adored her, the woman that had taken care of Alizon without ever having to. Choice would always be the most important aspect of life.

Alizon glanced back at Vlad, without meeting his gaze, and shrugged a little.

"No, it's not her. We-"

And before she could stop herself, Alizon fell back into Aunty Windwater's arms and began to gently cry. Her aunty gave a short sigh and rubbed Alizon's back, clenching her tight and making small sounds of comfort.

"Oh dear, love, whatever's the matter? What's happened? You tell us if you want to, no need if not, but cryin's best for these moments."

"It's just..." Alizon sobbed. "Vlad and I – we all had a...a dark time the other night. Vlad thought it best I get rest wherever I could." Alizon stepped back and wiped her eyes. "We lost someone close to us. I told him this is where I come to get my head straight, I hope we're not intruding."

"Girl, of course you're not, I've already said welcome! It's terrible about your friend – sorry, I'm happy to meet you, Vlad," Aunty Windwater said, holding out her hand.

Vlad took it and shook – hard calluses, the hands of hard work and harder dedication – and he felt a shiver run up the woman's arm. Her eyes glinted. She looked at his face properly, the pale skin, the sunken cheeks, the way he held himself.

"Been a while since I met a vampire," Aunty Windwater said quietly, her voice faint and knowing.

"You are not afraid?" Vlad asked, his hand still clasped in hers.

She blew her lips a little and smiled.

Blood and Biscuits

"Any vampire that can stand in daylight and is held in such regard by Alizon ain't a vampire to be afraid of. Get inside and we'll sit a while, get some views of one another. And some crumpets."

"Ooh, do you have the salty butter!" Alizon cried excitedly as they walked in, Vlad bowing his head humbly.

"Of course, it's been out the fridge a while so it's just on the soft side, too."

Vlad looked round the low-ceilinged kitchen. It would have been a large room were it not stuffed with mismatched wooden furniture, strange, colourful ornaments of dragons and goblins, and hundreds of charms hiding the walls. However, it was no claustrophobia nightmare but instead rather cosy as Vlad sat at a rough-hewn oak table and smiled at Alizon.

"I had a sense somebody might be coming," Aunty Windwater said, the adornments in her long dreadlocks jangling pleasantly as she set about preparing cups for tea and coffee. "I felt it in the waters of the airs after they settled in my streams. And the God above's gazing down bright and unfettered. Always a good sign. I take it you want a black coffee, my lover?"

"That would be splendid, yes. Do I detect a little accent?" Vlad asked boldly. "From the South-West?"

"Totnes," Aunty Windwater replied breezily as she placed a sloshing kettle on a gas hob. "Go back occasionally to get more elephant trousers," she added, flapping her baggy legwear merrily, its pattern of rhinos and flowers waving.

When they were sat with their respective drinks, Alizon with her buttered crumpets, the three got to talking. Both women surprised Vlad with their candidness, holding nothing back in the regaling of their lives. It transpired that they were unrelated, instead Aunty Windwater was an old friend of Alizon's father's. She had neither seen nor heard from him in years, she did not even know where he lived now, and had no contact details. Alizon's mother had seen to that when they had separated, removing all information before they had chance to know where he had moved. Not that

Alizon seemed bothered. She said nothing about it, choosing instead just to listen to her guardian talk brightly into the kitchen, her voice filling every last space not already filled, skipping between furniture and rooms and returning to Vlad's senses with a detailed map of the house's insides. They ended up talking about all manner of things, from Alizon's school to what films they liked, and even where Aunty Windwater bought the vegetables she could not grow herself.

"And then I saw his aura and decided he wasn't worth my time. Got my onions from someone else," Aunty Windwater finished, draining the last of her tea.

Vlad stared at her blankly as Alizon watched with awe, fascination evident in her motionlessness. Her hands, usually so lively with discomfort, were still.

"His aura?" Vlad repeated questioningly.

"Mmm," Aunty Windwater confirmed. She leant back and looked at Alizon. "You didn't tell your friend here about me?" Alizon shook her head and Aunty Windwater gave a short, musical laugh. "But he's a vampire! And he knows all about *your* powers! Why should I be left out?"

Aunty Windwater took a scone from a dish in the middle and began spreading clotted cream on it.

"Always do jam second," she said, adding raspberry and blackcurrant preserve on top of the cream. "Where I'm from, cream second is punishable by death. Right, so what Alizon forgot to mention," she continued, taking a bite out of her freshly prepared scone, "was that although I'm a practicing Wiccan, I've got an added talent for reading auras. Bet you didn't expect *that*."

"Oh, no I very much did not," Vlad said thinly, wondering if he was supposed to know what that meant. "Unfortunately, for once I am at a loss. I know relatively little about Wiccan magic; Alizon had to explain much about herself to me after we started getting to know one another."

"And a wonderfully skilled weather witch she is, too, she grew up in the right conditions out here and under the tutelage of her senior channellers at Emberlash College in Wales. I was raised different, a woman of a particular gift born under just the right circumstances. My gift's separate from my Wiccan knowledge, it's a *Perspective*, a natural-made talent in someone. It can happen in literally anyone, oftentimes in non-magical folk. You see, auras are a particular energy created by living things, Mr Vlad, energies I can see around them, and I reckon I've figured them out over these years. Never knew what it was as a child but now I've got an adult's outlook. It's why talents're called Perspectives, because you can never understand them until you learn enough from life to frame 'em proper."

Vlad leaned in, hands wrapped about his mug intently.

"What is this energy?" he asked almost breathily. "What do you see?"

"I see a sort of...well, *aura*. As I said, it's an energy, like a faint shimmer, never seems to go away."

"Like a sort of cloud?" Vlad suggested.

"Not really, it's a lot less dense. It's more like flames: they come from fire and give off light but they're not really a *thing*, they're more a process. Auras are like flames, images of deeper processes."

"Now that I understand. Do auras ever change?" Vlad asked.

"All the time. Some people have strong auras, some weaker. Babies've got extremely small auras, hardly there at all, but it quickly grows as they age. Get the imagination about 'em, the quick fancies of children. When people die, though, when they *stay* dead, then their auras disappear completely, they go into the earth."

"So it is life force, then," Vlad guessed but Aunty Windwater shook her head.

"No, but I did once guess that. See, I learned to live with this, I can't ever turn it off. It's a type of sight, a beautiful *in*sight into people, like a secret only I know. Auras are different when you sleep, when you concentrate, when you laugh and cry, when you sing, play instruments...in the end, auras represent people as they are, in their state of mind, how they're thinking."

"Yes but what *are* they? What do they do?"

"Auras, ultimately...are nothing. They do nothing, anyway. They're merely representations of your intelligence. They're thought, Vlad, pure thought. The more people use their brains, the more they *think*, the stronger their auras. Their energies flow from them and into the ground, like it's pouring down with gravity and back into the world. I don't know how it works, I've never found information on it, it's just..."

"It's a gift," Alizon finished. "It always has been, even when I was small and you could tell me all the funny shapes you saw around people. You used to make me laugh with our ice creams at the park."

"You remember! Oh, that's so wonderful, Alizon, those are my fondest memories of you, you know." Aunty Windwater sipped her lemongrass tea, finishing her scone. Vlad let her gather her thoughts and wondered what *her* aura looked like, or if she had ever seen it in a reflection. "My gift is nothing compared to raising Alizon, though, and her natural powers so intricate as they are, but it's my own little corner of wonder. I love it, it gives me such deep understanding of people."

"It truly is a wondrous ability, a window into the mysteries behind the soul itself." Vlad leant in closer and grinned slyly. "And I noticed you mentioned fully dead people have no auras, so what do you see of *my* cursed thought?"

Aunty Windwater smiled and sipped her lemongrass tea.

"I make a point never to tell anyone their aura. It'd be rude to assume their intelligence." Her eyes glanced all about Vlad with clever interest. "But nice try, all the same."

Alizon sat back and sighed in satisfaction, searching round the room with wide eyes. Vlad, meanwhile, was intent on learning more. He opened his mouth to speak but Aunty Windwater held up her hand.

Blood and Biscuits

"I don't know how any of it works, Vlad, before you ask - I can see you're a man of questions."

"He really is," Alizon said bluntly. "Certainly gets everyone at the group talking."

"And it's important to talk, just like I taught you," Aunty Windwater said. "I'm glad you've had such a strong influence on my niece, Mr Vlad. I'm happy she's found good friends in her adulthood, it's something I've never been able to truly give her."

"It seems like you have done more than anyone should ever have asked of you," Vlad said quietly, seeing love line every angle of Alizon's face.

"Nobody ever asked me to do anything," Aunty Windwater said, squeezing Alizon's hand.

Week Ten
History Soaked into the Walls

CASTLE LAEGORIA,
MONDAY, 18:00

Vlad walked the castle halls and found himself smiling. He was in some form of peace. The heavy drag of his depression tried to weigh him down and drown him, and he fought it off with every step. But Cuthbert would not suffocate him today.

Thoughts of Sarah skimmed Vlad's mind as he wandered the winding corridors, staring in wonder at stained-glass windows and old tapestries hanging lifeless. Battles were evident in much of the iconography, huge wars between creatures of Earth and beasts of other worlds raging across the creations. Thousands of the older pieces of art bore images of great achievements and representations of painful and beautiful truth and deep-set imagination. From vast stone sculptures of gods and people united in creation to ornaments upon plinths detailing love in its many forms.

Vlad stopped to admire an intricately ornate fountain crafted out of a south wall, a great thing made to seem as if a forest pool had grown from the stone, petrified in time. He ran a pale finger along the pool's edge and sat for a moment, interlacing his fingers in thought, head bowed in remembrance of Sarah and all she had represented. Vlad recalled her face as she departed this world, that *relief*, and he wondered how that felt, how that truly felt.

Blood and Biscuits

"To be released from this life and to find peace…that is an adventure I may never know. Or perhaps I already know it, given the image of myself in the afterlife. What did *that mean? Am I actually in my own version of hell and that was a vision of me in purgatory? No, that is not possible. If I ponder too much it will drive me insane."*

Though the act caused him great pain and guilt, Vlad pushed aside thoughts of Sarah. If he dwelt on her any longer, his peace would end, he would topple from his knife-edge balance, and Cuthbert would come for him. In that instance, Vlad would lose control and descend into utter rage. The last time that happened, Vlad had found himself off the coast of Sennen, in Cornwall, and screaming his darkness at the sky.

There had been a great storm that night. To his great shame, Vlad had been too violent of mind to assist the lifeguards sent out to rescue the trawlers.

He stood and journeyed west along the last of the long hallway. He turned north and headed up the crafts workshops of Laegoria. The hallway expanded into vast rooms once used for the creation and development of artefacts and contraptions of influence. Now the mezzanines hung empty, the machines and forges cold in their housings, doing nought but gathering dust.

When at last Vlad came to the grand staircase, he stood for a moment and gazed down the two hundred and seventy-five steps, which he had counted long ago out of boredom. Every fifty-five steps there were wide landing stretches leading down more winding corridors and serving as places to stop and admire of the castle's history and ornateness, with more sculptures and towering paintings taking up far too much wall space, Vlad realised.

The vampire looked to the stairs and shook his head, more at himself than anything else. It was not something anybody would notice right away but at the back of each step, etched into the riser, there was a different historical scene set in marble. Very difficult to see and even more hellish to study without a huge amount of time at one's disposal. Thankfully, Vlad's immortality allowed for such things and so he had committed two months of tireless analysis until he had formed a detailed account of each stair. He had then compiled these into a book with sketches and wonderings of his own, and then set the book on a lectern on the ground floor.

Vlad wondered just what exactly drove him to do such remarkably ridiculous things. He supposed it was simply another effect of his despair, finding extensively detailed objects then uncovering everything he could about their every facet and history. To many it would seem arrogant or obsessive, but Vlad knew he was staving off the feelings of personal darkness.

He sighed and descended the staircase, noting the time, knowing his friends would arrive soon. He wished to show them around his home and finally start making the castle feel some way alive again. Vlad wished to fill the empty halls and rooms of cold memory with laughter and music and conversation, the way it must have been long ago when Laegoria was built. He came to the cavernous atrium at the bottom and walked to the colossal entrance doors.

"Come, let us make new history together," Vlad said quietly to the doors, and he hauled them open using the spell-driven wheel and chain system to one side.

Great bronze weights, shaped and engraved as gigantic bianzhong bells descended on ropes, hauling the doors open with their sheer mass. They rang and boomed beautifully, announcing the opening of the castle. The doors would close again when the chain wheel was reactivated, hidden spells working in ways too complex for Vlad to understand.

Deep sun poured in, bathing the atrium in its golden brilliance, evening light that would have obliterated a much younger, less capable vampire. Vlad stepped out to meet it and felt the warmth on his dead skin, breathing in automatically and smelling the sweet scent of the river on the air, mixed with the soils of the wastelands beyond and the thousands of other senses from the skies above. He heard the birds calling and felt the vibrations through the ground as the earth shifted in its myriad ways far below, and Vlad experienced joy arriving from the abyss of his despair as he came to face a new day.

His demon lurked close behind him now, an omen waiting to pounce and drag him down into the ever-yawning chasm that awaited him, mocking him for his role in Sarah's passing. The spectre of her face equal parts comforting and taunting him, thanking and blaming him.

A short while passed before Vlad sensed the arrival of a banshee, a human-form werewolf, an enchantress, and a wraith. Since the night of the afterlife, Vlad had meditated and realigned his connection to Ellin's Island and as he concentrated on that renewed bond, he felt the river lands change with their arrival. The island became *aware* of a supernatural surge, and Vlad knew Fable was with them. He knew not her breaths but he recognised the stir of air before her, eddies swirling gently around her body. Vlad read the vibrations of the ground and counted the footsteps of five people. They were all in good spirits.

Waiting patiently, Vlad absorbed the day and wondered where he would begin with the tour of the castle. They saw little after the Rite of al-Mawt, for everyone had been tired and Vlad had felt himself spiralling into gloom. He had needed three blood packs to recover.

In fact, all they had really seen was the chapel, where the new support sessions would be held, and the kitchens. Cain had nearly fallen over himself at the sight of fifty boxes of Jaffa cakes and Alizon and Fable had practically drooled over the mountains of foreign herbal and fruit teas available in the cupboards.

Before long, the Support group appeared as silhouettes. Vlad saw them raise their arms and point to the castle; he caught snippets of conversation on the wind, their emotions influencing Vlad's senses. He discerned awe and fascination, joy and trepidation, all the normal things people should feel when faced with the prospect of spending time in something as truly ancient and dominating as Laegoria.

Vlad heard Fable first.

"...and that's the way of it, I'm afraid. We shall have to ask nicely."

"He's definitely the accepting type. I reckon Vlad'll go for it."

Vlad smiled strangely and wondered what they were talking about as Alizon offered something.

"Well, perhaps it's a matter of perspective. I think it's taller than it looks, if that makes sense."

"That's ridiculous!" Jacob clearly said as Lucy chuckled, and Vlad sensed a thread of sadness unravel itself from Alizon. Jacob evidently noticed her withdraw in some way because he quickly added: "No I'm sorry, I didn't mean it like that. What I meant, Alizon, was that I can't see what you mean. You mind explaining?"

Vlad sensed another thread from Alizon, this one of pride, and she said:

"What I mean…things like this can be very deceiving. I know the castle's lowered its illusion magic – I don't know much about that stuff, before you ask, I'm a weather witch – but that doesn't stop its sheer size from confusing your eyes. I think it's taller than you say, and a lot, *lot* deeper. There'll be some really interesting things in there, given what Vlad said about it and his reluctance to admit that he doesn't know everything about the place. We should ask what Cain wants and maybe we'll get a better idea."

Before they continued, somebody obviously saw Vlad waiting by the huge entrance doors. The mood of the group immediately shifted into one of collective guardedness, as if they thought Vlad had heard their every word.

"*They are right, of course,*" he thought, "*but they need not be worried about it.*"

The group approached silently. Vlad opened his arms welcomingly.

Blood and Biscuits

"Good afternoon to you all, though it might yet be evening soon. Please, enter and warm yourselves up."

"It's not that cold, actually," Lucy stated as they walked into the castle's atrium, their feet treading lightly upon the deep-red carpet. Cain looked down and stepped away immediately, his face turning the same shade of crimson as the carpet, wet, muddy boot prints shining darkly on the once-spotless material.

"Oh bugger, Vlad, I'm sorry about that. Christ, it's gone right in the plush, that's gonna' be a proper job scrubbin' that out."

Vlad snorted.

"I care not for such things, Cain. You can do what you like with it – you can *burn* the bloody thing, for all I care. There is some deep enchantment laid down that cleans and repairs that sodding carpet every night, come the stroke of midnight, and for the death of me I have been unsuccessful in my attempts to destroy it permanently. I am quite serious," Vlad added at their incredulous faces, "I have even tried tearing it up and dissolving it with acid during some of my fouler mood swings but to no avail. I even ripped out the whole thing and flew it to France, only to find it once more in the atrium the next morning. I can only surmise that whoever protected that carpet was somebody of either unhinged paranoia or outrageous arrogance. Either way, it is a waste of magic, if you ask me."

Alizon bent down and, as the electrical smell of power filled the air, she channelled a single unit of weather magic. An ice-white, sharp-pointed equilateral triangle appeared and turned the air into a hair-thin knife. Fascinated, Vlad watched Alizon slice off a corner of carpet along with a golden tassel; she held it up and dangled the tassel thoughtfully.

"We shall see," she said seriously, and Vlad inclined his head.

"As you wish," he intoned simply. He turned to the others as he closed the great oaken doors again, the chains sliding back into the floor as the wheel stopped spinning. "So, what is it Cain wished to see of the castle you all worried would be too much for me to bear?"

Cain's face turned red again and Lucy laughed.

"He wants to see how high you can go. I don't know why, given he's afraid of heights, but there you go."

"I'm fascinated with tall buildings," Cain qualified. "Always have been. Maybe it's the height thing, God knows." He paused and looked at Vlad out the corner of his eye. "So, is it possible to go high up?"

"Of course, why would it not be?" Vlad queried. "What a foolish thing to worry about, I already said I would provide you all a tour of the place, did I not?"

"Well I dunno', I was worried the tallest tower might've been your bedroom or something! Then Alizon said it was taller than it really was and I got confused."

Cain glanced round and folded his arms defensively. The vampire smiled.

"We can start the tour at ground floor level and finish at the top, how does that sound?"

"Sounds crackin'," Cain said. "Can head back down and properly end with the chapel, then, and do the support stuff."

"An excellent idea!" Vlad said. "I shall truncate much of the tour, the castle is beyond vast and there is plenty I have yet to properly explore and define. Therefore, you shall have the abbreviated and abridged version, so please keep all questions for the end."

"You sound like you're about to start a rollercoaster," Jacob said, the chuckle not quite masking his worry.

"You are in for quite a ride, then, as some doorways you should genuinely not put your arms or legs through," Vlad commented, smiling grimly. "Now, there are five portions to the castle, and from what I can tell, each serves a very different, yet broad, function. We have 'Low Ways', 'Mid-realms', 'Irons', 'Pathacs', and 'Octothers'." He pointed to two passages at the east side of the atrium, the left one a wide stone staircase leading underground. A message inscribed above read '*Aut viam inveniam aut faciam*'.

"That is the 'Low Ways'," he explained. "The first section. It comprises a warren of catacombs stretching long and winding beneath Ellin's Island, travelling distances I have yet to determine, though I have mapped a little. The primary purpose of the Low Ways is to confuse me greatly and reveal nothing, for there are endless stores of ancient weaponry and armour down there, amongst other things, with no history of battles fought around these immediate parts. Then there are humungous chambers and halls fit for sub-level kings still bedecked with moulding finery, as if great monarchs once resided beneath this island instead of above. And not to mention the glowing runes written along every wall detailing a huge story in poetic form. It is all *most* obscure, I assure you."

"That's a lot of information to take in, you should consider condensing your explanations," Alizon said.

"Oh I am, to a severe extent," Vlad replied. He pointed to the towering archway on the right of the winding stairs leading to the dungeons, the message '*Transire, cibus est, expectans*' inscribed in the arc. "The old dining hall and master's study chambers; possibly the most intact rooms in the castle, aside from the Jade Chapel."

Vlad continued in that vein, naming the castle's second portion, 'Mid-Realms', the central castle keep, totalling seven floors. The ground floor was for living: kitchens, chapel, washrooms, et cetera. The top floor was for learning and productive work, displaying dozens of workshops and classrooms of different kinds for the maintenance and creation of all manner of things. The rest of the five floors, sitting between the ground and top floors, Vlad said he would describe as they moved up the grand staircase.

With the first floor, Vlad simply tried to show what he could of the more intricate and interesting features, beginning with a devilishly complex water system he believed ran the entire length, breadth, and depth of the castle. Some of it was visible through doorways of the north-facing walls along the wider corridors of the first floor and Vlad let silence fall so they could hear it humming merrily in every direction. This solved the problems of water deliverance in its many forms.

There were huge rooms with stone-based arenas, seating levels of oak boards and teak beams stacked around their edges. Smaller chambers were filled to the brim with dusty old scientific and practical equipment, and pieces of artistry long-since abandoned. Strange little throughways ran to other sections of the first floor but they were too intricate to follow then. There were hundreds of rooms, too many to visit now, some too dangerous to enter, a few too magically sealed to open.

"It is like this castle was a school, a rudimentary hospital, a place of worship, and a hub for combat training all in one," Vlad mused openly as they ascended to the second floor. "Perhaps it was all of those things, over the years, a gigantic place re-appropriated each time somebody else came along with a purpose that needed fulfilling. And that is just what we have seen already. You wait for what comes next."

On the second floor, the corridors became winding and complicated, with strange offshoots leading seemingly nowhere and others ending in balconies overlooking the sloping rooftops or offering staggering views of the towering turrets and expansive wastelands of Ellin's Island. Vlad opened door after door and showed the Support Group the sorts of things he meant, the castle offering up broken pieces of history in droves as the secrets and mysteries piled on top of one another, begging for answers with no hope of success. Vlad showed doorways hidden behind tapestries and passageways concealed by paintings.

At the very end of the second floor corridor there was a three-foot high door that would not open, and Vlad commented on it.

"One of the many I cannot access, sealed by some spell. I have tried many times but I might as well shout at it for all the good my darkness is against it. Most frustrating."

Blood and Biscuits

Alizon crouched and eyed the door interestedly.

"*These* particular stairwells lead between floors but there are enchantments on them that seem to change," Vlad explained, pointing to several open staircases, their interiors dark. "I swear I have been up them many times but they keep changing floors; one journey will lead to the third floor, another time the same stairwell goes straight to the sixth, or even into rooms I cannot find using conventional methods."

"Why would they do that?" Lucy asked, peering at the thin, winding stairs as they passed them.

"I suppose you are supposed to enact the right spell and the stairwells take you to whatever floor or room they are magically connected to. However, this castle is so old, and has been alone for so much of its life without the care and supervision of true magic casters, the ancient spells designed into its features and architecture have gone a bit…have gone a bit funny, I call it."

Suddenly, one of the stairwells ejected a blast of air and gave a noise like a gasping explosion. All but Vlad leapt and darted away from the empty stairwell. Vlad shrugged.

"You see? That one just sneezed at you, it is clearly backfiring. I have seen one speaking French, another pretending it is shut, and even one that blows raspberries, it is very immature. There is a suit of armour that is supposed to give directions but all it does now is sneak around the fourth floor, trying inexpertly to hide behind things when you look at it. He is very bad at it, I have made many a game out of his attempts."

"You're bloody mad," Cain grunted, his eyes peering down the second floor corridor worriedly.

"You get quite lonely here, it is good to have people inside these walls for the first time," Vlad said offhandedly.

He moved on, continuing the tour enthusiastically.

"I think, perhaps, the second floor was some form of communal sleeping arrangement." They climbed the grand staircase to the third floor. "It makes no sense to me, for people require privacy when they sleep, and this castle is more than large enough to accommodate such proceedings. I think I might be missing something, if that is the case."

"Were kids ever evacuated here during the war?" Jacob asked

"Which one? To a vampire centuries old you cannot just say 'the war'. I assume you refer to the Second World War?"

Jacob nodded and Vlad thought back over seventy years.

"Yes, as a matter of fact. A good few dozen came to Ellinsgate from London and Plymouth and made the north their home – many stayed permanently, finding new lives in the safety and peacefulness the countryside offers, these beautiful parts teaching so much to children that only knew poverty and fear. But I know not of any that would have found themselves in this castle; remember, I was still roaming these halls back then. I would have been fully aware of children running free inside the castle walls within an instant."

They continued to the third floor but Vlad stopped on the landing, his head swivelling to the east and west entrances.

"Oh for God's sake, not again. Both sides as well, bloody hell."

"What? Oh, there's…a garden…" Lucy said, coming to stand next to Vlad.

Where a corridor should have been instead there was an endless expanse of sun-drenched gardens, lush alien trees and bright flowers not of Earth in every direction. It defied the laws of physics, unbound by the confines of the castle's structures.

"How the hell's this here?" Jacob asked, poking his head through the doorway into the vastness beyond. "Looks very nice, whatever it is."

"It should not be here, the third floor ran away. It obviously got nervous at your presence and disappeared, it was here when I came down earlier to meet you all. Damn it, it does this sometimes. When it gets used to you, I am sure it will return, but the entire third floor is somewhere in the Inbetween, the place between places. Instead, please enjoy these gardens that it sends as a replacement; I do not know *where* it steals them from but I am fairly sure a denizen on another world is currently missing part of their property."

"Could we get lost on another world if it comes back and we're in the gardens?"

"Oh no, highly unlikely. The third floor would absorb you and put you in a cleaning cupboard for safety. It did that with me once…"

"Honestly, this place is more appealing than you think," Lucy said, a smile on her face. "It's *adorable* that a corridor's hiding from us, absolutely adorable."

As they left to walk upstairs, Vlad saw Fable stroke the doorway fondly, as if to reassure the third floor that everything was fine.

Above the entrance to the fourth floor was the inscription '*Ageōmétrētos mēdeìs eisítō*'. The fourth floor was where Vlad surmised many of the classrooms for schoolwork would have been, but again he had no idea what sort of education had occurred if so. Nor, he pointed out, did he know *who* would have been taught. He simply spent his days lingering on in utter confusion, exploring more of the floors in his spare time and discovering only more questions, never answers.

As they walked, there came a sudden, distant *clank* and everyone stopped, eyes darting nervously. Vlad gave a thin smile and slipped a sliver of darkness into his voice.

"*We have guests, Sir Terrence, please do not scare them. I know exactly where you are, you are unsuccessfully hiding behind the statue of Lady Gastaway. That is very rude, you know she despises such things. She gave you a slap last time.*"

The *clank clanked* again, and then the sound of *clanking* disappeared down the corridor as something heavy and metallic ran away.

"Apologies, he was going to try and sneak up on you, he has not seen new people since I came here two hundred years ago. That is his way of being polite."

"Sir Terrence?" Lucy asked.

"Oh yes, Sir Terrence Millington of Potley, or at least his suit of armour. Please, do not dwell on him, he will only think your interest flattering and redouble his efforts and become quite the nuisance."

The fifth floor lost all trace of the notion of corridors and rooms and, instead, became a vast and complex labyrinth of tunnels and "systems", Vlad called them.

"Another hiding floor?" Cain asked.

No, this is supposed to be here. The fifth floor is quite literally a maze," the vampire explained as he showed the Support Group both entrances leading east and west, deep into the castle. "I have yet to plumb it fully but I have gone a fair way in, and what I can tell you is it is full of the most unusual surprises. I would highly recommend none of you enter for I had to use quite a bit of my power to sense the escape."

"Jesus, how long were you in there?"

"Four days, give or take," Vlad admitted with a note of shame.

"Four days!" Jacob cried, leaning back from the west doorway where he had been peering into the maze curiously.

"Oh yes, and I had not moved very far in at all. I am certain the labyrinth's walls and enigmas shift and move according to their spell lyrics. Tremendous magic would be required to produce such complexity and, given my limited knowledge, you might fathom how far I have gotten with unravelling *those* particular mysteries."

"Sounds like it took you long enough with the illusion keepin' the castle under wraps," Cain said, looking in through the maze's east doorway. He looked back quickly. "No offence, mate."

"None taken, I assure you. We must all be aware of our shortcomings and one of mine, unfortunately, resides in the understandings of magic. I have a keen interest in the subject, do not misunderstand me, and much of what I study revolves around this castle in particular, but until I *know* the spell or the magical basis, I am at a loss at finding a starting point. This is where I have developed no small amount of envy for those born into magic in its many flavours. For this, I suppose I must apologise to Alizon and Fable in case I ever appear to be a little too interested in you or if I sound standoffish. I mean no offence, rather like Cain when he so aptly points out my flaws."

"Alright, I didn't mean it like that," the werewolf growled but Vlad snorted a short laugh and Alizon cut in before anything else was said.

"That's ok," she smiled. "I don't mind. To be here and study this place alongside you would bring me great joy. I can feel the power of the castle beating away like a drum, almost calling to me despite our differences in disciplines – weather magic is hardly ever used in the creations of things and so I often find myself at quite a loss, too, Vlad."

"Then we find kinship, you and I," Vlad commented easily and Alizon shrugged.

As they walked the stairs to the next floor, Vlad kept in time with Alizon and spoke quietly.

"You know, there is plenty of room should you so wish to stay. It would give you more than enough space to practice your magic and you would want for nothing. I would ask nothing *of* you, too, other than the odd 'Hello' in the morning and perhaps a conversation or two of an eve. I would otherwise leave you to your devices and give you free reign of the castle, aside from a few chambers and passageways that are too dangerous."

Alizon did not look at the vampire but instead gazed up the stairs and then glanced at the ceiling, as if measuring the entire place. She sighed and turned her hands over and over, the barest spark of magic twisting from them, imperceptible to all except Vlad's senses.

Blood and Biscuits

And Fable, it would seem, who Vlad realised had suddenly looked in their direction.

"That is most kind of you to offer, Vlad, but I can't."

"No?" he asked as they reached the sixth-floor landing. He motioned for everyone to enter the east doorway, to a torrent of dim natural light beyond. He lowered his voice and hoped Alizon would not take him for snooping. "Is it the spectre of your mother hanging over you?"

Alizon shook her head immediately.

"No, I wouldn't base my decisions on her. I do love her, in my own way, but that doesn't mean I live my life *because* of her. I hope she understands that." Vlad thought on the terrible bruising across Alizon's torso, which he still sensed pained her, and doubted it highly. "No, I can't stay here, I feel like the magic isn't present enough," Alizon finished.

"How do you mean?" Vlad continued as the group strolled through a wide corridor towards the light ahead.

"Well…it's all hidden, isn't it? Even you, after two hundred years, cannot find much of it. I feel I'd be lost in a palace of nothingness, empty promises of secrets lurking behind doors that might never be revealed. It sounds like a great temptation that would ultimately lead nowhere but disappointment."

Alizon held up the piece of fabric and tassel she had removed from the atrium carpet and waggled it pointedly.

"I have a thousand ways of attempting to convince you otherwise," Vlad said, "but I know they would be futile. You must act as you decide and I will simply hope that, one day, you will see this place for what it truly is. I honestly believe you would do great things here, Alizon, and perhaps in the future Fable may see this, too. For one thing, if I get the time, I would so like to encourage a huge and ornate garden to grow across the wastelands, if that might tempt you yet."

"That does sound lovely but I fear it isn't enough. What's the point of it? You said as much yourself about this carpet," she added, letting the cut piece of fabric fall limp in her grasp. "Magic needs purpose, it cannot just be for vanity or arrogance. Besides, Fable seems happy living with Jacob," Alizon pointed out.

"Indeed, she does," Vlad replied simply as the light ahead washed over them.

The sixth floor was for the study of all things flora. Stretching west were strange alchemical laboratories, dry stores, and convoluted potion-making facilities for learning and experimentation. Stretching east were enclosures set out as gigantic greenhouses and running for hundreds of feet, their plants dead and rotted away long ago. Great troughs of soil were all that remained now, their dirt still moist even after all these years; columns that would have seen vines growing upon them now stood bare and empty, green-stained metal supporting a ceiling that was panelled glass, besmirched with grime and rain spots. It allowed little light through, casting everything in an eerie gloom.

In a corner sat a towering bell plant, its thick and fibrous body sitting fat as vines and wide leaves draped across the floor. It had somehow remained alive, its tissue rigid to the touch, deep-green veins thrumming within its flesh. Vlad had always thought it looked tropical but he had not heard of a plant that size and type before. It had simply motionlessly for as long as he had known, minding its own business as he had hardly minded his.

At the very end of the greenhouses, a looming pair of deep wooden doors sat closed and ominous, embedded with decorative runes and gemstones.

"Oh, these glass rooms would have been astonishing," Lucy breathed, her head turning to take in the finely detailed walkways above and thin ironwork embellishments. "And still are, actually, in a way that reminds me of my mansion. There's loads more beyond that far wall, too. Such a shame it's all died away."

"Ahh but if you listen carefully," Vlad said quietly, leaning over one of the huge troughs of soil and staring down into its depths, "you can still hear life feeding these rooms. There is that water system rushing beneath all of this. That is why the soil has stayed damp all these years; it must be connected to the river somewhere. This castle is still alive, after all these centuries, its heart still beats and thrums, and it is strong. I find these matters *fascinating*."

"As do I!" Fable exclaimed, joining Vlad by the trough. He moved closer.

"Do you mind if I take your hand a moment?" he asked gently and Fable shook her head.

"No, not at all."

Vlad carefully lifted Fable's long, blackened hand and pressed her palm firmly to the trough. She made a slight sound of pain, the tight and damaged skin wrenching her frayed nerves, so Vlad controlled the pressure with a little more consideration. He waited a moment and then, with absolute command over the control holding back the surge of his darkness, Vlad pushed the smallest amount of power into his veins and fed his strength into Fable. The faerie gasped and shivered as she suddenly became aware of everything about her, her senses heightened just as Vlad's were, and she stared all around in deep admiration of the glass rooms, and of the world.

"Can you feel that power beneath your skin? The thrum of the heart?" Vlad asked and Fable gazed down at the soil. Such a simple thing to wonder upon and yet the smile growing upon her face more than satisfied the moment. "Yes, I know that look. That is the feeling of strength rushing beneath you, something you would otherwise be blind to. Is it not perfect?"

"I just…" Fable stammered, her hand gripping the side of the trough as if for dear life. "Is this how you feel every day, Vlad?"

"Yes. It never ends and sometimes I wish that it might, even for but a minute. Yet I would miss it, too, for I would suddenly not feel as you feel now, and experience all that is small and hidden of this world. Consumed by my despair."

"It is like no magic I have ever experienced, even recalling the days of when I had full command of my Light. It is too much, I fear."

Fable removed her hand and looked at it, the black and puckered skin still causing her pain as it always did. Yet for one moment, Vlad was convinced he had taken that agony from her and given her something else, something greater.

"Is this all part of your attempts to cure us?" Fable whispered.

Vlad nodded.

"Yes. There is an answer to you all, and to all of this," he added, indicating the vast greenhouses. "All we need be patience and they will give themselves up, one way or another. It would seem that after Sarah I must amend my previous thoughts and admit that I have arrived at a new conclusion: those with body *and* soul might yet be cured. That is all of you, despite your deaths," and here he nodded to Lucy and Jacob. Their eyes flickered with deep emotion and respect.

"But what about you?" Lucy asked, the realisation dawning on her, the dim light through the ceiling casting her sharp features in stark relief. "Where does that leave you? Sarah was given her cure, the one she sought the most, but you say you can't find the same relief."

Vlad smiled twistedly.

"I gave up believing myself capable of walking free of this curse centuries ago. And after seeing another me in the afterlife I fear I was right to do so. That imposter, I think, bore no immediate ill will but I did not trust his image. Though my wife and daughter were happy, and seeing their faces again after so long, shining down at me with nothing but love in their eyes, and…forgiveness…" Vlad struggled over the word, choking at its depth. He swallowed back his pride and started again. "Seeing their faces was like a second chance for me. I simply wish I had been prepared, to answer the doppelgänger with meaning, like magic with purpose."

Blood and Biscuits

"You still have no idea what he meant? I was sure you'd have an answer now, you seem to have books on everything," Jacob said delicately.

Vlad shook his head.

"No clue, I am afraid. Still, best not to dwell on it, especially now with so much to do. Come, would anyone else care to try?"

One by one, each of the Support Group came to the side of the trough, and Vlad fed them a minute section of his darkness so they might perceive the rush of water beneath the soil, that raw influence of nature harnessed by intelligent creation. Even Cain allowed Vlad to touch his hand, which surprised the vampire for reasons he was ashamed to admit stemmed from old beliefs surrounding masculinity.

The greater moment, however, was a mark of how far *everyone* had come, not just Cain.

Once the moment was over, everyone stared round the empty greenhouses thoughtfully, drinking in the strange designs of the place as warm, humid air permeated throughout.

"So what's through them doors at the end?" Jacob asked, nodding through the long greenhouses to the great wooden entranceway sealed solidly.

"The belfry," Vlad replied, voice haunting the dirtied glass rooms. "The great clock tower of the castle. It is one of the five portions, known as Irons."

"Well there's gotta' be more stuff inside this belfry place," Cain grunted, taking a step towards the great wooden doors. "Ain't that how the rest of this worked? You just walked in and started gatherin' information if and when you found it."

"Yes, for most places except the belfry," Vlad said, putting his hand on Cain's shoulder and pulling him back gently. "You see, I have never been inside Irons, nor has anyone I have ever read about in the library. It barely gets a mention. Oh, there are histories and explanations galore on the gargoyles and grotesques decorating the outside, and there must be a huge bell somewhere within its vast

Blood and Biscuits

depths, but for the death of me I have found nothing on it. It certainly has never tolled. I found one rumour suggesting the bell rings when the master of the castle dies. As far as I am aware, Irons is an enigma, from its name to its namesake, from its roots to its stem to its flower."

"If you can't get through the doors then there's magic on them, blocking your way," Alizon offered. "Give me a bit of time in the future and I will find an answer."

However, Vlad shook his head.

"You will find nothing for there is nothing of magic of those doors." Alizon's face fell in disappointment, a rare showing of facial emotion that matched common usage. Vlad smiled at her. "And there is no shame in not knowing," he added, "for I have looked upon those doors for two hundred years and come up with nought. I should hardly expect anyone else to find something. Still, one day it would be nice to cross that dreaded threshold and see what Irons contains."

"You could just fly up the outside and see for yourself. Just smash in through a window or summat'."

Vlad gazed round at Cain.

"I have already tried that, scores of times, and yet the castle rejects my attempts. I cannot see within and I cannot possibly know what lies inside. Irons is counted amongst the few places in this castle I simply cannot get into, for one reason or another. It also happens to be the largest by quite a margin – you saw from the outside the belfry is enormous. I think it is its sheer size that frustrates me the most for there must be such knowledge inside."

"Maybe fortunes will change now you have us around," Fable pointed out and Vlad smiled.

"Indeed," he said, inclining his head. "But for now, we will continue with the tour I have yet to finish. The tour that includes places we can actually get into, I might add. Come, I believe we have the tallest tower to climb, do we not?"

Cain's eyes lit up.

Vlad showed them back to the grand staircase and up to the seventh and final floor that stretched only west. A large window in the east wall showed down through the tops of the greenhouses far below on the sixth, the last rays of the day's light following them as they headed along the top of Mid-Realms, into the castle deeps. He showed the Support Group down the long, winding corridors, the paths snaking round and round in crooked manners as hallway after hallway produced dozens of side corridors and doors to other fascinating places. Many of them sat as old stores for working materials, shelves and high cupboards stacked far to the ceilings: a few rooms stood filled with piles of different types of raw rock and worked stone while others held processed carbons or metal ores sorted on wooden racks. There were even three chambers dedicated to the several hundred varying tools required for fine craft, each with a given purpose.

Many more rooms were laid out like lecture halls, lined with viewing platforms and decorated with words in phrases from long-forgotten languages. Some contained arches of stone and metal, others built to house constructs of physical magic. Vlad led the group past hundreds of sculptures and other works of art marking the hallways as Lucy and Jacob tried to stop and admire each and every one, both finding different expressions in the pieces, opinions formed from lifetimes of subjective interpretation. Vlad listened to them as they walked and gathered more of an idea of who they were as individuals, solitary minds building the collective conscience of the group. Individuality is important in most aspects of life, though judging by the Support Group it was clear that the whole was a thousand-fold greater than the sum of its parts. That much was proven during the Rite of al-Mawt.

Vlad toured the group through the workshops of machinery and contraptions, the forges drawing the attention of Cain and Alizon as the others focussed on the finer details of artisanship, design, and craft still littering the floors and workbenches. Cain finally approached one of the deep forges in the north corner of the fourth workshop and expressed interest in the black iron tools and heavy anvils.

Blood and Biscuits

"Ahh yes, a metalwork station," Vlad said, his hands behind his back as he surveyed Cain. The man picked up one of the hammers and hefted its weight. He swung it a few times and Vlad smiled. "You have a firm arm and steady hand; these things were made for people of your physical confidence, you know. One day we might fire a forge back up and see if you have the spirit of a smith residing within you."

"Ooh, now I like the sound of that," Lucy called over suggestively and Cain blushed a little. He put the hammer back down on the edge of the forge and shrugged.

"Doubt it," he mumbled, walking away. "I reckon all I'm good for is liftin' boxes and gettin' told off for having bad manual handlin' technique. Bend with the knees is where I get stuck."

"That's pretty much the majority of it," Jacob said, "so if that's where you bugger up there's no hope for your back."

"Nobody is truly aware of their capabilities until they try themselves against absolutely every possibility," Vlad commented. As Cain rejoined the others, Vlad added: "You know, these workshops are where I pilfered many of the items I required for my laboratory in the library. I also plundered the depths of the extractor's workshops further west to obtain the necessary test tubes, dried ingredients, brewing pots, et cetera."

"Extractor's?" Cain asked as they advanced through the workshops and up another, smaller, flight of stairs into the higher reaches of the castle. "What's that?"

"Somebody that distils and brews and mixes lots of different herbs and elements and liquids together, to concentrate the most potent qualities of specific ingredients, or to create entirely new qualities from new combinations."

"Oh, so like potion making?"

"In a sense," Vlad said as they climbed a further ninety-eight stairs to the castle's third section: 'Paths of Academia', or *Pathacs*. This was the learned portion of the castle, the place where one went to study alone and in peace, encompassing the vast library, the cold

Blood and Biscuits

and unused alchemical rooms, and so much more. "However, potions generally combine ingredients to make a large amount of one fluid, used for one purpose. Extractors *do* make potions but that is only a single part of their journey. To possess the greatest quality of every possible combination from every natural substance, one must learn hundreds of different extraction methods, for many thousands of different ingredients, producing hundreds of thousands of combinations, and millions of results. And no, before you ask, Alizon, I cannot explain them all as I have not the knowledge. You shall have to mull the notion over with a cup of tea in a little while. Ahh, here we are."

The group walked from the narrow marble staircase and out into a dimly lit, cavernous library.

"Wow," Jacob whispered, turning round and round as he took it all in. "This is…"

Fable and Alizon were speechless, eyes scanning every line of the library hungrily.

"Can barely see a thing in here," Cain grunted. He pointed up. "We're high up but there's hardly any windows in that fancy-painted dome."

"Why'd you think that is?" Jacob asked and Cain shrugged. Then he held up a finger as he realised something.

"Wait, natural light damages books, right?"

"Correct in one," Fable said pleasantly and Cain smiled to himself, pride leaching from him.

Jacob and Lucy suddenly leapt back in fright as something flapped enthusiastically overhead, an almost wooden-like *squawk* ejecting from the thing.

"This place is attacking us!" Jacob cried. Cain laughed at him.

"Relax," Vlad said calmly, "it was only a wordpecker, a library helper. You will find this place far too vast, too complex, to search by yourself – wordpeckers and bookworms were created long ago to aid people. Yes, Jacob, *wordpeckers*, I am not making this up,

Blood and Biscuits

you nearly lost an eye to one just now. You signal for one of them and then give them a list of books to find, though like everything else enchanted here they do not *quite* operate as they should anymore."

Vlad gazed contentedly at the endless shelves, book-stuffed rows stretching high and far, towering two hundred feet above. Some shelves actually *touched* the ceiling, the hand-painted stone preventing their bent and rickety stacks crashing to the ground. Others lined the huge walls, looming in gigantic towers of tomes and volumes, parchments, papyruses, and many other pieces of knowledge in dozens of different forms. Helical staircases of worked bronze curled up to stone levels built haphazardly throughout the library, suspension bridges linking many together, support columns so messy it appeared that much of the library was being held up by books alone.

All of it was there to be stored and to be read, but mostly to be protected.

"This is amazing," Jacob whispered excitedly. "To think, this has all been here since before we started coming to the island, hidden away with the lovely sculptures and paintings in the corridors. I need more time here."

Fable mirrored Jacob's mood.

"I've never in all my days witnessed such a place, and I grew up around the Sun Palace. I've experienced opulence and I've seen grandiosity yet this dwarfs it all."

"I'm going to see if Vlad's got stuff on art history," Jacob said enthusiastically, skittering away immediately.

"Try Row R! It's behind the doors with the naked nymphs!" Vlad called to him as Jacob disappeared amongst the shelves.

Alizon followed Jacob a little while before her interest was suddenly taken by a small door. She opened it and disappeared into the depths of Row F, swallowed up by the library. Vlad knew she would be content simply roaming through the complex tunnels, entertained by floating oil lamps, pulling books down methodically, examining them intensely.

Blood and Biscuits

"What's through this tunnel past these big stacks of books?" somebody called from somewhere near the back of the library, their voice tiny.

"You shall have to be more specific!" Vlad called back.

"There's Greek messages on arches here, does that help?"

"Ahh yes, there is only a hidden repository of knowledge there. She is slumbering right now, I shall wake her for you another day!" Vlad replied.

Pacing the library, Vlad watched the group to soak it all in. However, Cain seemed unperturbed by the staggering volume of books and wealth of knowledge and instead walked past the shelves and mobile ladders to head straight for the makeshift laboratory Vlad had set up decades before. The vampire followed, a small smile upon his face, and watched Cain quickly locate the delicate vial in which he had delivered his own blood to Vlad. Eventually, his eyes settled on the distillation equipment, the apparatus standing cold.

"Is this what I think it is?" he asked, pointing at the vessels. Vlad nodded.

"Yes, my experiments into the nature of your blood. Would you like to know what I have so far?"

Cain nodded and Vlad motioned him to another table, where a microscope stood beside a rack of carefully prepared glass slides. Vlad picked up one, labelled '𝔖𝔲𝔟𝔧𝔢𝔠𝔱, 𝔠𝔞𝔦𝔫: 𝔭𝔯𝔢-𝔪𝔦𝔵, 𝔠𝔲𝔯𝔰𝔢'; it had a crimson powder residue caught between the two glass plates.

"This," Vlad began, "is the distillation of your cursed blood *before* I added wolfsbane. It looks like any other blood, if a little darker; the redness derives from iron-bound haemoglobin molecules in your blood cells. Care to look through the microscope?"

Cain shook his head slightly.

"I'll take your word for it today. Not really feelin' the detail, you know?"

"Just an overview, as you wish," Vlad said. He restored the slide in the rack and picked out two others. One contained a pure white powder residue while the other held a grey powder, and they were labelled '𝔖𝔲𝔟𝔧𝔢𝔠𝔱, ℭ𝔞𝔦𝔫: 𝖕𝖔𝖘𝖙-𝖒𝖎𝖝, 𝖇𝖑𝖔𝖔𝖉' and '𝔖𝔲𝔟𝔧𝔢𝔠𝔱, ℭ𝔞𝔦𝔫: 𝖕𝖔𝖘𝖙-𝖒𝖎𝖝, 𝖈𝖚𝖗𝖘𝖊' respectively. Vlad held up the grey powder slide. "This is the split curse I told you about, after wolfsbane was added to your blood then steam-distilled in the suspension fluid. This remained in the first vessel, where the curse always stays. It is precisely the same as the first slide, except now there is no blood – the blood split from the curse with the wolfsbane addition. Clear so far?"

"Yeah, I'm golden," Cain muttered unconvincingly.

"Good. Now this is where things get interesting, my friend, for *this*," and here Vlad held up the slide with white powder, "is also what resulted. This evaporate is derived from the post-distillation of the wolfsbane-changed blood suspension."

"Ok, *now* I'm not following," Cain said. "Gettin' really complicated."

Vlad hissed at himself and reordered his words.

"My apologies, I know this is difficult when you have no experience, and you have already told me you struggled with science."

"Did I?" Cain asked confusedly.

"You were drunk. Now, let me explain again. The red powder is your dried blood, with a little moonglow tincture to help the precipitate set, amongst other properties. This is before I added wolfsbane, so the curse is still bound to your blood and therefore appears unremarkable. With me so far?"

"Actually, now I am."

"Excellent. Now this is the curious part, Cain. These next two slides are *after* I added the wolfsbane. Normally, you would see a simple split, where the distilled blood turns brown-red and the remaining curse a grey powder. This is true for all werewolves I have studied before."

"But you ain't got that in those fancy slides," Cain said, pointing to the two results in Vlad's hands. The vampire gazed at them thoughtfully.

"No indeed. Your blood, when separated from its curse, does not turn red, like anybody else's would, but instead dries pure white."

Cain looked to the workbench and saw the flasks of white fluid there.

"But *they're* white," he said, pointing at the flasks. "You sure that's not normal?"

"Those are the suspension fluids of your blood, and they are white because of the additions that help keep the cells and virus alive, for purposes of the experiment. However, all other werewolf blood types dry to become a blood-coloured powder after the wolfsbane is added but yours turns white, *even whiter* than the fluid. This means, in no uncertain terms, that your curse is not the only thing in your blood, and I am not referring to a disease, before you ask. That, Cain, is beyond unexpected. It is...miraculous, I suppose is an apt term.

"You see, I have seen this before, a long time ago, but it had nothing to do with werewolves. I could not allow this to end here and so I applied what I knew," and here Vlad picked up a tiny jar from the workbench and showed it to Cain. It contained a clear, light-golden fluid so thick it hardly moved when upended. A label said '𝕸𝖆𝖓𝖓𝖆 𝖔𝖋 𝕬𝖘𝖍'.

"Ash is a tree, I know that much. But manna?" Cain asked.

"Indeed," replied Vlad slowly. "Tree sap, from an ash in Greece. I collected this a week ago – it has but a month's experimental life before its freshness is lost and the entire batch must be discarded, hence why I have no stores of it. This sap goes by another, far more ancient name: 'blood of heaven'." Cain's eyebrows rose worriedly as Vlad added, "I applied a single drop to your wolfsbane blood, post-distillation, and this happened."

Vlad picked out two more slides and held them up. One was another red powder while the second contained a dot of powder so small it was hardly visible, so diamond-white it was piercingly bright – this second slide was labelled '𝕾𝖚𝖇𝖏𝖊𝖈𝖙, 𝕮𝖆𝖎𝖓: 𝖕𝖔𝖘𝖙-𝖕𝖔𝖘𝖙-𝖒𝖎𝖝, 𝖇𝖑𝖊𝖘𝖘𝖎𝖓𝖌'.

Blood and Biscuits

"This red slide is your blood *after* wolfsbane and *after* manna. This white one? That is what remained behind."

Cain said nothing and Vlad began to worry. He heard the others of the group talking about different discoveries in the library and he sensed the vibrations of their moods as they explored, but Vlad focussed his attentions on Cain.

"Is everything alright?"

"Yeah, yeah…" Cain began unconvincingly. "It's just a lot to take in. I've gotta' ask, otherwise it'll eat at me all day and I'll get told off by Lucy for moping: what does the white blood *mean*? That tiny bit after the, err, heaven blood – the manna. Am I ill? Have you seen it before?"

"No, you are not ill – far from it, actually. And yes, as I said, I have seen this once before," Vlad replied honestly. He had decided to be frank with Cain; hiding facts about the man would not help in any way. "It was from the blood of a pure being, a creature of absolute divinity. A Serafere, of the ancient world."

"Wait," Cain said quietly, knuckling his forehead as he thought back through something. "I've heard of those. Aren't they from God and such?"

"In the Bible, yes," Vlad responded easily, "but this is not what I mean. Firstly, you are thinking of the seraphim, high angels to God. What I speak of are 'Serafere'. It is both singular and plural, like sheep, to give a rather basic example. Serafere were creatures of a bygone time; many of my ilk believe they were the real-world basis behind the notion of angels and heavenly beings. Nowadays, you would not find a Serafere."

"I get your point," Cain said. "So where'd they all go, and why?"

"Well, since humanity rose and established itself as the dominant species several thousand years ago, taking over the physical world, creatures like the Serafere diminished from the mortal planes."

Blood and Biscuits

Vlad sensed the others moving back to the front of the library, most likely full of questions and excitement, but he saw Cain's eyes brim with worry and fear. He reeked of self-doubt.

"You're sayin' I'm not normal," he started but Vlad quickly shook his head as Cain stammered on. "You're sayin' I'm one of these Serafere things, back from old times like some demon trapped inside me?"

"No, Cain, my God no! That is not even *possible*, let alone true. I did not make my point clear: Serafere were blessed, they were creatures with *blessing* in their blood. As far as I know they gained this blessing through the righteousness of their souls and it bound to their blood just like your virus has done. A blessing is the precise *opposite* of a curse, and acts rather like a protection, if you will, rather than a dragging weight."

"Oh," Cain said, and a segment of his fear removed itself from his emotional standing. "So I'm not a Serafere?"

"No," Vlad chuckled. "I would have sensed it in you immediately and you yourself would have been aware of such a union long ago, my friend. I am saying that your blood as *akin* to theirs, in that you are blessed in some way."

"Ahh…hang on, I've got special heaven blood, too? That's not right, otherwise it'd force my curse down, surely. You said it just then, these blessing thingies act as protections but if I've really got one whizzin' round my systems then I'd get some of its magic defence."

Vlad looked at Cain strangely and then decided on a matter,

"The first time I met you, Cain, when you staggered down into the basement of St Ellin's church, all covered in blood, I smelled something. I smelled the werewolf in you, yes, but I also detected a second thing, a foreign matter, something I had never smelled before."

"And that was my blessing. You can actually *smell* a blessing in someone's blood, Vlad, that's kinda' messed up."

Blood and Biscuits

"No, Cain, no I did not smell it at all. Your powdered blessing is odourless. No, what I detected on the air that night, what I smell every time I encounter your blood, is your curse. Both smells from your curse, *two* odours from the same thing, distinct and different from one another. I tasted it when I drank your blood in the Parrot and Cracker and I smell it here again, in your curse powder."

"Great, so now I've two things to worry about: a curse you don't know about, when you're supposed to be an expert on werewolves, and a blessing I'm not supposed to have." Cain sucked his teeth, a pale slice of fear cutting from him. "Did I make the right decision asking you to research this about me, Vlad?"

"Yes, you most certainly did. Cain, the Support Group should be evidence enough that if we can help you understand who you are then you should take that path. Not just who, though-"

"But what I am as well, yeah I remember," Cain interrupted, stroking his unshaven cheek nervously. "Ok fine, I guess if anyone's gonna' get to the bottom of all this business," he continued, indicating himself up and down, "then you're best placed for it. You really sure this is what your science experiments showed?"

"It is as much as I can surmise, yes. It might not feel it, Cain, but this blessing has somehow affected your blood in the same way your unique curse has, and the two have been warring for as long as you have been infected by the werewolf virus. The blessing *is* doing all it can to counteract your curse. I have a hunch this is why your relationship with Lucy has also formed as a deep bond in your transformed state, meaning she can influence command over you. It would seem this blessing allows you to feel love for another whilst transformed, though I wish not to sound mawkish. It is the very first instance I have heard of such in a werewolf."

Cain only looked at him, relief and anxiety battling for victory over his mind. Vlad hoped to strike a balance in the man.

"And so when I distilled your blood after splitting the curse with wolfsbane your blessing became visible in the resultant. I only needed to cleave *that* with manna to confirm my suspicions. It is remarkable, truly remarkable. And I think with the right persuasion, and enough time, this could go a long way to explaining what makes you…*you*. I hope this will suffice for now for it is all I have at this time."

"It's enough for now," Cain said with a smile. "It's enough for a long while, Vlad, I'm gonna' need time getting over it, actually. Part of me still regrets asking."

"Never regret asking questions, Cain," Vlad said, replacing the slides in the rack and clapping him on the shoulder, ignoring his natural vampire urge to attack him. "Never. Not unless you have asked directions from a stranger, you may regret those times."

Cain barked a laugh at the unexpected joke and Vlad decided it was probably best to continue the tour upwards.

"Come, we still have quite the climb ahead of us and time is ticking on. It is the cruel and merciless march of the fourth dimension, I am afraid."

"Surely there's more of this Pathacs to see," Alizon said half-questioningly, looking beyond the library, eyes landing on several doors leading off from the huge chamber. "There can't be just books and a weird lab."

Vlad ignored the tone. Alizon only sounded rude to the untrained ear.

"Oh, there is *much* more to see of Pathacs, that I can assure you. And there is plenty more of the castle in total, but if we are to see the tallest tower and still have a support session then I suggest we return another day to resume our explorations."

Alizon grumbled something as they left the library, Cain glancing back with unreadable seriousness at the extensive research equipment strewn across the workbenches, and continued on up the staircase to a large, sixteen-sided room of deep onyx and marble insets. Including the entrance, there were eight doorways, each set in every other wall of a perfectly formed hexadecagon; seven statues of green-shining jade stood magnificently against the blank walls,

Blood and Biscuits

looming over the chamber strangely, all turned towards the doorways they stood beside.

In the room's centre there was a wooden lectern, unremarkable and, therefore, hugely interesting to Vlad. A large, leather-bound book sat atop the stand and a bell jar covered the entire thing, its iridescent, flawless glass reaching the floor.

"Bloody hell, Vlad," Jacob said, stepping out into the chamber. "I can't focus at all! It's like walking into a dream."

"I know," Vlad replied humbly. "Do you not feel as if you could spend several days mapping it all out and admiring the artistry and imagination in the symbols above the doorways, the statues and those same symbols on their plinths, the murals upon the ceiling high above?"

"You're gonna' tell us that's what you've done, right?"

"I might not have been," Vlad said indignantly. His flitting eyes betrayed him and Lucy caught the lie.

"Come on," she said with a sly smile. "How long did you spend in here in one go?"

Vlad sighed.

"Three days."

Cain and Jacob snorted and Fable made a whistling noise – Vlad thought it was of appreciation.

"And what did you do with the information you gathered?"

"I compiled it in a short book and put it on display next to that statue of the mermaid with her eyes bound in cloth," Vlad admitted awkwardly, pointing to the north-north-eastern wall. There was indeed another lectern, this one cast from bronze, next to a huge sculpture of a blinded mermaid, her hands raised, mouth cast in a grim line. "It is a sickness, I feel. I see something interesting and I suddenly must know everything about it, and then I have to go one step further and document the bloody thing and *then* have the arrogance to put it on display!"

Lucy patted Vlad on the shoulder, almost sadly.

"We all have our vices," she grinned, winking at Jacob.

Blood and Biscuits

An odd note of sadness permeated the group, something that wonders and marvels could not quite mask. Vlad watched them as they moved and spoke, registering their bodies and faces for the tiniest, subtle signs of lethargy and despondency, finding evidence wherever he looked.

'*It is hardly unexpected*', he noted silently, thinking on the afterlife and what they had all lost.

"So, now we've established another of Vlad's weird habits, let's hear what this section's called," Jacob remarked with slightly false cheerfulness. "Seven doorways, each leading to what I presume is seven towers, each with a statue next to them and weird symbols. Given your, um, obsessive behaviours, Vlad, I'd imagine this bit has a name, too?"

"Of course it does, but *I* did not name any of these places. I found most of them scrawled in various locations or in some of the books regarding the castle, and so I pieced together the mysteries that I could in the hopes of restarting the history of Laegoria. But to answer your question, the complex that is this room and its connected towers is known as 'Octothers'. Why is beyond me – I get the 'Oct' prefix, meaning 'eight', as there are eight doorways including the entrance here – but the rest of the name bewilders me."

"Anything in that fancy thing worth mentioning?" Lucy asked, pointing at the central bell jar and thick, leather-bound book within. Vlad shrugged.

"I cannot say, I have been unable to get the damned thing open. For all I know, that could be the book with all of the answers to the castle."

"Or some batty old sorcerer's favourite beetroot soup recipes," Cain grunted.

"Precisely," Vlad said. "It could be anything so it is worthless speculating on. Therefore, as you can imagine I have spent about half of my time here speculating on it."

"Well, I for one think Octothers is fascinating," Fable said quietly.

Vlad led them through the south-south-west doorway, which had carved above it a strange symbol of an eight-pointed compass, each arrowhead represented by a different letter of yet another unknown language. The compass-like symbol matched the one on a plinth of a troll beside the doorway, one three-fingered hand clutching a long staff, a look of deep intelligence and passivity on the creature's long-snouted face.

Deep steps wound up in a spiral staircase, the passage narrowing with every passing doorway – further rooms too complicated or dangerous to go into.

When at last they reached the top of the tallest tower, every one of the group was out of breath save for Vlad, Lucy, and Jacob.

Vlad pushed open the heavy door at the top and light broke out across the Support Group, spilling forth down the stone and illuminating the gloom. Vlad looked back and smiled.

"Are you ready?" he asked.

Everynone nodded then walked into the bright sunlight of the tallest tower, to see what awaited them. What they had not anticipated was how far *beyond* the tower they would see.

It was truly a magnificent sight to behold.

THE JADE CHAPEL,
LAEGORIA.
THE START OF THE SUPPORT GROUP.

Vlad smoothed out a non-existent crease in his shirt and gazed round the group. They sat upon the finest chairs of wrought gold and white velvet, Laegoria's previous occupants apparently sparing no expense in the furnishings as well as the complex layout and magical enchantments. Opulence had never been important for Vlad but as he looked round the chapel, its deep-green sculptures of gods and creatures sitting upon onyx altars, jade inserts radiating shimmering light from tall columns of black stone, he admitted that

𝔅𝔩𝔬𝔬𝔡 𝔞𝔫𝔡 𝔅𝔦𝔰𝔠𝔲𝔦𝔱𝔰

lavishness had the strange effect of making one feel rich and comforted in a false sort of way.

There was a new table by the edge of the room, packed with different teas, coffees, biscuits, cakes, and savoury snacks. All waiting for a werewolf, a banshee, a wraith, a faerie, and a witch to tear into them, destroying Vlad's lovely organisation. He had already accepted entropy would haunt him beyond the grave.

All eyes had gone from taking in as much of the room as possible to training on him with complete focus, each pupil unwavering, every face rapt with attention as Vlad cleared his throat. He saw them, and he saw how far they had come, his group of death, blood, and life. Vlad noticed the empty chair somebody had pulled up to align with where Sarah had once sat in their circle in honour of her memory, and he smiled a thousand meanings.

And then he spoke.

He delivered the sentence that had brought them all together in the first place, those few words drawing them all in as one, binding them in the same ship to ride the waves of their problems. It was the first sign of hope that they would one day accept who they were not only as supernatural entities but as individuals, too. People.

"So, how was everyone's week?"

CASTLE OF THE BLACK SKIES.
TUESDAY, 01:32AM.

"Jeez, I can't believe what time it is!"

"I know, the problem arises from when a good conversation is begun and everybody can get involved. And the chapel has no windows so the natural passing of time is lost."

"Ahh, like Ikea."

"If I knew what an Ikea was, I would agree with you."

"Shame Lucy had to leave for her mansion, her bloody binding really screws her over."

Blood and Biscuits

"At least Cain went with her. That was the right thing to do."

Vlad saw everyone to the front entrance of Laegoria and released the oak doors with their locking chain wheel. The great bronze bianzhong bells descended and the huge doors opened smoothly. Jacob stepped outside and breathed in the freezing air, early-December clutching at Ellin's Island like an icy hand.

"Christ, that's cold," the wraith said, rubbing his arms and looking all the world like he wanted to stay inside the gigantic, warm castle. "Still, got to get home. More things to sell online."

"Oh yes, how *is* the business going?" Vlad asked, leaning against the stone doorway. Fable nodded enthusiastically.

"It appears we've gotten the hang of this merchant stuff, for the money's increasing. We're keeping track of our income for…oh, what was it?"

"Taxes," Jacob completed. "Just say taxes. Get it over with."

"Taxes," Fable said, a triumphant smile on her face.

"Ahh, the only thing other than death that remains a certainty," Vlad said. "And trust me on that, I know how the Romans operated."

The group looked at him strangely, but they let the comment go. Vlad leaned out into the night and smiled thinly, thinking of the time of year that approached and how everyone would be celebrating in all of their different ways. He had seen hundreds of yuletides and watched as people grew throughout the decades, changing in their vast and in their minute ways.

"I bid you all a very good night," he said happily, waving them off from the castle's front doors. "And a very, merry Christmas in a few weeks. I hope you find peace; I wish I could be around for it but I have made up my mind about something and shall not be available. However, if you find you are lonely, that you are scared," and here, Vlad looked to Alizon automatically, "or you simply wish to feel just an ounce of love, then find one another. Go to Galloway's Mansion and spend the day together, drink cider or martinis or mushroom tea, do whatever it is you paranormal people do to find peace. I will send you a message about the next support session; it will not be long, I am sure."

"Can't believe we're not coming back next week," Jacob muttered. "Feels strange."

"Yes but I have many things to do this month and I cannot commit to anything at the moment. Beyond Christmas, however, I shall be available every Monday again, that I promise."

"Merry Christmas, Vlad," Jacob and Fable said together and they walked from the castle. Vlad turned to head back inside but he found Alizon there, staring down at the floor.

"Is everything alright?" Vlad asked gently, approaching just enough without appearing dominating.

She pointed and Vlad looked down, and he realised what she was concerned with. The red carpet of the atrium floor was clean and repaired again, Cain's muddy footprints gone and the corner she had sliced away now recovered. It was perfect.

Alizon mumbled something incoherent and Vlad chose to speak, hoping to allay her worries.

"Yes, I did warn you, I am afraid. There is no getting round the enchantment on this God-forsaken carpet. I cannot fathom why it irritates me so. I think it is the brazen use of magic for such a pointless feat, perhaps. Anyway, you will find the piece you had, tassel and all, now gone from your belongings. I was not lying before, and the castle is crammed *full* of bits of magic just like this, many of which I have still not *found*, let alone identified. Some seem to serve no purpose at all save for one small thing while others serve grand and wholly mysterious purposes, yet all combine to make this place what it is: a an ever-moving wonder of magical history."

Alizon looked up at Vlad and grinned.

"Would it be possible to maybe change my decision on your offer of staying here, Vlad? To take up the position of studious researcher and give myself my own thinking room?"

The vampire recoiled in surprise but returned the smile.

"Of course it would. Whatever altered your mind?"

Blood and Biscuits

"The carpet, of course," Alizon responded curtly, as if Vlad was slow. "I said before I didn't think this place could offer me anything but I think I was distrustful, like I didn't believe its secrets were real. I see now I was wrong and I'd like to set aside the life I've been living to join you here. Just for a short while, if that's still alright?"

"As I said," Vlad pointed out as the night air blew softly over them, "you are most welcome here, and I shall not get in your way with whatever it is you feel you must do to keep your mind occupied. However, I cannot offer you a bed tonight for there is nothing to sleep upon at the moment. Could you give me until, perhaps, after Christmas so that I can organise myself and then get a room nicely sorted? You may bring whatever comforts and furniture you wish, too, the castle will not mind that."

Alizon nodded, her eyes still never meeting Vlad's.

"That sounds satisfactory. I look forward to it. I hope the third floor corridor can trust me and return home."

"I am sure it will," Vlad said simply and Alizon bade him good night so she could catch up with the others. Vlad wound the chain wheel round and the doors boomed shut, and the vampire moved to lean against them for a moment. He pressed his brow to the thick, heavy oak and felt the thrum of the castle again, the deep, distant, endless movements of water and magic flowing through thousands of walls and rooms as they had always done since he had arrived.

He thought back to the day he had landed on Ellin's Island – it had been Westmire-Fields back then – and the face of Sarah returned to his mind. With no one there Vlad had no distractions, he had no choice but to acknowledge all that haunted him, the thing that dogged his every step, refusing to diminish until he finally recognised and accepted it.

He turned from the doors, shoulders slumped in the vastness of the castle, and a mask of utter rage transformed his face, and the demon that was his despair leapt upon him. The vampire felt

Blood and Biscuits

Cuthbert's strangling claws throttling the life from his emotions, squeezing all joy and serenity that had become him, arresting his thoughts and howling with laughter as Vlad's control on his power dissolved and he became the vampire, the monster he truly was.

Darkness enveloped him.

Wings burst from his back, shrouding him in ragged shadow. Horns ripped from his forehead. Fangs slid sickeningly from his jaws. Vlad lost his mind as the memory of Sarah's face consumed him, and he disappeared from the atrium, howling through the corridors in choking desolation.

Reappearing in one of the last abandoned rooms at the far eastern end of the castle, a dark place of gloom and misery, the beast unleashed its darkness and its fury on everything in sight. He was nemesis.

Sarah was gone and for that Vlad slammed his fists against the ancient tables and stacks of wood frames, cried his fury at the grime-streaked windows and bare piles of rusting iron, tore the stone and rafters from the ceiling, and dragged his black metal claws down the walls, wood and paint splintering across the floor.

Then he stood in the centre, anger devouring him, and erupted in power.

So much power, all for the woman that had departed this world. It burned through the room like hellfire, obliterating everything in its path, turning wood, iron, and stone to ash. Vlad blazed in the unquenched black flames of night, roared until the very corridors quaked beneath the gaze of his wrath.

The vampire was alone, his family gone.

He thought on the spirit image of himself with his wife and daughter in the afterlife, enjoying their love as he lingered on, lost and reasonless, and he screamed blood and ire as the room tumbled about his shoulders, burying him in dust and stone. The fact that the magic of the room would repair it again the next day only enraged him further, glass turning to sand in his fury.

No. 76, Waterbarrow's Road, London, 17:00, 25th December

Two booted feet landed upon the cold wet ground. There was no snow. There was never any snow. The songs constantly lied; Christmas was getting greyer with every passing year.

The street was long and curved, as many upscale London roads were, and the houses were tall, thin, and deep. Their white walls shone in the lengthening evening, pearlescent columns adorning their porches. They were very expensive houses.

Vlad shook himself down, heavy cloud droplets cascading from his dark-brown trench coat, and he walked across the road quickly. The streets were silent, the lights from homes twinkling in different colours as the silhouettes of occupants moved within merrily, their comfort and joy almost overpowering Vlad's senses.

The vampire came to number 76 and hesitated, his fist held before the door as he suddenly realised he was nervous. *Why* was he nervous?

Vlad straightened his thoughts and chided himself a fool. He rapped his knuckles smartly upon the door then held his hands firmly behind his back, waiting patiently.

There was a pause. When the door opened a little, a pair of tired, kind eyes appeared. The aged gaze looked up and found Vlad's face, and then the eyes grew wide with a bright smile.

The door opened and in the frame, there stood a tall man of Afro-Caribbean descent, face loosened by age but losing none of the laughter and love it had seen for over seventy years. The man threw his arms wide and boomed a deep laugh, his voice the same as it had always been. A voice that had spent its life helping people. An influential voice.

"Vlad!" he cried.

"John," Vlad said, his own face breaking out in a grin. Before

Blood and Biscuits

he could react, John threw the door wide, strode out, and seized the vampire in a hug. "It's – *oof* – good to see you, friend," Vlad managed.

"Oh I missed you, man," John said, finally releasing the vampire and stepping back. He looked into the house and shouted: "Moira! Oh Moira, there's a young man 'ere to see you! Moira, get yourself down here, woman!"

A voice called from somewhere in the house.

"Alright, you daft old sod, I'm comin' as fast as I can. That turkey's weighin' me stomach down, for God's sake. I think it was fed *lead* rather than seed. Tasty, though, I'll give Vlad our best for it."

"Funny you should mention him," John smirked.

Moira walked out from the soft light of the house and framed herself in the doorway, and Vlad beamed down at her, her eyebrows raising in surprise. It was good to see her out of Antarctica and somewhere warm again. Well, warm relative to the South Pole.

The homeliness of normal life suited her far more than the coldness of a distant land.

"Vladislav Eliade," Moira said quietly, folding her arms and smirking. "We didn't expect to see you here. How's it been since I last saw you? Did you…move your Sarah on?" she ventured hesitantly.

"Yes," Vlad muttered, hat twirling in his hands agitatedly. "She is at peace now."

"So the ritual worked," Moira confirmed. John glanced between them gravely; Vlad wondered how much he knew, though it was obvious he understood the tone of the matter. Moira gave a tight nod. "I am glad for her and sorry for your loss."

"It is alright. She has found her happiness, and that is enough for me now, though I have much to discuss, if you would grant it some time?" Moira nodded again and Vlad glanced down the street simply just to look away for a moment. Moira reminded him of good times and he was not in the right frame of mind for that. He turned

Blood and Biscuits

back, suddenly resolute. "I am not here to bring down the mood. I am not quite Father Christmas but I hope I will do for the evening."

"Wait, you wanna' join us tonight?" John asked, his white eyebrows raised.

"Would that be...alright?" Vlad asked. "I wish not to be alone and I know no one else who would have me. I did not want to disturb you but it has been so very long since I have heard people laughing at this time of year, and-"

Moira suddenly clapped her hands and laughed, her breath misting upon the night air.

"You silly man, of course you can come in! It's a time for family, isn't it? Come on, John, bring the vampire inside from the cold before he camouflages into the snow, and get your best whiskey out. He can come and smell the turkey he gave us, if he can't taste it."

"Right you are, woman. Oh what a beautiful evening this'll be," John said, showing Vlad inside warmly and clapping him on the shoulder, taking his coat and hanging it on a hook on the wall. "The kids'll be thrilled to see you again, Vlad, they've asked about you so much over the years. God you haven't aged at all, I can see that better in the light. It's no wonder Moira liked you back in the day."

"I...I..." Vlad stumbled, at a rare loss for words. However, John only laughed louder and shut the door.

"You really need to get over that, man," John said, showing Vlad through to a large living room, an eight-foot tree standing proudly in the far corner and beautifully decorated. "I've told you time and time again I never cared. You're family, far as I'm concerned, and so think the others, too!"

As he finished, they walked into the spacious open-plan lounge-dining room and five faces turned round from the table, five adult faces Vlad had known since they were born. And some of them had their own children now. Every one of them broke out into the most radiant smiles, and in that moment, Vlad did not feel alone. He hugged each and every one of Moira and John's children and was handed a sleeping baby to hold and a large glass of whiskey as he was barraged with a hundred questions on vampirism and informed many times that none of them had told anyone his secret. And right then Vlad felt happy.

Right then, all was well.

THANK YOU

This is a dedication to everyone that has helped me bring this story, these characters, the settings, and the front and back cover – and all else required to make a novel what it is – to life. None of this could have been made without them constantly telling me how awful certain bits were, how well other bits read, and how middlingly average almost the rest of it was if I lost focus, as I usually do when I ramble. But not only this, people that have read other stories that have given me advice that has carried onto Blood and Biscuits, I give you thanks too. Your support taught, encouraged, and transcended.

To my sister, Elizabeth, who could not have been a better friend, mentor, and person. She helped raise me and she guided me through so many of life's tricky situations. We might have fought on occasion but we're best friends now; thank you for letting me gross you out as often as humanly possible.

To my mother, Althea, who raised me through the thickest and thinnest. I don't know how you dragged two kids up whilst studying at the same time but I'll always remember our Sheffield days. You are the best and you make me proud.

To my step-dad Joel, for always being at the end of the phone with questions on the narrative, for being unafraid to tell me whenever I was wrong, for delving into every nook and cranny of every chapter, and for teaching me never to mix my metaphors.

To my dad for reading through it all, week-by-week, and trying his best to critique me – he managed one spelling mistake!

Martinis at Midnight

To my friends, who stand by me despite everything I find repulsive about myself. To Dan and Lewis, for our endless conversations that keep me sane (go sports), and for reading all the random pieces of nonsense I sent at all hours of the day and night, and commenting on what works and what doesn't. For helping my designs, redesigns, creations, and recreations. And for being there through the good and tough times.

To Jess W, who was there from the beginning of Vlad and particularly liked Cain's arc. To Lucy T (who shares but a namesake with my banshee), who taught me her own magics and mythologies, and who helped with the cover designs. To my boss, Nathan W, for being a good friend through many situations and for understanding when I wasn't at my best. To Harry P and his fearless criticisms: you were right, the book's better without the essays. To Wil and Harriet, who have been reading my nonsense for years and helping me shape my characters.

To my many colleagues over the years that are now absent from my life, as the passage of time so often separates us: we had wonderful days, our innumerable conversations helped shape this book into what it is. Never underestimate the power of talking to as many and as varied as possible.

To everyone at Andy's Man Club: your humanity made my monsters into people and helped them be seen. You were the inspiration behind this entire thing – how was your week?

And to my children, for always wanting to see my drawings, no matter how bad they are, and never failing to produce such faces of wonder, and then bluntly asking me why nothing looks right. They can be truly the most honest critics. They make my life complete.

Martinis at Midnight

And lastly to my wife, Esme, for somehow always being by my side and putting up with my ridiculousness, my selfishness, and the long evenings I have spent typing away instead of cuddling. You did everything the others did and more. You sat and taught me women's' perspectives, breastfeeding, emotional communication. You spent car journeys and evenings, when the kids were asleep, going over detail over mind-numbing detail. You told me when my drawings were rubbish and when they were passable. And you were the one that pushed me to get the help I needed when I wasn't right. I love you.

An aside to my toiling Instagram Book Community:

To George Ander (author of the upcoming To Those We Found) – you are sensible brain muscle and generosity.

To Chris Gielsing of A Dragon's Library – you are honesty and commitment.

To Gwyn Barber-Ross (author of Shadows of a Name) – you are twilight grandeur and poetic understanding.

Lotty Balfour (author of the upcoming Atlas Gate) – you are the straight-talking, no-nonsense, parent like me.

Danielle Paquette-Harvey (author of The Prophecy and Age-Old Enemies) – you are kindness and friendship.

Michelle Piper (author of the upcoming Price of Innocence, book one of Sonder's Song) – you are the amazingly insightful writer and ship wizard.

Rick Hardesty (author of The Battle for Terra Paradisum) – you are adventure and incredible humility.

Mad Malic (www.madmalic.com) – you are insight and empathy.

S. A. Smith (author of the upcoming The Rain Gypsy – you are spice and goodwill (never change Bill).

Thank you to everyone.

Printed in Great Britain
by Amazon

75929293R00302